BRAIN CAMP

SQUARE
FISH

An Imprint of Macmillan
175 Fifth Avenue
New York, NY 10010
mackids.com

BRAIN CAMP.
Text copyright © 2010 by Susan Kim and Laurence Klavan.
Illustrations copyright © 2010 by Faith Erin Hicks.
All rights reserved. Printed in China by RR Donnelley Asia Printing Solutions Ltd.,
Dongguan City, Guangdong Province.

Square Fish and the Square Fish logo are trademarks of Macmillan
and are used by First Second under license from Macmillan.

Square Fish books may be purchased for business or promotional use.
For information on bulk purchases, please contact the Macmillan
Corporate and Premium Sales Department at
(800) 221-7945 x5442 or by e-mail
at specialmarkets@macmillan.com.

Cataloging-in-Publication Data is on file at the Library of Congress
ISBN 978-1-250-06292-5 (paperback)

Originally published in the United States by First Second
First Square Fish Edition: 2015
Book designed by Colleen AF Venable
Colored by Hilary Sycamore and Sky Blue Ink
Square Fish logo designed by Filomena Tuosto

10 9 8 7 6 5 4 3 2 1

AR: 2.4 / LEXILE: GN250L

BRAIN CAMP

WRITTEN BY SUSAN KIM & LAURENCE KLAVAN
ARTWORK BY FAITH ERIN HICKS
COLOR BY HILARY SYCAMORE

SQUARE
FISH
First Second
NEW YORK

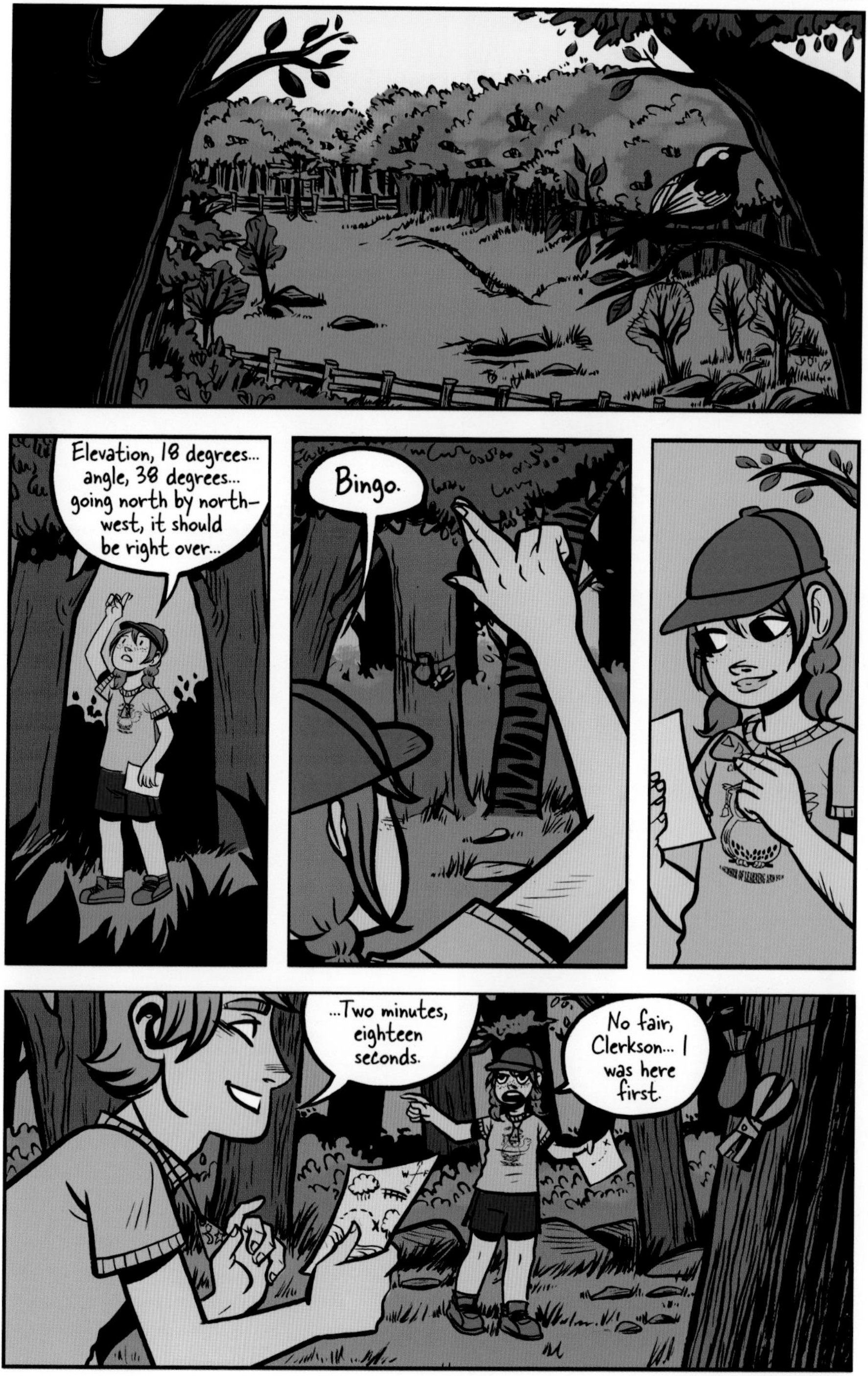
Elevation, 18 degrees... angle, 38 degrees... going north by north-west, it should be right over...
Bingo.
...Two minutes, eighteen seconds.
No fair, Clerkson... I was here first.

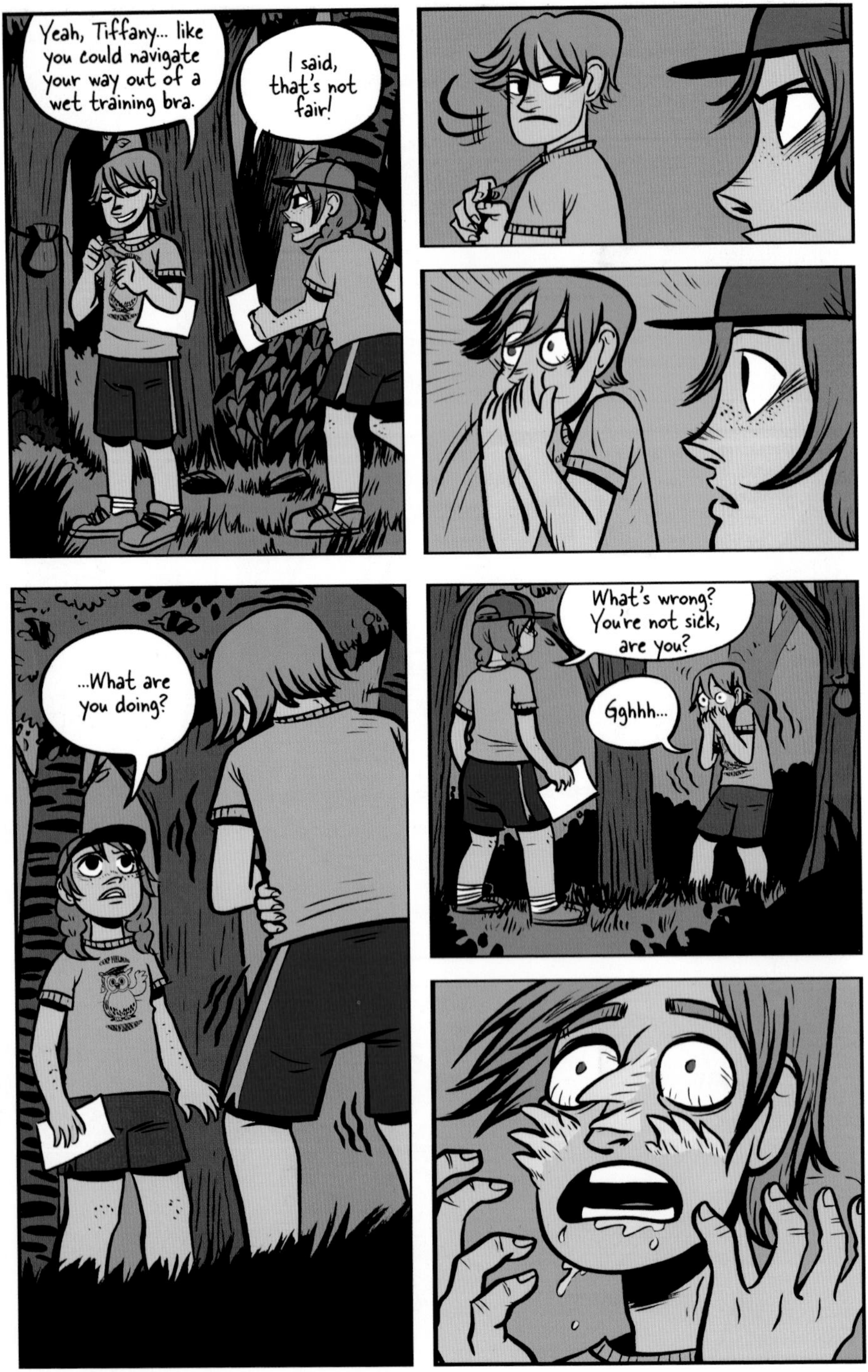

Yeah, Tiffany... like you could navigate your way out of a wet training bra.
I said, that's not fair!
...What are you doing?
What's wrong? You're not sick, are you?
Gghhh...

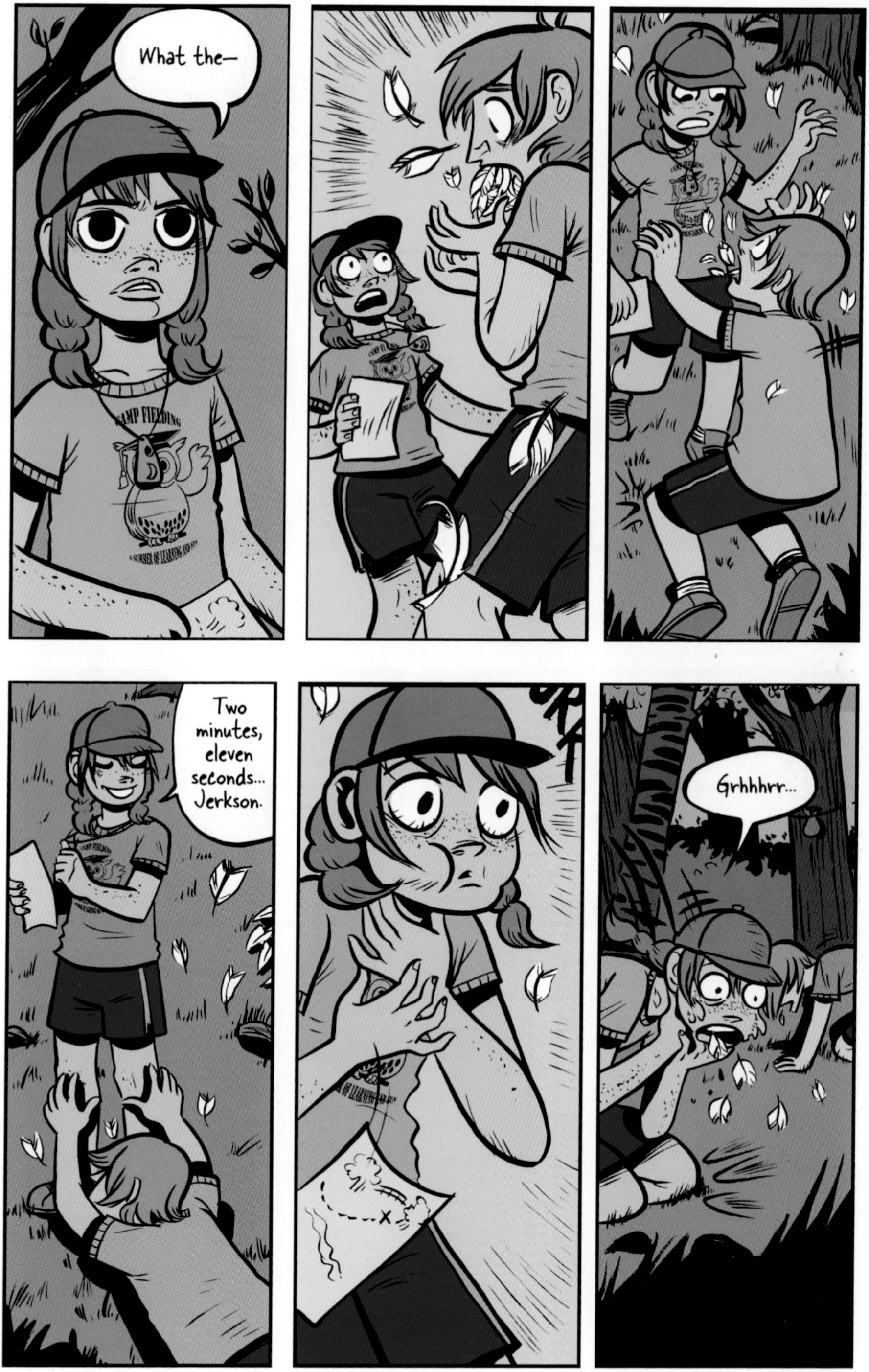
What the—
Two minutes, eleven seconds... Jerkson.
Grhhhrr...

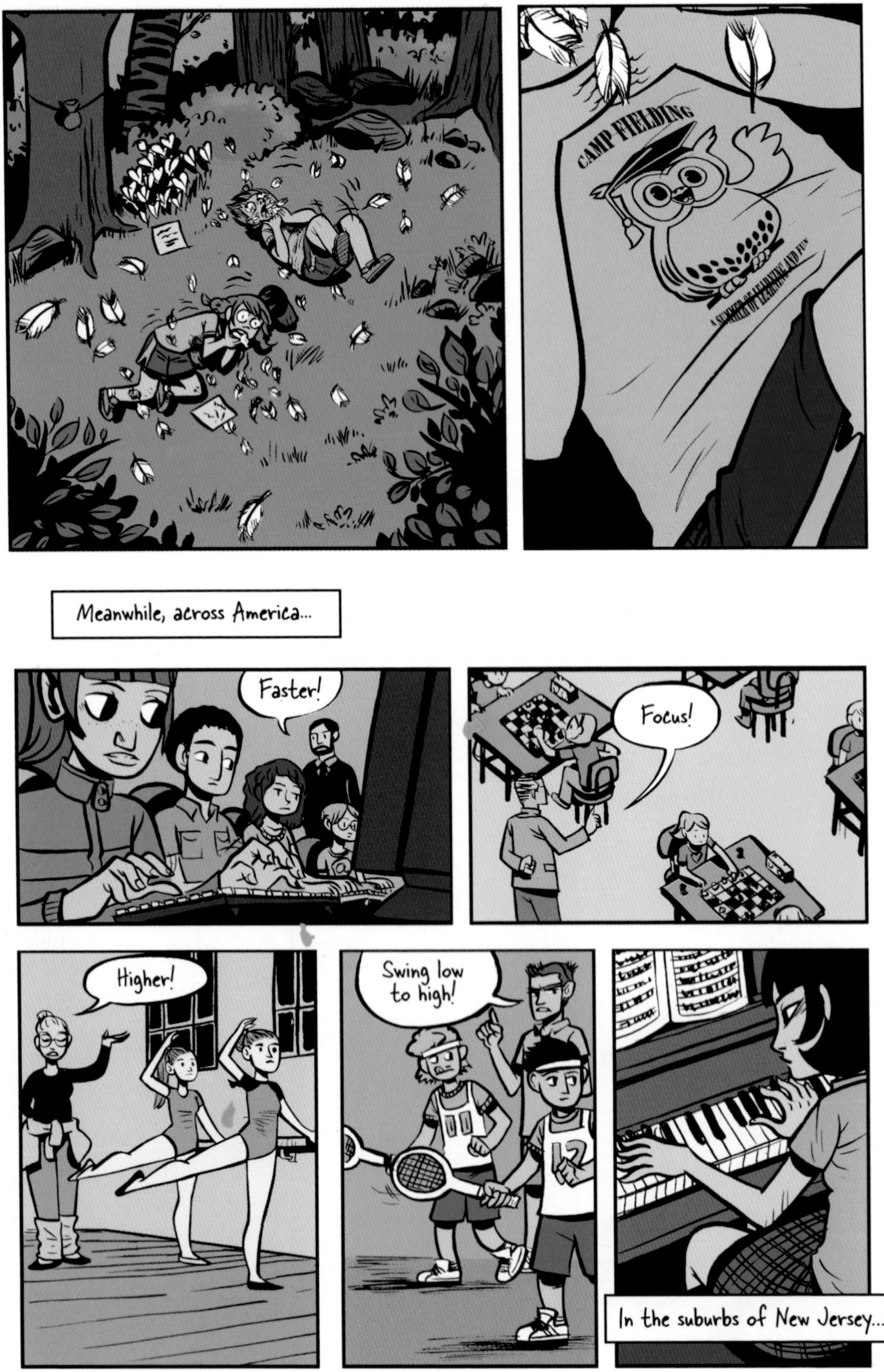
CAMP FIELDING
A SUMMER OF LEARNING AND FUN
Meanwhile, across America...
Faster!
Focus!
Higher!
Swing low to high!
In the suburbs of New Jersey...

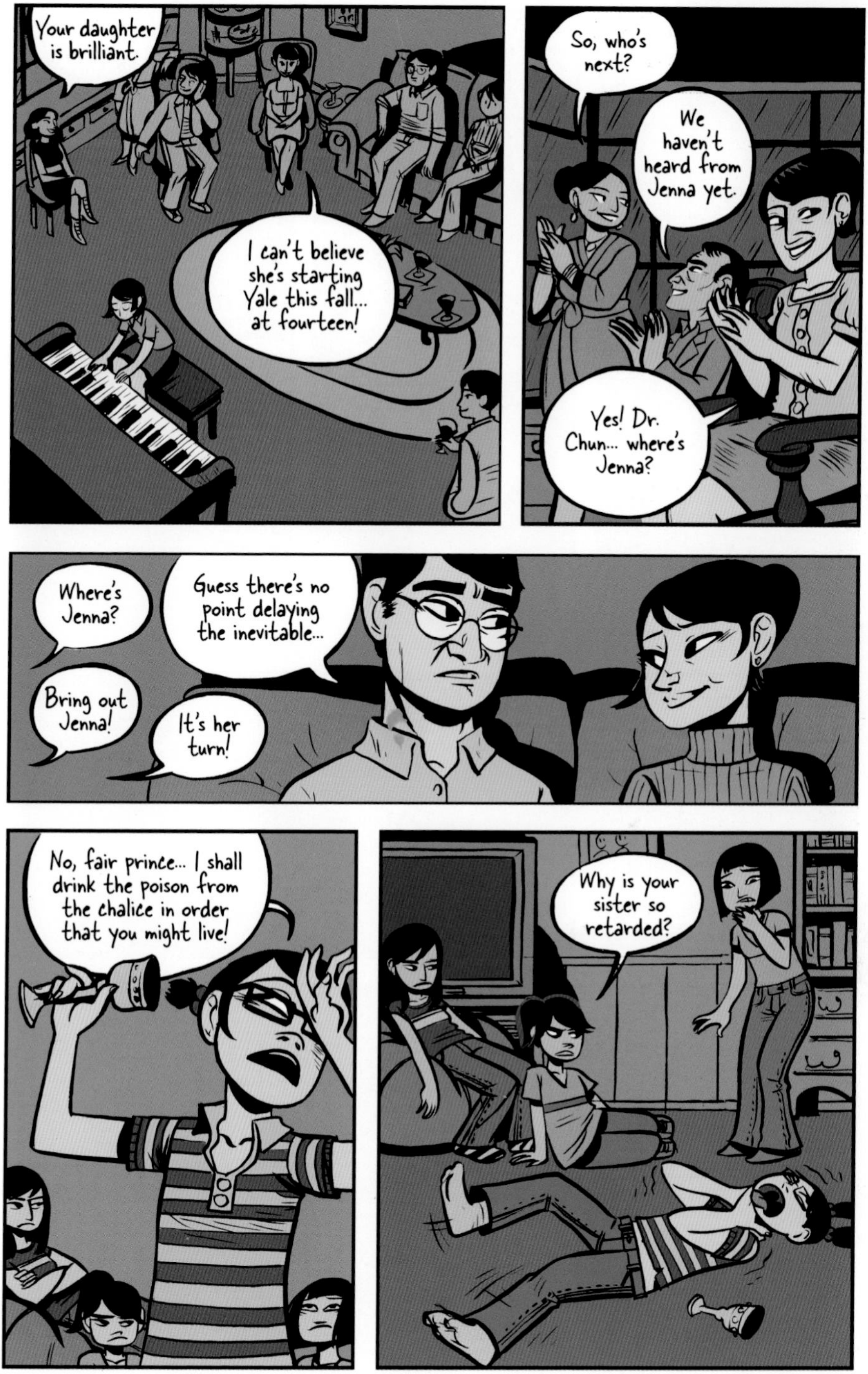
Your daughter is brilliant.
I can't believe she's starting Yale this fall... at fourteen!
So, who's next?
We haven't heard from Jenna yet.
Yes! Dr. Chun... where's Jenna?
Where's Jenna?
Bring out Jenna!
It's her turn!
Guess there's no point delaying the inevitable...
No, fair prince... I shall drink the poison from the chalice in order that you might live!
Why is your sister so retarded?

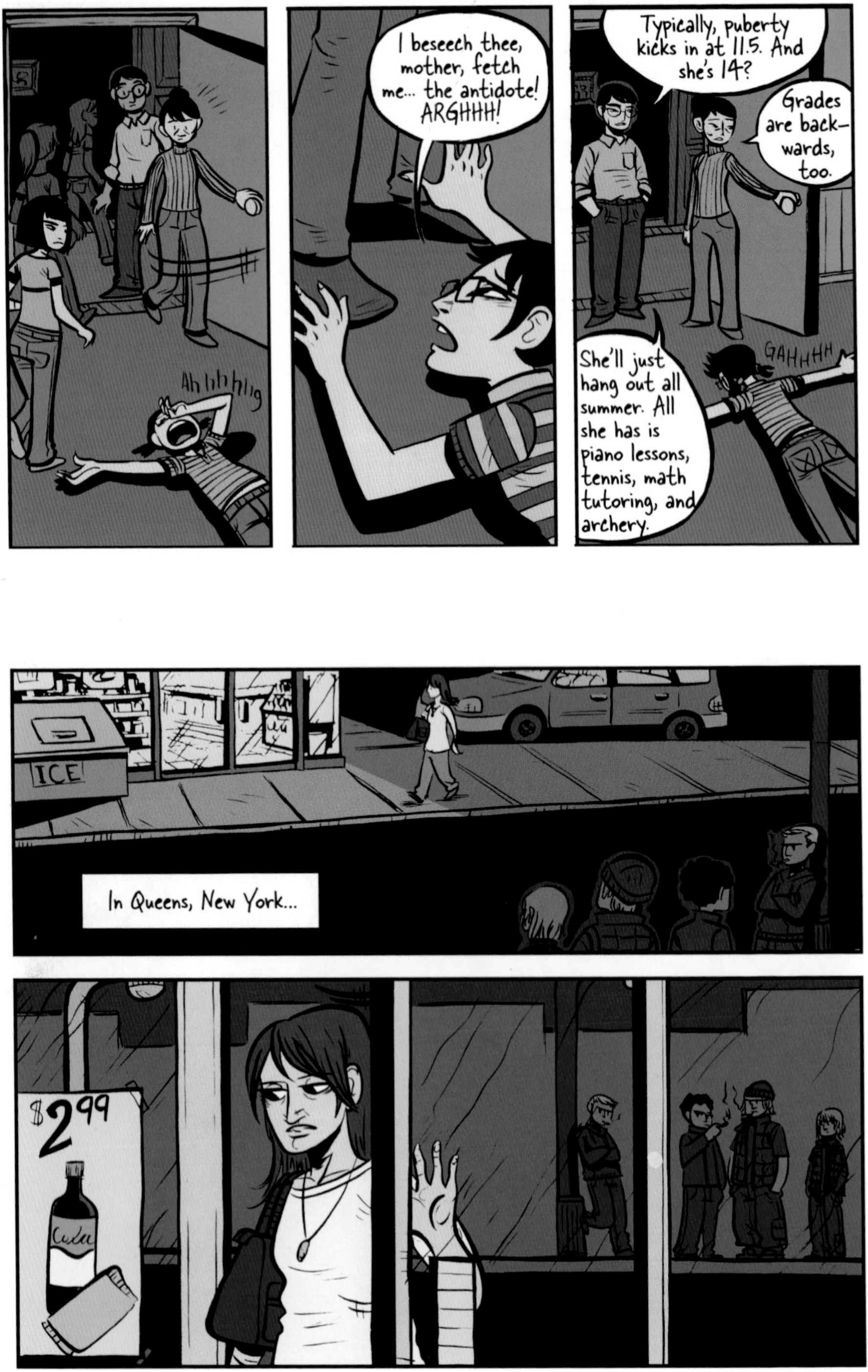
I beseech thee, mother, fetch me... the antidote! ARGHHH!
Typically, puberty kicks in at 11.5. And she's 14?
Grades are back-wards, too.
She'll just hang out all summer. All she has is piano lessons, tennis, math tutoring, and archery.
GAHHHH
ICE
In Queens, New York...
$2.99

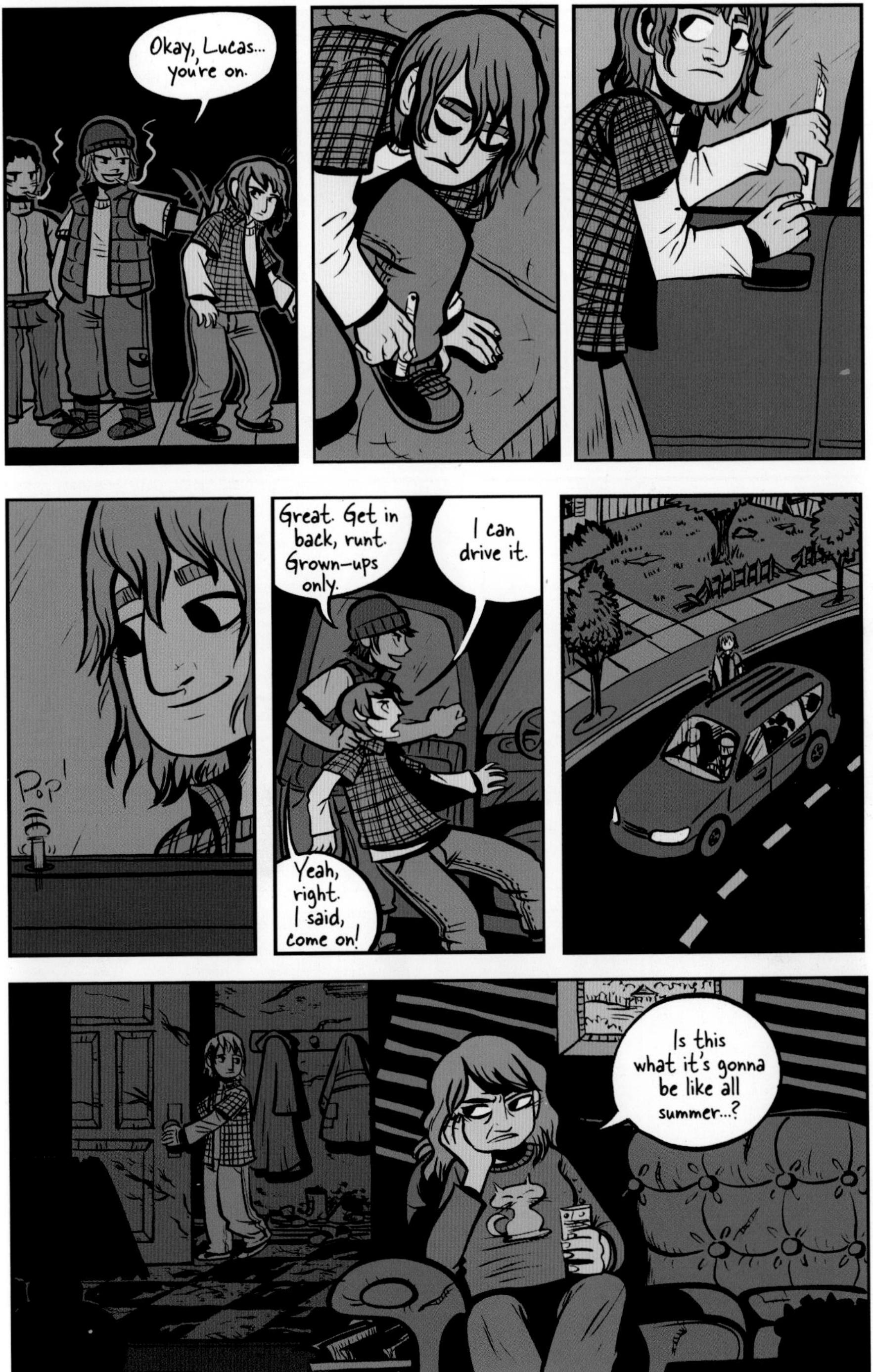
Okay, Lucas... you're on.
Pop!
Great. Get in back, runt. Grown-ups only.
I can drive it.
Yeah, right. I said, come on!
Is this what it's gonna be like all summer...?

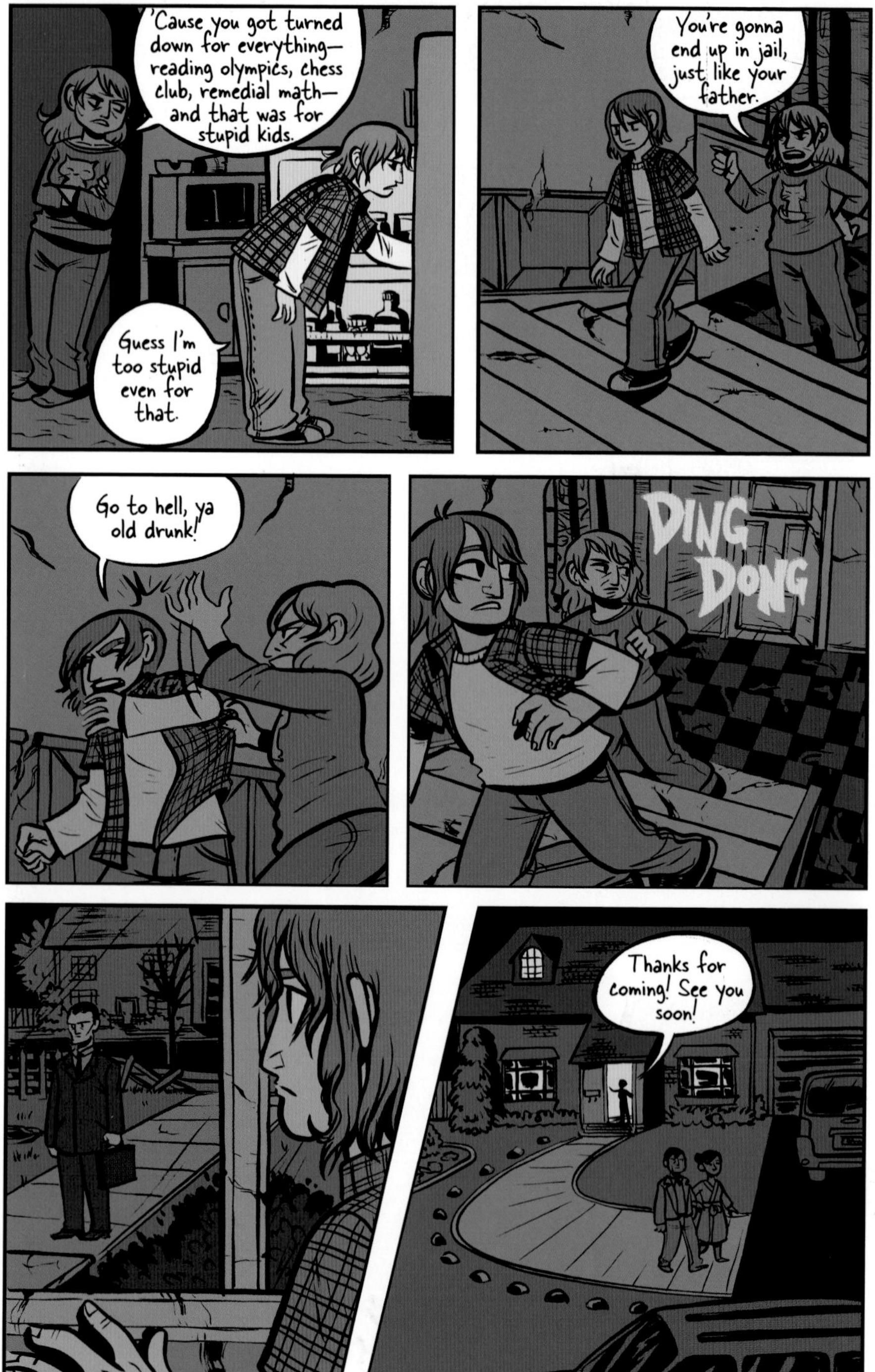
'Cause you got turned down for everything—reading olympics, chess club, remedial math—and that was for stupid kids.
Guess I'm too stupid even for that.
You're gonna end up in jail, just like your father.
Go to hell, ya old drunk!
DING DONG
Thanks for coming! See you soon!

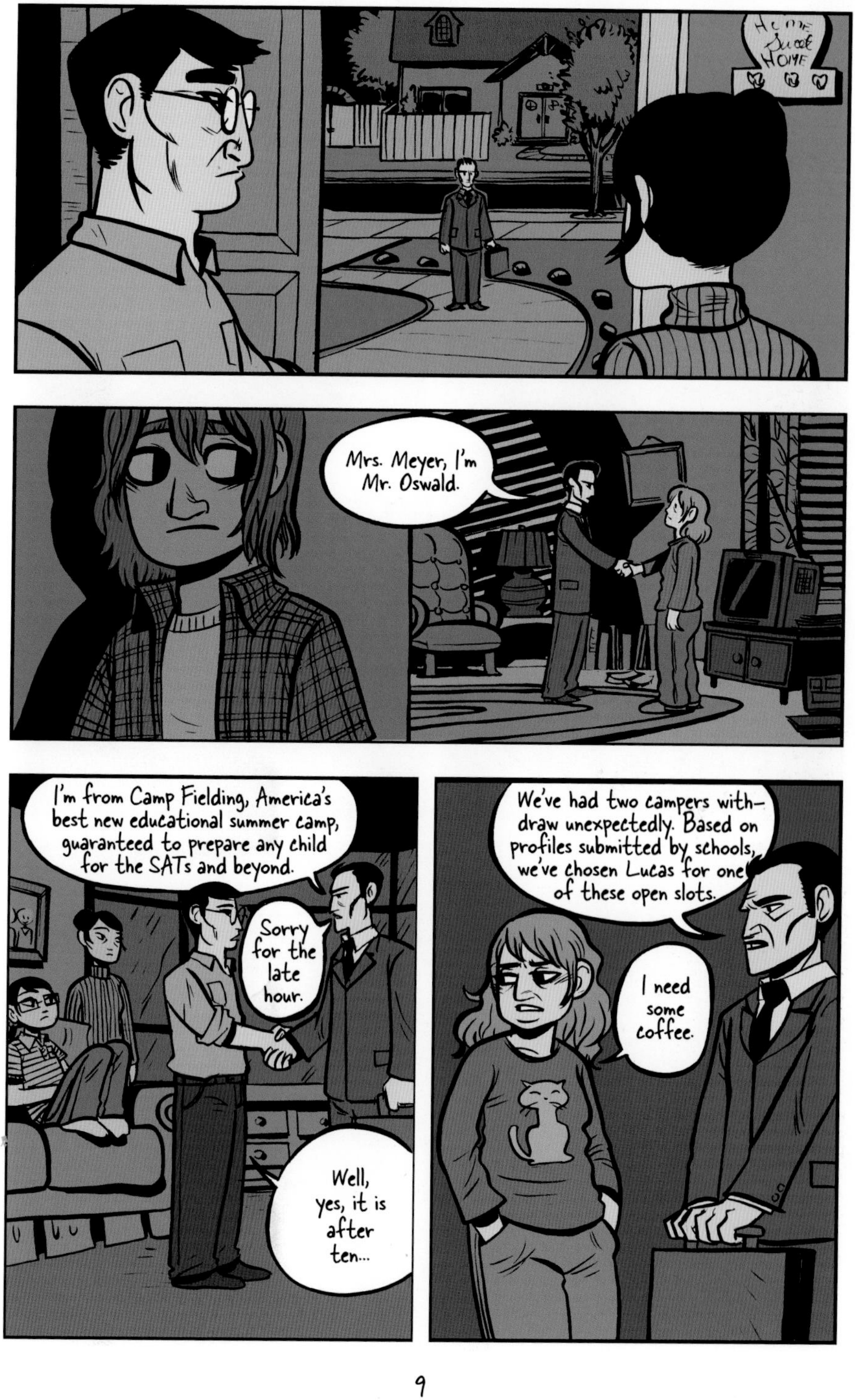
HOME Sweet HOME
Mrs. Meyer, I'm Mr. Oswald.
I'm from Camp Fielding, America's best new educational summer camp, guaranteed to prepare any child for the SATs and beyond.
Sorry for the late hour.
Well, yes, it is after ten...
We've had two campers with-draw unexpectedly. Based on profiles submitted by schools, we've chosen Lucas for one of these open slots.
I need some coffee.

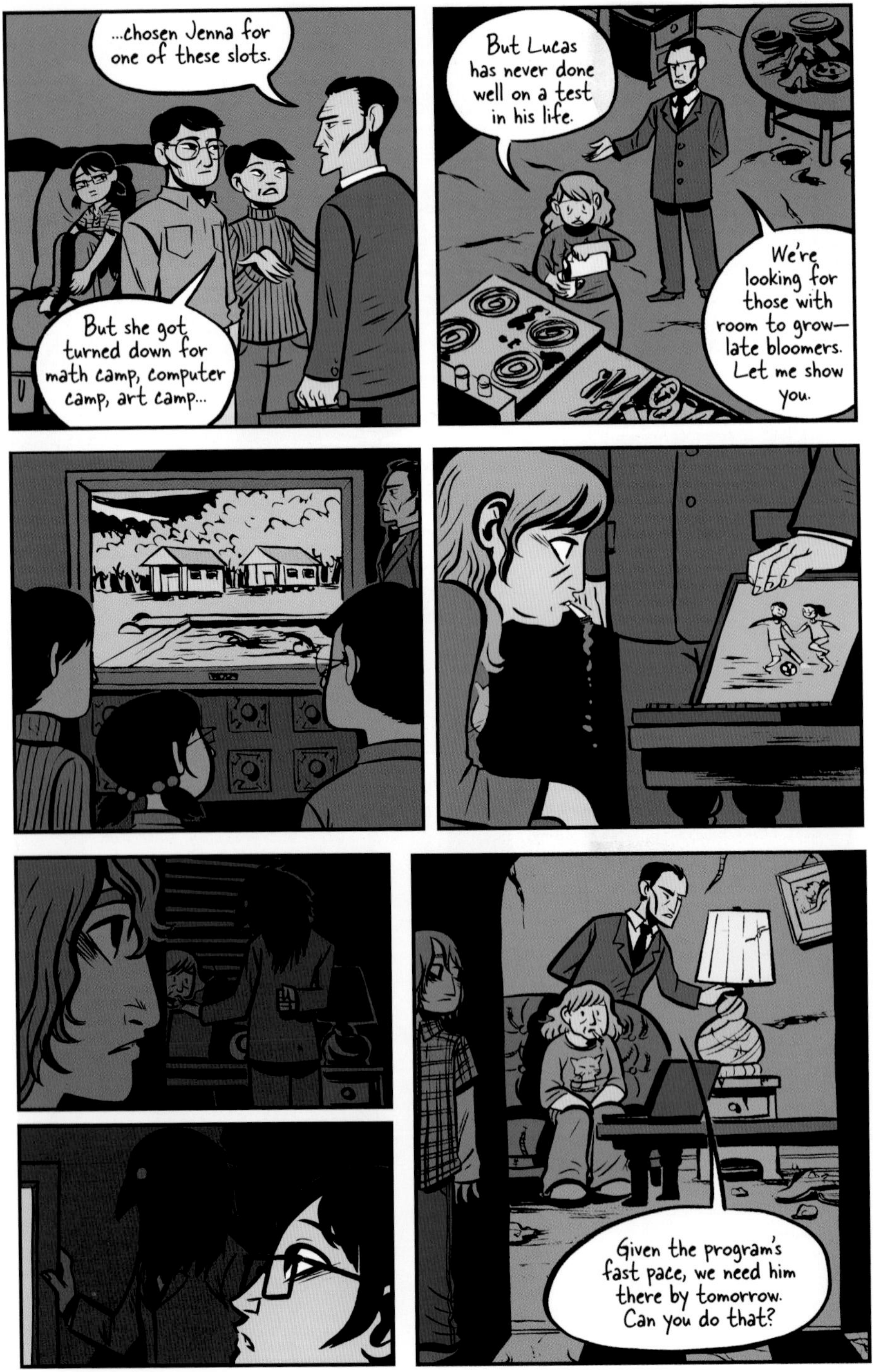
...chosen Jenna for one of these slots.
But she got turned down for math camp, computer camp, art camp...
But Lucas has never done well on a test in his life.
We're looking for those with room to grow—late bloomers. Let me show you.
Given the program's fast pace, we need him there by tomorrow. Can you do that?

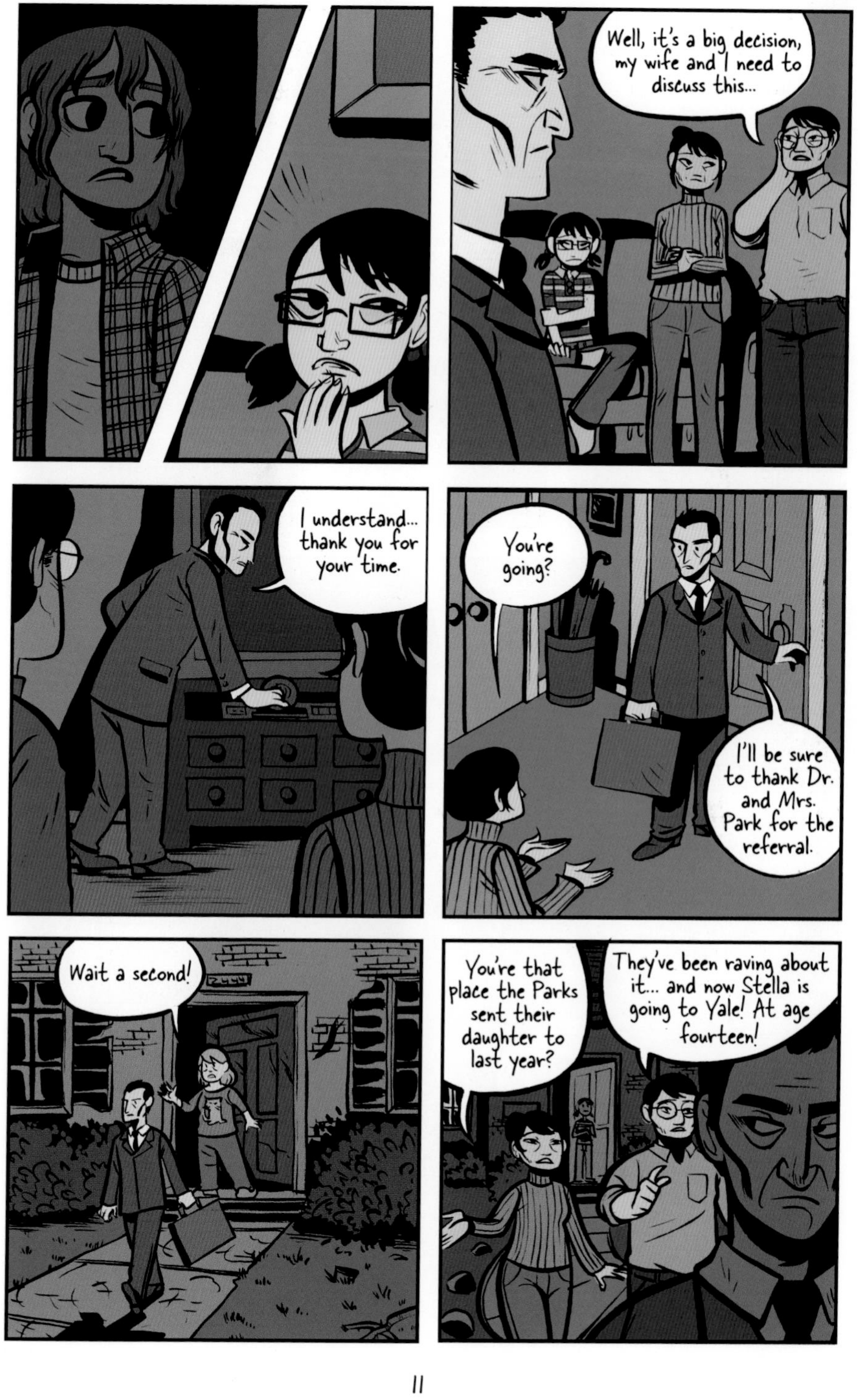
Well, it's a big decision, my wife and I need to discuss this...
I understand... thank you for your time.
You're going?
I'll be sure to thank Dr. and Mrs. Park for the referral.
Wait a second!
You're that place the Parks sent their daughter to last year?
They've been raving about it... and now Stella is going to Yale! At age fourteen!

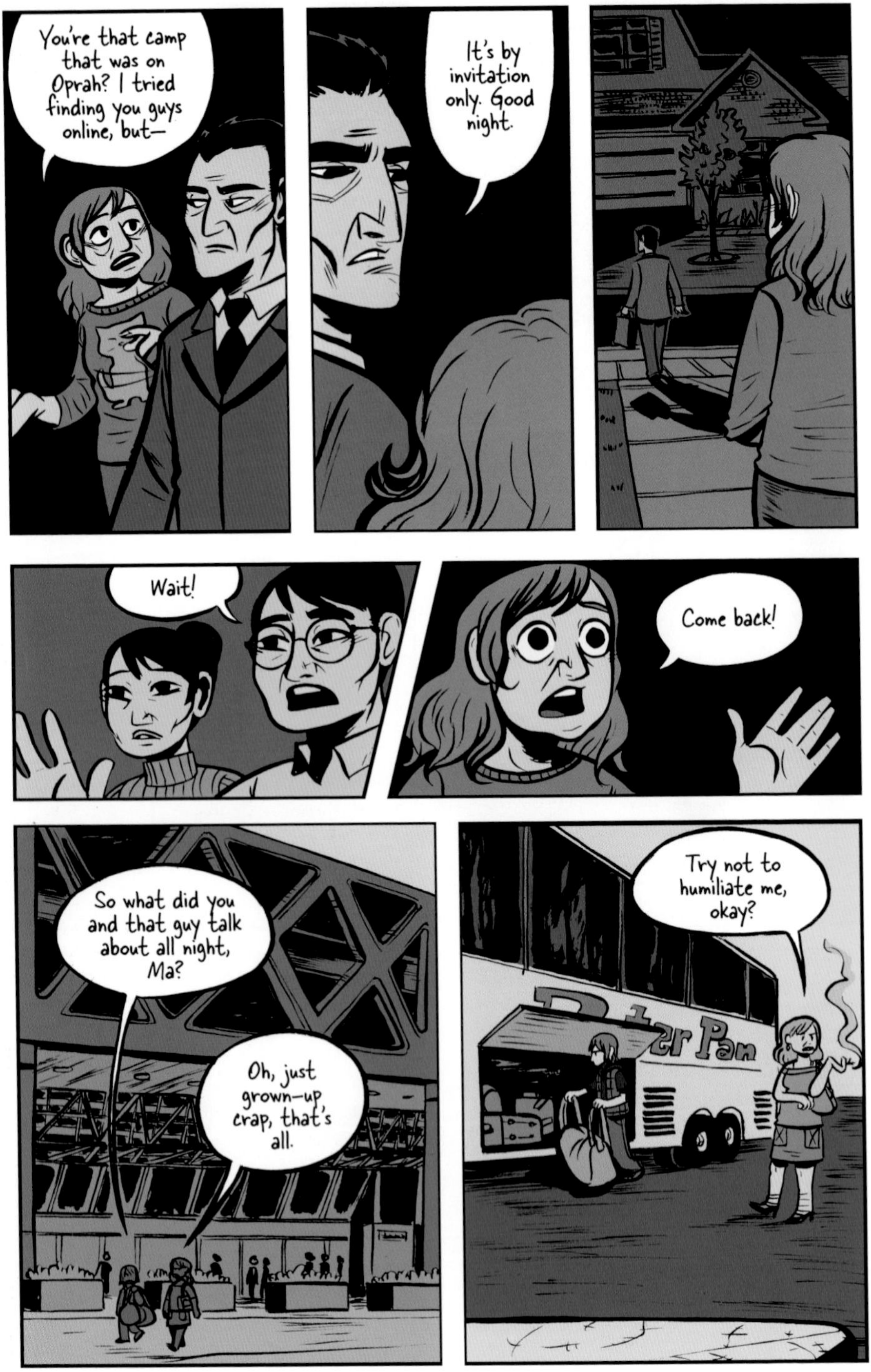
You're that camp that was on Oprah? I tried finding you guys online, but—
It's by invitation only. Good night.
Wait!
Come back!
So what did you and that guy talk about all night, Ma?
Oh, just grown-up crap, that's all.
Try not to humiliate me, okay?

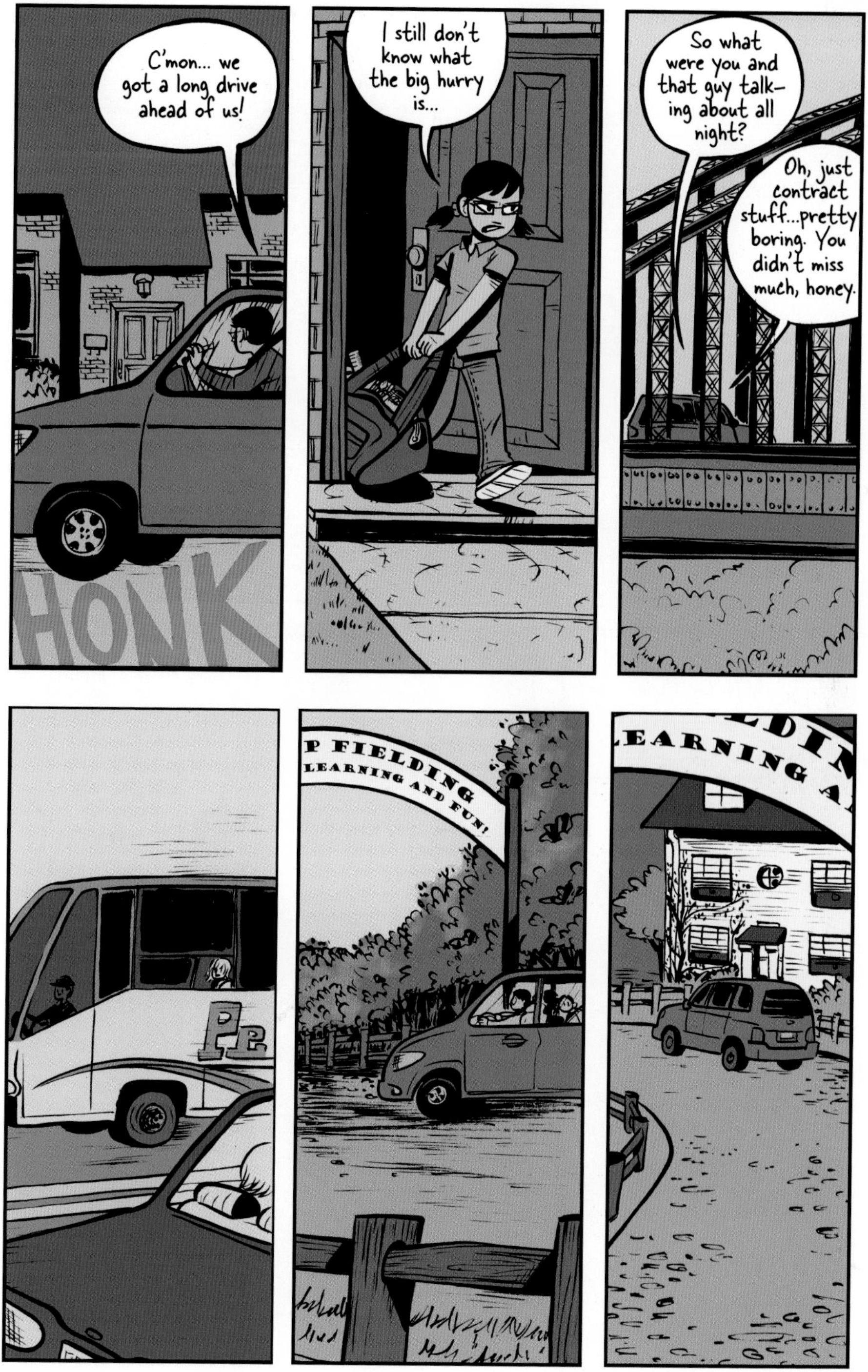
C'mon... we got a long drive ahead of us!
HONK
I still don't know what the big hurry is...
So what were you and that guy talk-ing about all night?
Oh, just contract stuff...pretty boring. You didn't miss much, honey.
P FIELDING
LEARNING AND FUN!
ELDIN
LEARNING A

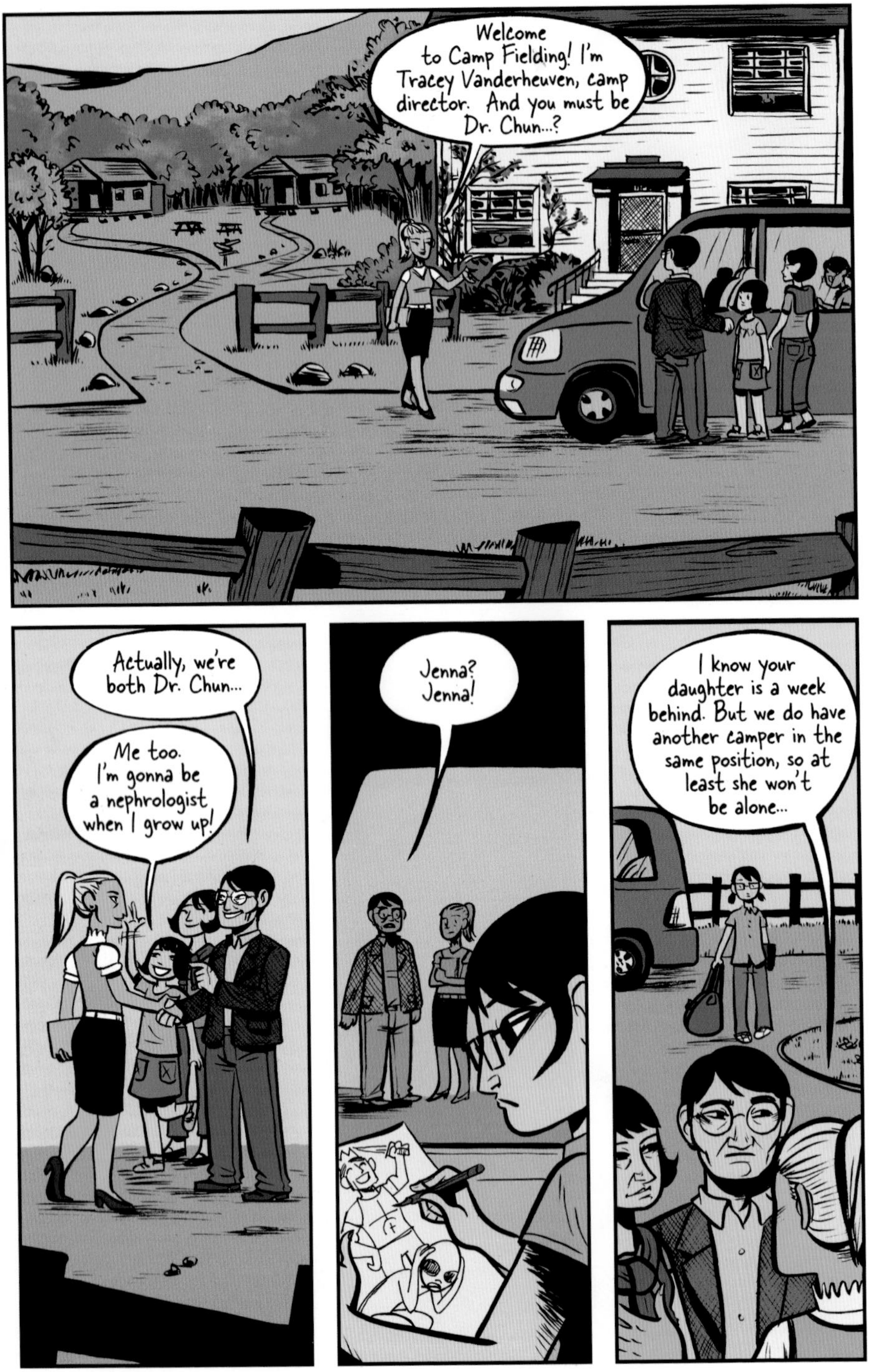
Welcome to Camp Fielding! I'm Tracey Vanderheuven, camp director. And you must be Dr. Chun...?
Actually, we're both Dr. Chun...
Me too. I'm gonna be a nephrologist when I grow up!
Jenna? Jenna!
I know your daughter is a week behind. But we do have another camper in the same position, so at least she won't be alone...

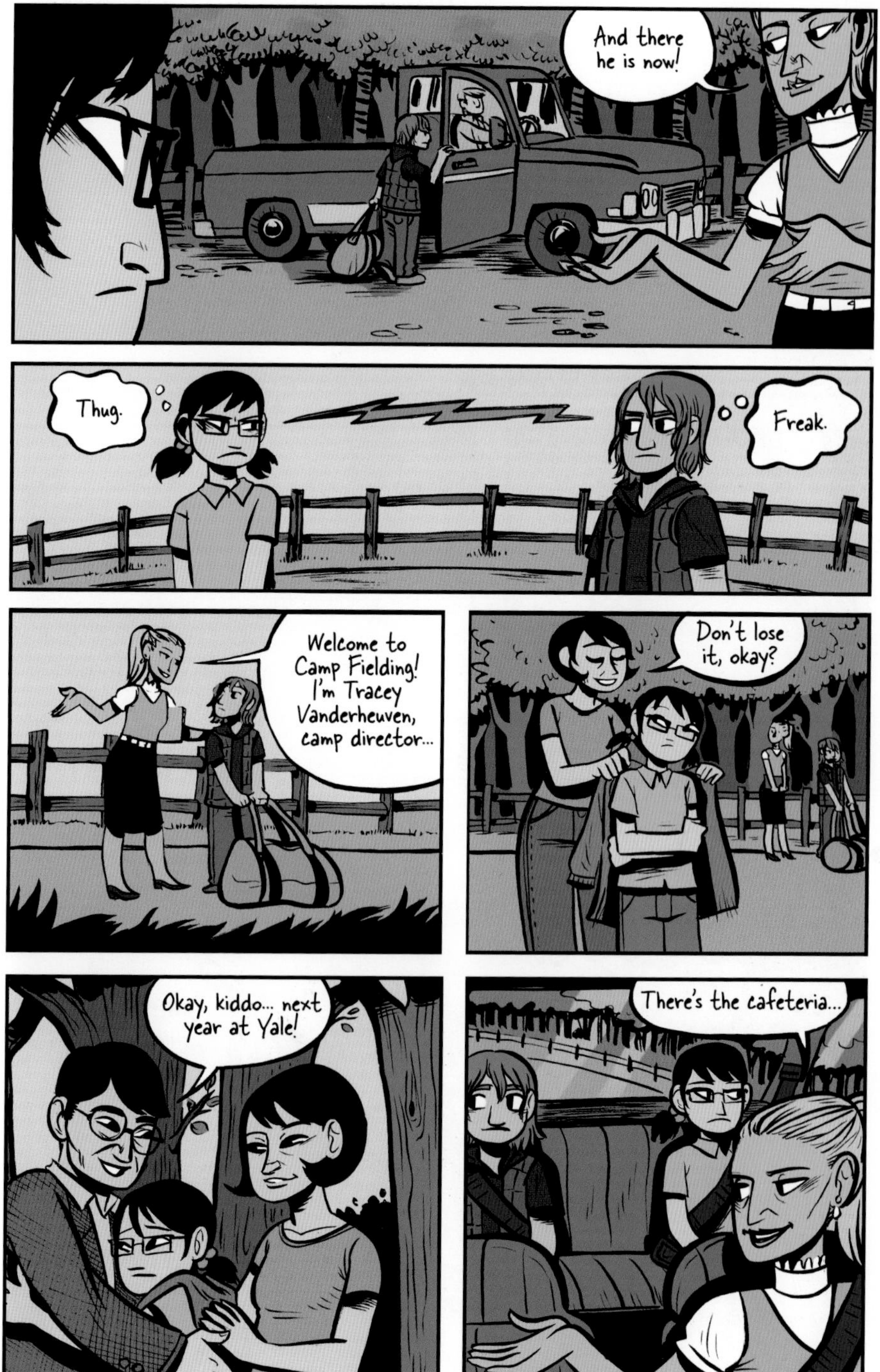
And there he is now!
Thug.
Freak.
Welcome to Camp Fielding! I'm Tracey Vanderheuven, camp director...
Don't lose it, okay?
Okay, kiddo... next year at Yale!
There's the cafeteria...

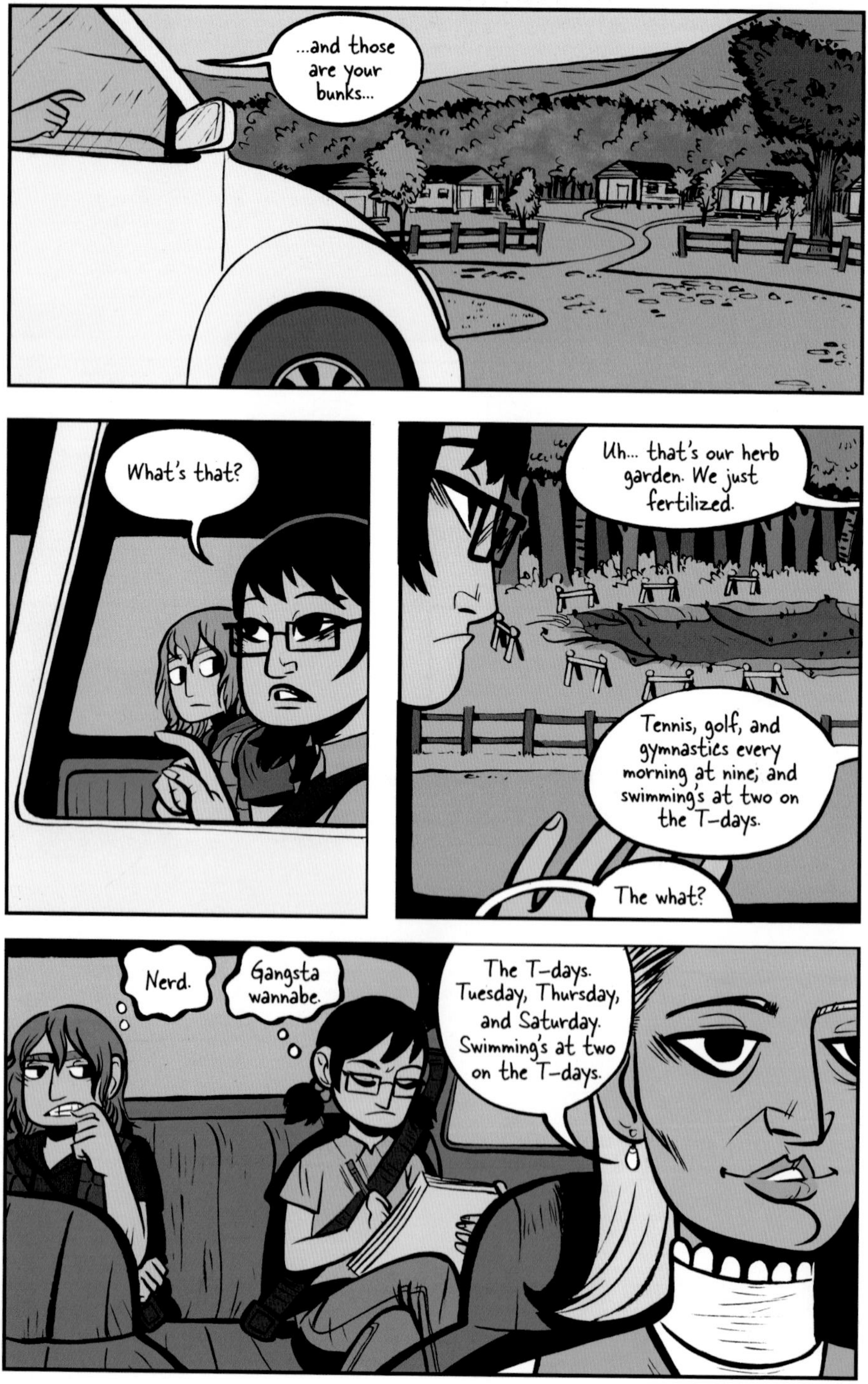
...and those are your bunks...
What's that?
Uh... that's our herb garden. We just fertilized.
Tennis, golf, and gymnastics every morning at nine; and swimming's at two on the T-days.
The what?
Nerd.
Gangsta wannabe.
The T-days. Tuesday, Thursday, and Saturday. Swimming's at two on the T-days.

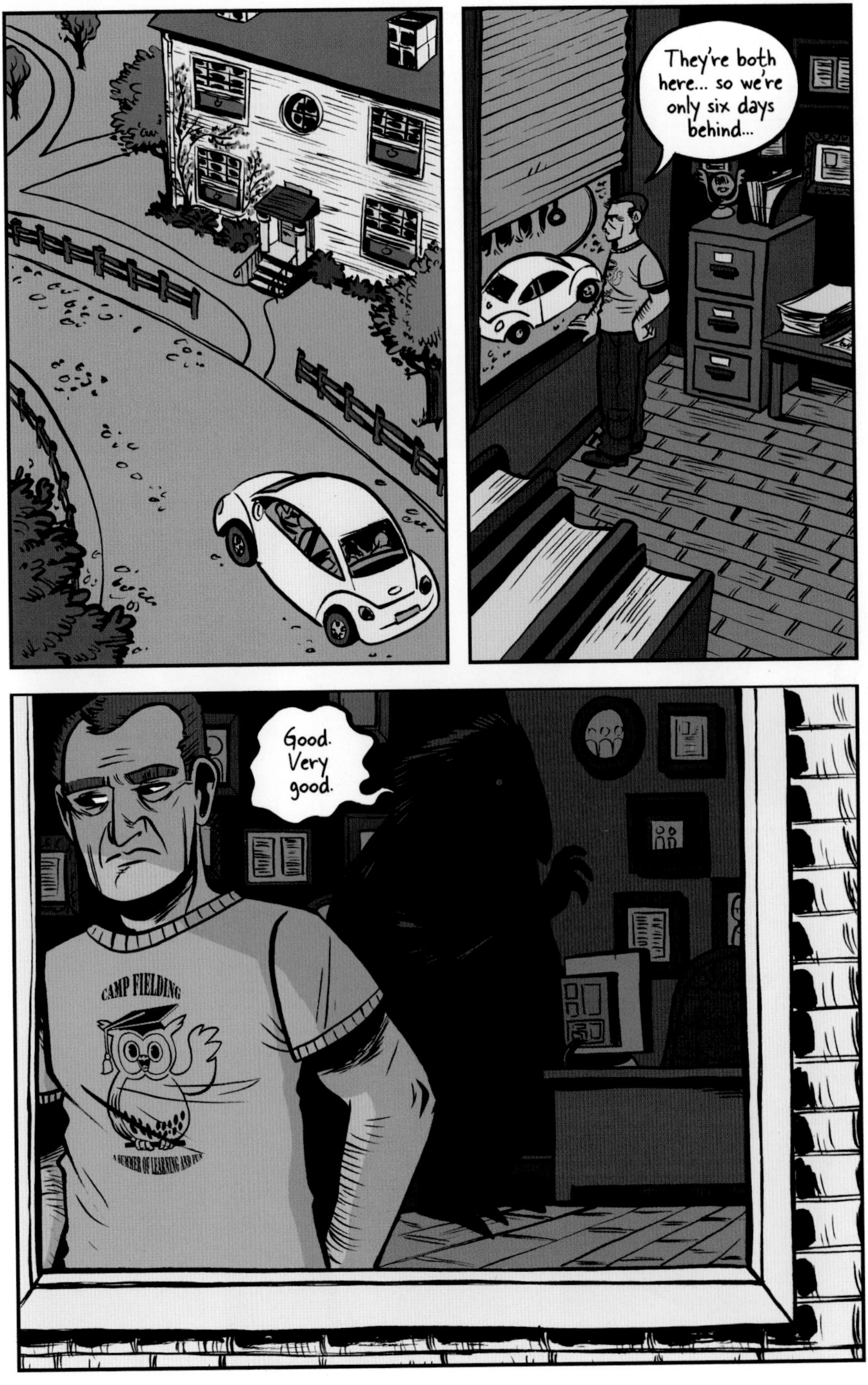
They're both here... so we're only six days behind...
Good. Very good.
CAMP FIELDING
A SUMMER OF LEARNING AND FUN

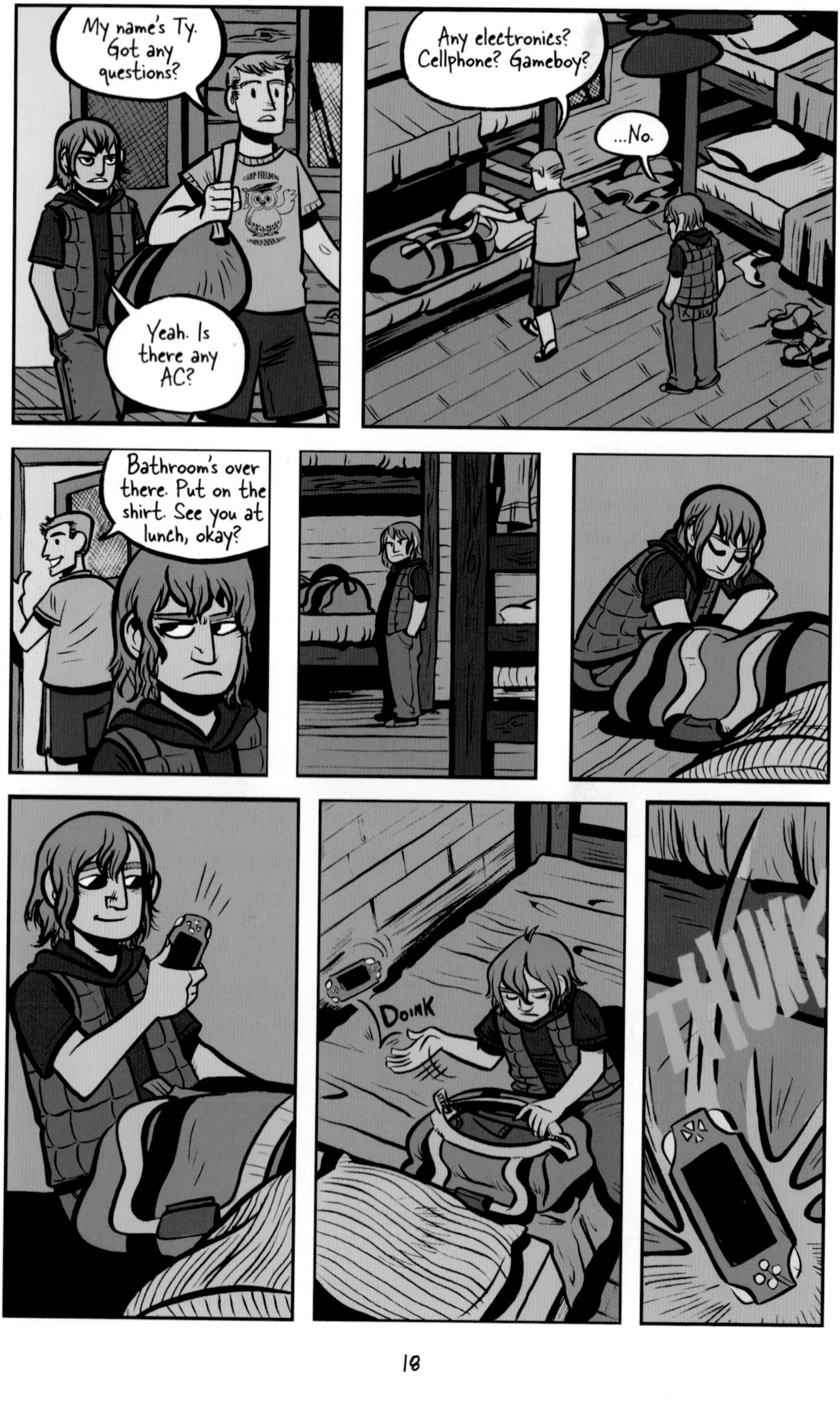
My name's Ty. Got any questions?
Yeah. Is there any AC?
Any electronics? Cellphone? Gameboy?
...No.
Bathroom's over there. Put on the shirt. See you at lunch, okay?
DOINK
THUNK

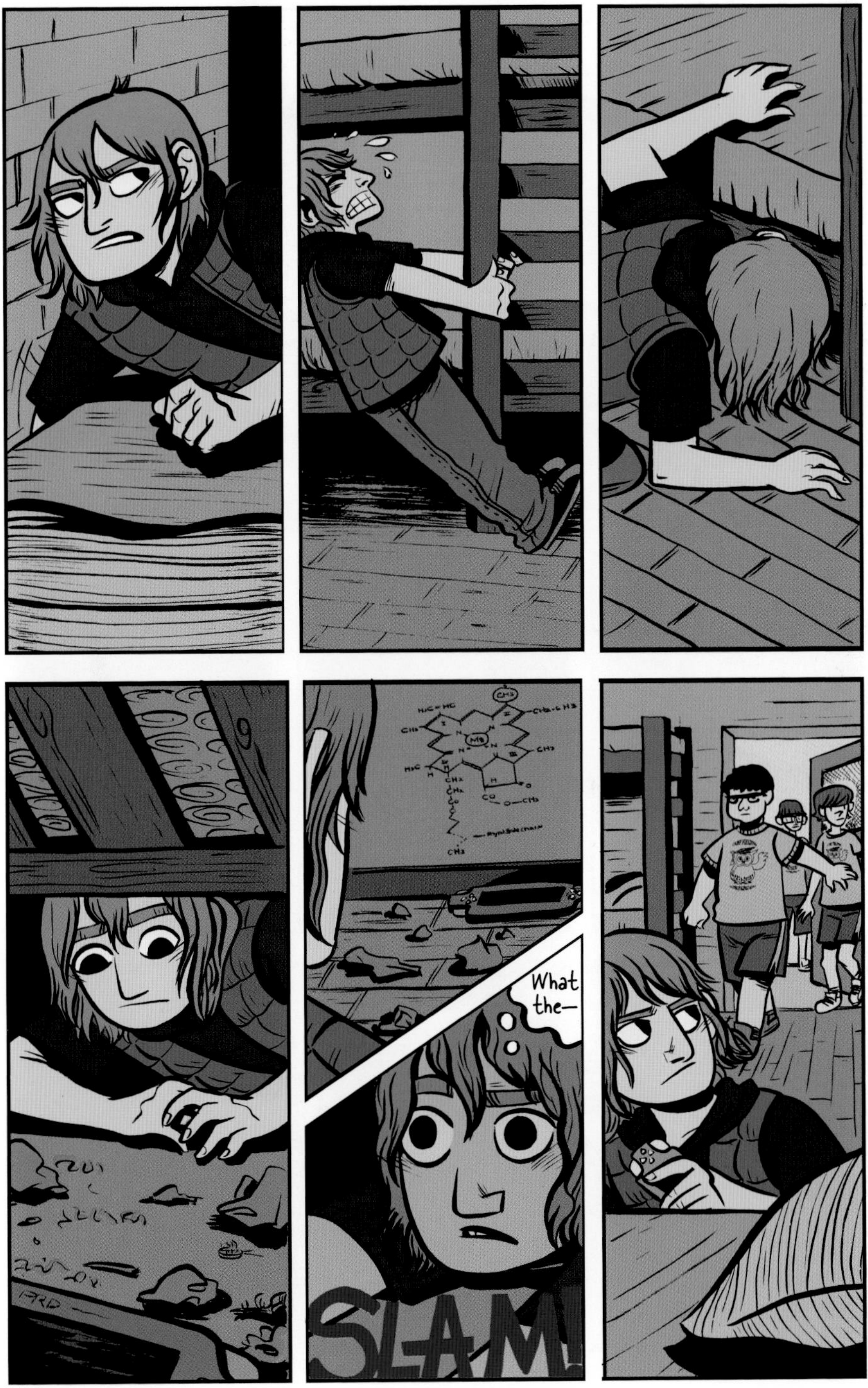
What the—
SLAM!

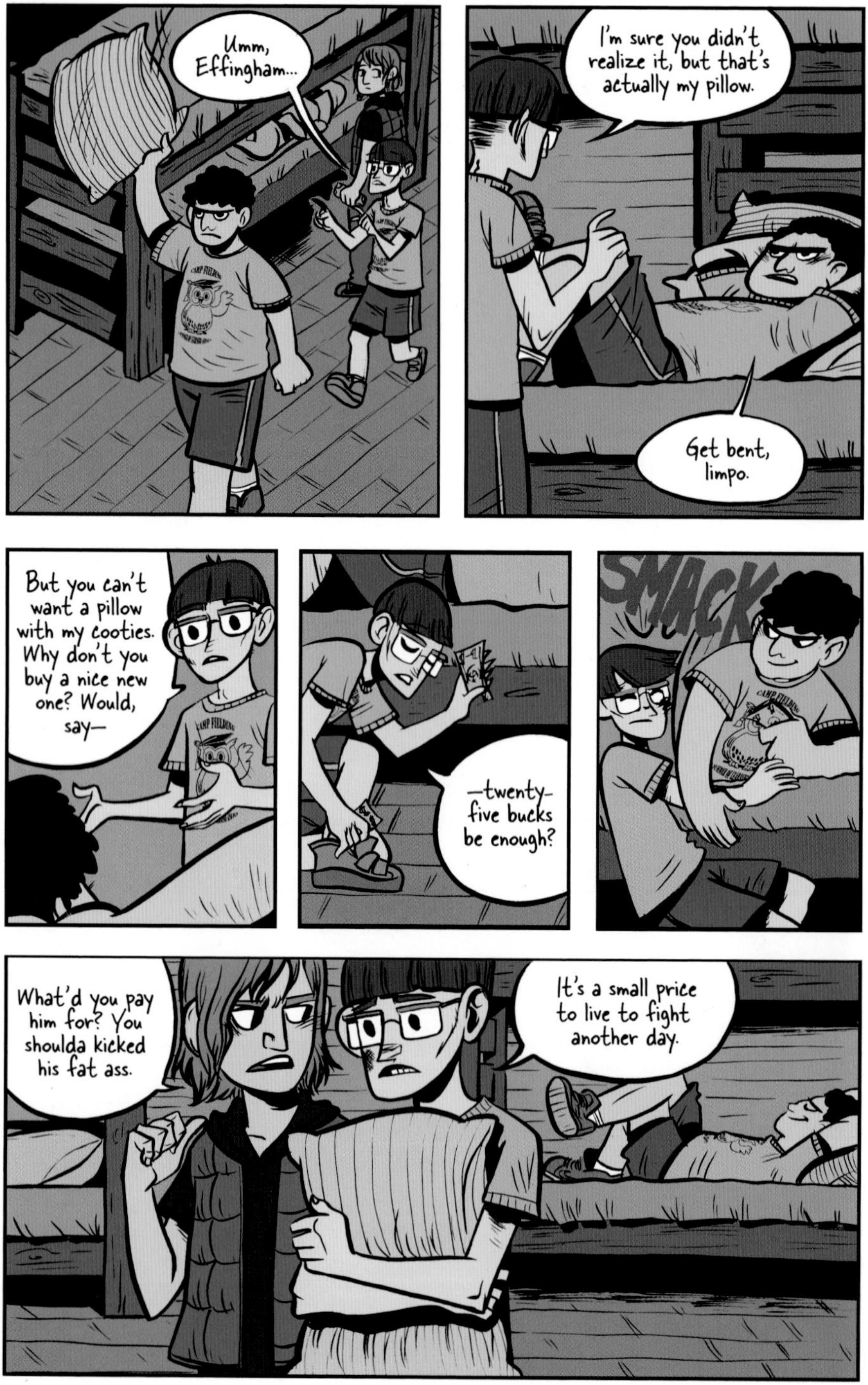
Umm, Effingham...
I'm sure you didn't realize it, but that's actually my pillow.
Get bent, limpo.
But you can't want a pillow with my cooties. Why don't you buy a nice new one? Would, say—
—twenty-five bucks be enough?
SMACK
What'd you pay him for? You shoulda kicked his fat ass.
It's a small price to live to fight another day.

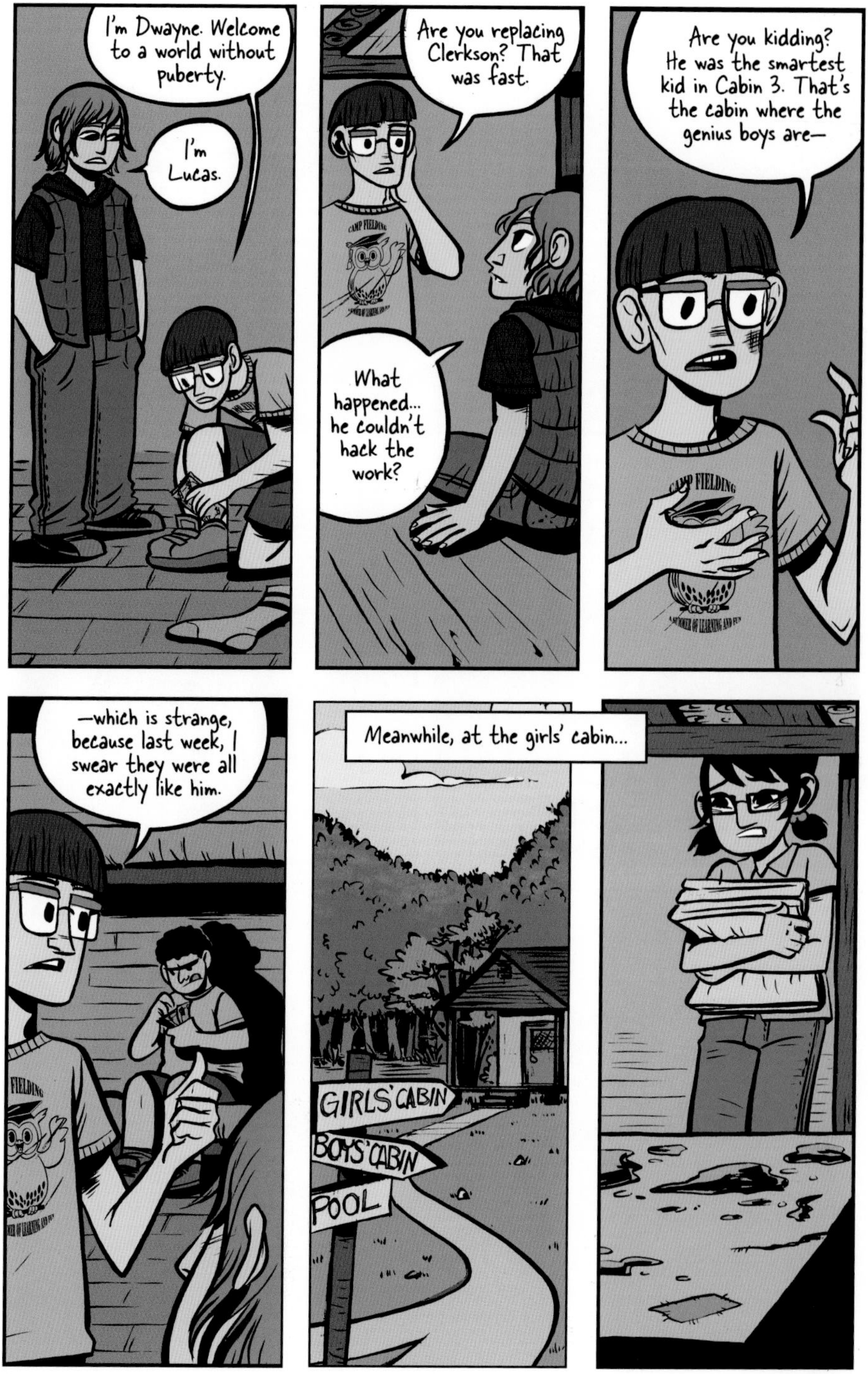
I'm Dwayne. Welcome to a world without puberty.
I'm Lucas.
Are you replacing Clerkson? That was fast.
What happened... he couldn't hack the work?
CAMP FIELDING
Are you kidding? He was the smartest kid in Cabin 3. That's the cabin where the genius boys are—
CAMP FIELDING
A SUMMER OF LEARNING AND FUN
—which is strange, because last week, I swear they were all exactly like him.
Meanwhile, at the girls' cabin...
GIRLS' CABIN
BOYS' CABIN
POOL

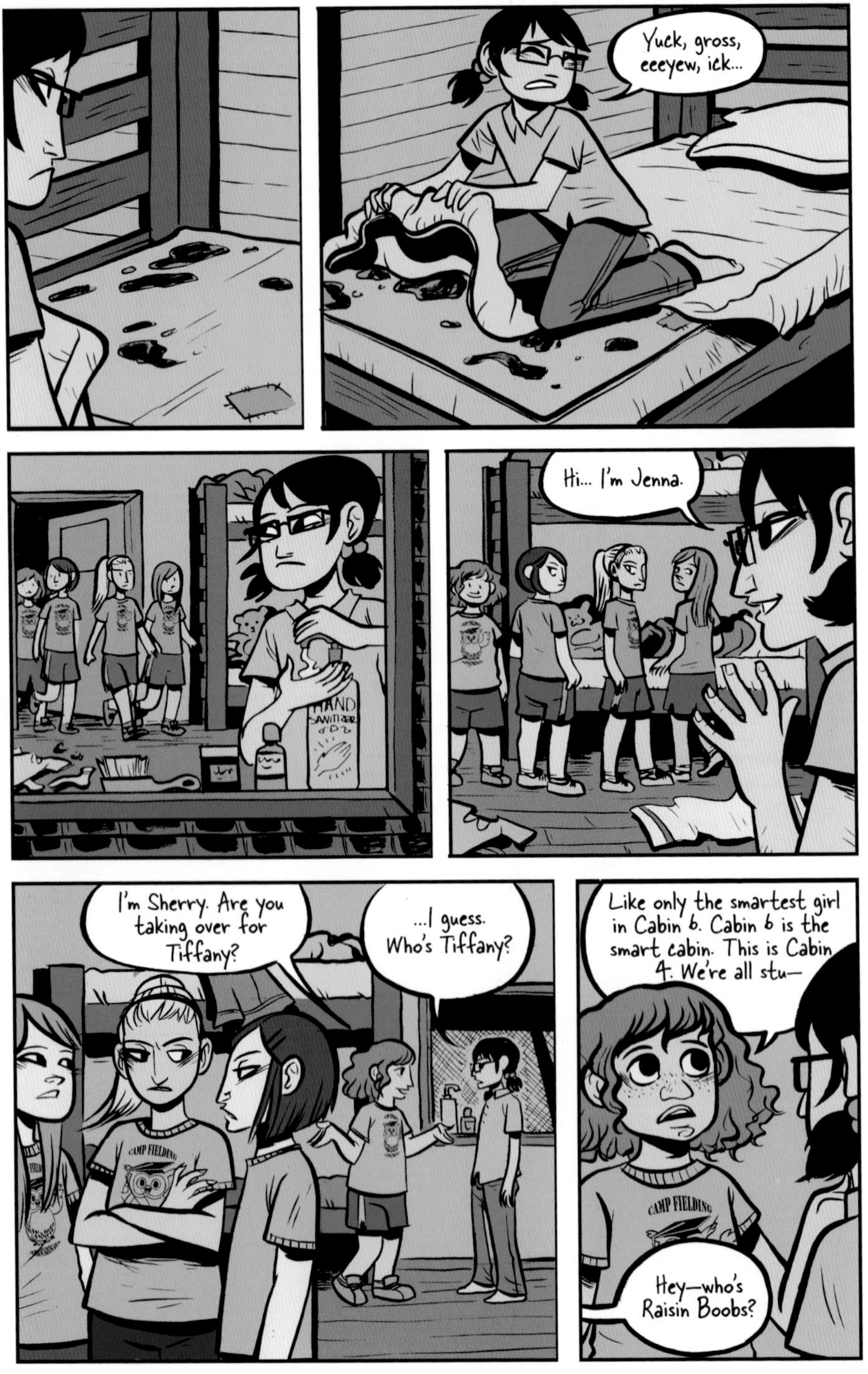
Yuck, gross, eeeyew, ick...
HAND SANITIZER
Hi... I'm Jenna.
I'm Sherry. Are you taking over for Tiffany?
...I guess. Who's Tiffany?
CAMP FIELDING
Like only the smartest girl in Cabin 6. Cabin 6 is the smart cabin. This is Cabin 4. We're all stu—
Hey—who's Raisin Boobs?

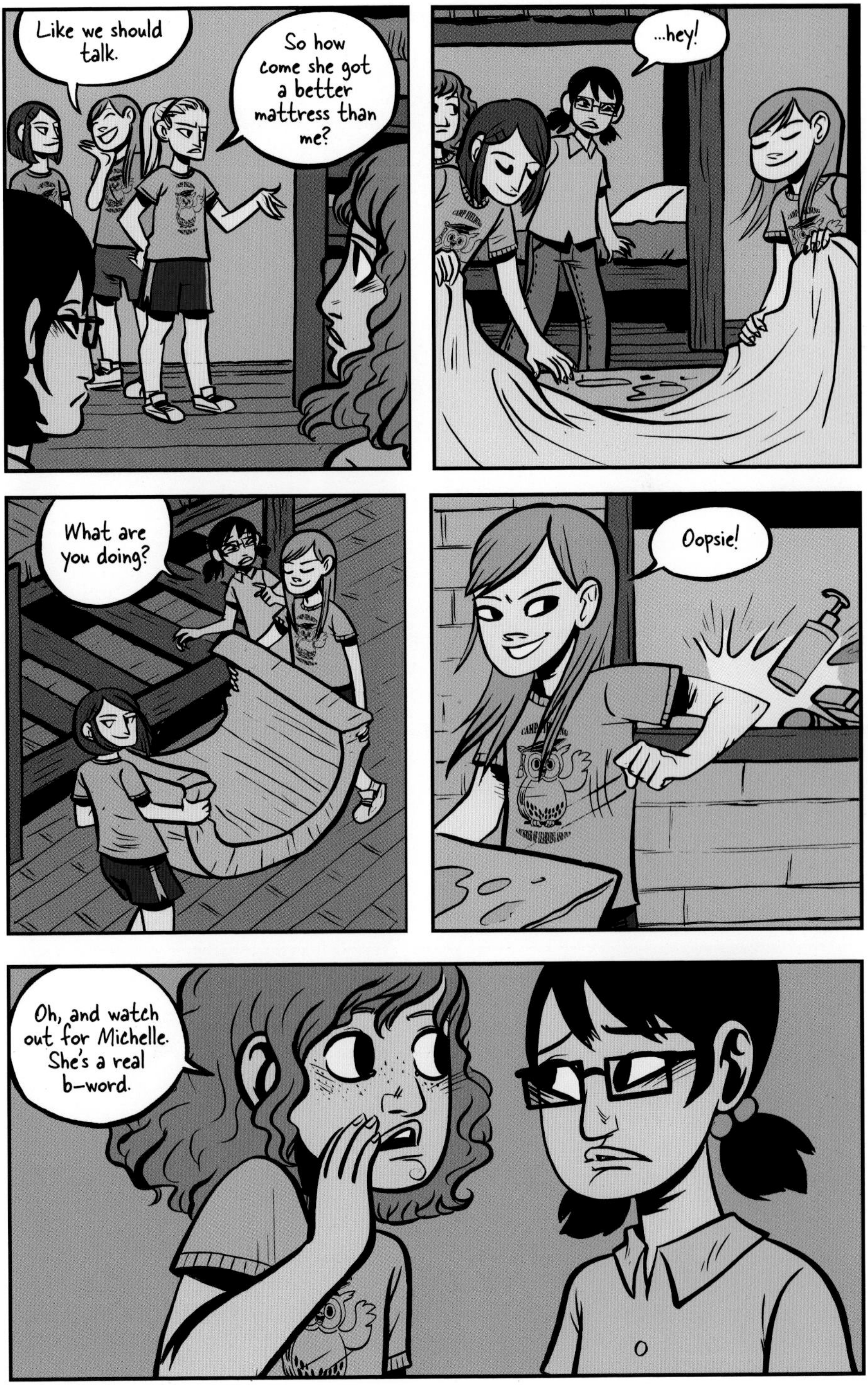
Like we should talk.
So how come she got a better mattress than me?
...hey!
What are you doing?
Oopsie!
Oh, and watch out for Michelle. She's a real b–word.

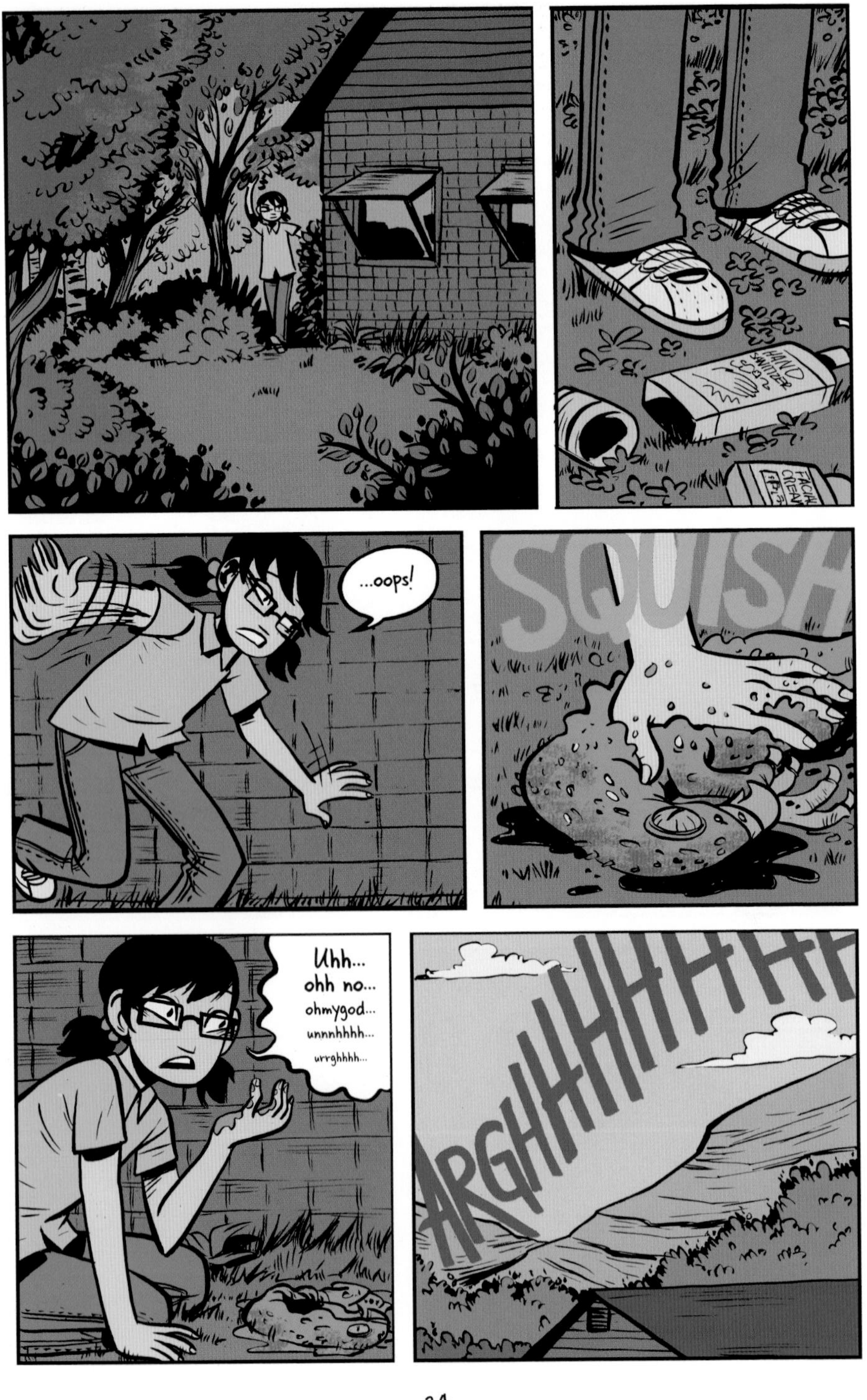
HAND SANITIZER
FACIAL CREAM
...oops!
SQUISH
Uhh... ohh no... ohmygod... unnnhhhh... urrghhhh...
ARGHHHHHHH

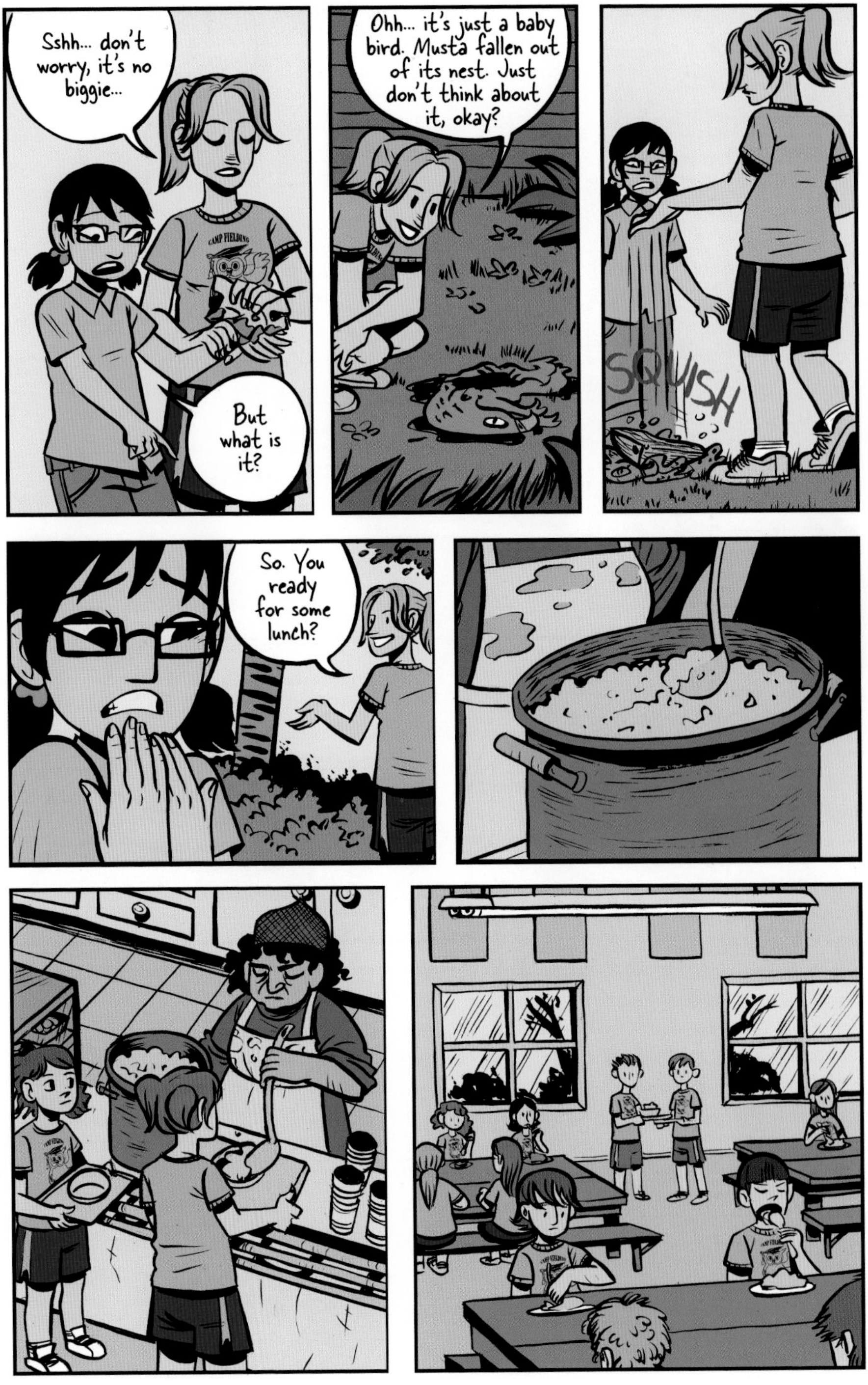
Sshh... don't worry, it's no biggie...
But what is it?
Ohh... it's just a baby bird. Musta fallen out of its nest. Just don't think about it, okay?
SQUISH
So. You ready for some lunch?
CAMP FIELDING

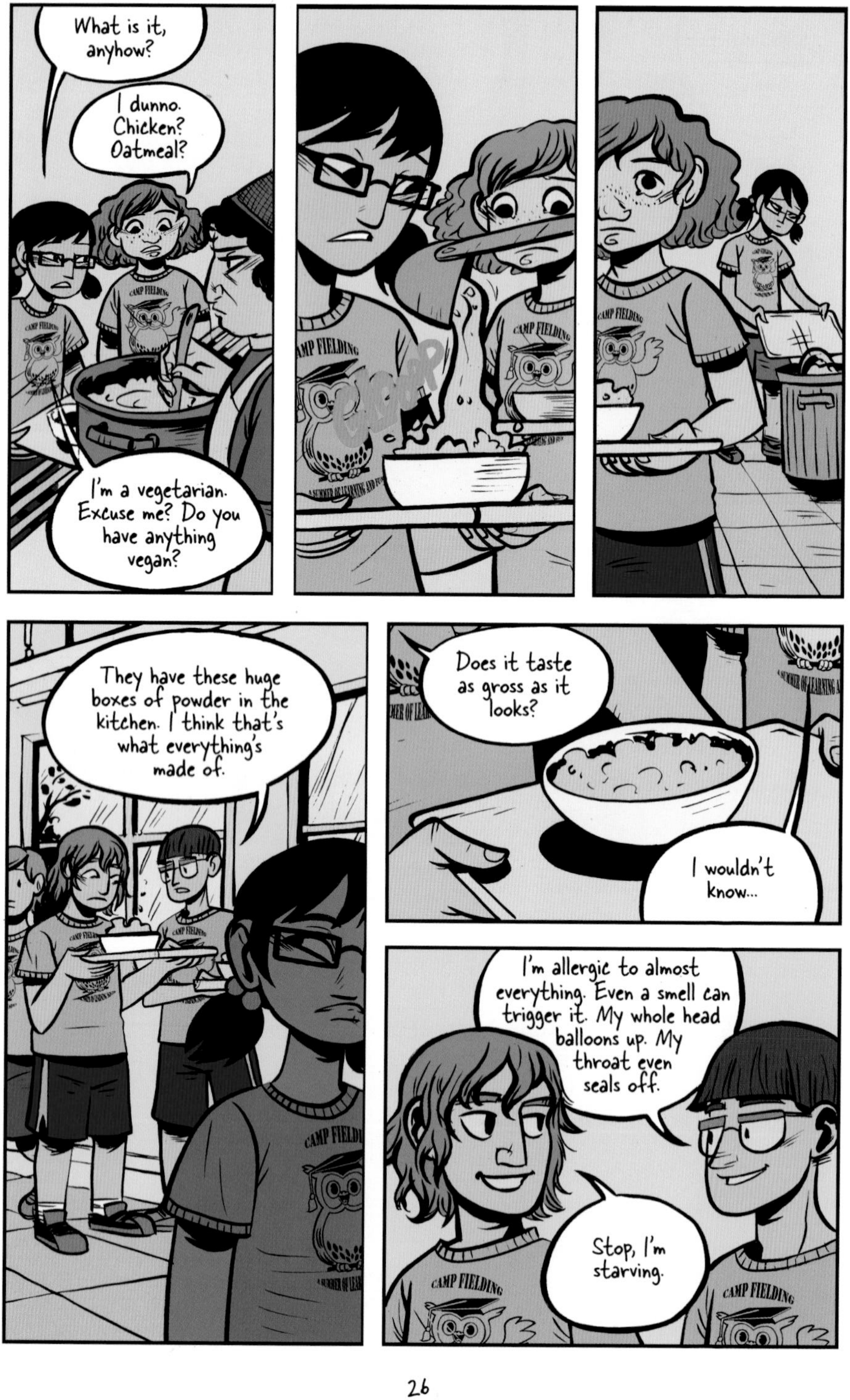
What is it, anyhow?
I dunno. Chicken? Oatmeal?
I'm a vegetarian. Excuse me? Do you have anything vegan?
CAMP FIELDING
They have these huge boxes of powder in the kitchen. I think that's what everything's made of.
Does it taste as gross as it looks?
I wouldn't know...
I'm allergic to almost everything. Even a smell can trigger it. My whole head balloons up. My throat even seals off.
Stop, I'm starving.

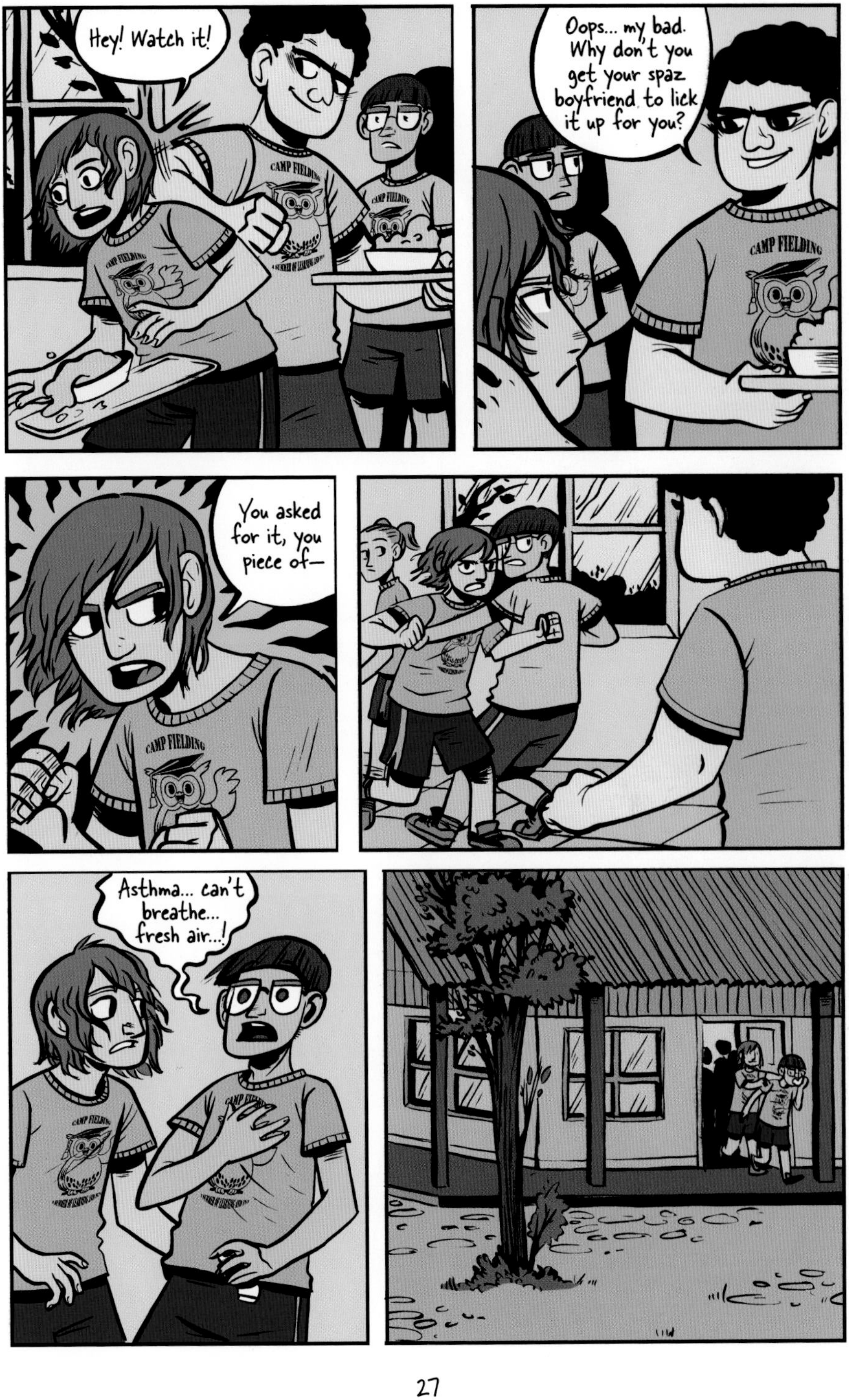
Hey! Watch it!
Oops... my bad. Why don't you get your spaz boyfriend to lick it up for you?
You asked for it, you piece of—
Asthma... can't breathe... fresh air...!

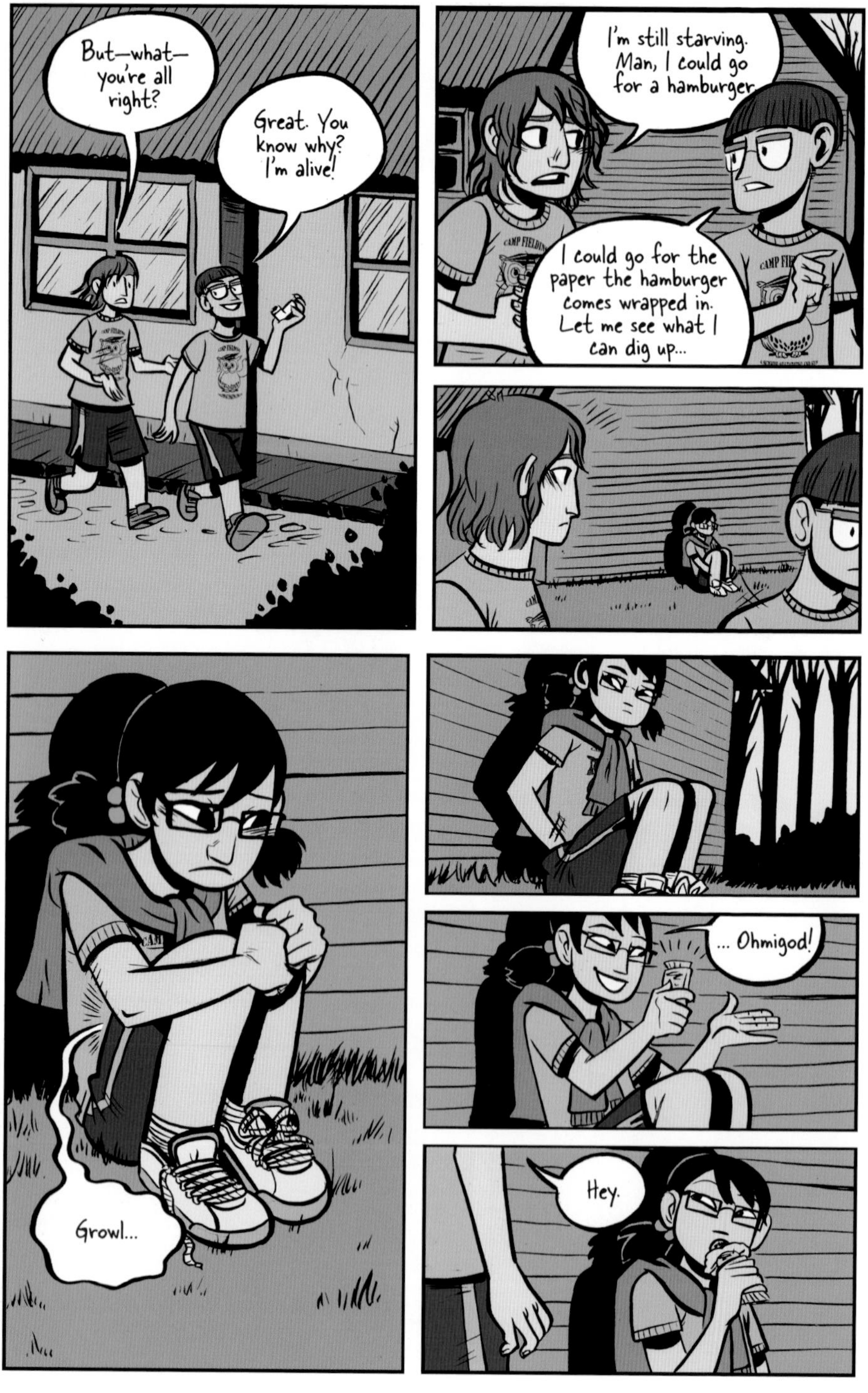
But—what—you're all right?
Great. You know why? I'm alive!
I'm still starving. Man, I could go for a hamburger.
I could go for the paper the hamburger comes wrapped in. Let me see what I can dig up...
CAMP FIELDING
Growl...
... Ohmigod!
Hey.

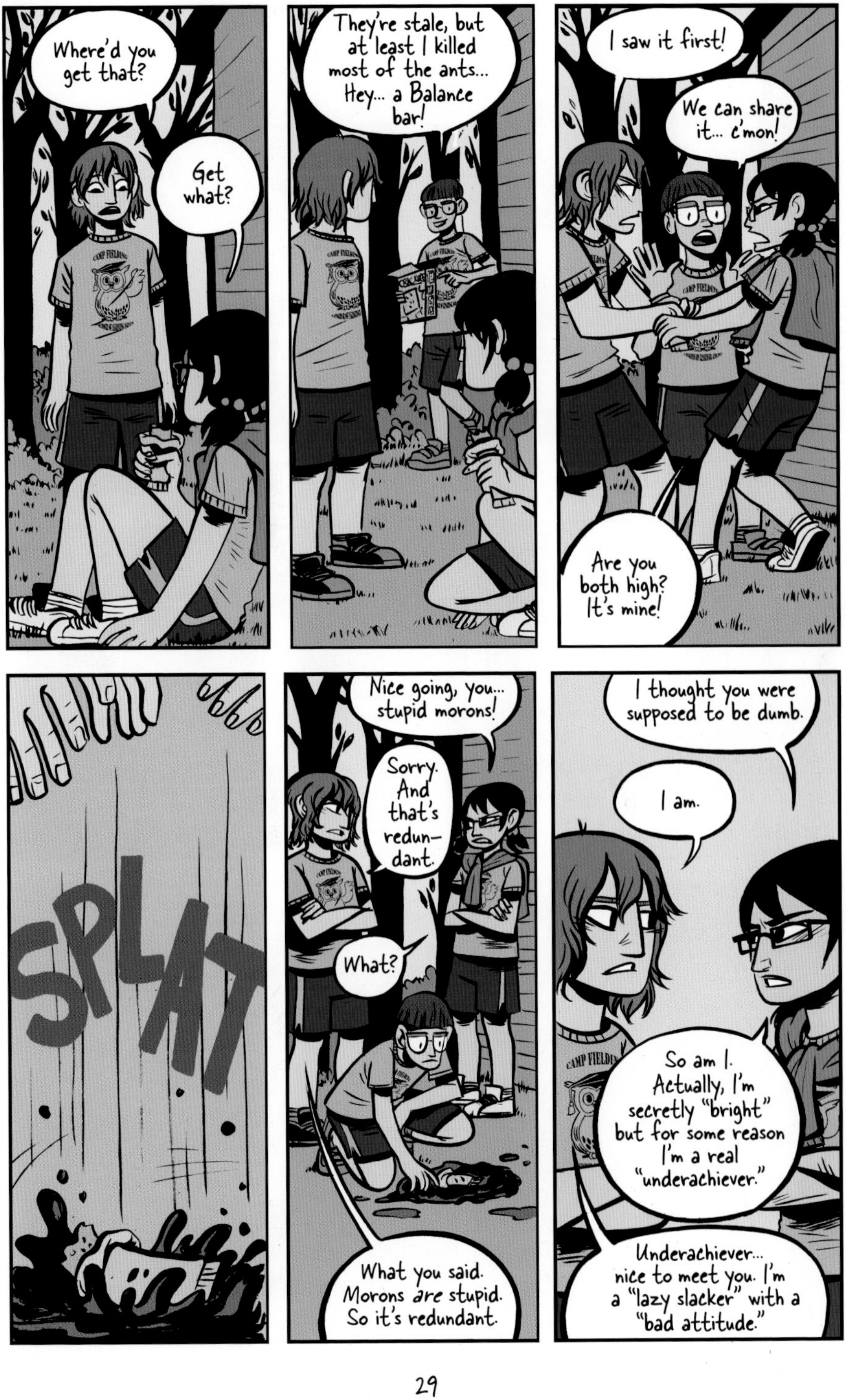
Where'd you get that?
Get what?
They're stale, but at least I killed most of the ants... Hey... a Balance bar!
I saw it first!
We can share it... c'mon!
Are you both high? It's mine!
SPLAT
Nice going, you... stupid morons!
Sorry. And that's redun-dant.
What?
What you said. Morons are stupid. So it's redundant.
I thought you were supposed to be dumb.
I am.
So am I. Actually, I'm secretly "bright" but for some reason I'm a real "underachiever."
Underachiever... nice to meet you. I'm a "lazy slacker" with a "bad attitude."

—and I'm "hyper" and "clueless."

Okay, people... listen up!

You get five minutes to finish up. Then it's time for the afternoon's activities!

Trust me... she doesn't mean volleyball.

The weird thing is, they don't teach at Camp Fielding. All they do is throw you into a subject and figure you'll just pick it up.

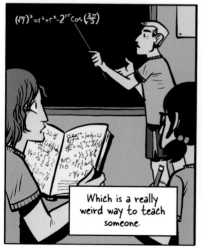

$(\sqrt{7})^2 = r^2 + r^2 - 2^{rr}\cos\left(\frac{2\pi}{3}\right)$

Which is a really weird way to teach someone.

Kunt u wat ik begrijpen zeg?

See what I mean?

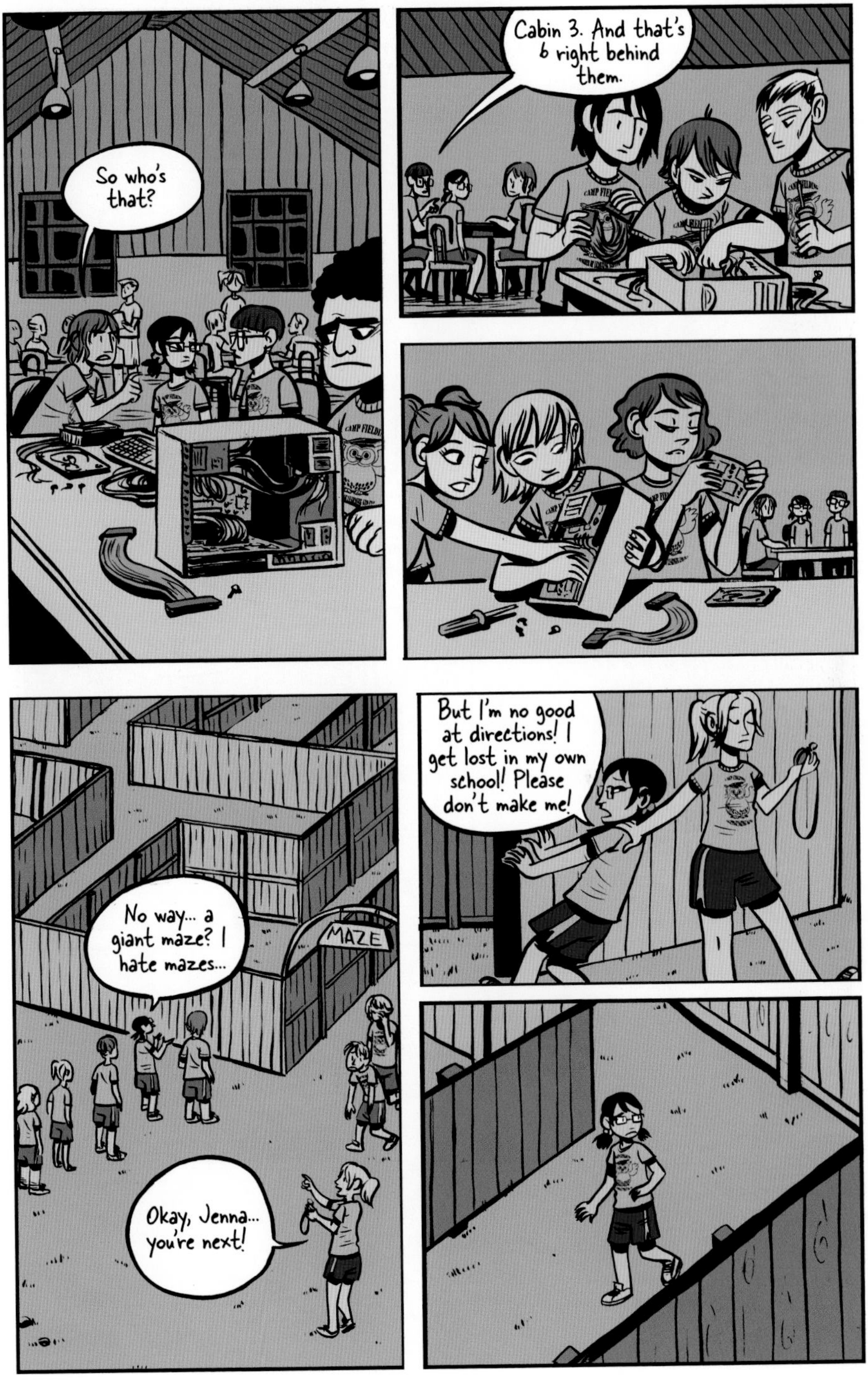
So who's that?
Cabin 3. And that's 6 right behind them.
CAMP FIELDING
No way... a giant maze? I hate mazes...
MAZE
Okay, Jenna... you're next!
But I'm no good at directions! I get lost in my own school! Please don't make me!

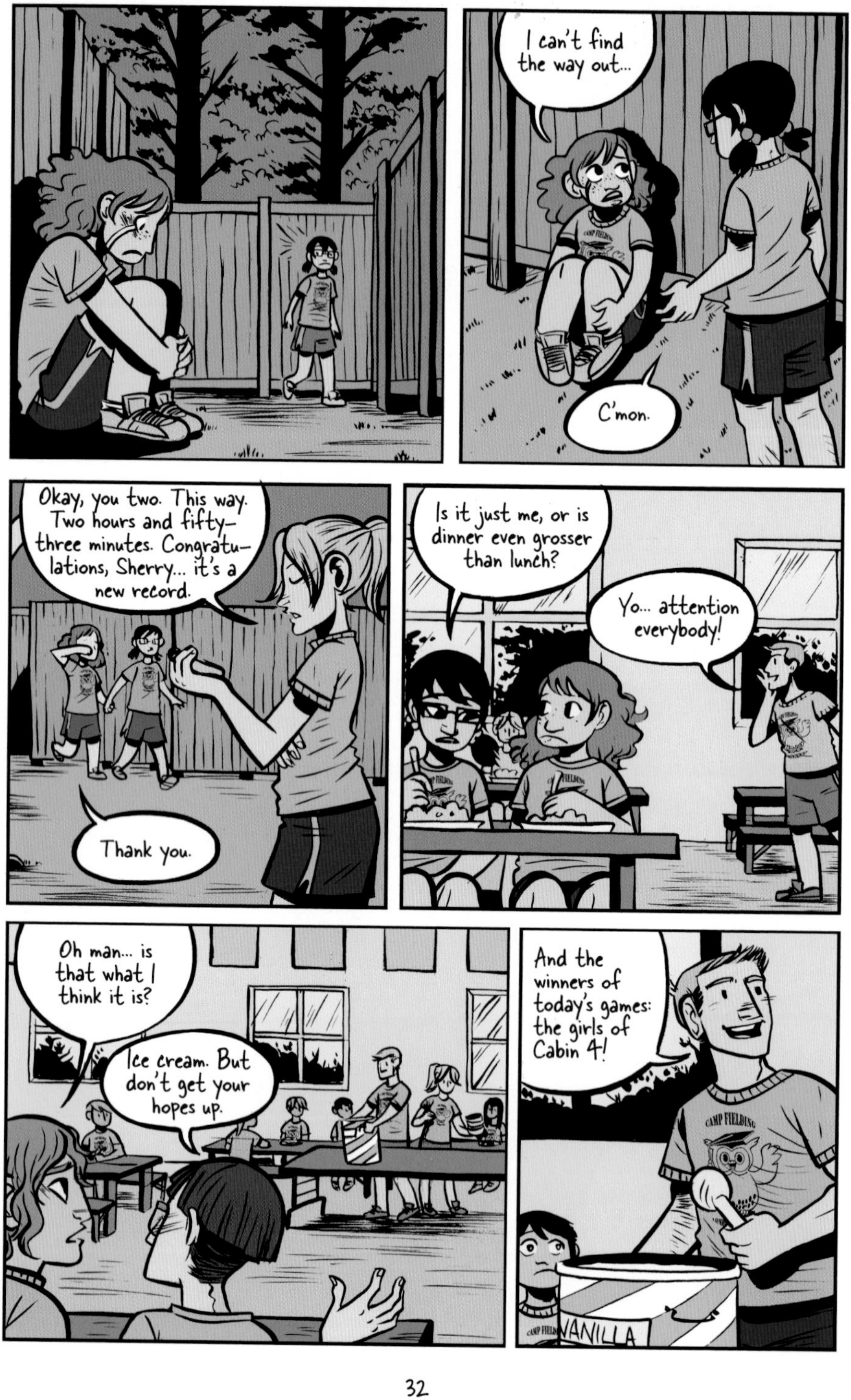
I can't find the way out...
C'mon.
Okay, you two. This way. Two hours and fifty-three minutes. Congratulations, Sherry... it's a new record.
Thank you.
Is it just me, or is dinner even grosser than lunch?
Yo... attention everybody!
Oh man... is that what I think it is?
Ice cream. But don't get your hopes up.
And the winners of today's games: the girls of Cabin 4!
CAMP FIELDING
VANILLA

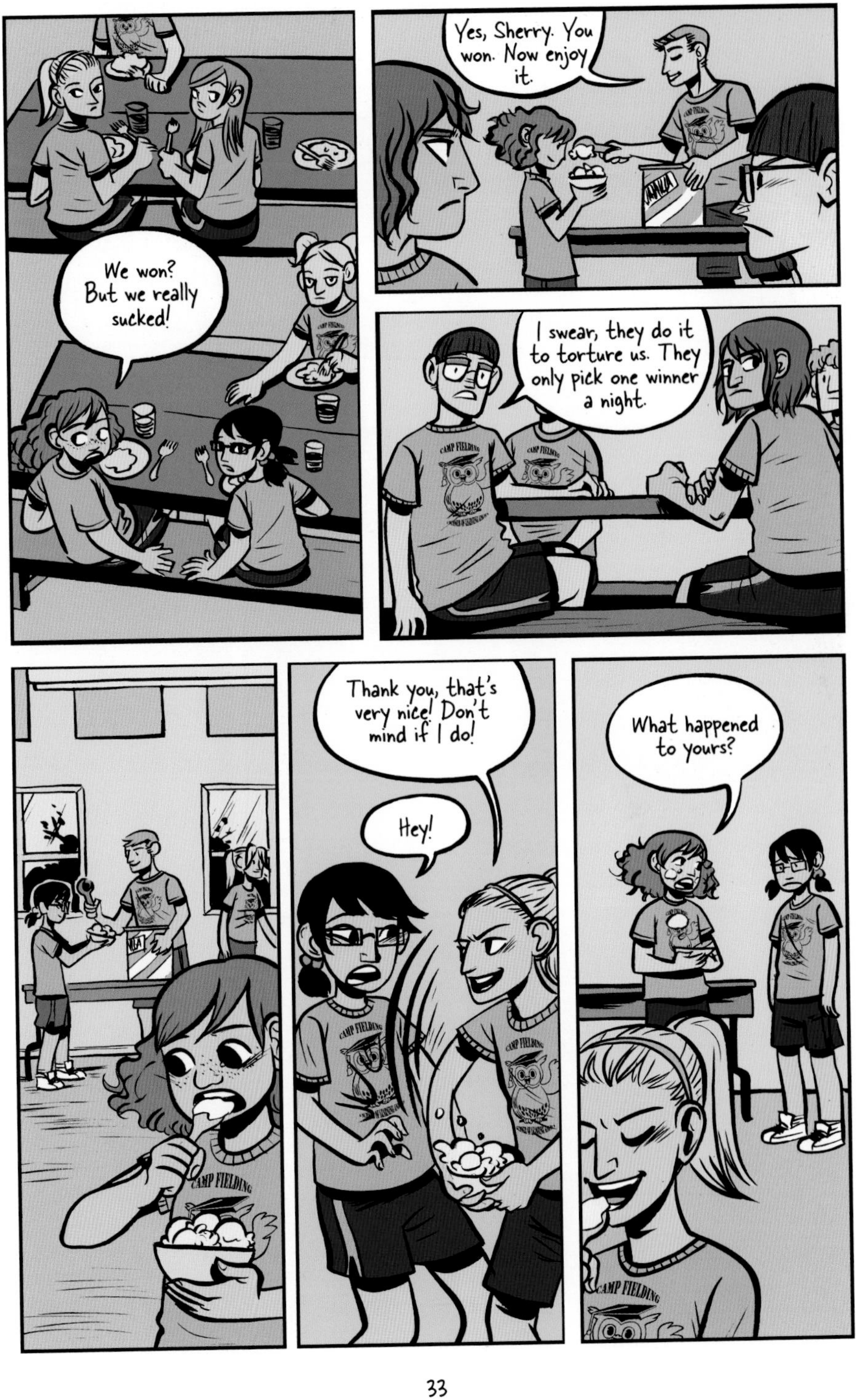
We won? But we really sucked!
Yes, Sherry. You won. Now enjoy it.
VANILLA
I swear, they do it to torture us. They only pick one winner a night.
CAMP FIELDING
Thank you, that's very nice! Don't mind if I do!
Hey!
What happened to yours?
CAMP FIELDING

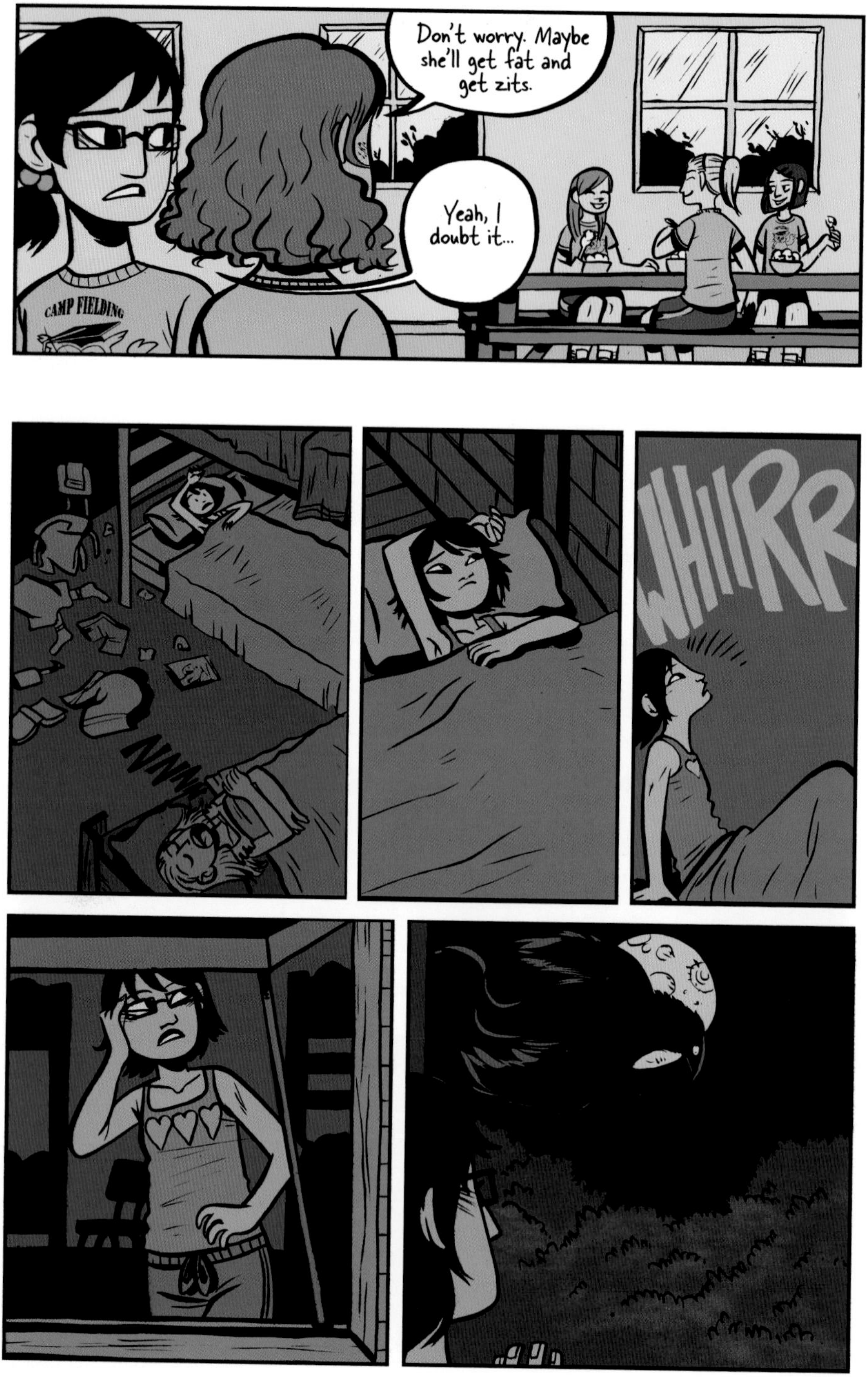
Don't worry. Maybe she'll get fat and get zits.
Yeah, I doubt it...
CAMP FIELDING
WHIIRR

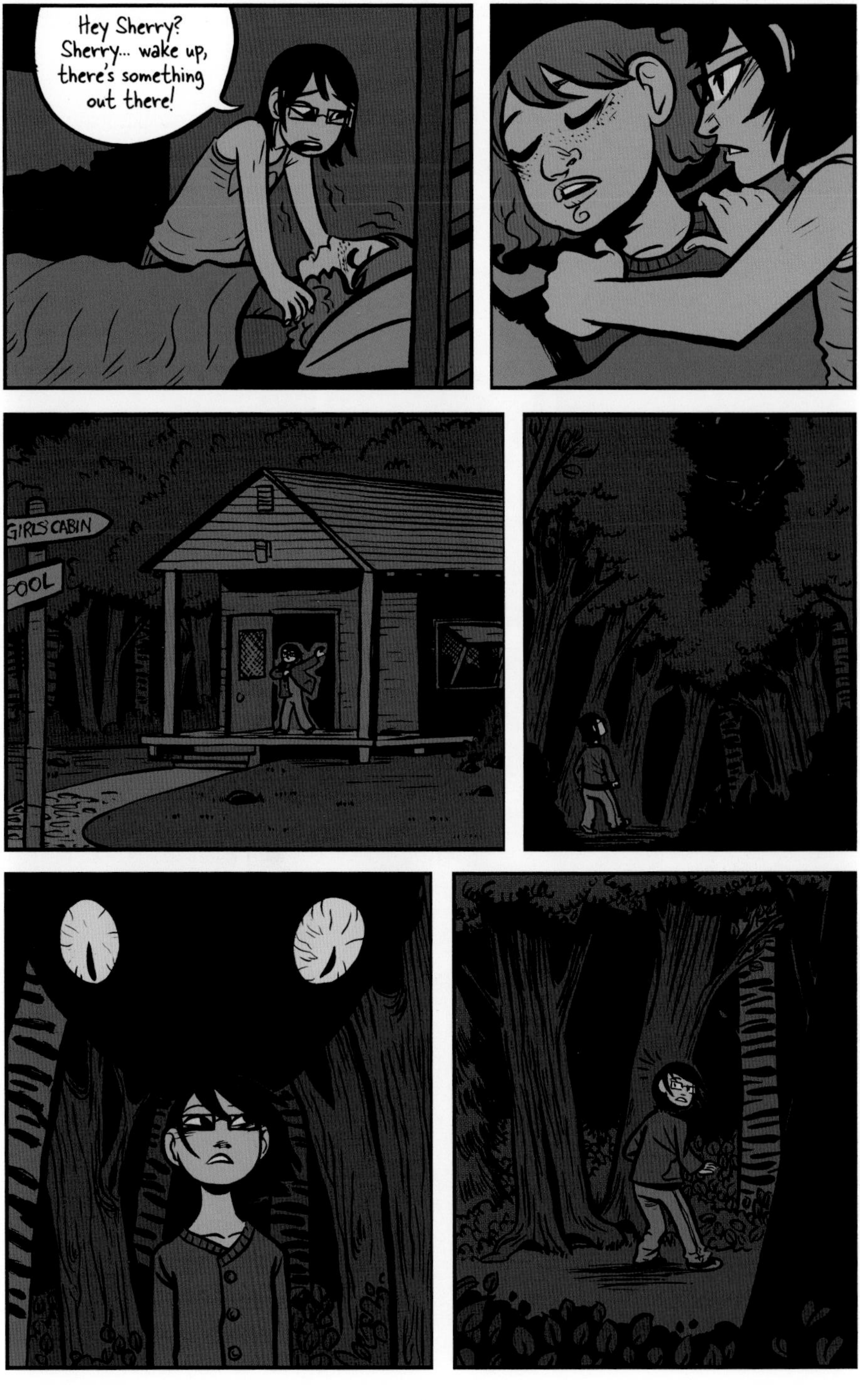
Hey Sherry? Sherry... wake up, there's something out there!
GIRLS' CABIN
POOL

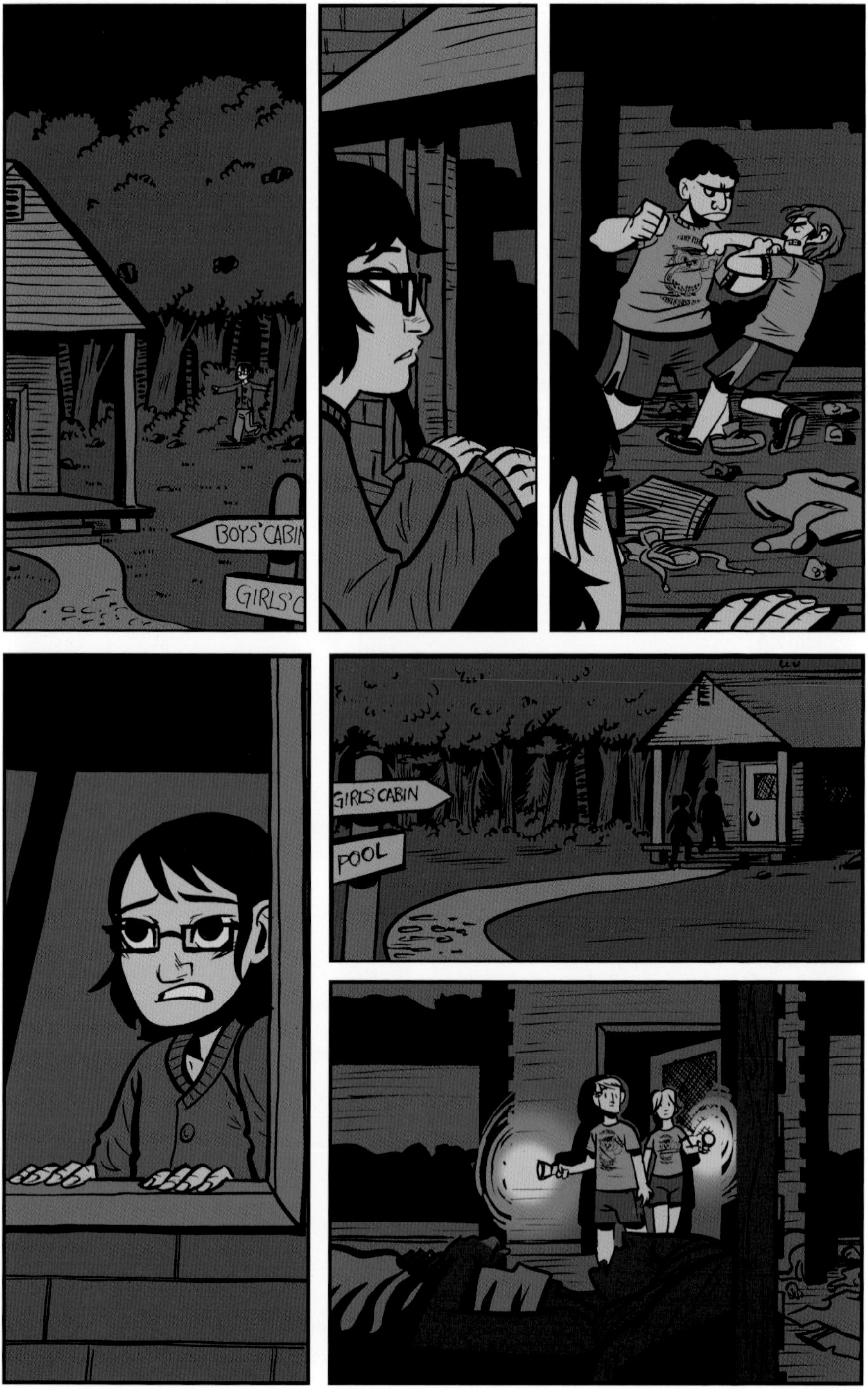
BOYS' CABI
GIRLS' C
GIRLS' CABIN
POOL

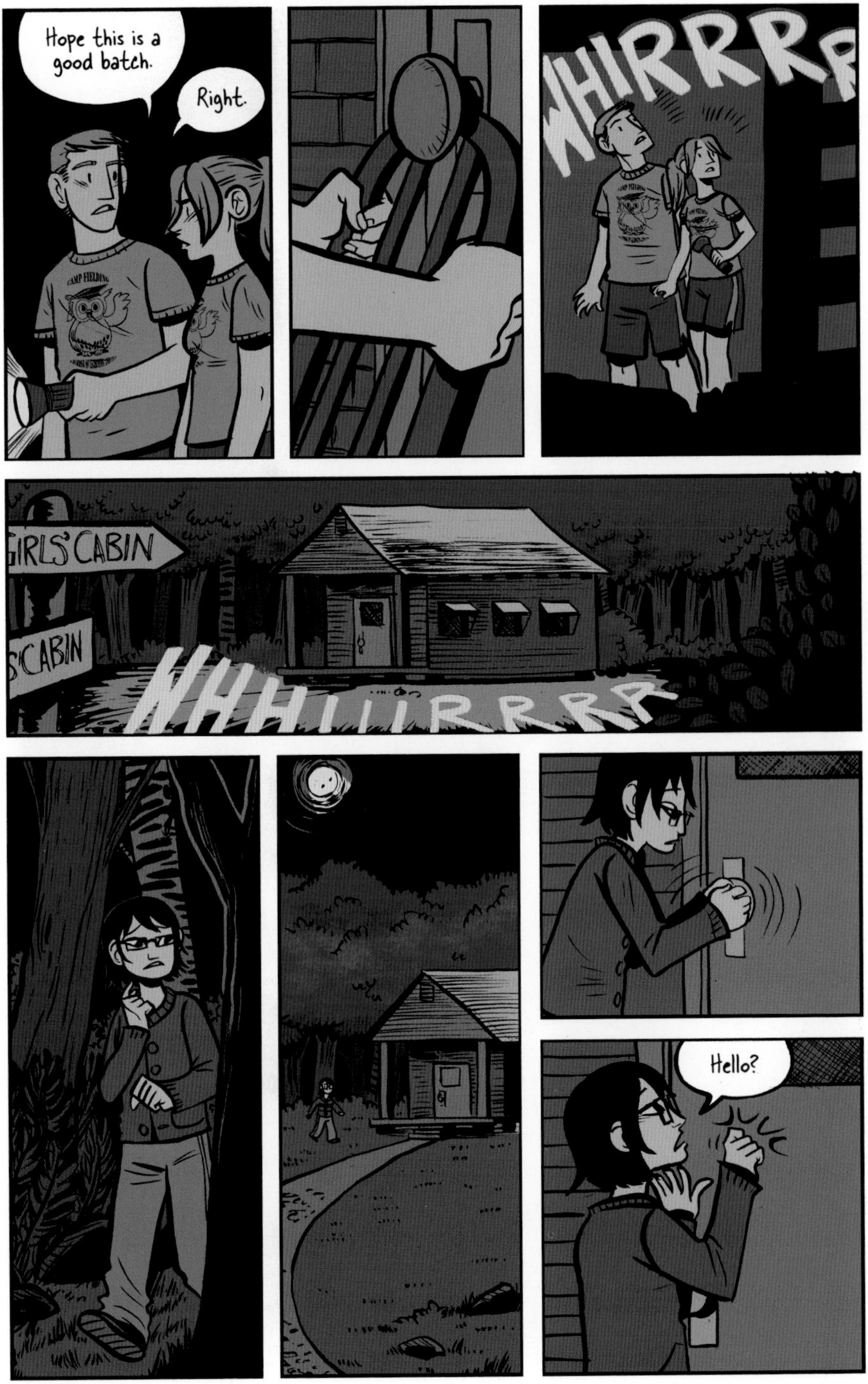
Hope this is a good batch.
Right.
WHIRRRR
GIRLS' CABIN
S' CABIN
WHHIIIRRRR
Hello?

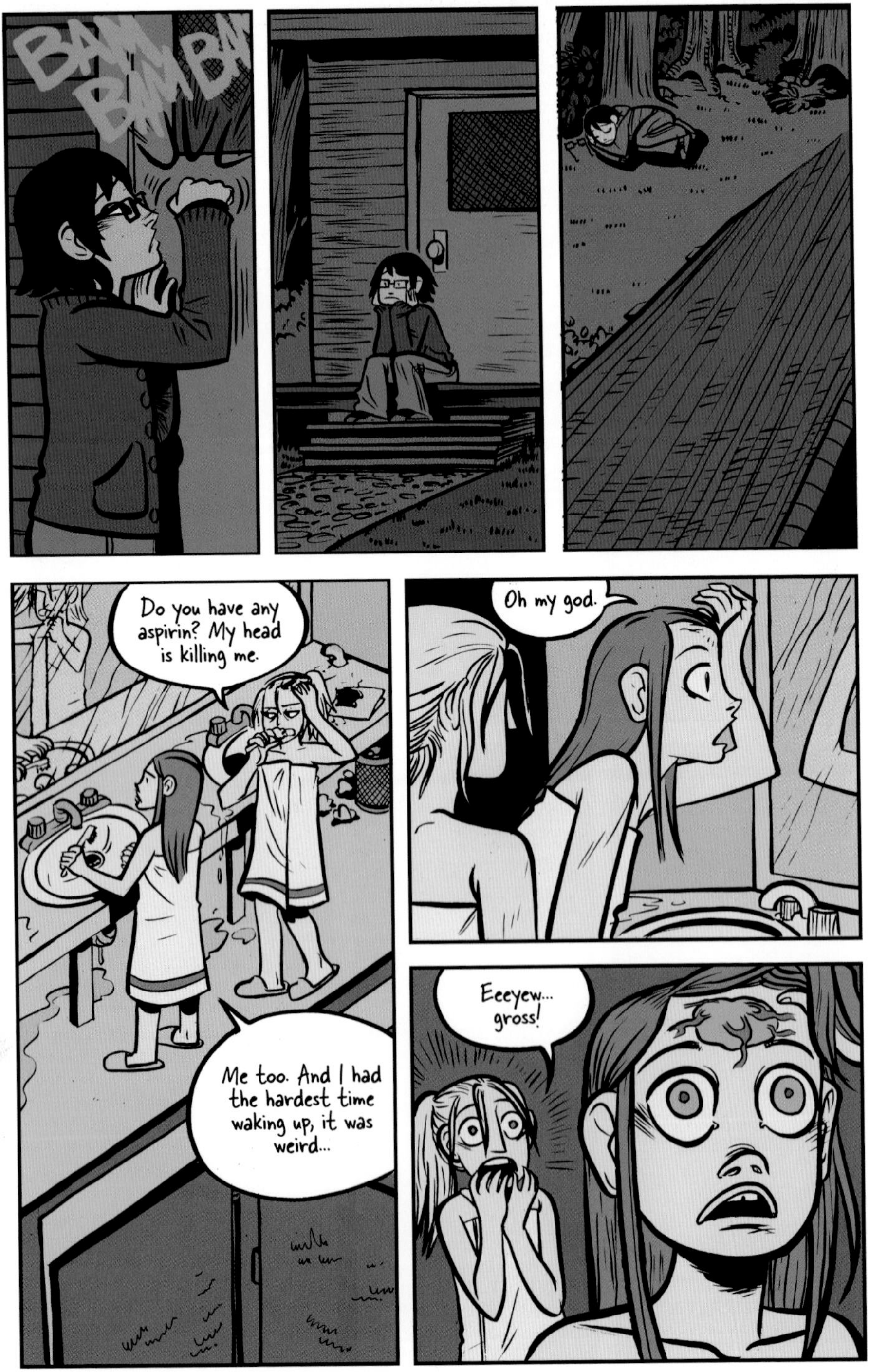
BAM BAM BAM
Do you have any aspirin? My head is killing me.
Me too. And I had the hardest time waking up, it was weird...
Oh my god.
Eeeyew... gross!

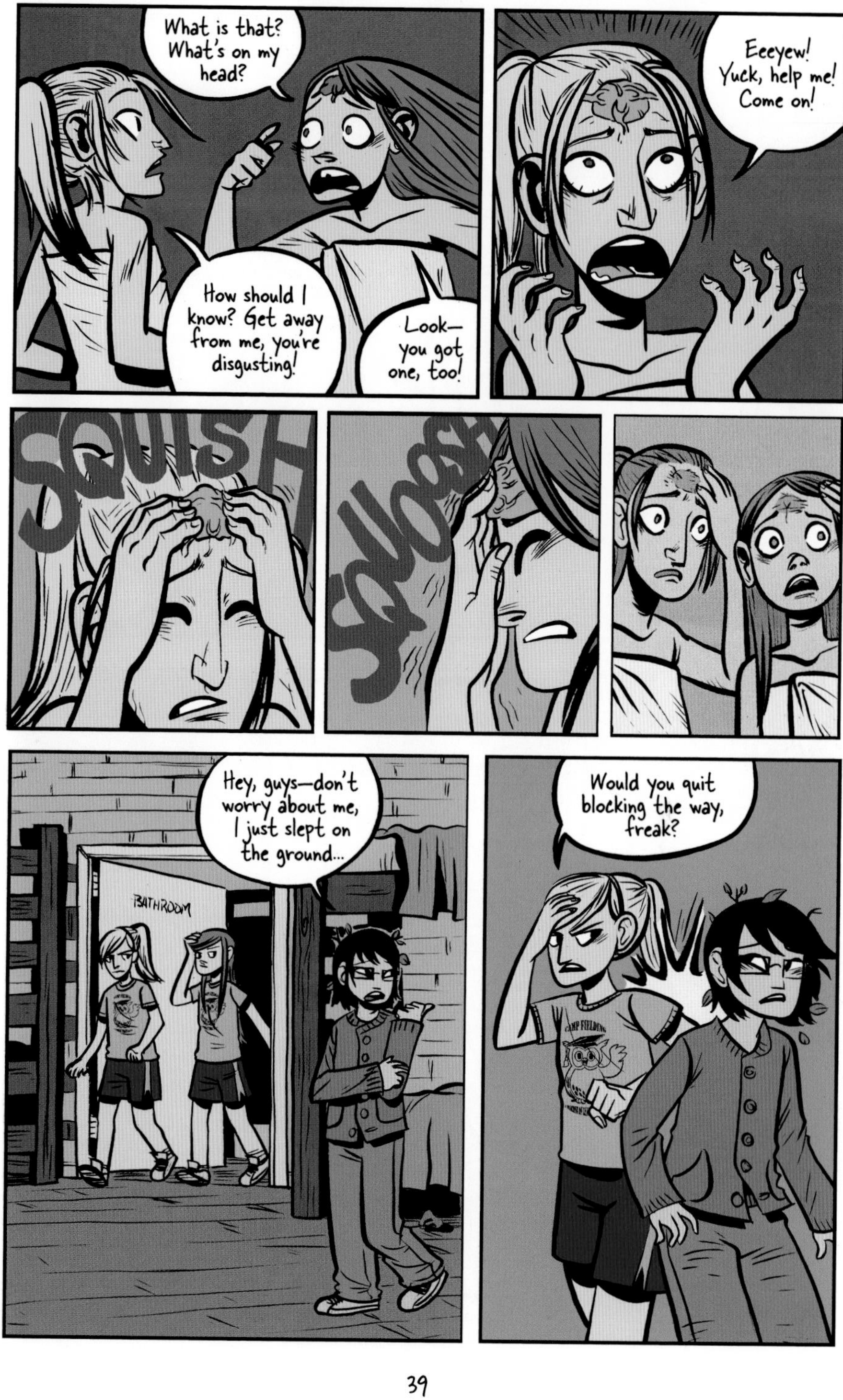
What is that? What's on my head?
How should I know? Get away from me, you're disgusting!
Look— you got one, too!
Eeeyew! Yuck, help me! Come on!
SQUISH
SPLOOSH
BATHROOM
Hey, guys—don't worry about me, I just slept on the ground...
Would you quit blocking the way, freak?
CAMP FIELDING

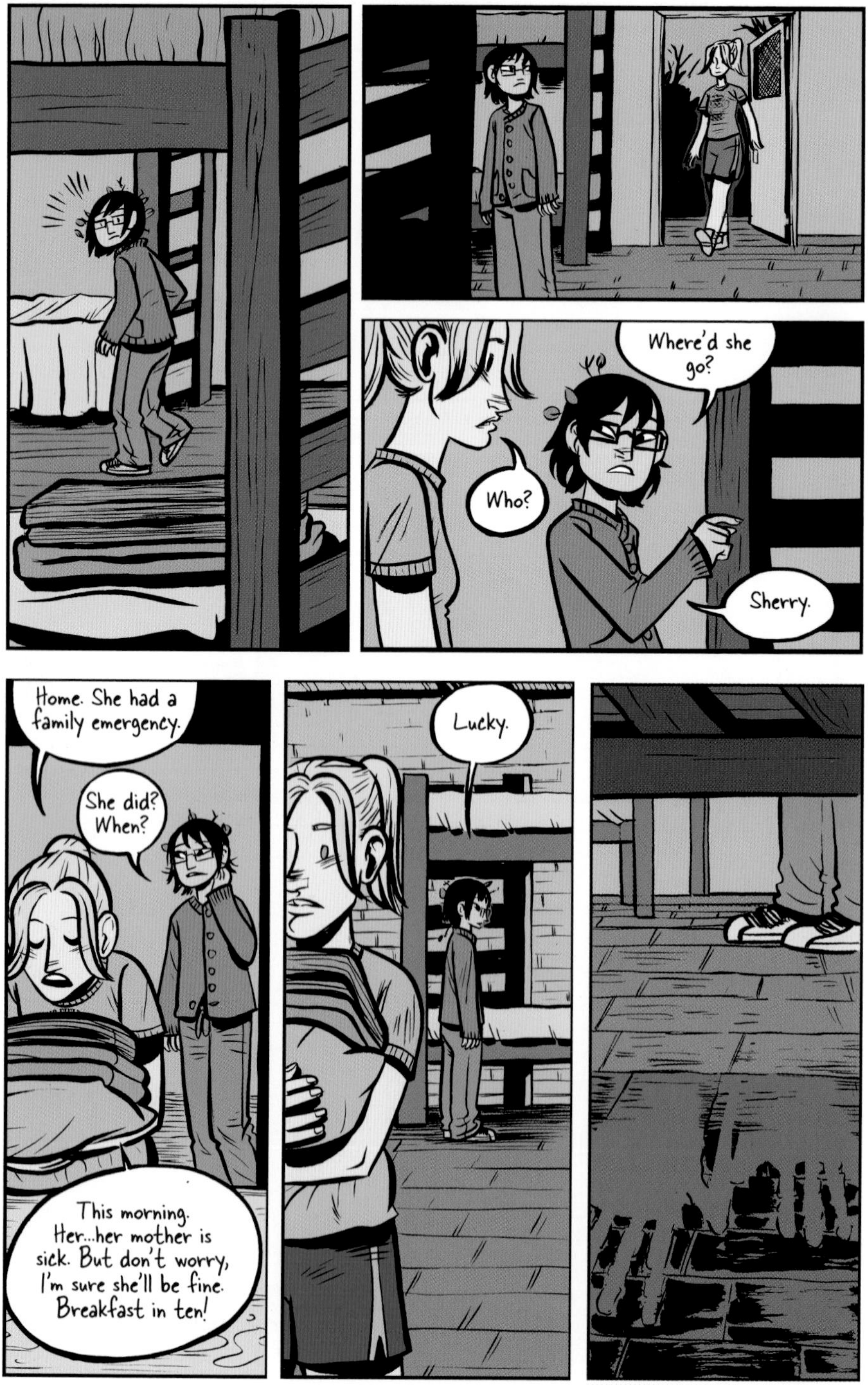
Where'd she go?
Who?
Sherry.
Home. She had a family emergency.
She did? When?
This morning. Her...her mother is sick. But don't worry, I'm sure she'll be fine. Breakfast in ten!
Lucky.

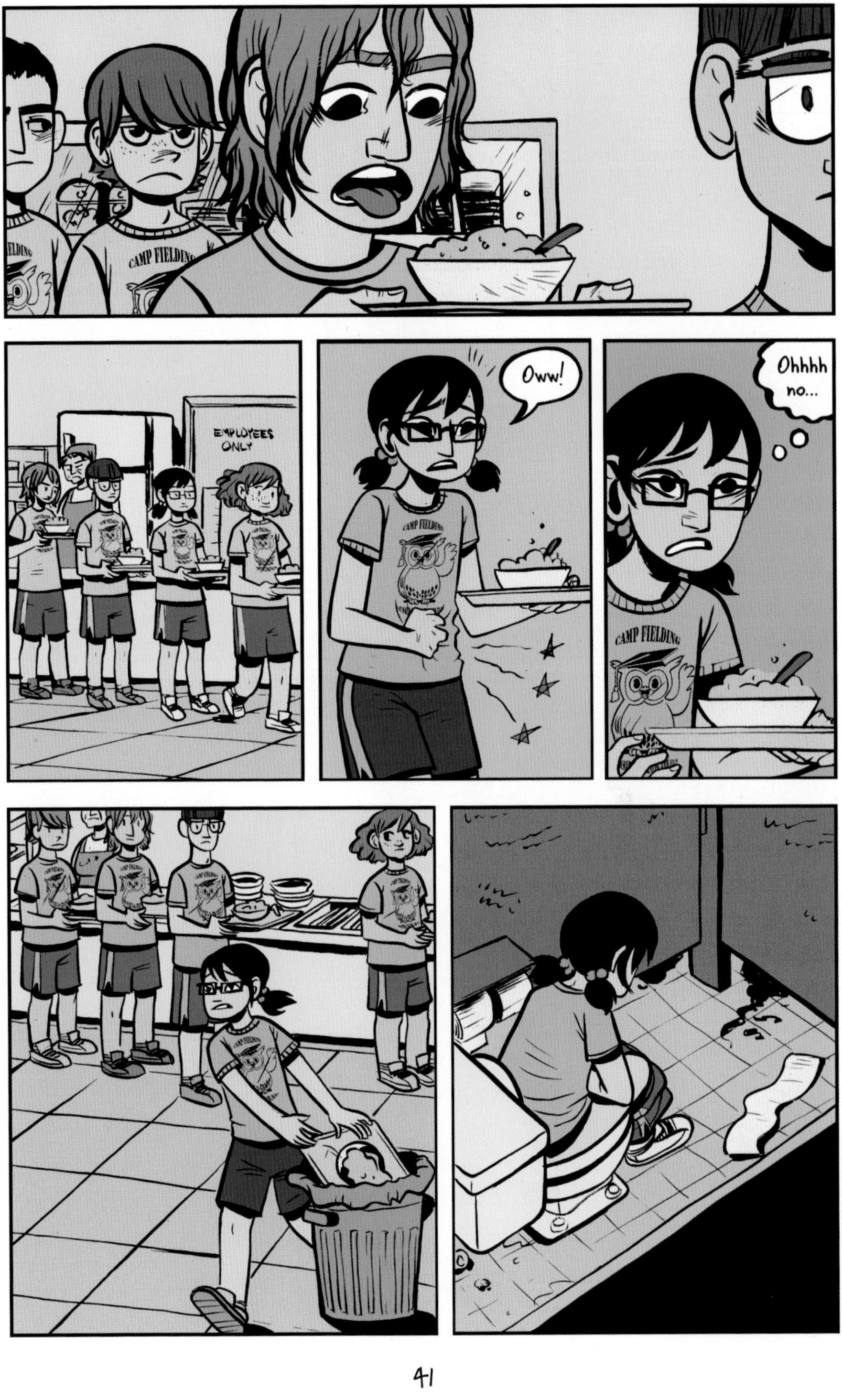
CAMP FIELDING
EMPLOYEES ONLY
Oww!
Ohhhh no...
CAMP FIELDING

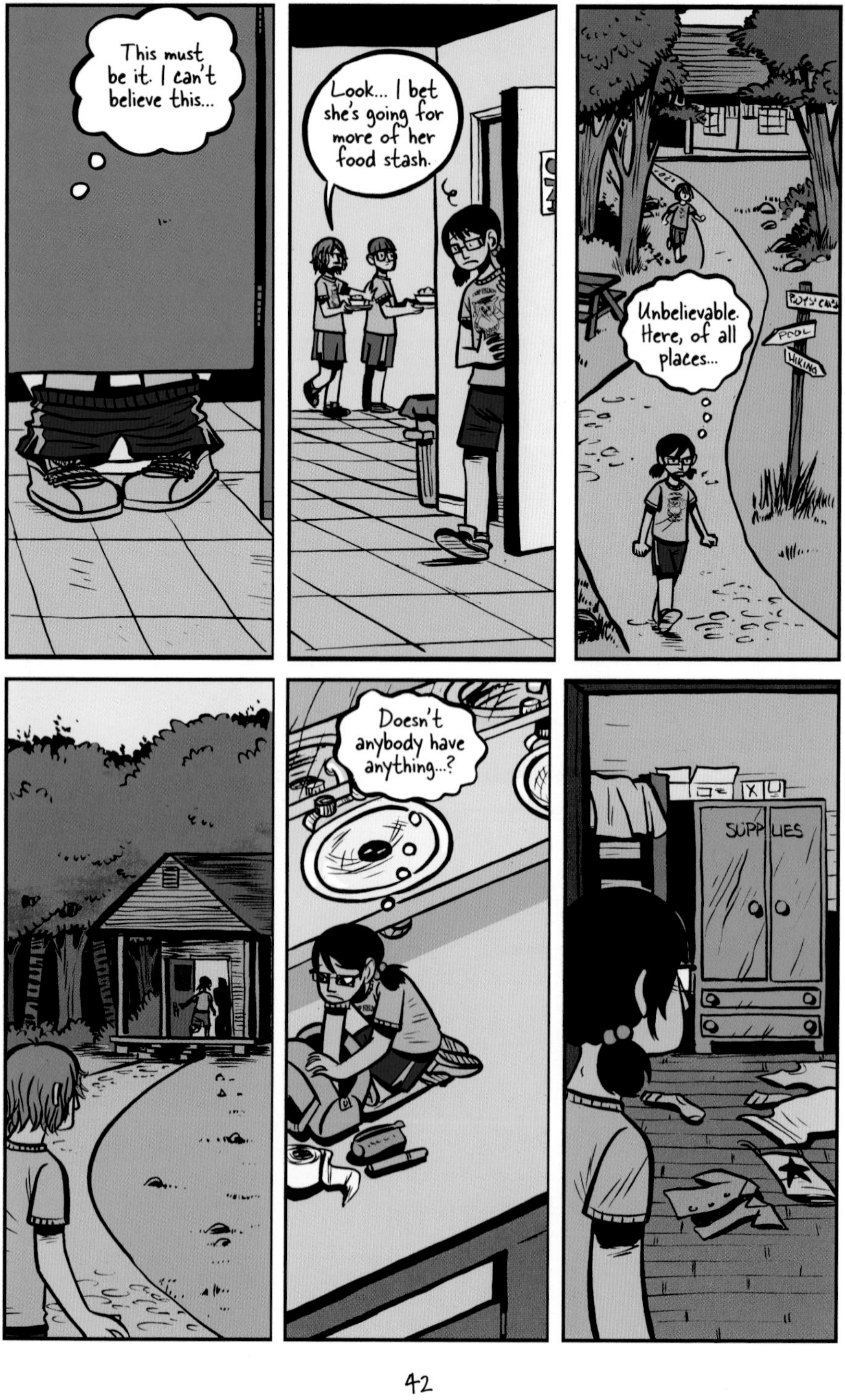

This must be it. I can't believe this...
Look... I bet she's going for more of her food stash.
Unbelievable. Here, of all places...
POOL
HIKING
Doesn't anybody have anything...?
SUPPLIES

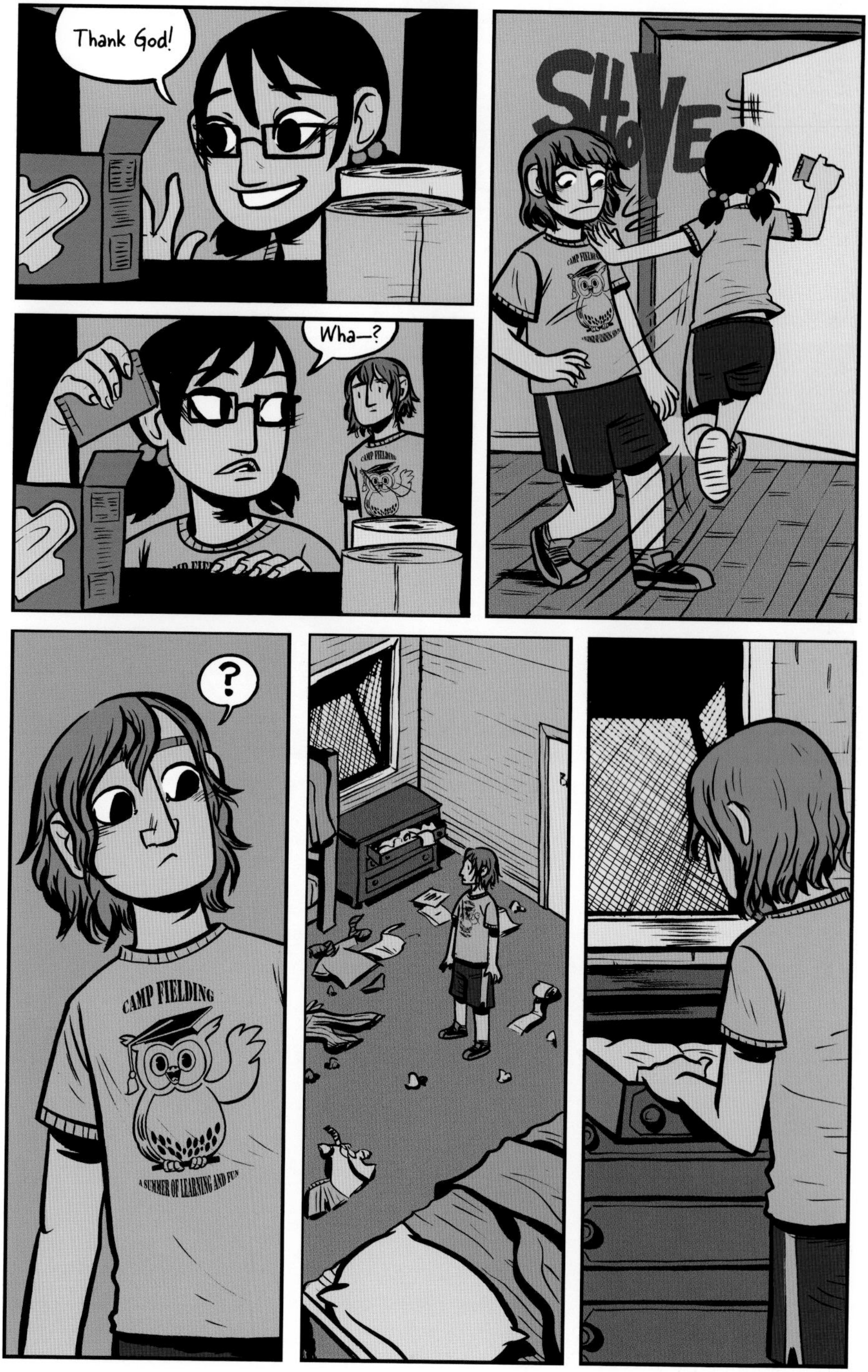
Thank God!
SHOVE
Wha—?
CAMP FIELDING
?
CAMP FIELDING
A SUMMER OF LEARNING AND FUN

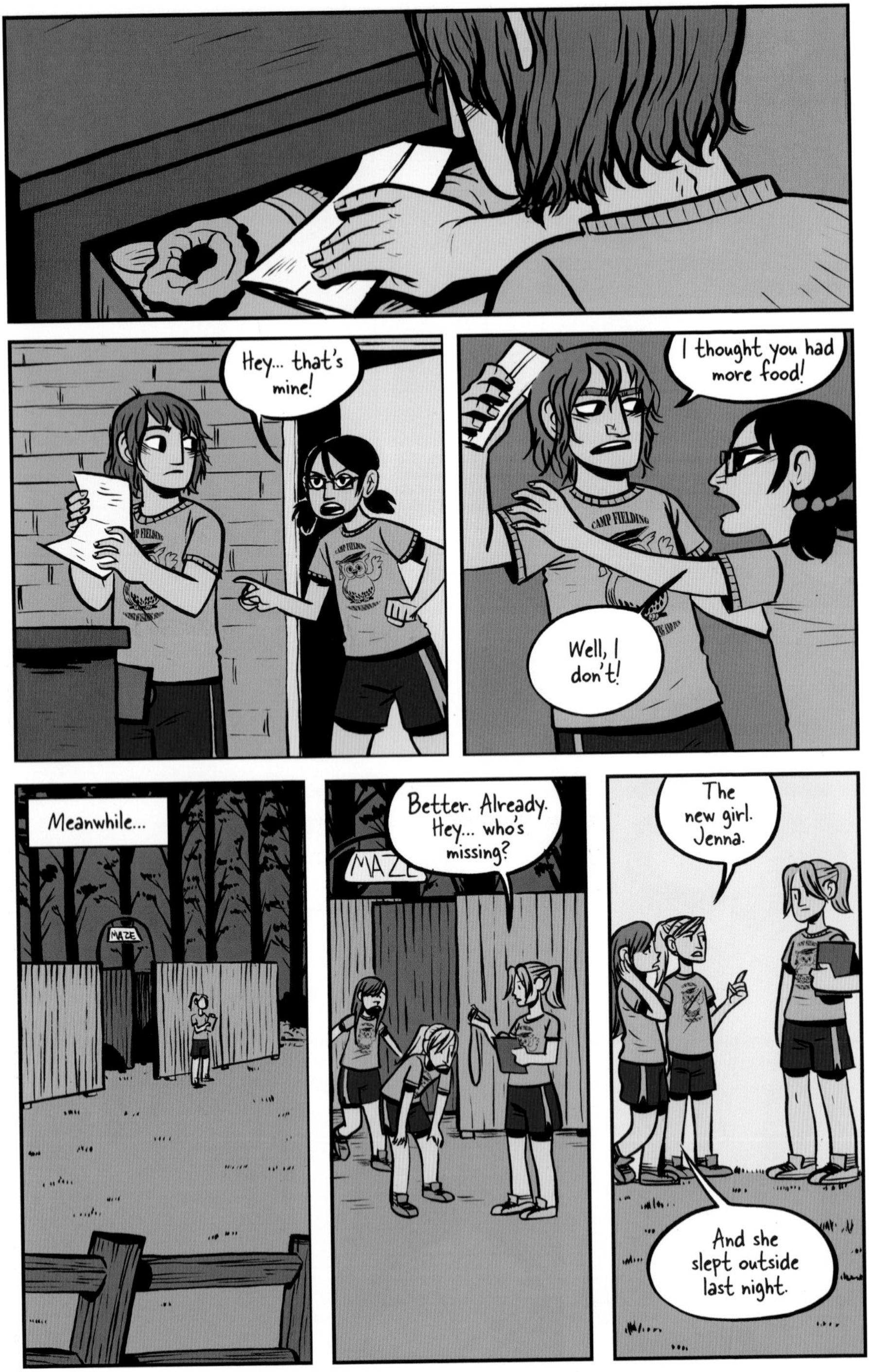
Hey... that's mine!
I thought you had more food!
Well, I don't!
Meanwhile...
MAZE
Better. Already. Hey... who's missing?
The new girl. Jenna.
And she slept outside last night.

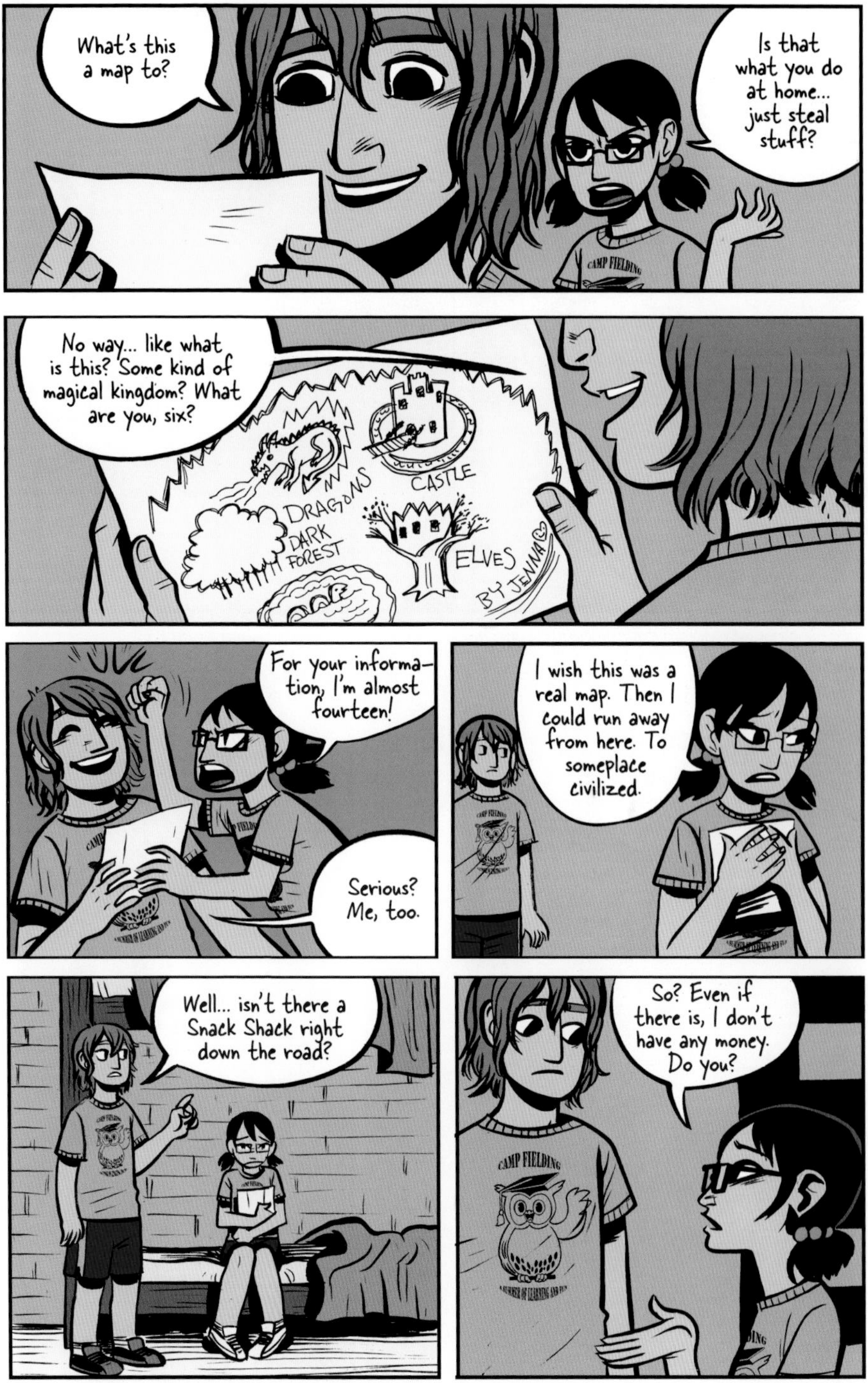
What's this a map to?
Is that what you do at home... just steal stuff?
CAMP FIELDING
No way... like what is this? Some kind of magical kingdom? What are you, six?
DRAGONS
CASTLE
DARK FOREST
ELVES
BY JENNA
For your information, I'm almost fourteen!
Serious? Me, too.
I wish this was a real map. Then I could run away from here. To someplace civilized.
Well... isn't there a Snack Shack right down the road?
So? Even if there is, I don't have any money. Do you?
CAMP FIELDING
A SUMMER OF LEARNING AND FUN

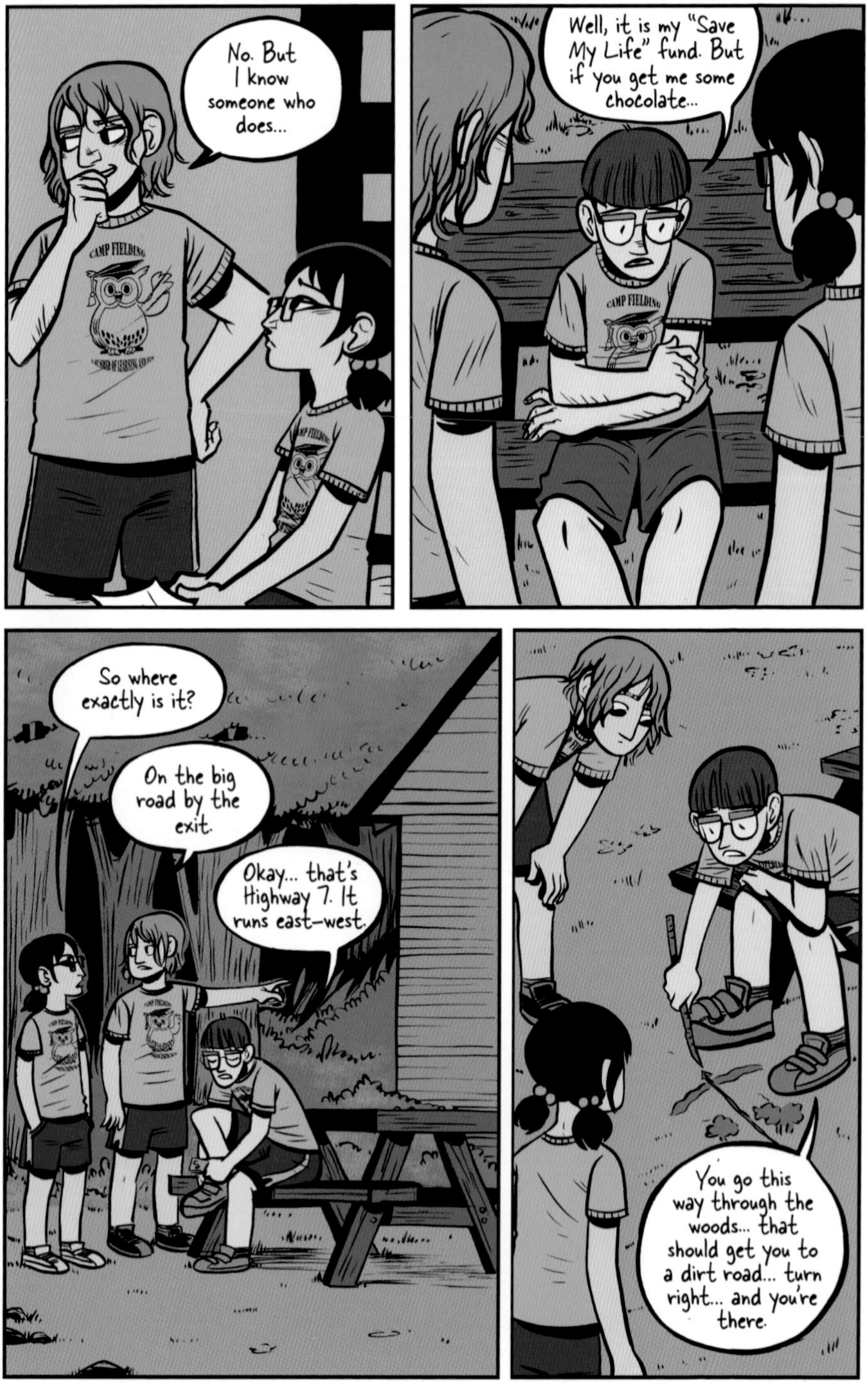
No. But I know someone who does...
Well, it is my "Save My Life" fund. But if you get me some chocolate...
So where exactly is it?
On the big road by the exit.
Okay... that's Highway 7. It runs east-west.
You go this way through the woods... that should get you to a dirt road... turn right... and you're there.

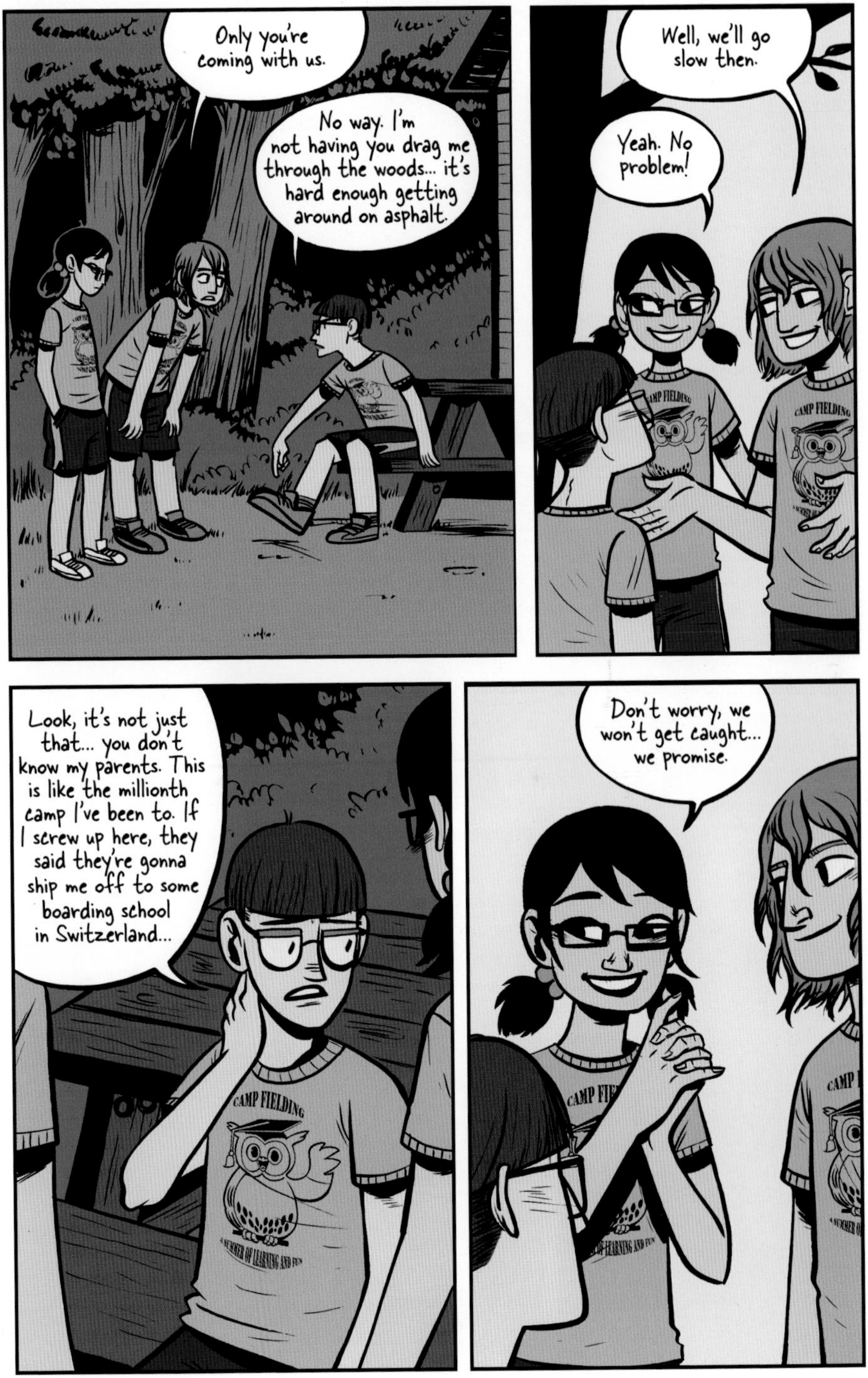
Only you're coming with us.
No way. I'm not having you drag me through the woods... it's hard enough getting around on asphalt.
Well, we'll go slow then.
Yeah. No problem!
Look, it's not just that... you don't know my parents. This is like the millionth camp I've been to. If I screw up here, they said they're gonna ship me off to some boarding school in Switzerland...
Don't worry, we won't get caught... we promise.
CAMP FIELDING
A SUMMER OF LEARNING AND FUN

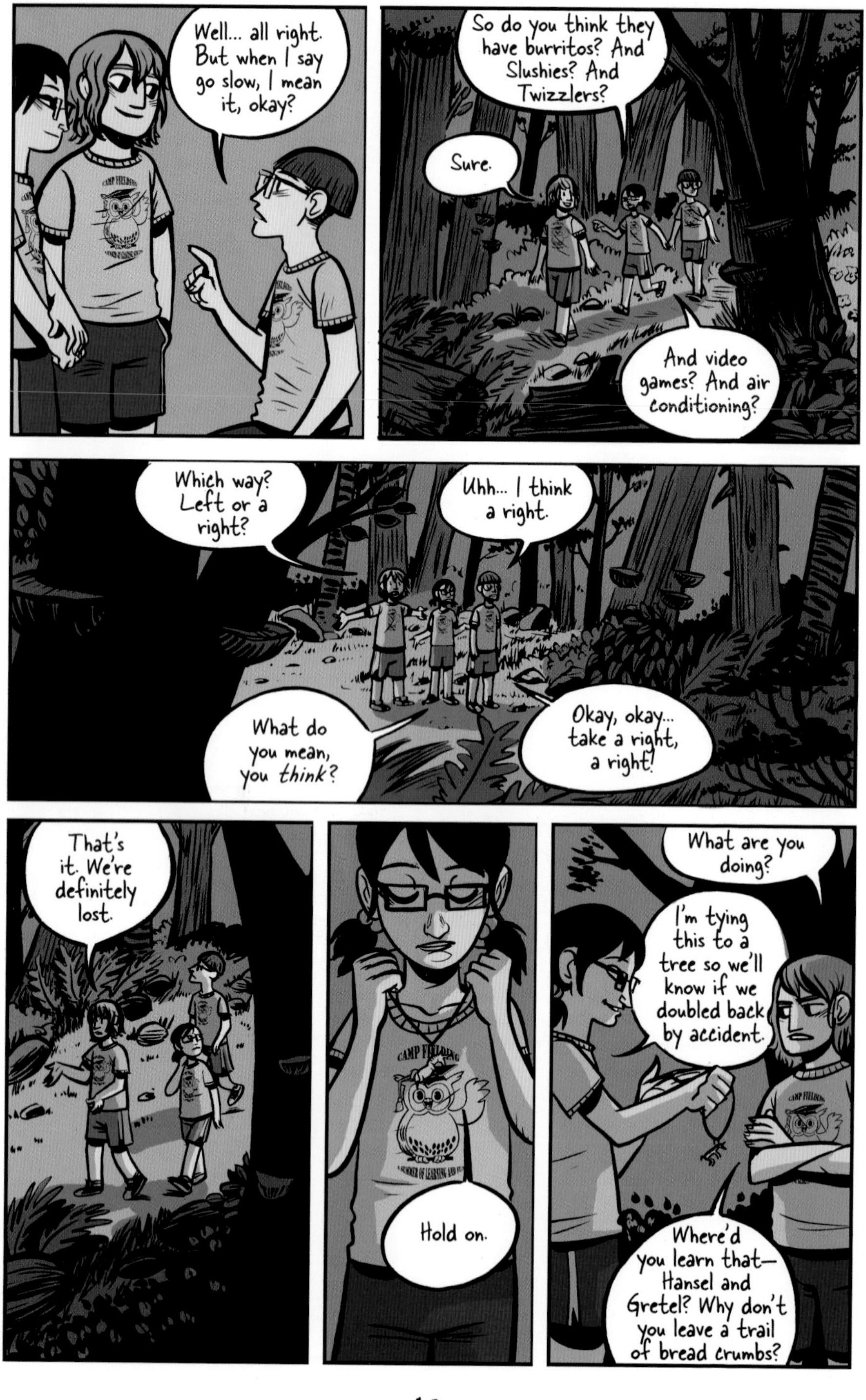
Well... all right. But when I say go slow, I mean it, okay?
So do you think they have burritos? And Slushies? And Twizzlers?
Sure.
And video games? And air conditioning?
Which way? Left or a right?
Uhh... I think a right.
What do you mean, you *think*?
Okay, okay... take a right, a right!
That's it. We're definitely lost.
Hold on.
What are you doing?
I'm tying this to a tree so we'll know if we doubled back by accident.
Where'd you learn that— Hansel and Gretel? Why don't you leave a trail of bread crumbs?

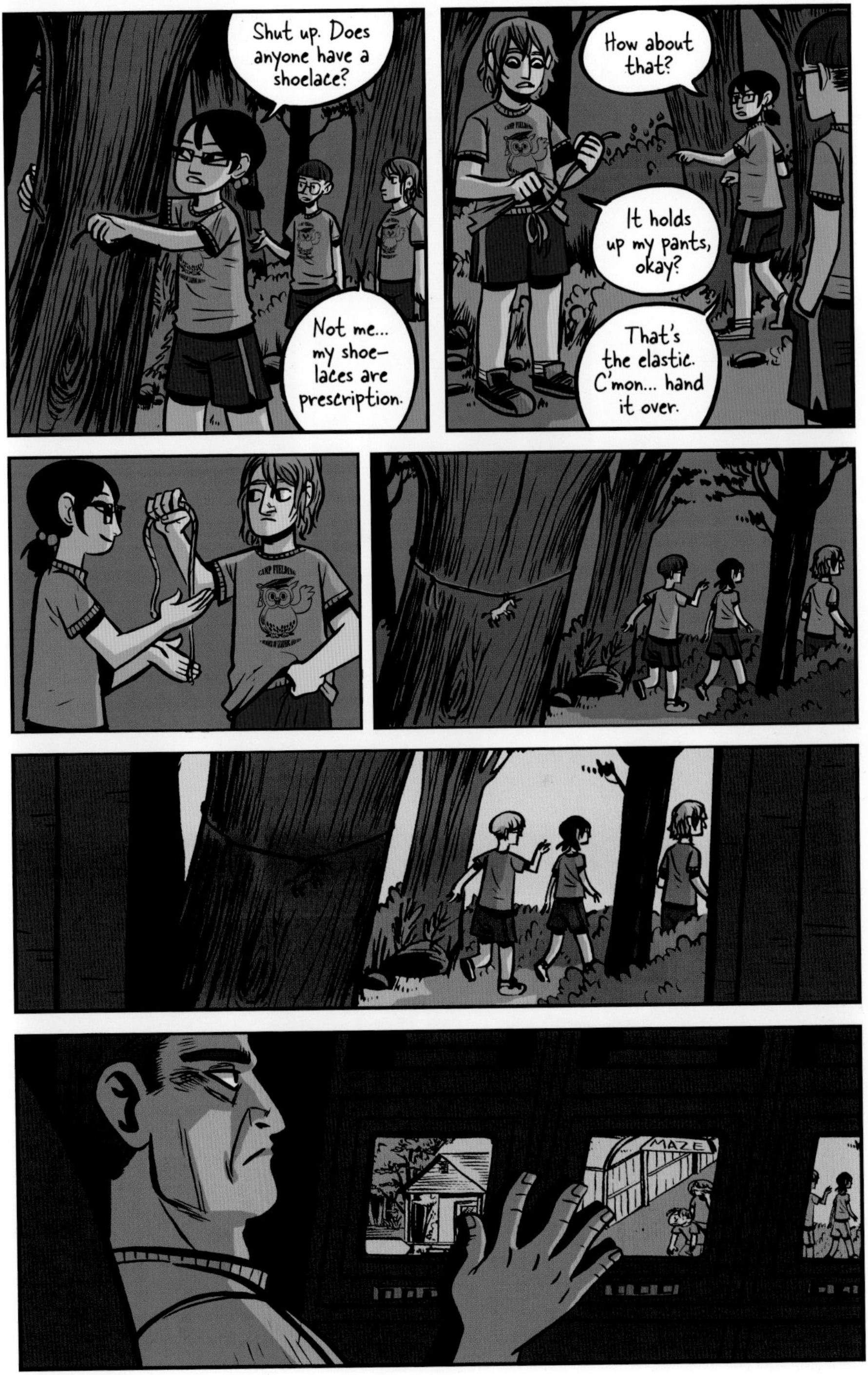
Shut up. Does anyone have a shoelace?
Not me... my shoelaces are prescription.
How about that?
It holds up my pants, okay?
That's the elastic. C'mon... hand it over.
MAZE

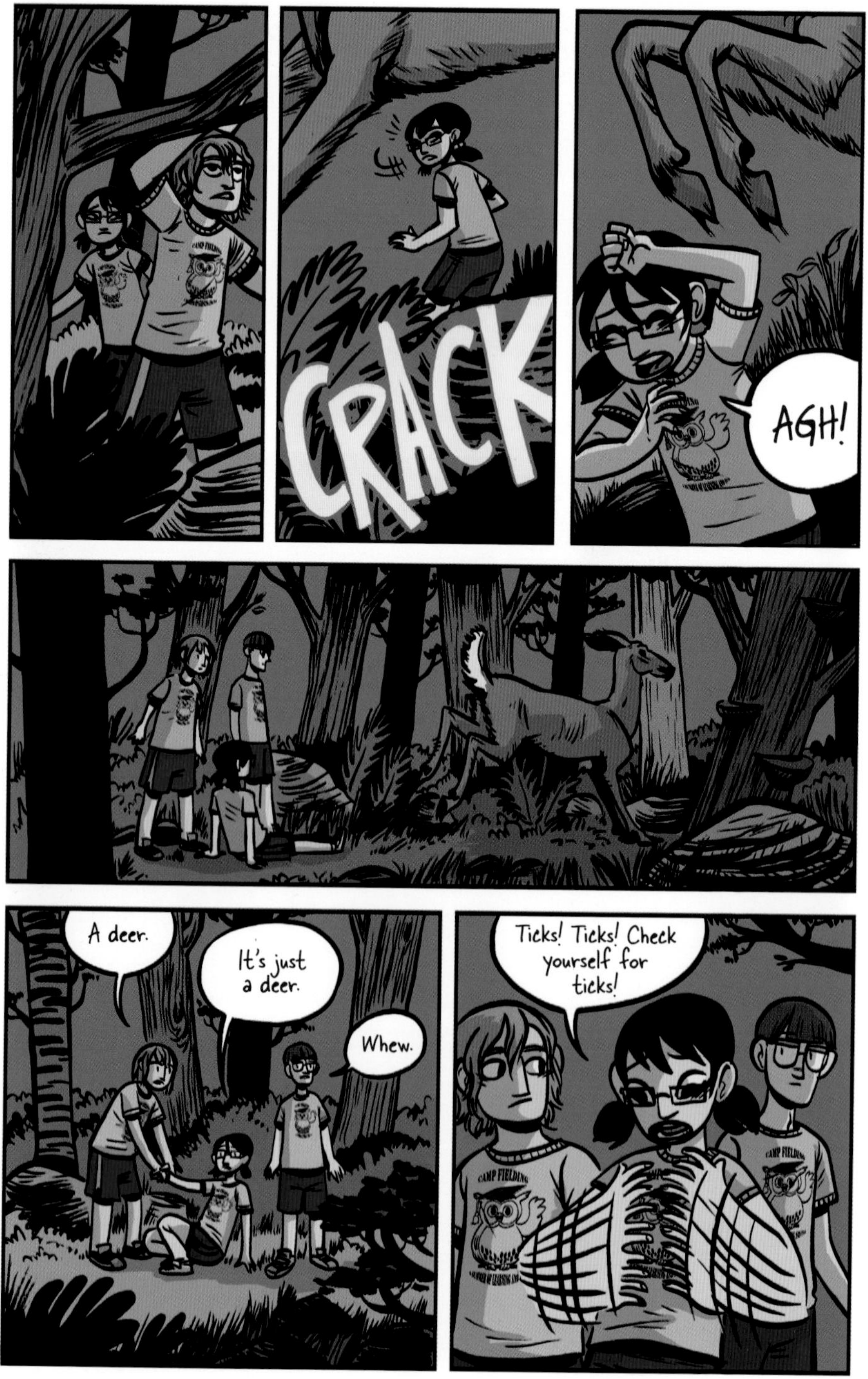
CRACK
AGH!
A deer.
It's just a deer.
Whew.
Ticks! Ticks! Check yourself for ticks!
CAMP FIELDING

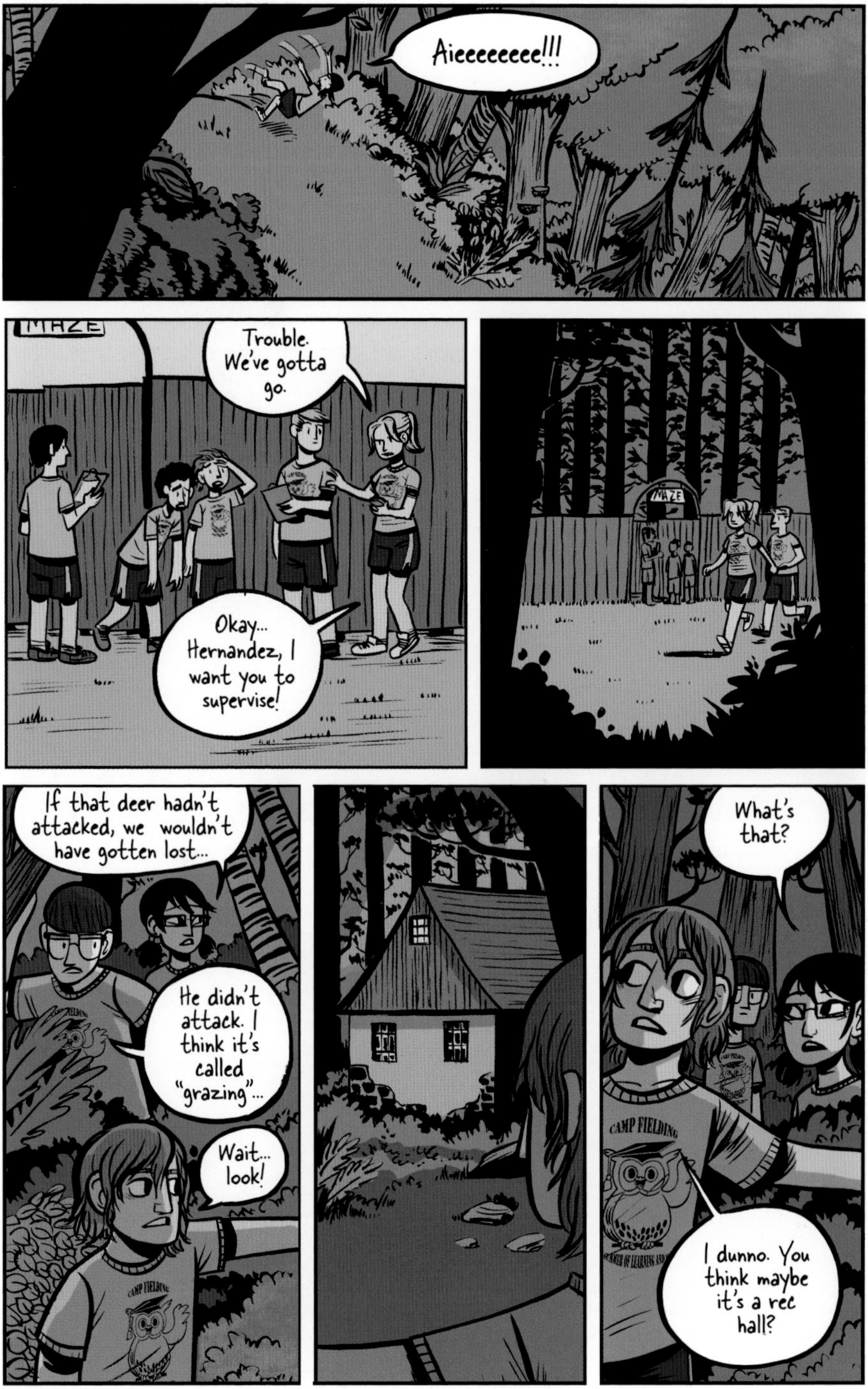
Aieeeeeeee!!!
MAZE
Trouble. We've gotta go.
Okay... Hernandez, I want you to supervise!
MAZE
If that deer hadn't attacked, we wouldn't have gotten lost...
He didn't attack. I think it's called "grazing"...
Wait... look!
CAMP FIELDING
What's that?
CAMP FIELDING
I dunno. You think maybe it's a rec hall?

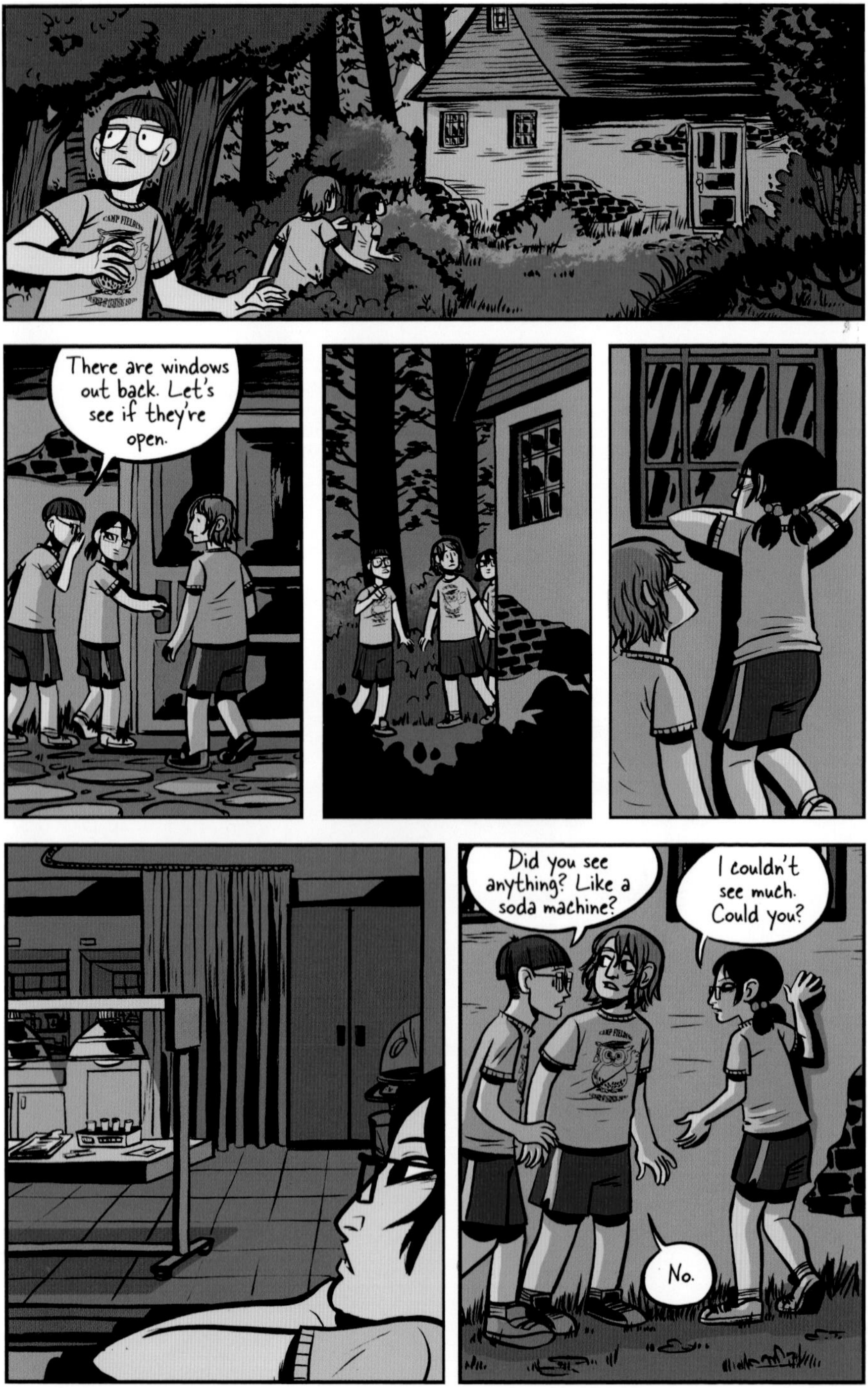
There are windows out back. Let's see if they're open.
Did you see anything? Like a soda machine?
I couldn't see much. Could you?
No.

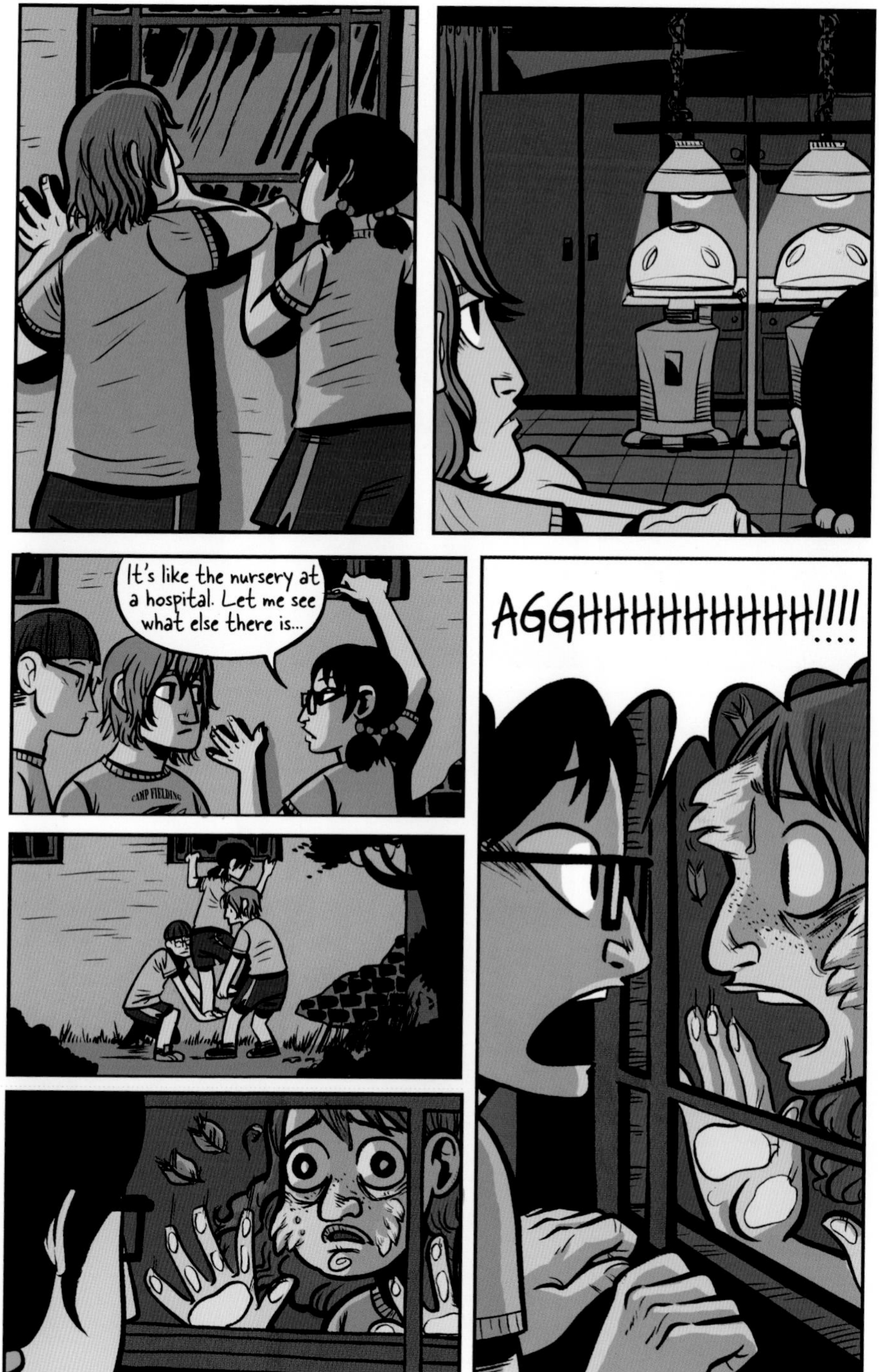
It's like the nursery at a hospital. Let me see what else there is...
CAMP FIELDING
AGGHHHHHHHHHH!!!!....

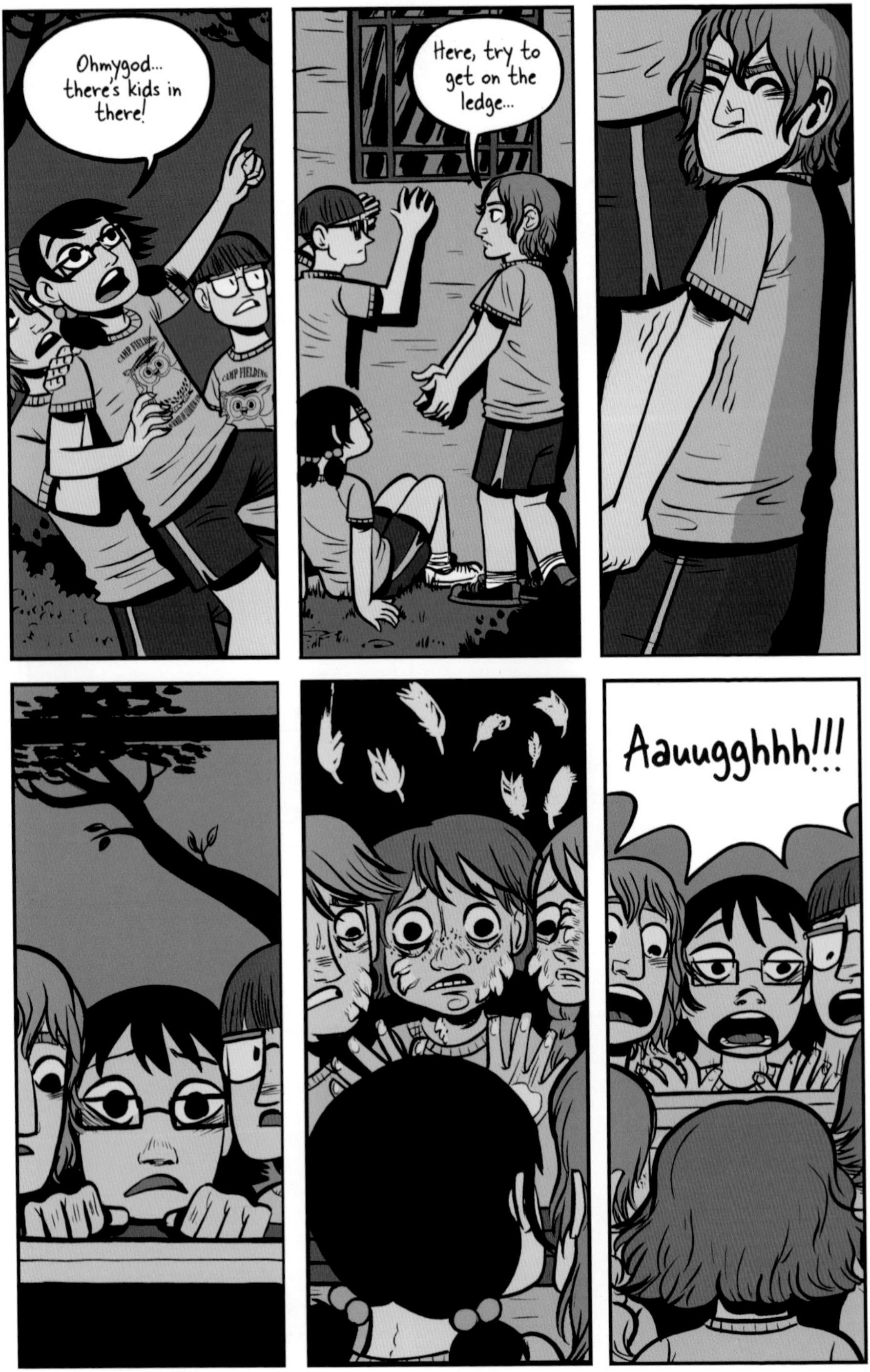
Ohmygod... there's kids in there!
CAMP FIELDING
Here, try to get on the ledge...
Aauugghhh!!!...

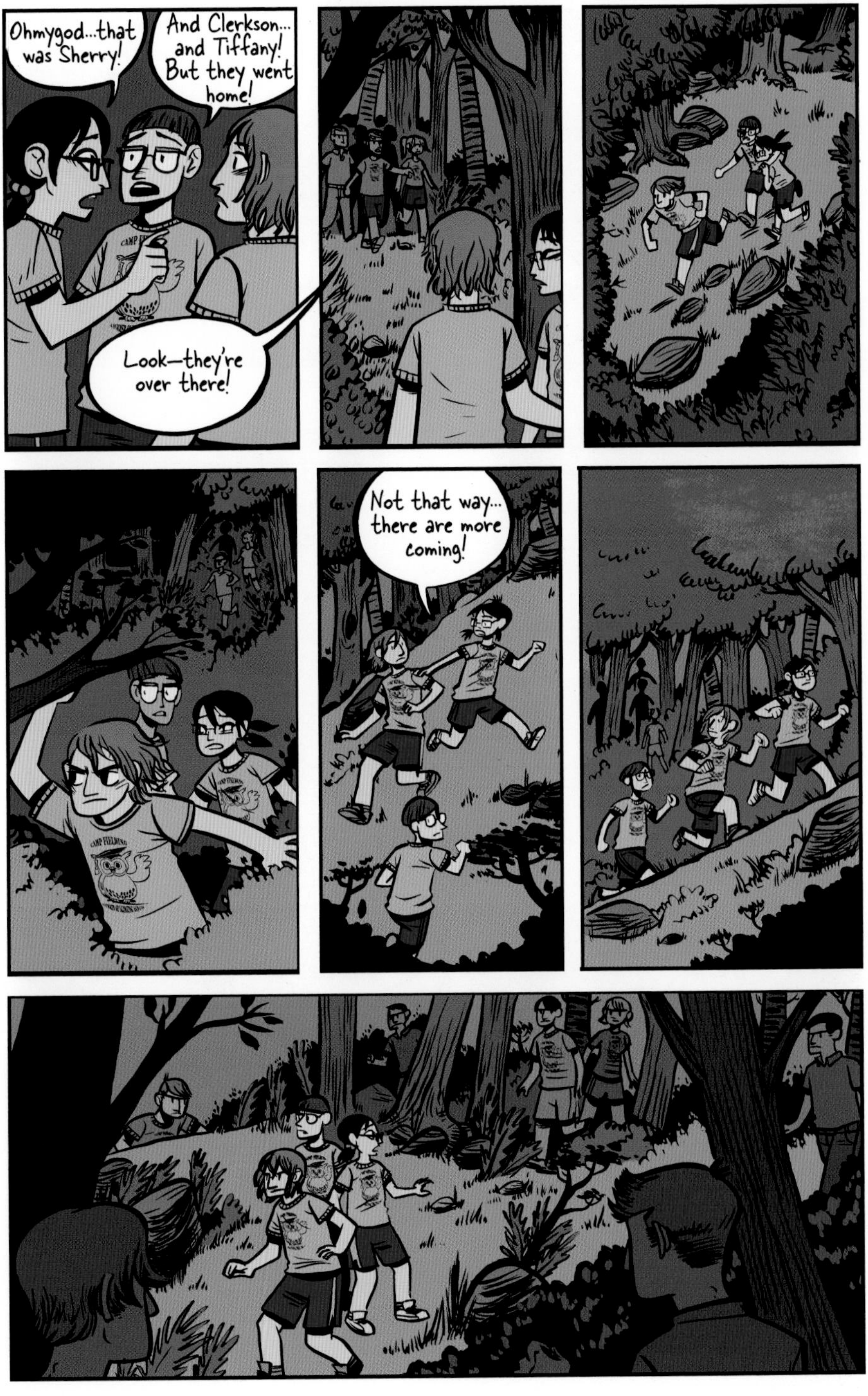
Ohmygod...that was Sherry!
And Clerkson... and Tiffany! But they went home!
Look—they're over there!
Not that way... there are more coming!

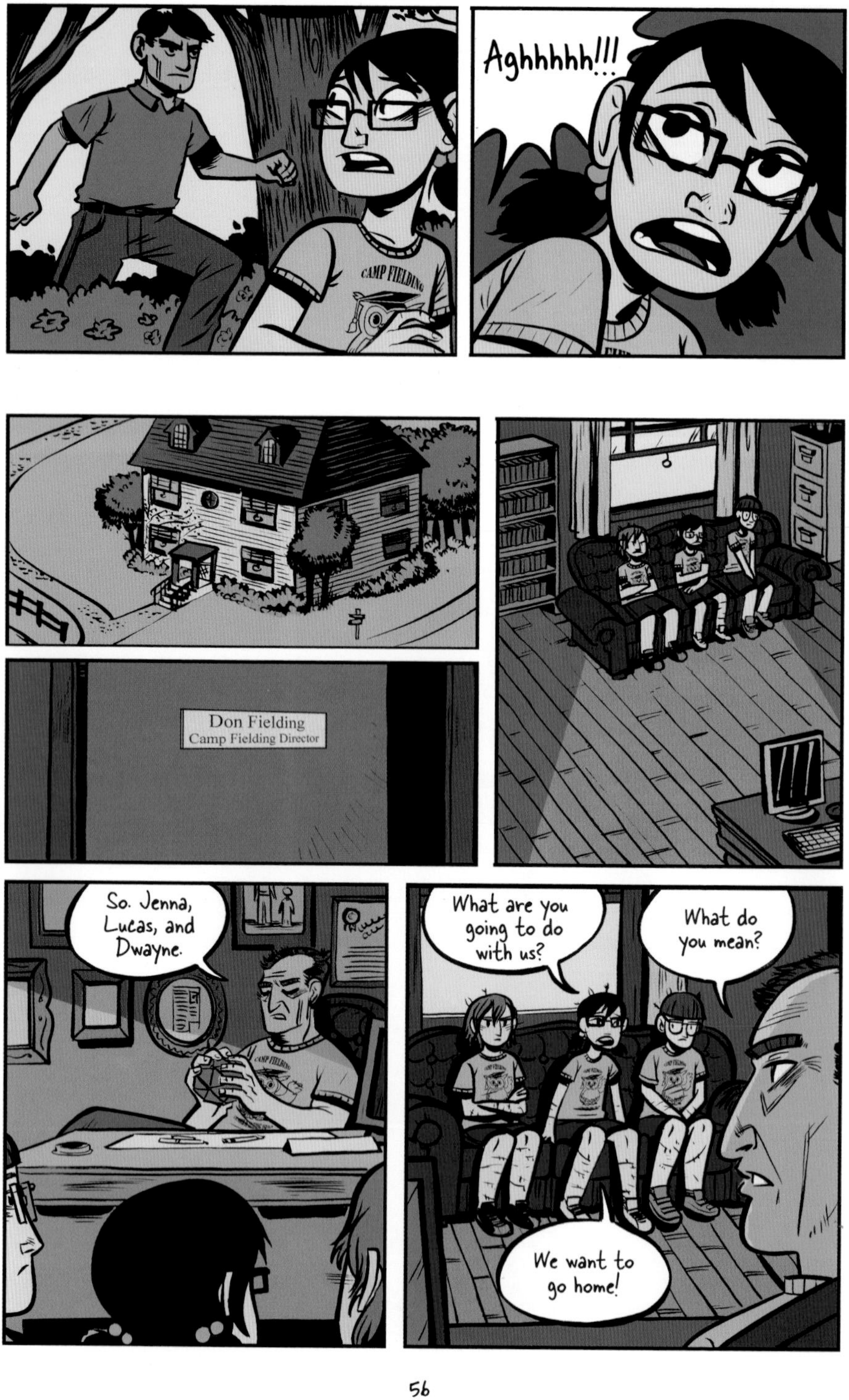
Aghhhhh!!!
Don Fielding
Camp Fielding Director
So. Jenna, Lucas, and Dwayne.
What are you going to do with us?
What do you mean?
We want to go home!

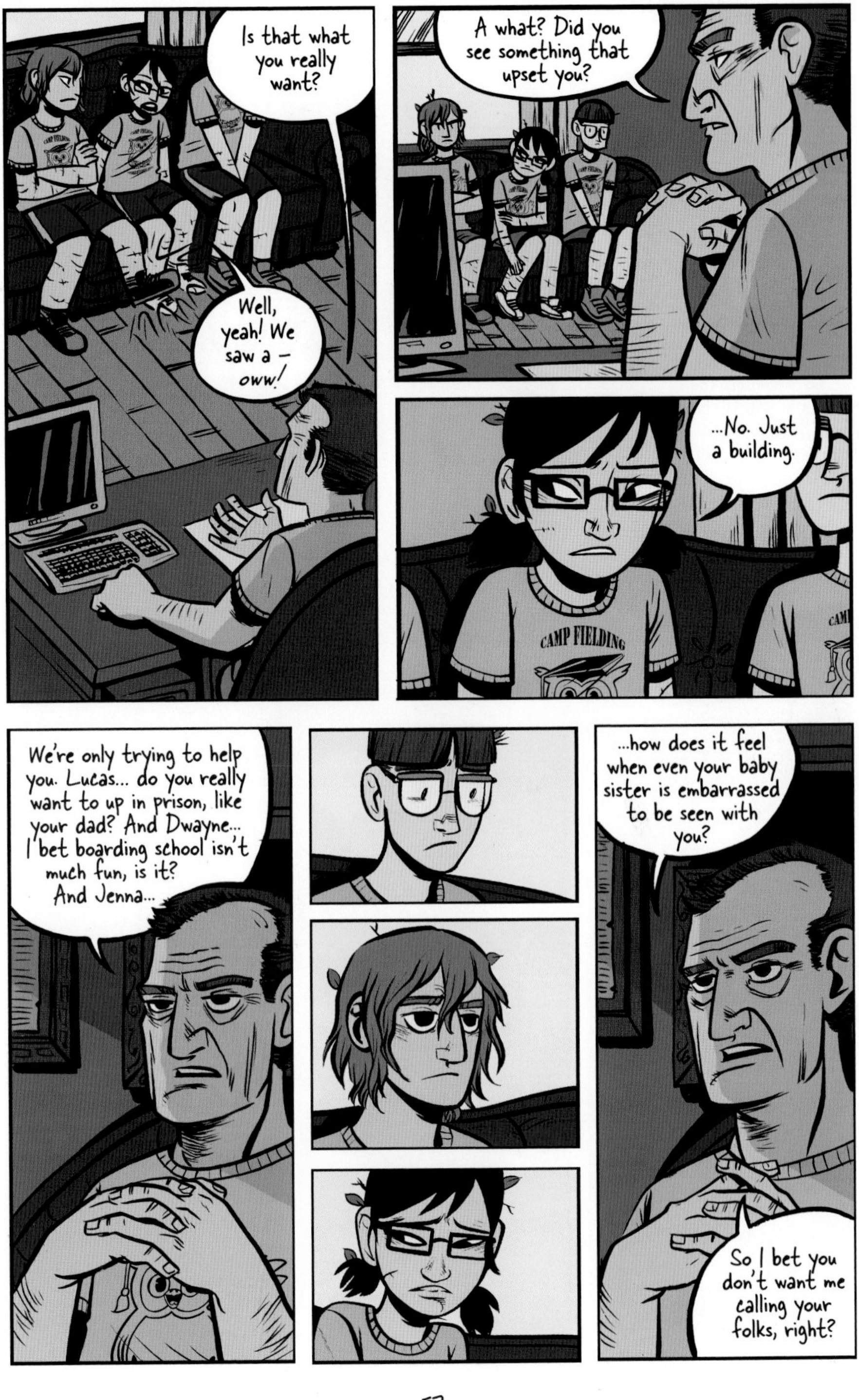
Is that what you really want?
Well, yeah! We saw a — oww!
A what? Did you see something that upset you?
CAMP FIELDING
...No. Just a building.
We're only trying to help you. Lucas... do you really want to up in prison, like your dad? And Dwayne... I bet boarding school isn't much fun, is it? And Jenna...
...how does it feel when even your baby sister is embarrassed to be seen with you?
So I bet you don't want me calling your folks, right?

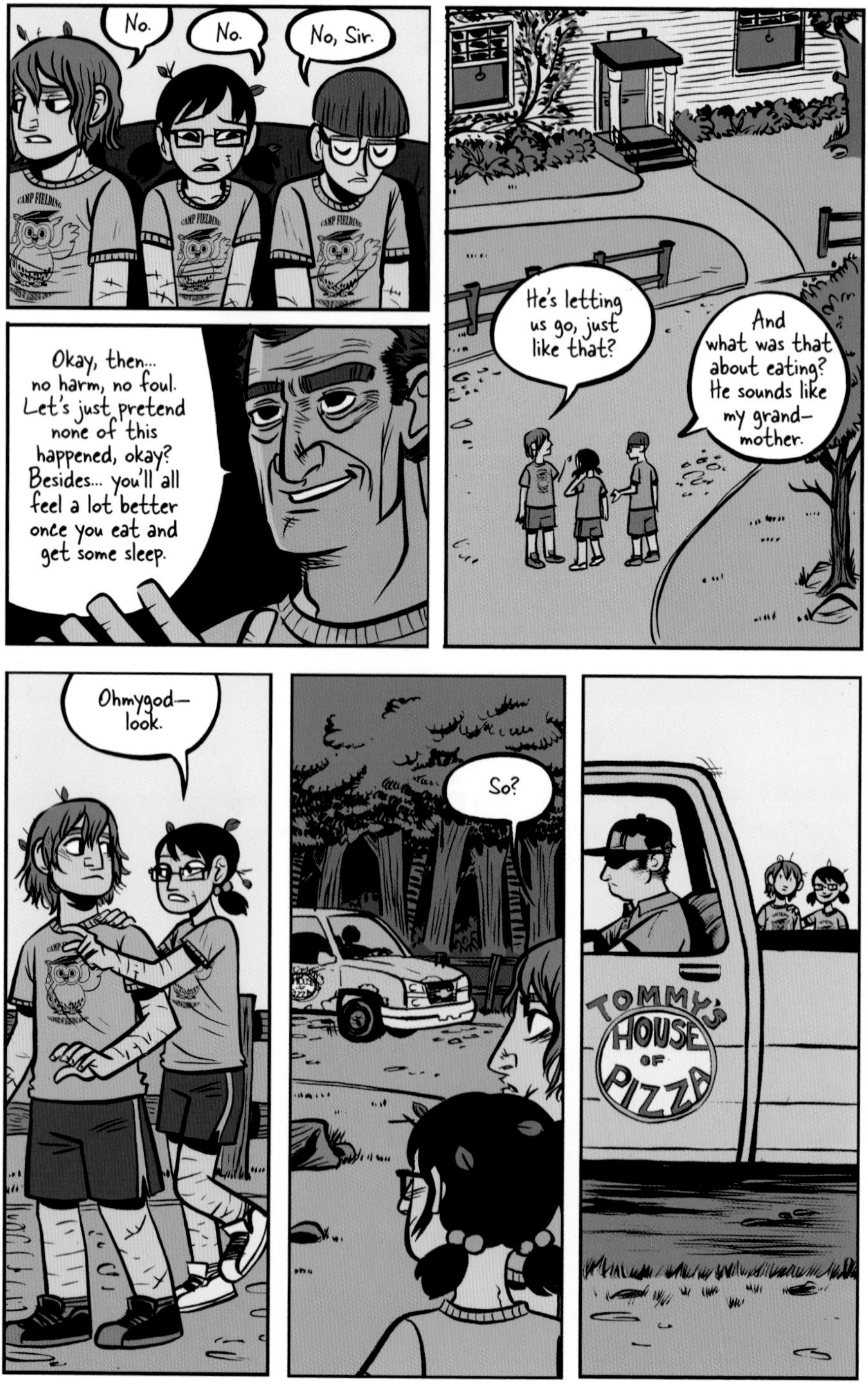
No.
No.
No, Sir.
CAMP FIELDING
He's letting us go, just like that?
And what was that about eating? He sounds like my grand-mother.
Okay, then... no harm, no foul. Let's just pretend none of this happened, okay? Besides... you'll all feel a lot better once you eat and get some sleep.
Ohmygod— look.
So?
TOMMY'S HOUSE OF PIZZA

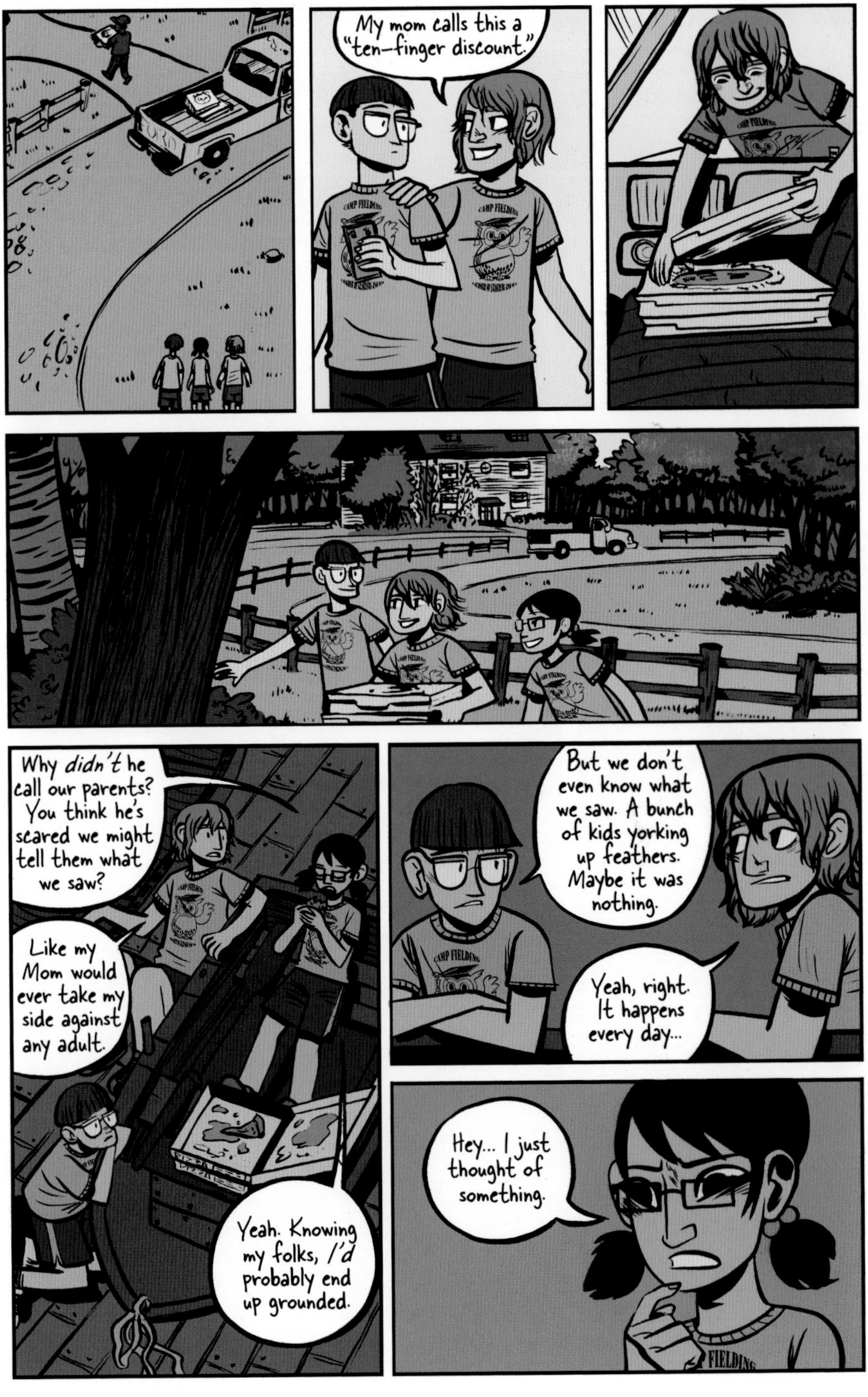
My mom calls this a "ten-finger discount."
Why *didn't* he call our parents? You think he's scared we might tell them what we saw?
Like my Mom would ever take my side against any adult.
Yeah. Knowing my folks, *I'd* probably end up grounded.
But we don't even know what we saw. A bunch of kids yorking up feathers. Maybe it was nothing.
Yeah, right. It happens every day...
Hey... I just thought of something.

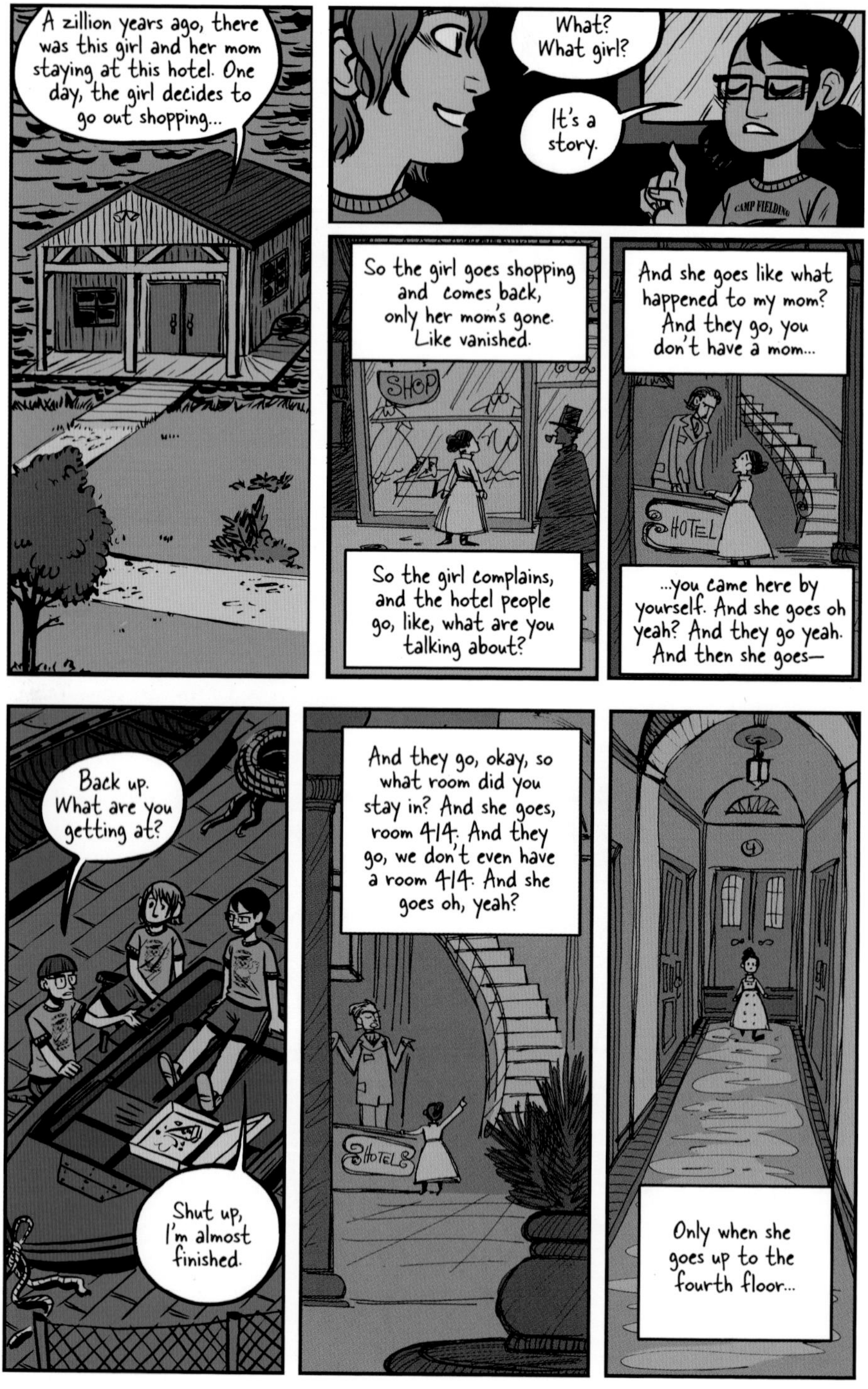
A zillion years ago, there was this girl and her mom staying at this hotel. One day, the girl decides to go out shopping...
What? What girl?
It's a story.
CAMP FIELDING
So the girl goes shopping and comes back, only her mom's gone. Like vanished.
SHOP
So the girl complains, and the hotel people go, like, what are you talking about?
And she goes like what happened to my mom? And they go, you don't have a mom...
HOTEL
...you came here by yourself. And she goes oh yeah? And they go yeah. And then she goes—
Back up. What are you getting at?
Shut up, I'm almost finished.
And they go, okay, so what room did you stay in? And she goes, room 414. And they go, we don't even have a room 414. And she goes oh, yeah?
HOTEL
Only when she goes up to the fourth floor...

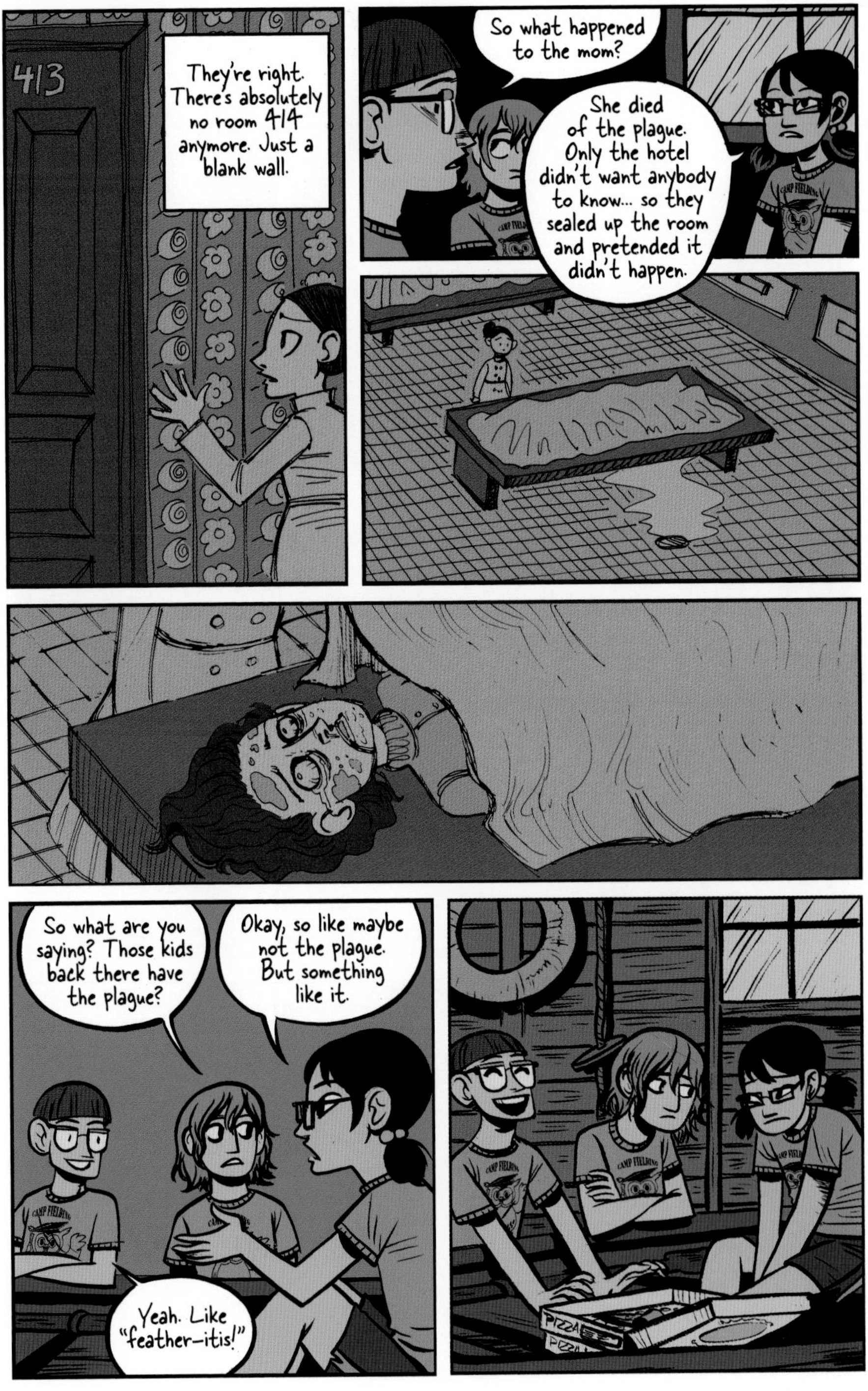
They're right. There's absolutely no room 414 anymore. Just a blank wall.
So what happened to the mom?
She died of the plague. Only the hotel didn't want anybody to know... so they sealed up the room and pretended it didn't happen.
So what are you saying? Those kids back there have the plague?
Okay, so like maybe not the plague. But something like it.
Yeah. Like "feather-itis!"
PIZZA
PIZZA

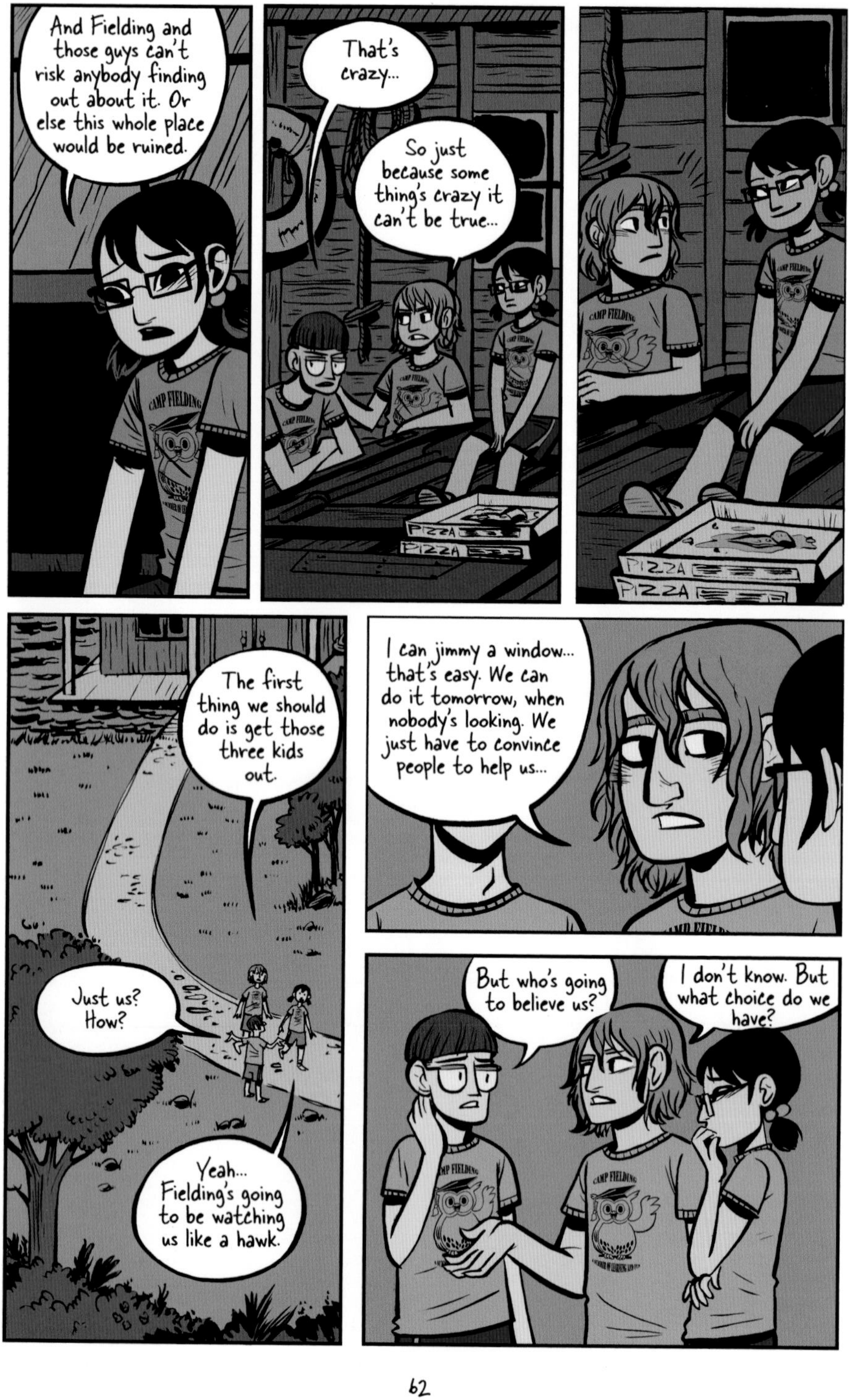
And Fielding and those guys can't risk anybody finding out about it. Or else this whole place would be ruined.
That's crazy...
So just because some thing's crazy it can't be true...
CAMP FIELDING
PIZZA
The first thing we should do is get those three kids out.
Just us? How?
Yeah... Fielding's going to be watching us like a hawk.
I can jimmy a window... that's easy. We can do it tomorrow, when nobody's looking. We just have to convince people to help us...
But who's going to believe us?
I don't know. But what choice do we have?

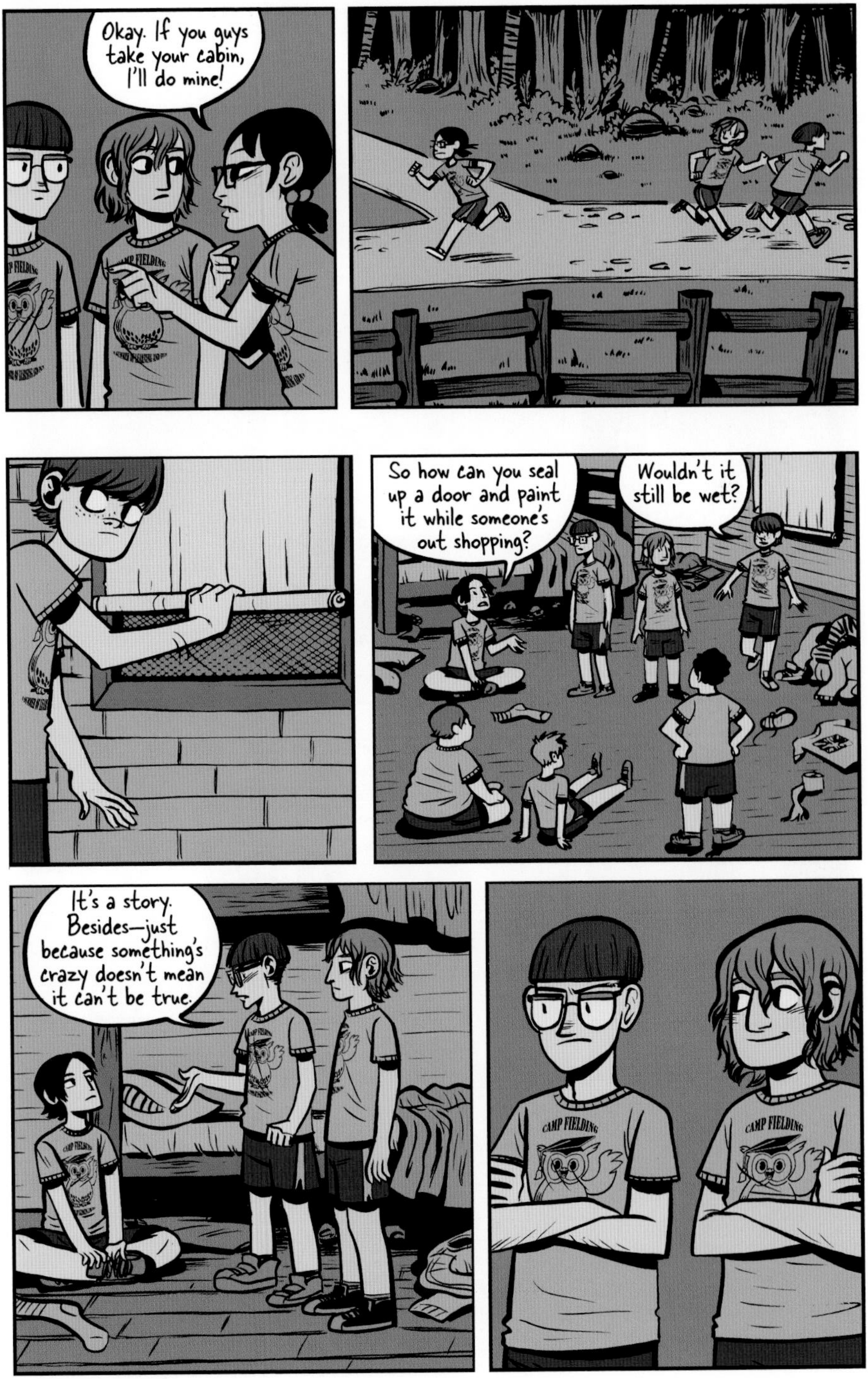
Okay. If you guys take your cabin, I'll do mine!
CAMP FIELDING
So how can you seal up a door and paint it while someone's out shopping?
Wouldn't it still be wet?
It's a story. Besides—just because something's crazy doesn't mean it can't be true.
CAMP FIELDING
CAMP FIELDING

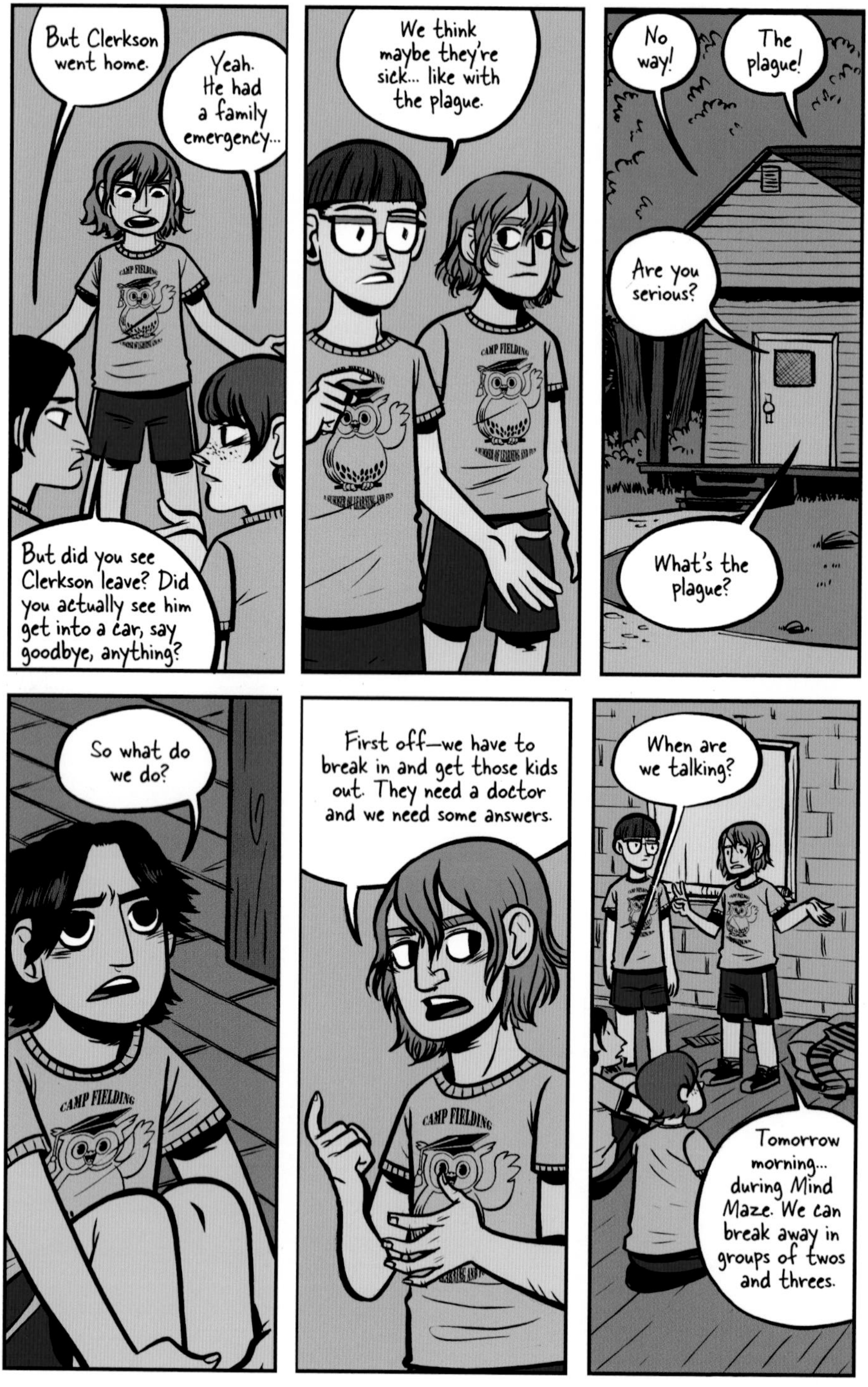
But Clerkson went home.
Yeah. He had a family emergency...
But did you see Clerkson leave? Did you actually see him get into a car, say goodbye, anything?
We think maybe they're sick... like with the plague.
No way!
The plague!
Are you serious?
What's the plague?
So what do we do?
First off—we have to break in and get those kids out. They need a doctor and we need some answers.
When are we talking?
Tomorrow morning... during Mind Maze. We can break away in groups of twos and threes.

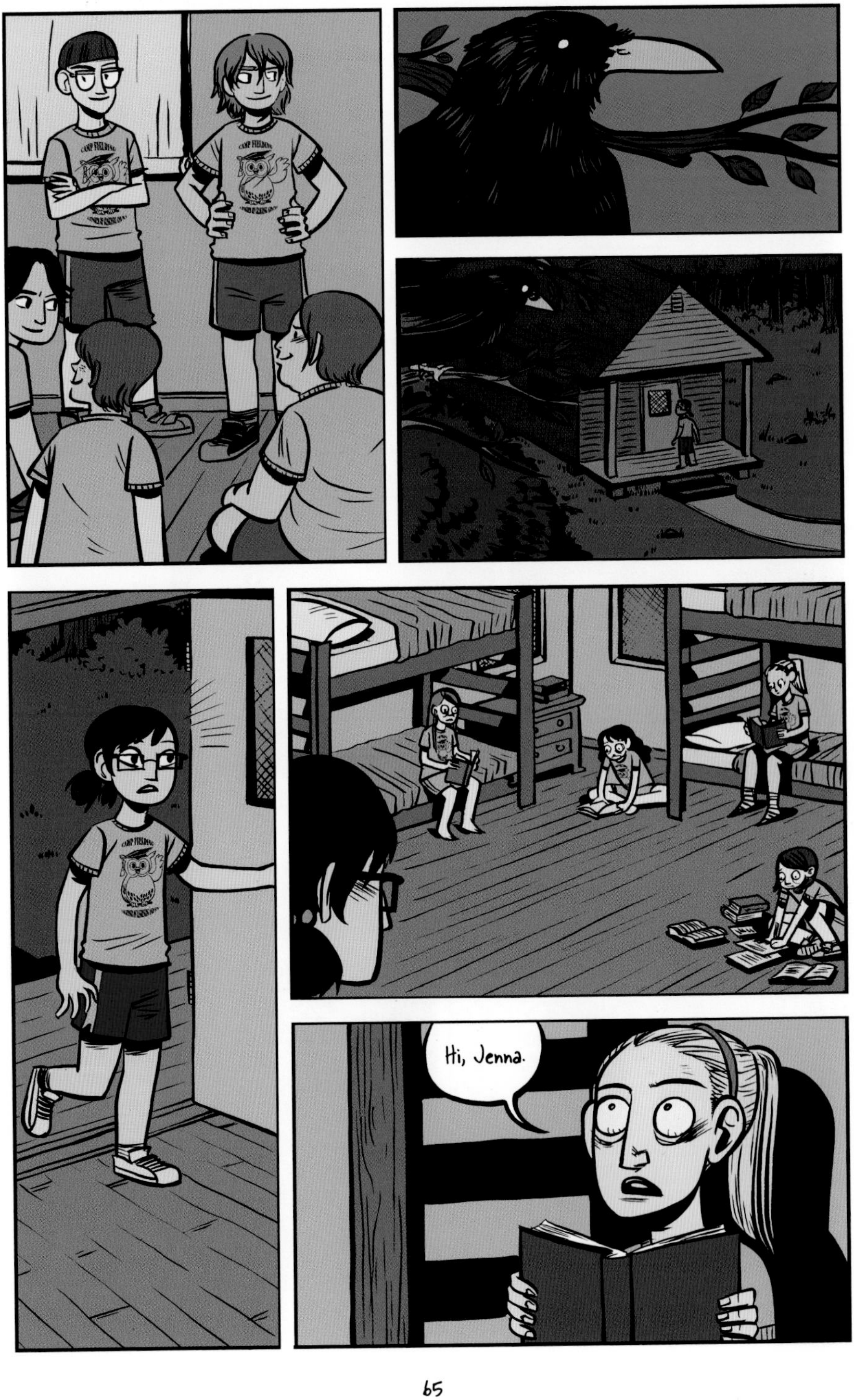
Hi, Jenna.

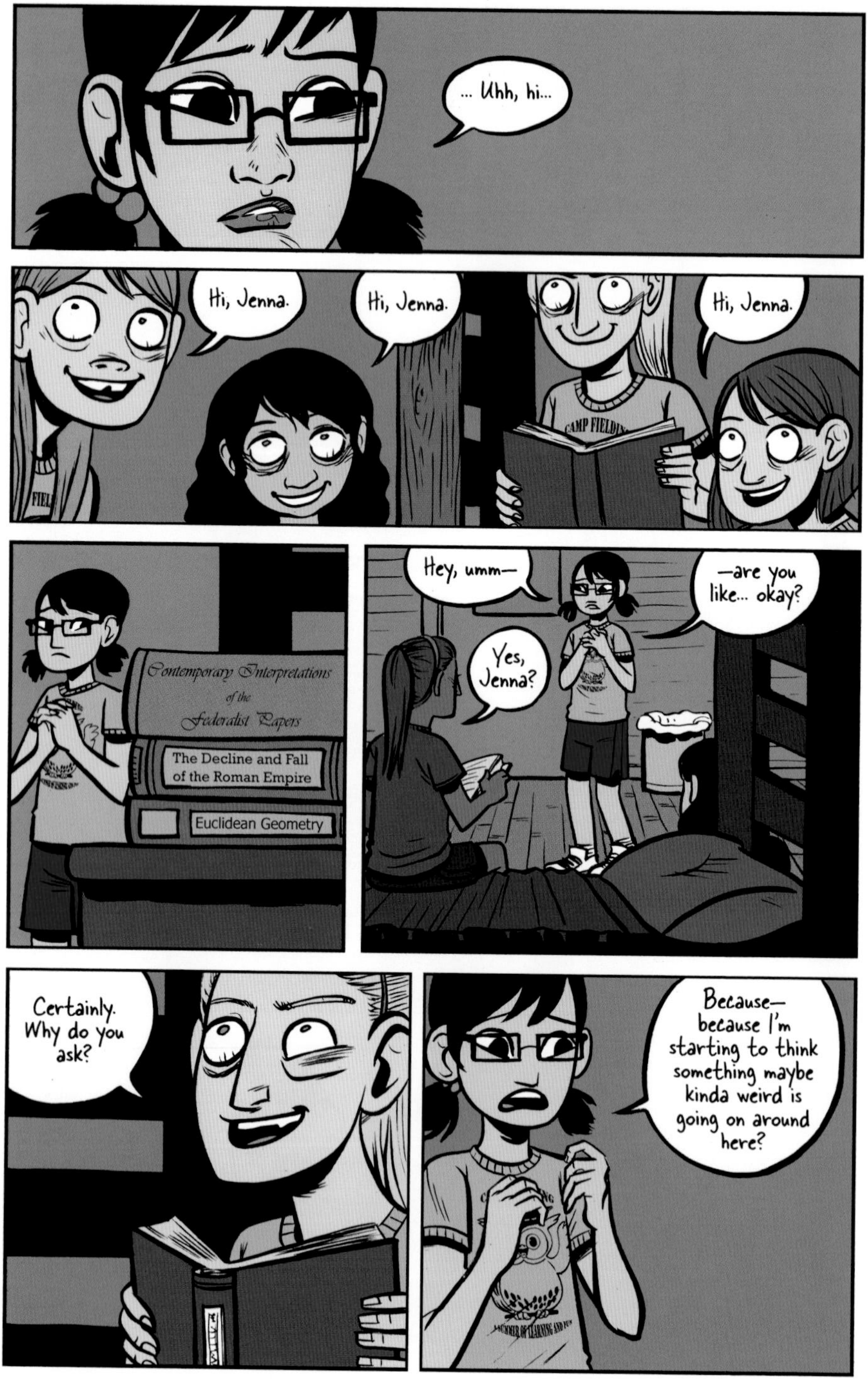
... Uhh, hi...
Hi, Jenna.
Hi, Jenna.
Hi, Jenna.
Contemporary Interpretations of the Federalist Papers
The Decline and Fall of the Roman Empire
Euclidean Geometry
Hey, umm—
—are you like... okay?
Yes, Jenna?
Certainly. Why do you ask?
Because— because I'm starting to think something maybe kinda weird is going on around here?

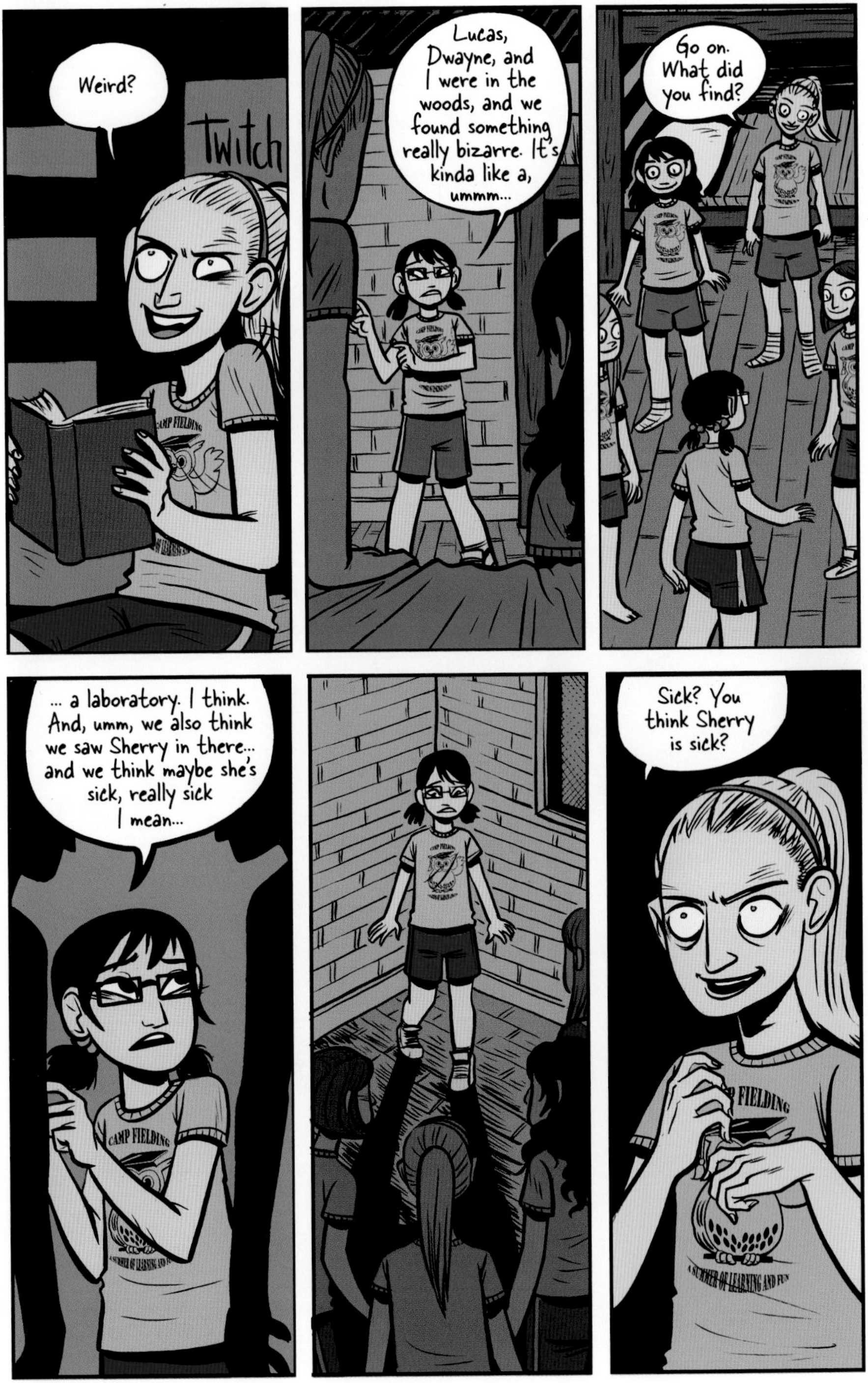
Weird?
TWITCH
Lucas, Dwayne, and I were in the woods, and we found something really bizarre. It's kinda like a, ummm...
Go on. What did you find?
... a laboratory. I think. And, umm, we also think we saw Sherry in there... and we think maybe she's sick, really sick I mean...
Sick? You think Sherry is sick?

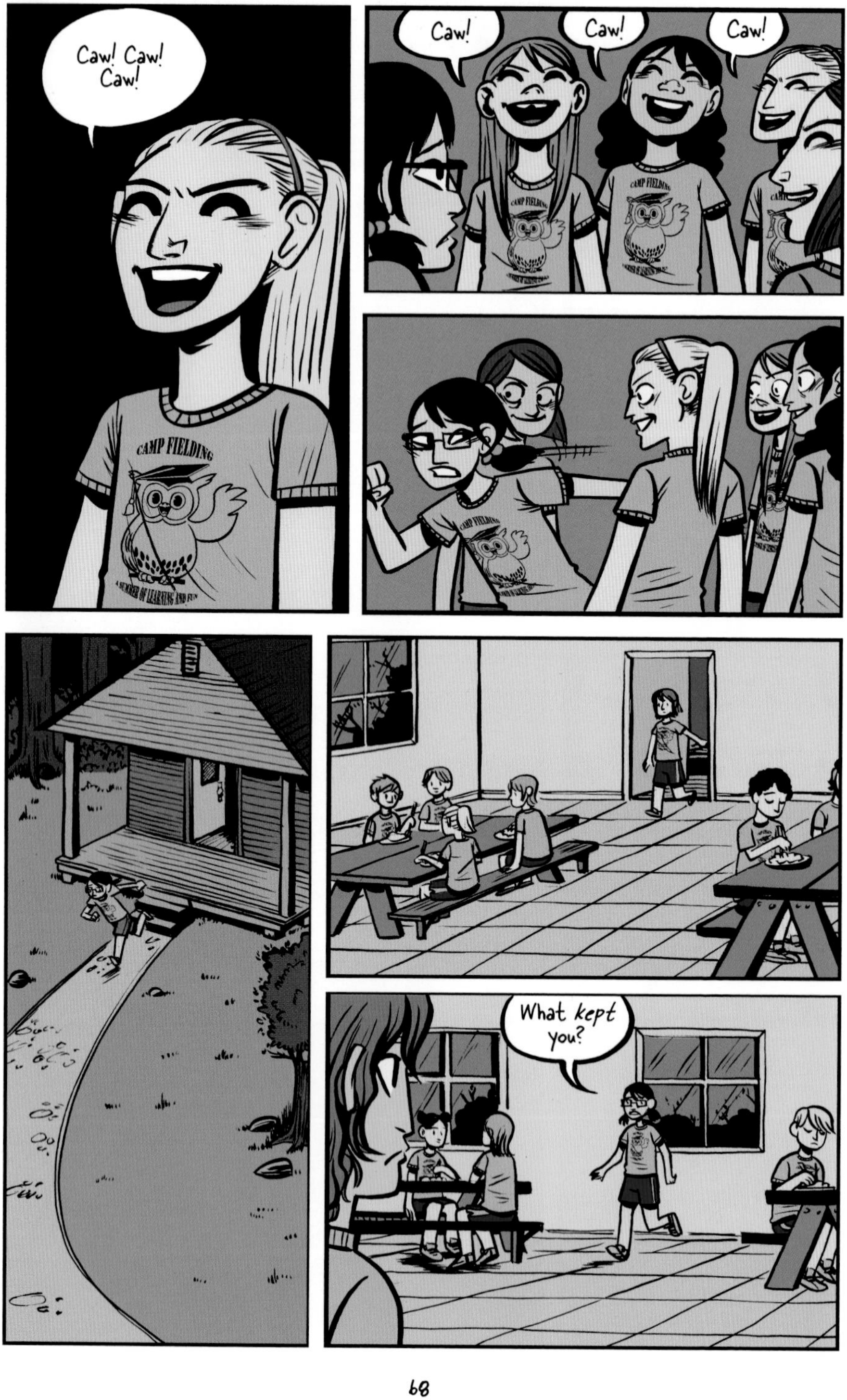
Caw! Caw! Caw!
Caw!
Caw!
Caw!
CAMP FIELDING
A SUMMER OF LEARNING AND FUN
What kept you?

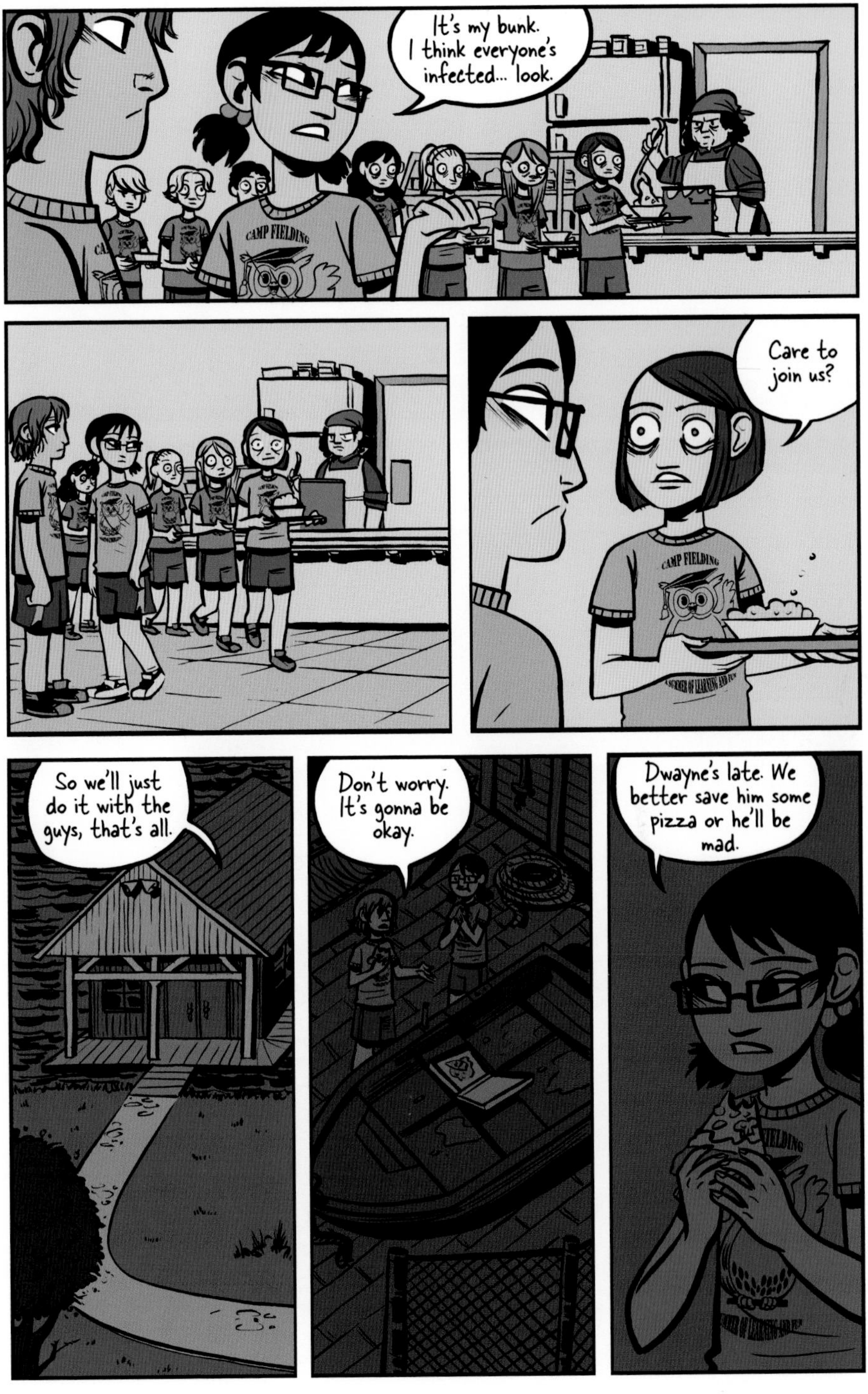
It's my bunk. I think everyone's infected... look.
CAMP FIELDING
Care to join us?
CAMP FIELDING
A SUMMER OF LEARNING AND FUN
So we'll just do it with the guys, that's all.
Don't worry. It's gonna be okay.
Dwayne's late. We better save him some pizza or he'll be mad.

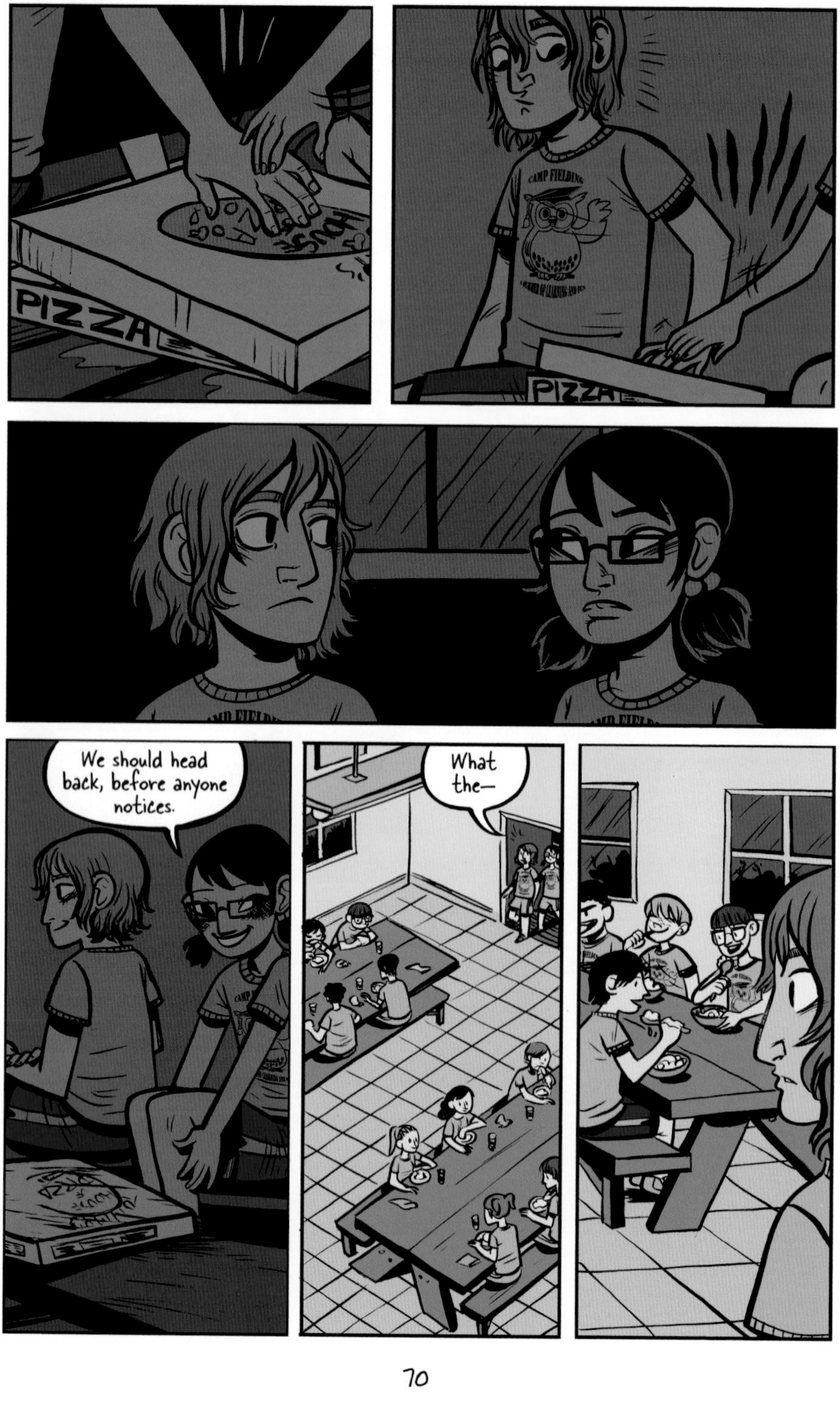
PIZZA
CAMP FIELDING
PIZZA
We should head back, before anyone notices.
What the—

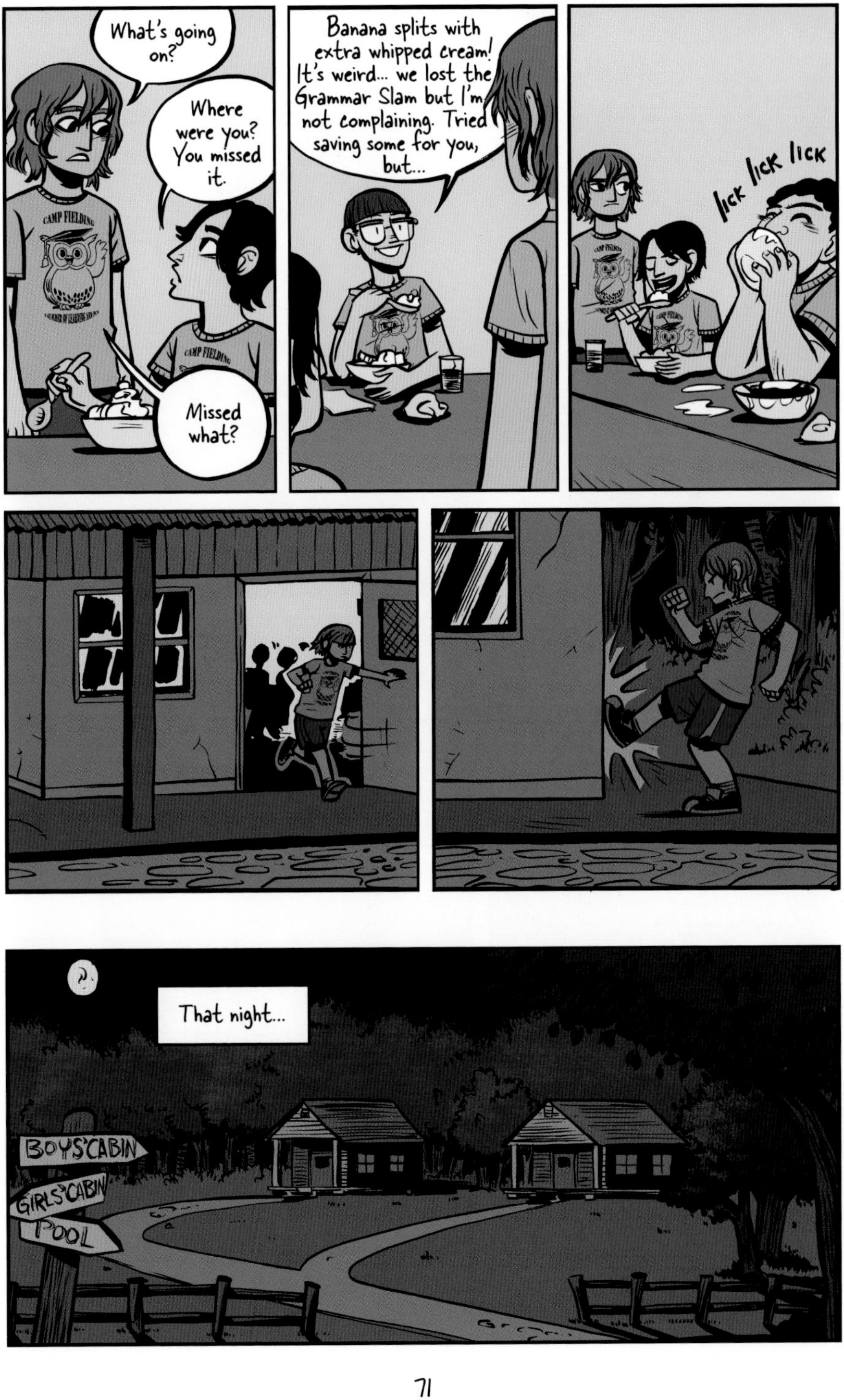
What's going on?
Where were you? You missed it.
Missed what?
Banana splits with extra whipped cream! It's weird... we lost the Grammar Slam but I'm not complaining. Tried saving some for you, but...
LICK LICK LICK
That night...
BOYS' CABIN
GIRLS' CABIN
POOL

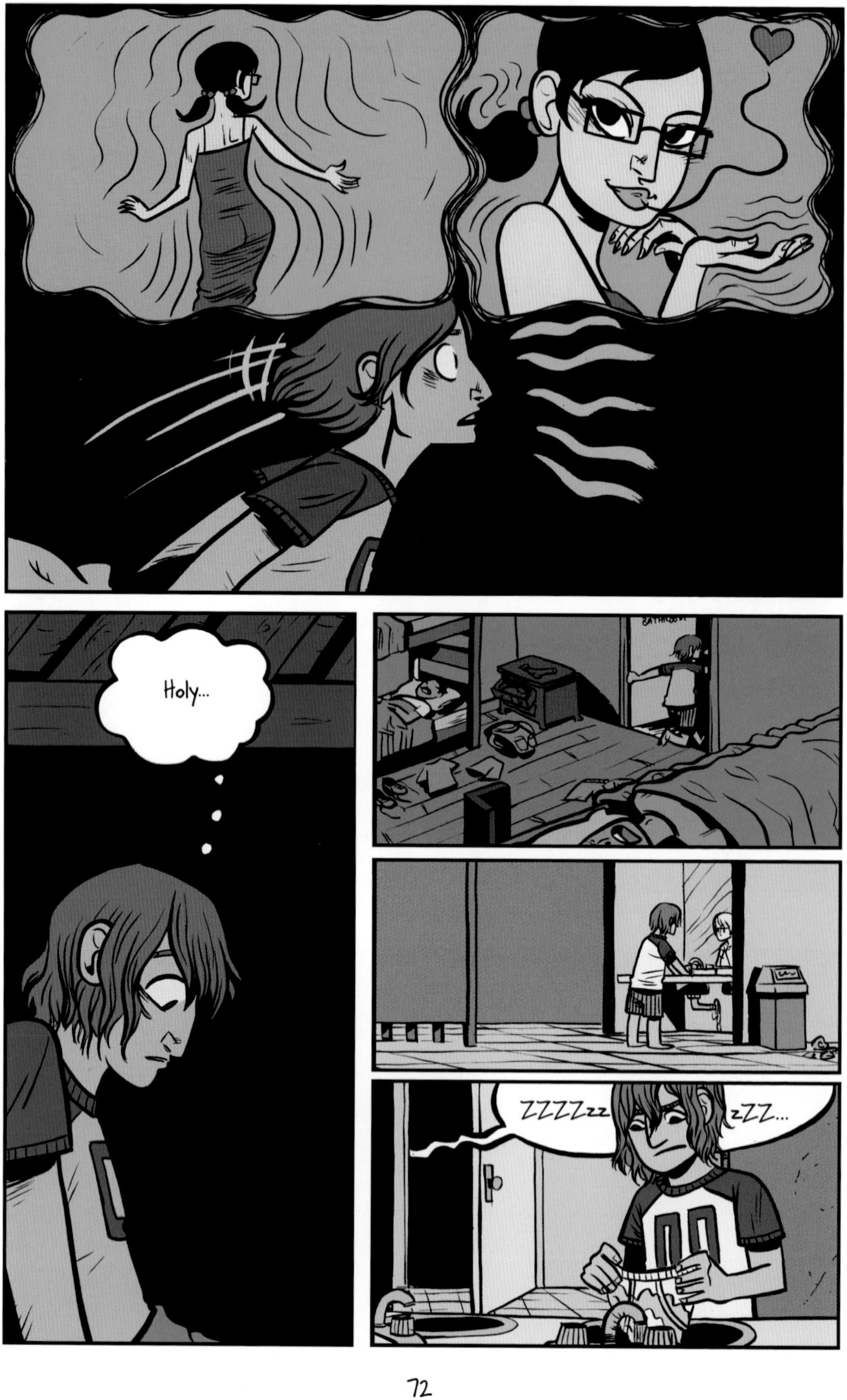
Holy...
BATHROOM
ZZZZzz
zZZ...

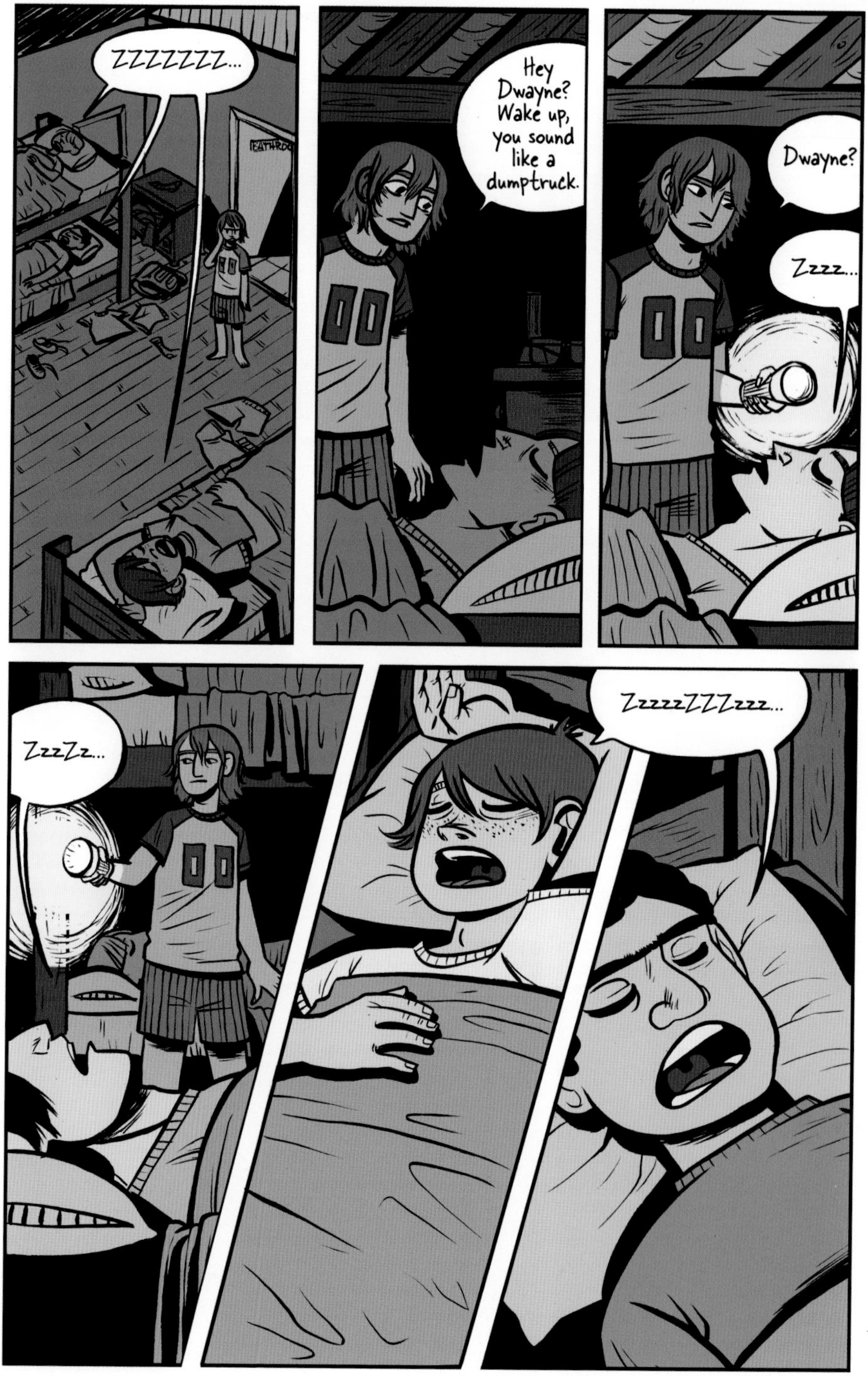
ZZZZZZZ...
Hey Dwayne? Wake up, you sound like a dumptruck.
Dwayne?
Zzzz...
ZzzZz...
ZzzzzZZZzzz...

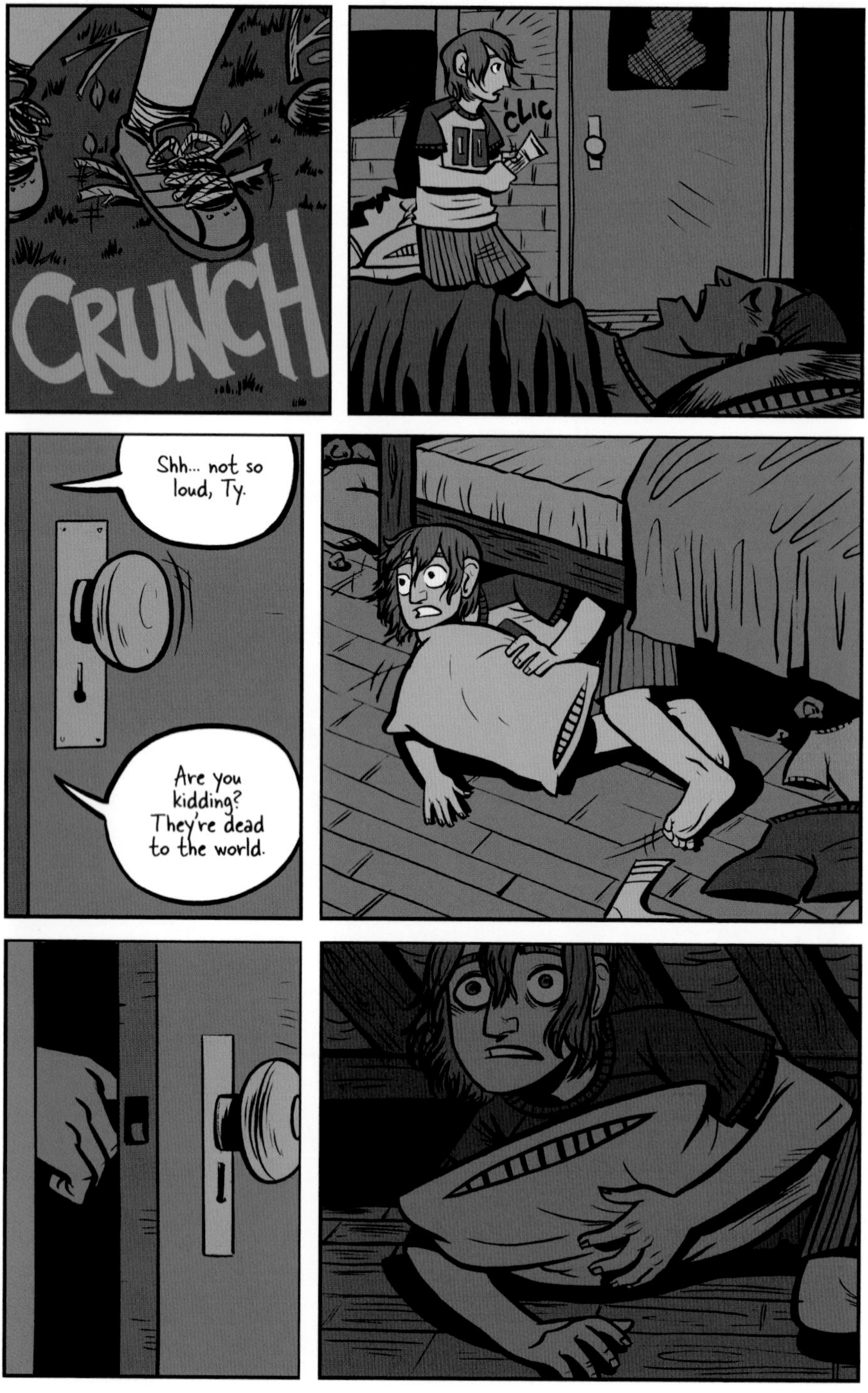
CRUNCH
CLIC
Shh... not so loud, Ty.
Are you kidding? They're dead to the world.

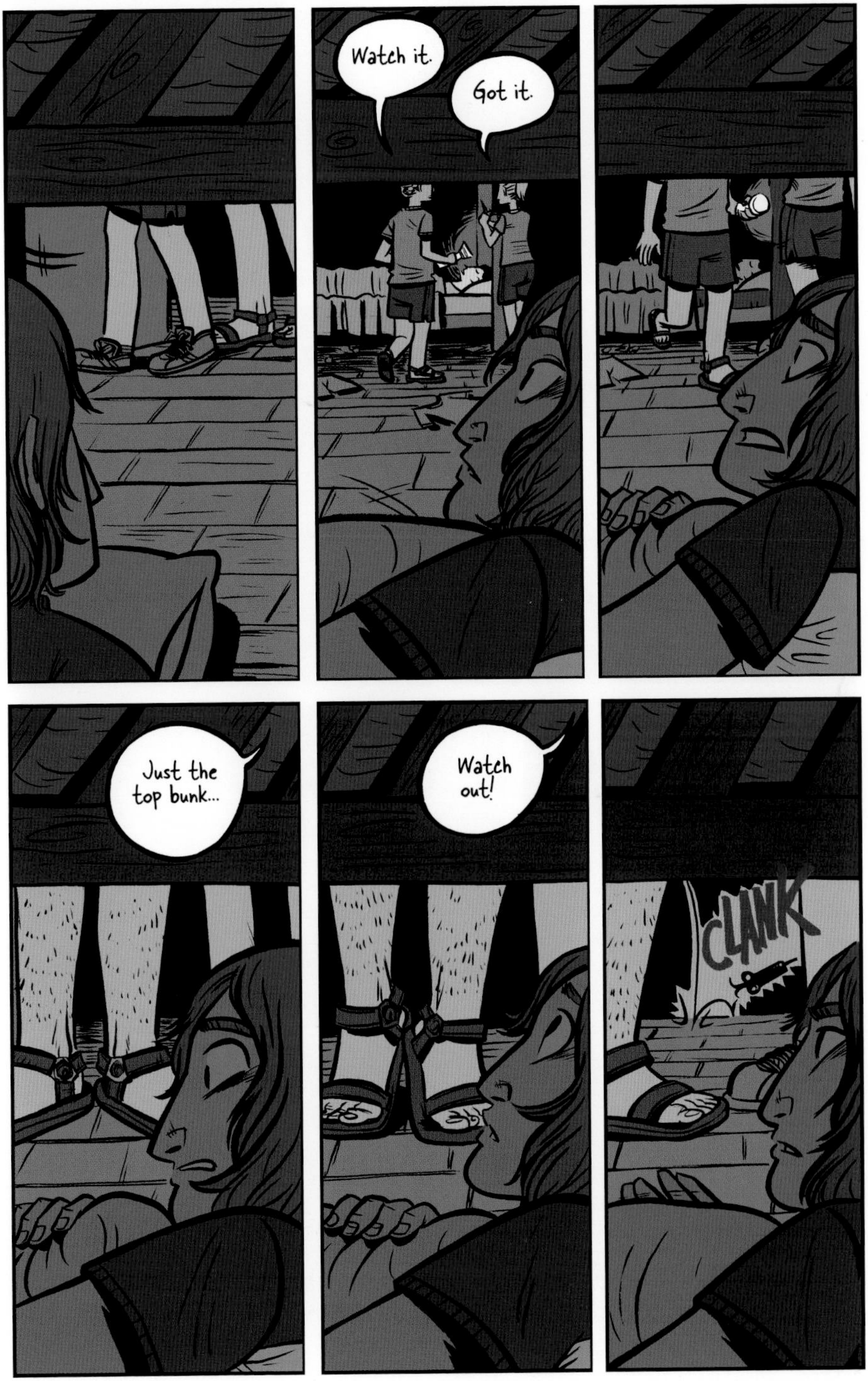
Watch it.
Got it.
Just the top bunk...
Watch out!
CLANK

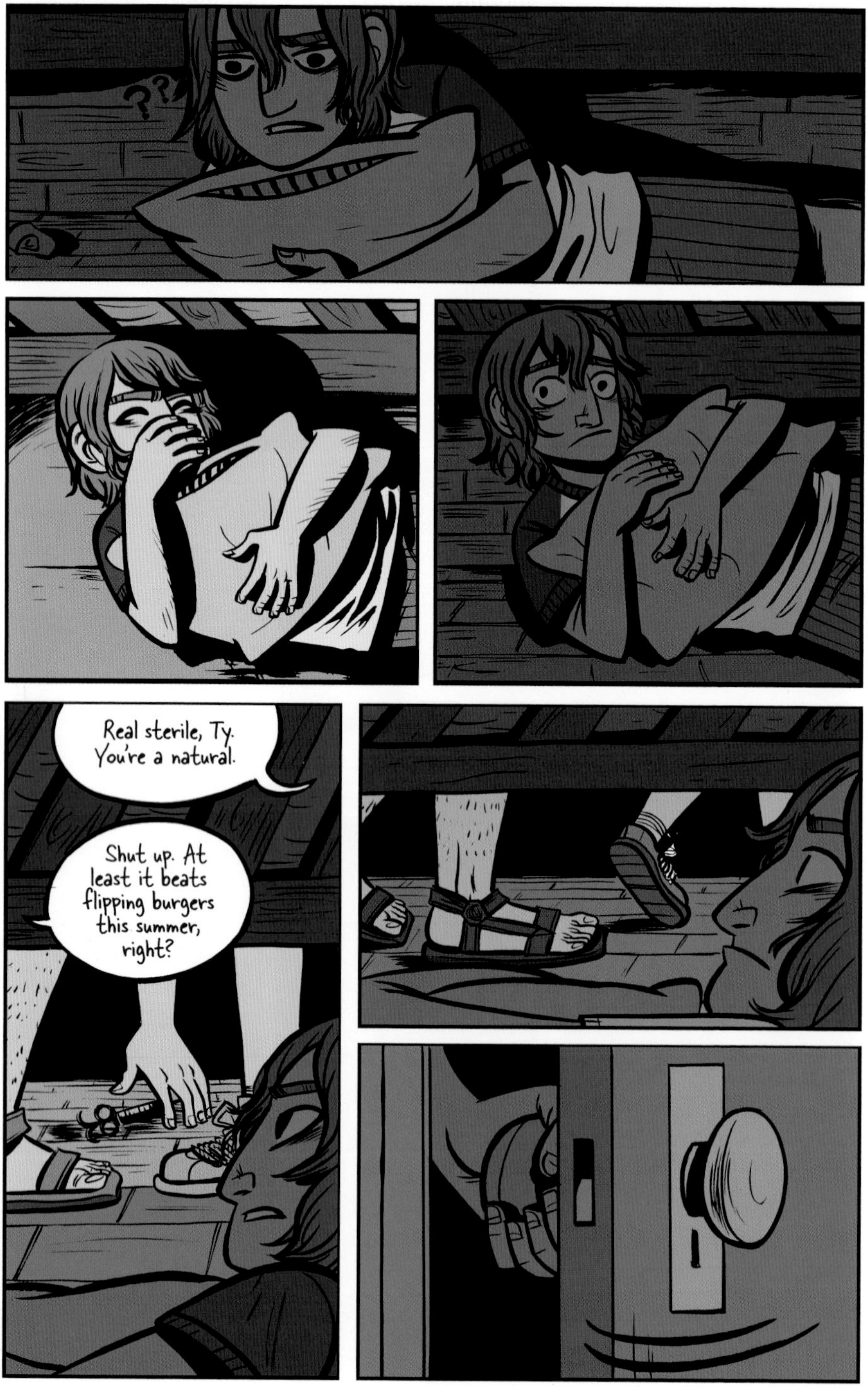
??
Real sterile, Ty. You're a natural.
Shut up. At least it beats flipping burgers this summer, right?

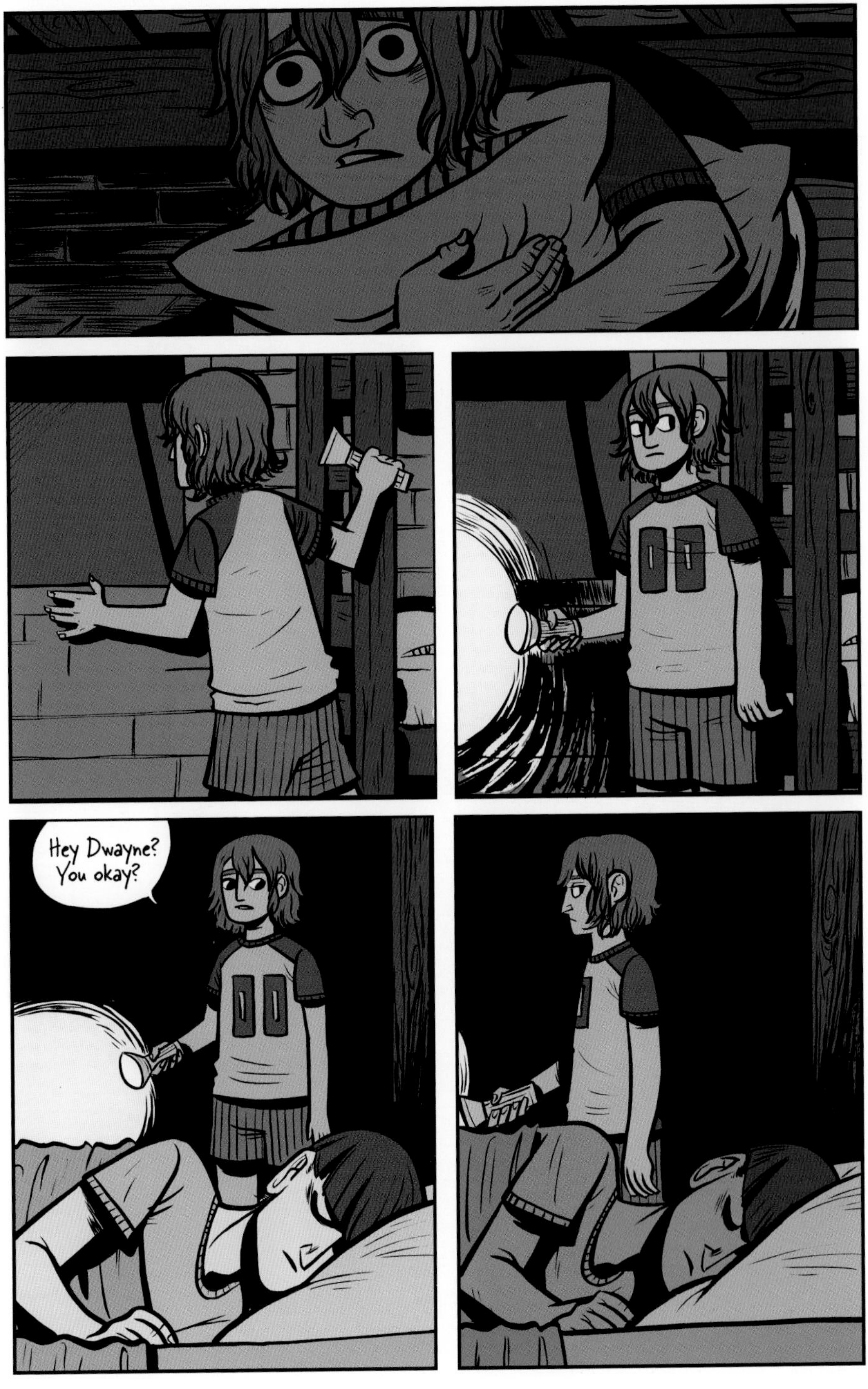
Hey Dwayne? You okay?

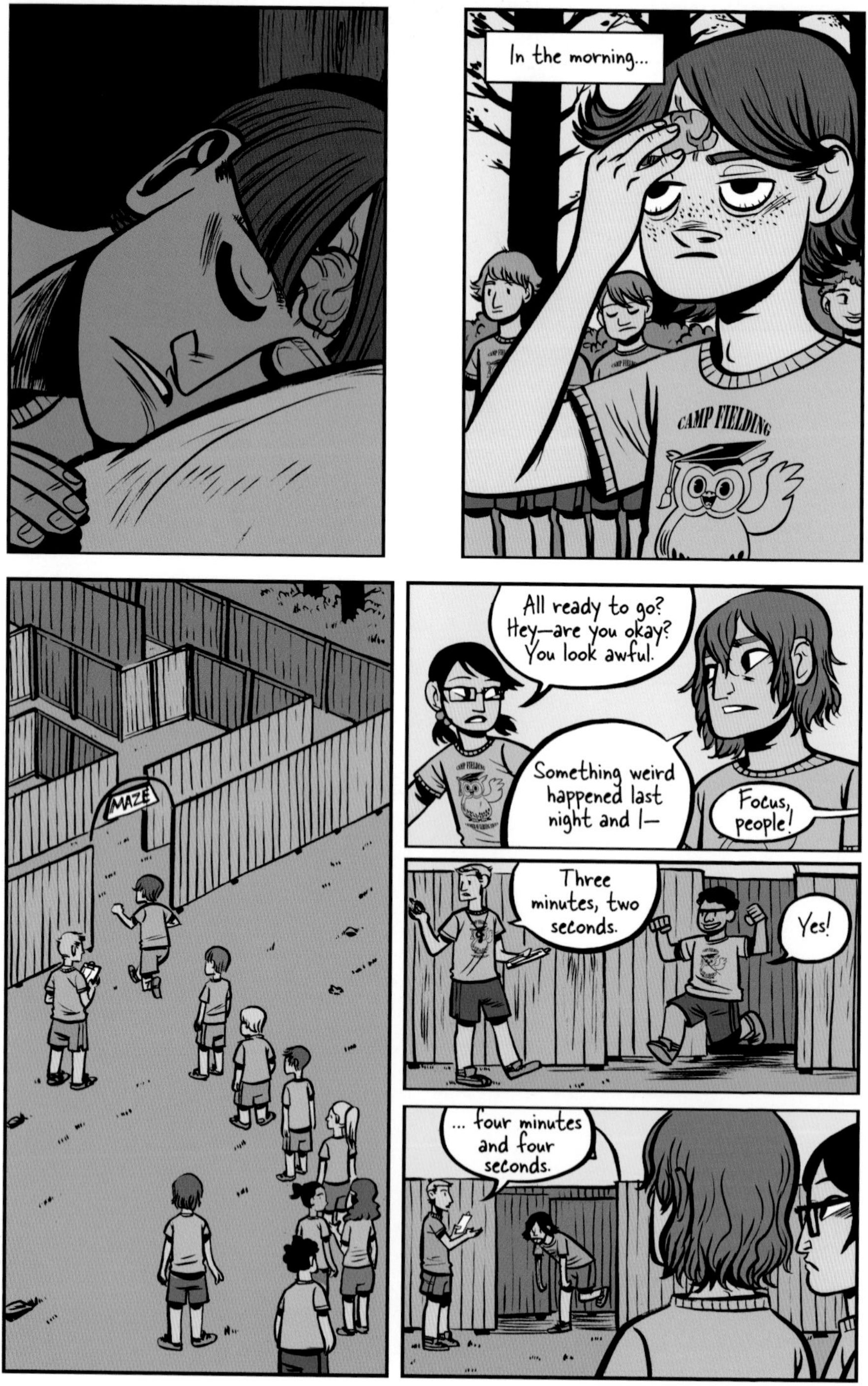
In the morning...
CAMP FIELDING
MAZE
All ready to go? Hey—are you okay? You look awful.
Something weird happened last night and I—
Focus, people!
Three minutes, two seconds.
Yes!
... four minutes and four seconds.

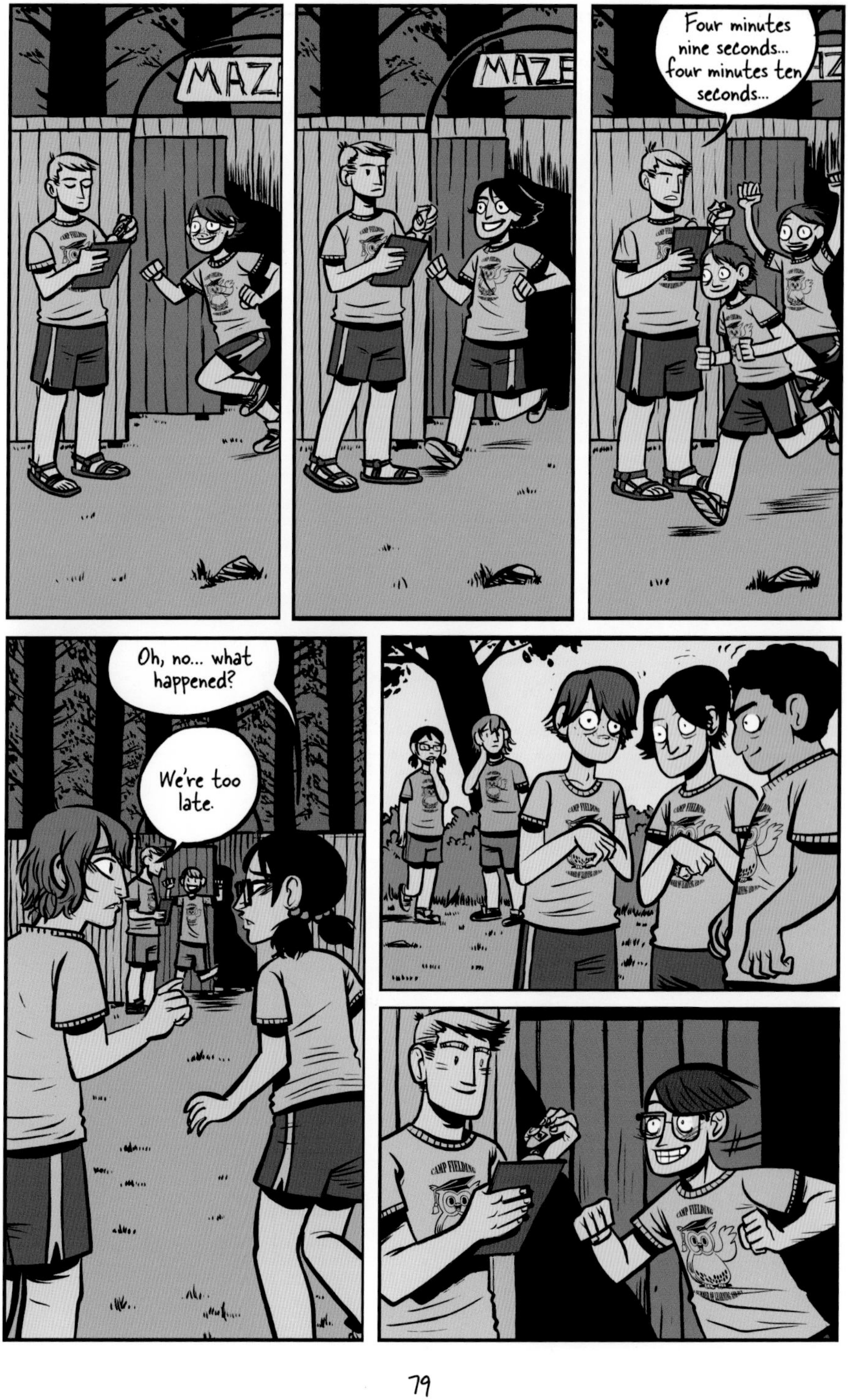
MAZE
MAZE
Four minutes nine seconds... four minutes ten seconds...
Oh, no... what happened?
We're too late.
CAMP FIELDING

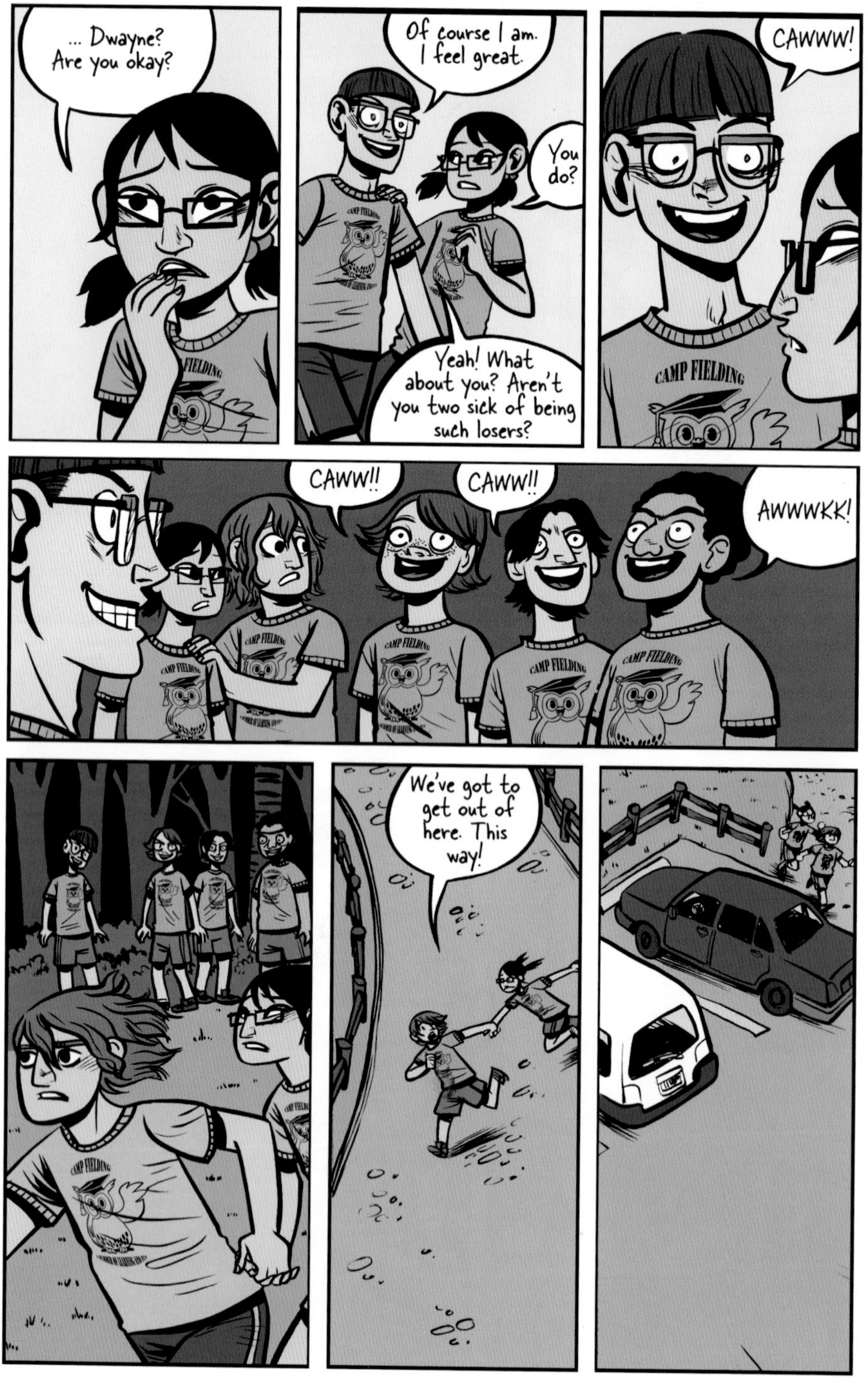
... Dwayne? Are you okay?
Of course I am. I feel great.
You do?
Yeah! What about you? Aren't you two sick of being such losers?
CAWWW!
CAMP FIELDING
CAWW!!
CAWW!!
AWWWKK!
CAMP FIELDING
We've got to get out of here. This way!

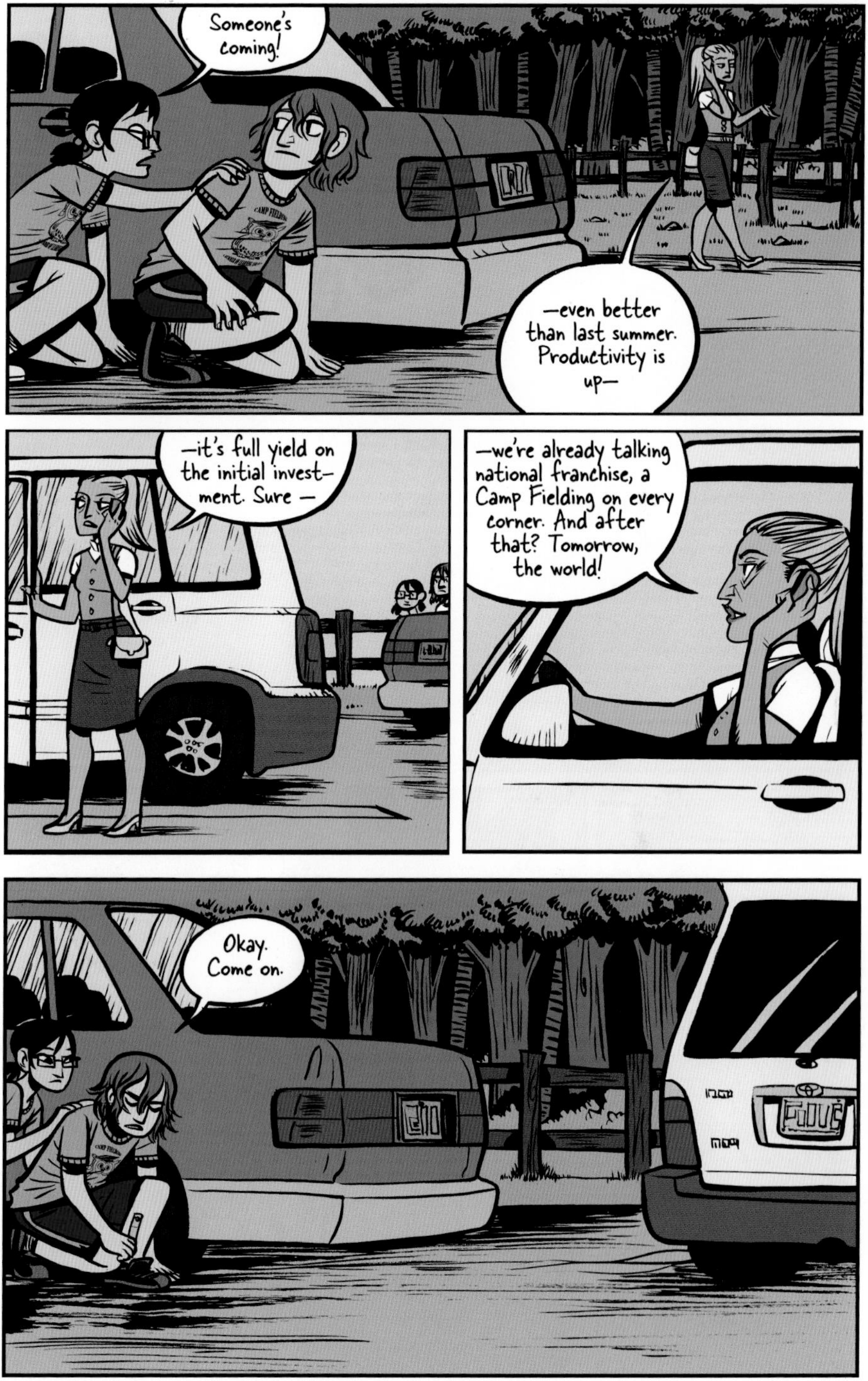
Someone's coming!
—even better than last summer. Productivity is up—
—it's full yield on the initial invest-ment. Sure —
—we're already talking national franchise, a Camp Fielding on every corner. And after that? Tomorrow, the world!
Okay. Come on.

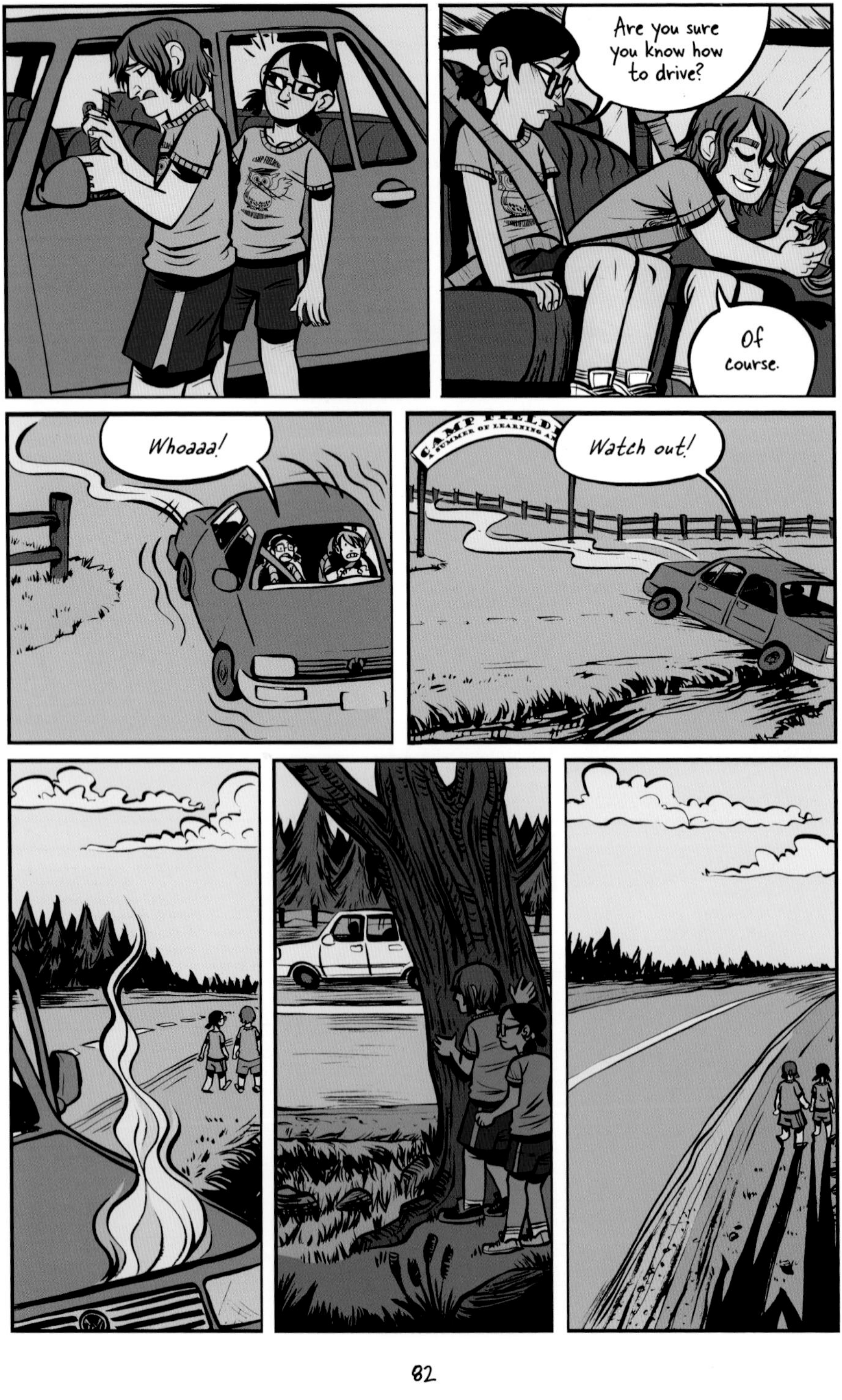
Are you sure you know how to drive?
Of course.
Whoaaa!
CAMP FIELDING
A SUMMER OF LEARNING
Watch out!

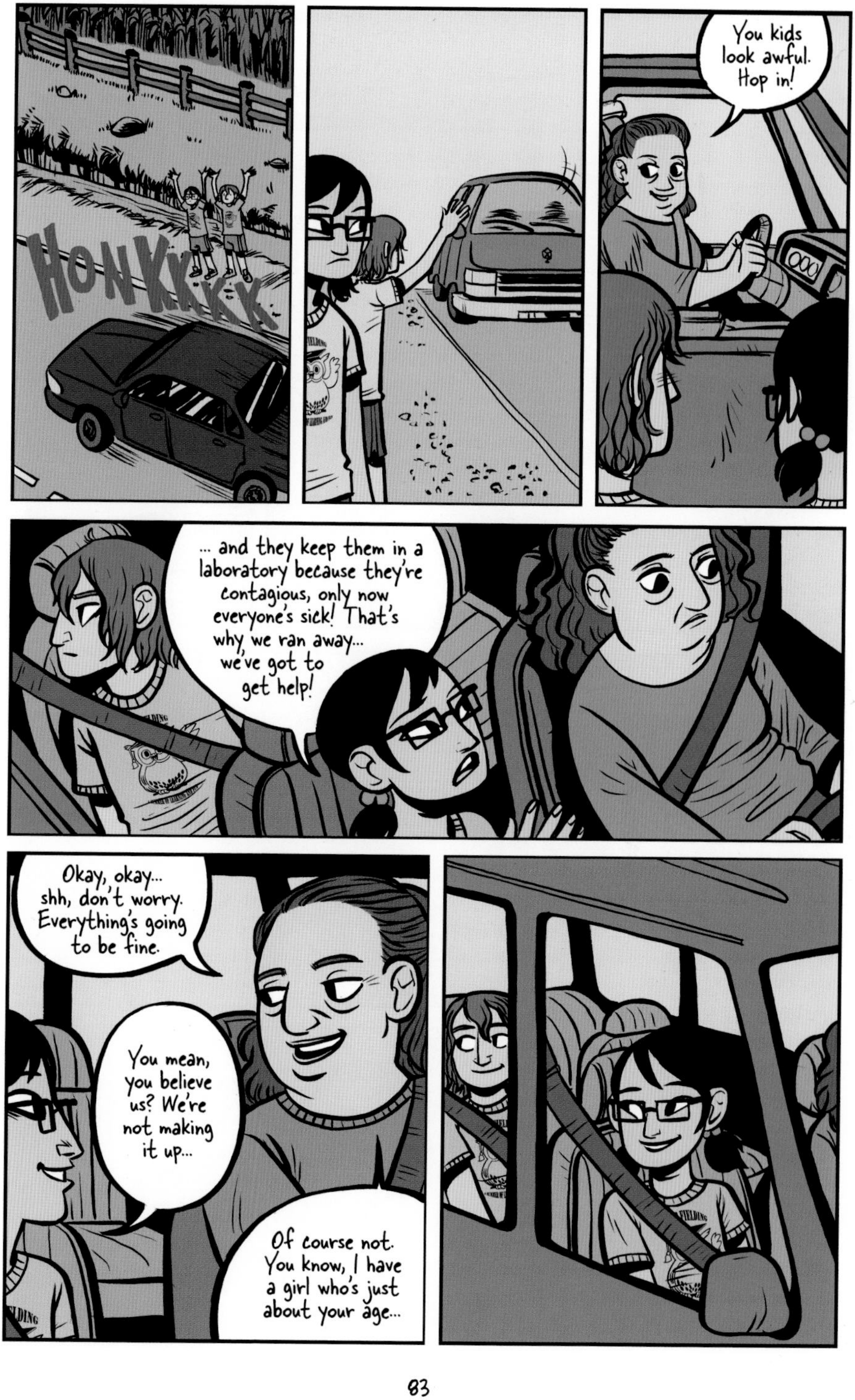
HONKKKK
You kids look awful. Hop in!
... and they keep them in a laboratory because they're contagious, only now everyone's sick! That's why we ran away... we've got to get help!
Okay, okay... shh, don't worry. Everything's going to be fine.
You mean, you believe us? We're not making it up...
Of course not. You know, I have a girl who's just about your age...

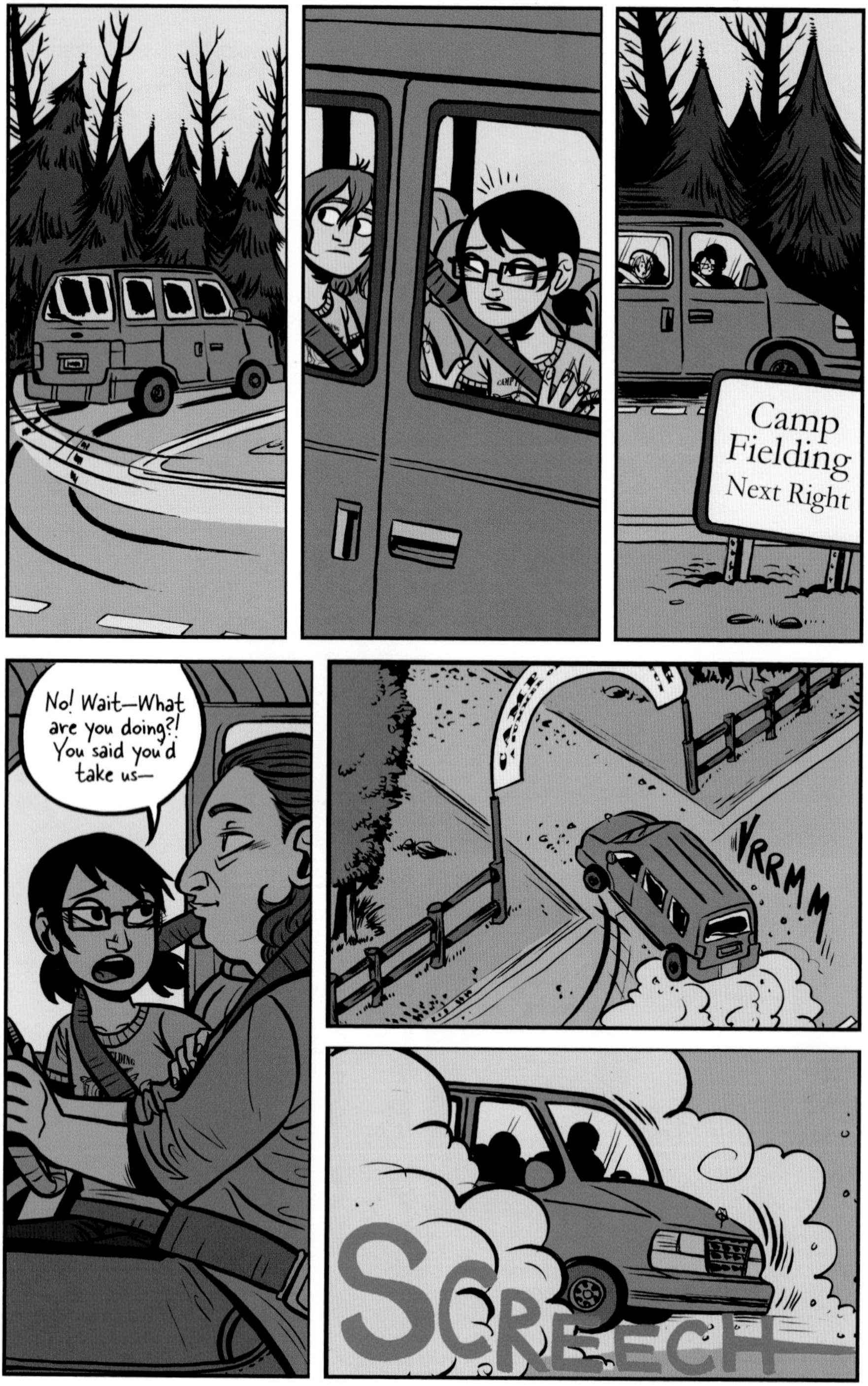
Camp
Fielding
Next Right
No! Wait—What are you doing?! You said you'd take us—
VRRMM
SCREECH

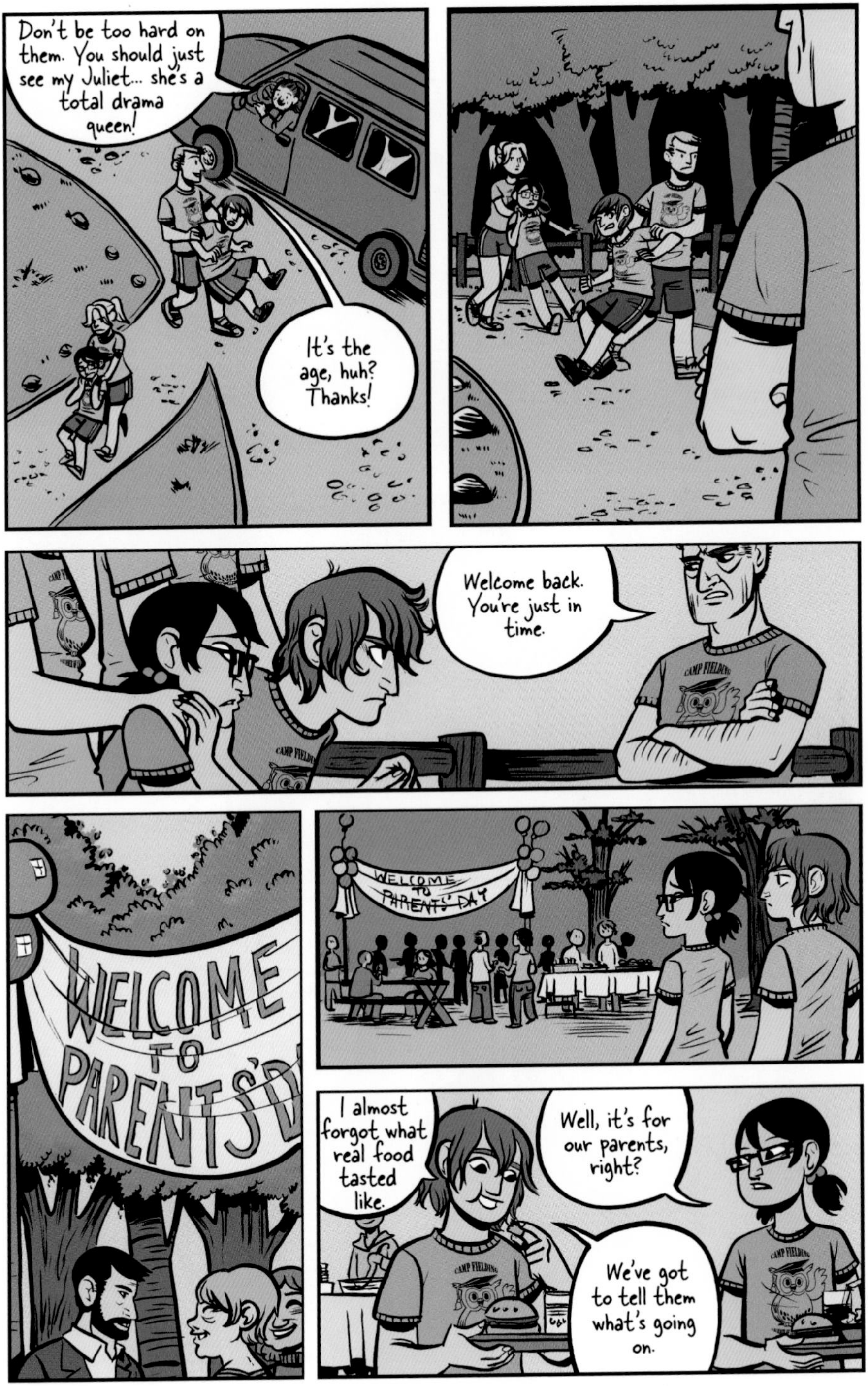
Don't be too hard on them. You should just see my Juliet... she's a total drama queen!
It's the age, huh? Thanks!
CAMP FIELDING
Welcome back. You're just in time.
CAMP FIELDING
WELCOME TO PARENTS'D
WELCOME TO PARENTS' DAY
I almost forgot what real food tasted like.
Well, it's for our parents, right?
CAMP FIELDING
CAMP FIELDING
We've got to tell them what's going on.

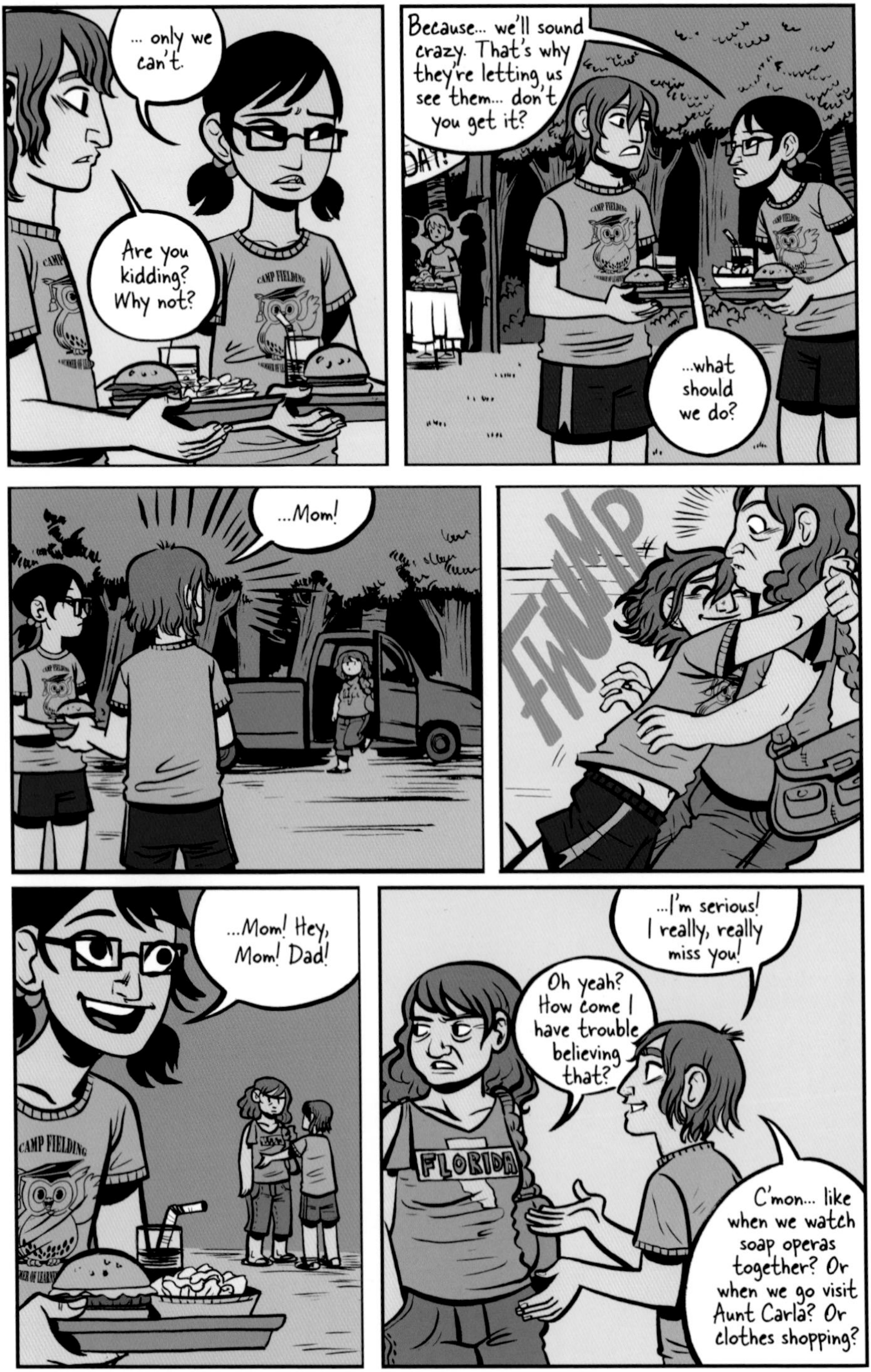
... only we can't.
Are you kidding? Why not?
Because... we'll sound crazy. That's why they're letting us see them... don't you get it?
...what should we do?
...Mom!
FWUMP
...Mom! Hey, Mom! Dad!
...I'm serious! I really, really miss you!
Oh yeah? How come I have trouble believing that?
C'mon... like when we watch soap operas together? Or when we go visit Aunt Carla? Or clothes shopping?
FLORIDA

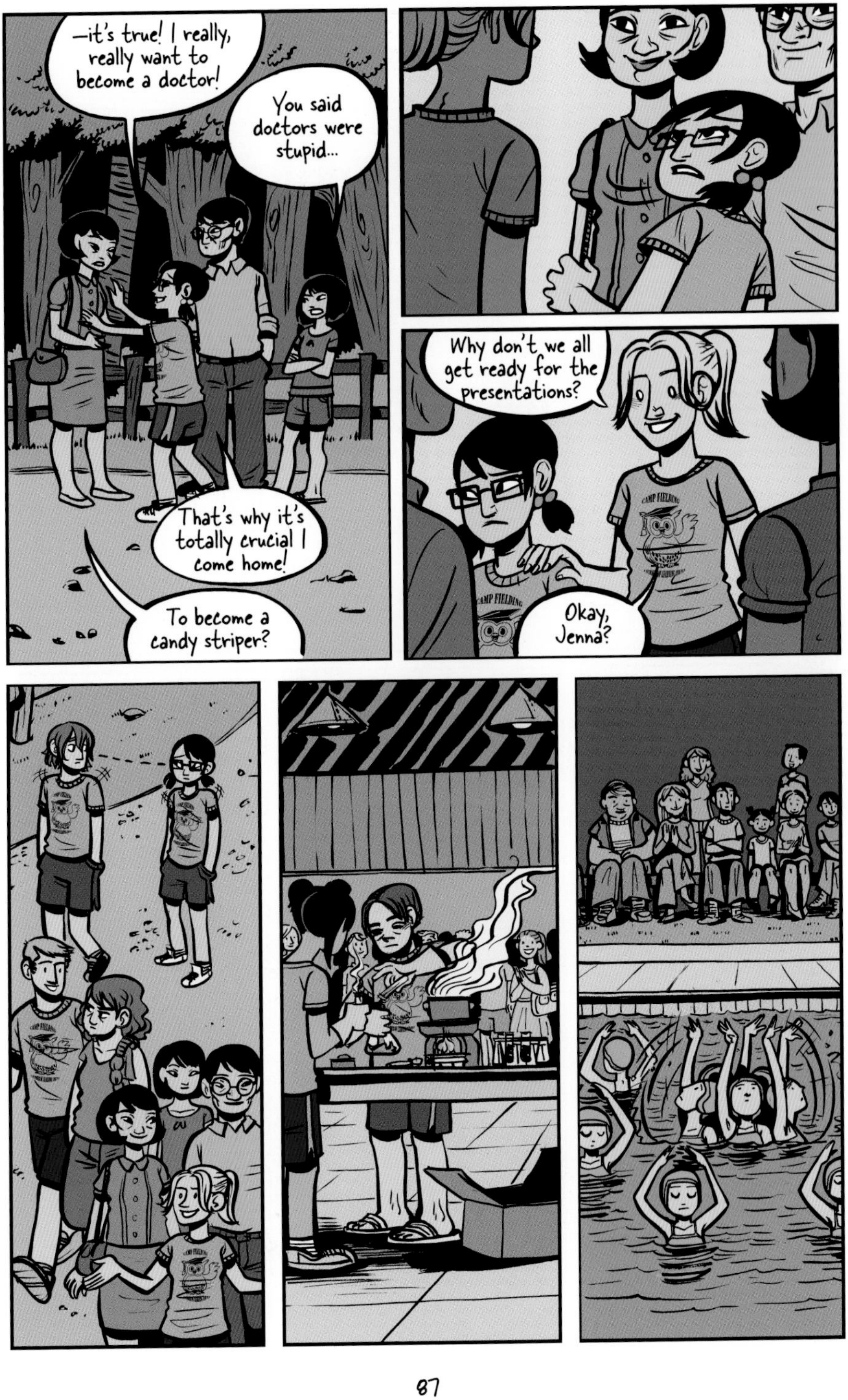
—it's true! I really, really want to become a doctor!
You said doctors were stupid...
That's why it's totally crucial I come home!
To become a candy striper?
Why don't we all get ready for the presentations?
Okay, Jenna?
CAMP FIELDING

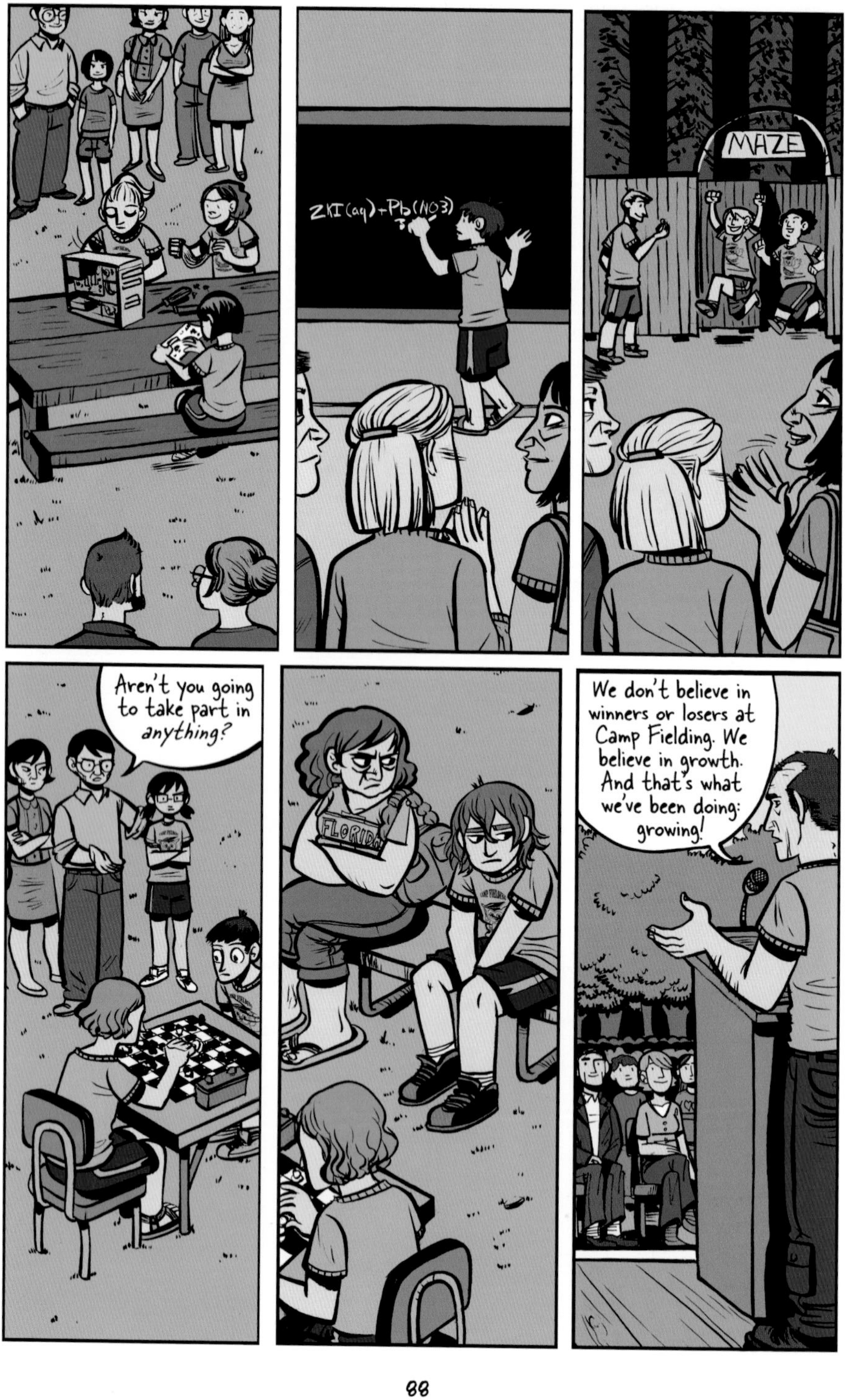
2KI(aq)+Pb(NO3)
MAZE
Aren't you going to take part in *anything*?
FLORIDA
We don't believe in winners or losers at Camp Fielding. We believe in growth. And that's what we've been doing: growing!

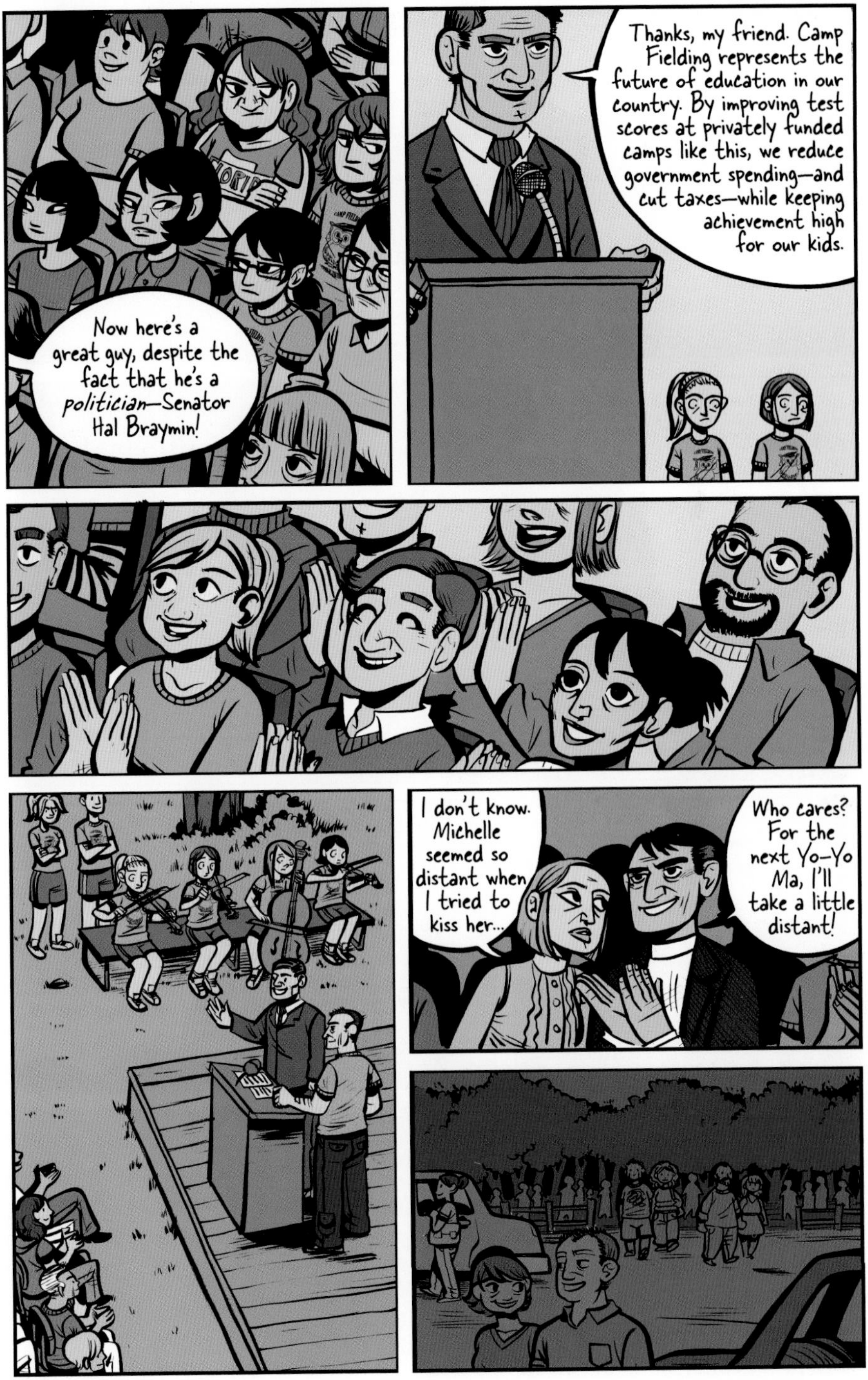

Now here's a great guy, despite the fact that he's a *politician*—Senator Hal Braymin!
Thanks, my friend. Camp Fielding represents the future of education in our country. By improving test scores at privately funded camps like this, we reduce government spending—and cut taxes—while keeping achievement high for our kids.
I don't know. Michelle seemed so distant when I tried to kiss her...
Who cares? For the next Yo-Yo Ma, I'll take a little distant!

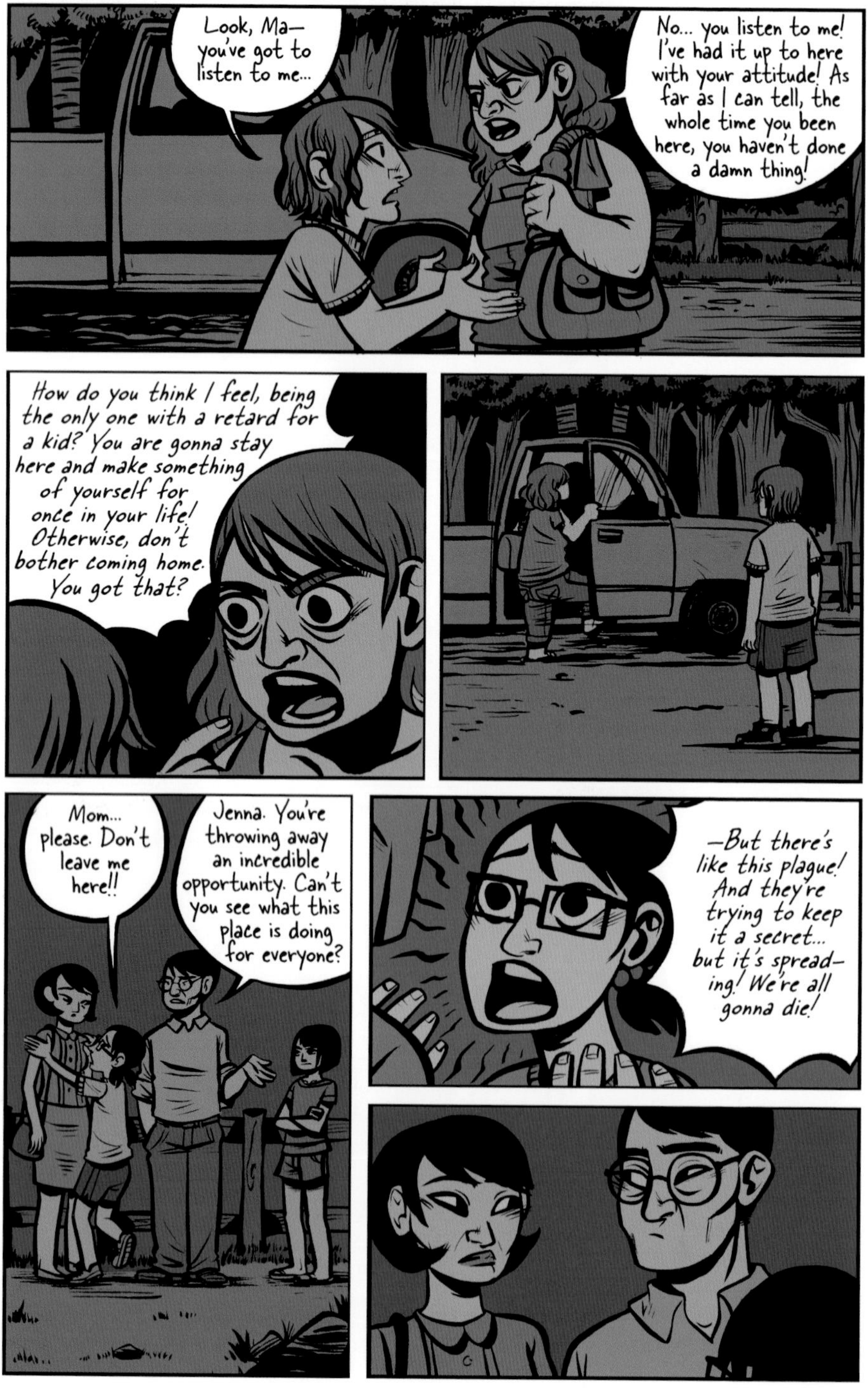
Look, Ma— you've got to listen to me...
No... you listen to me! I've had it up to here with your attitude! As far as I can tell, the whole time you been here, you haven't done a damn thing!
How do you think I feel, being the only one with a retard for a kid? You are gonna stay here and make something of yourself for once in your life! Otherwise, don't bother coming home. You got that?
Mom... please. Don't leave me here!!
Jenna. You're throwing away an incredible opportunity. Can't you see what this place is doing for everyone?
—But there's like this plague! And they're trying to keep it a secret... but it's spread-ing! We're all gonna die!

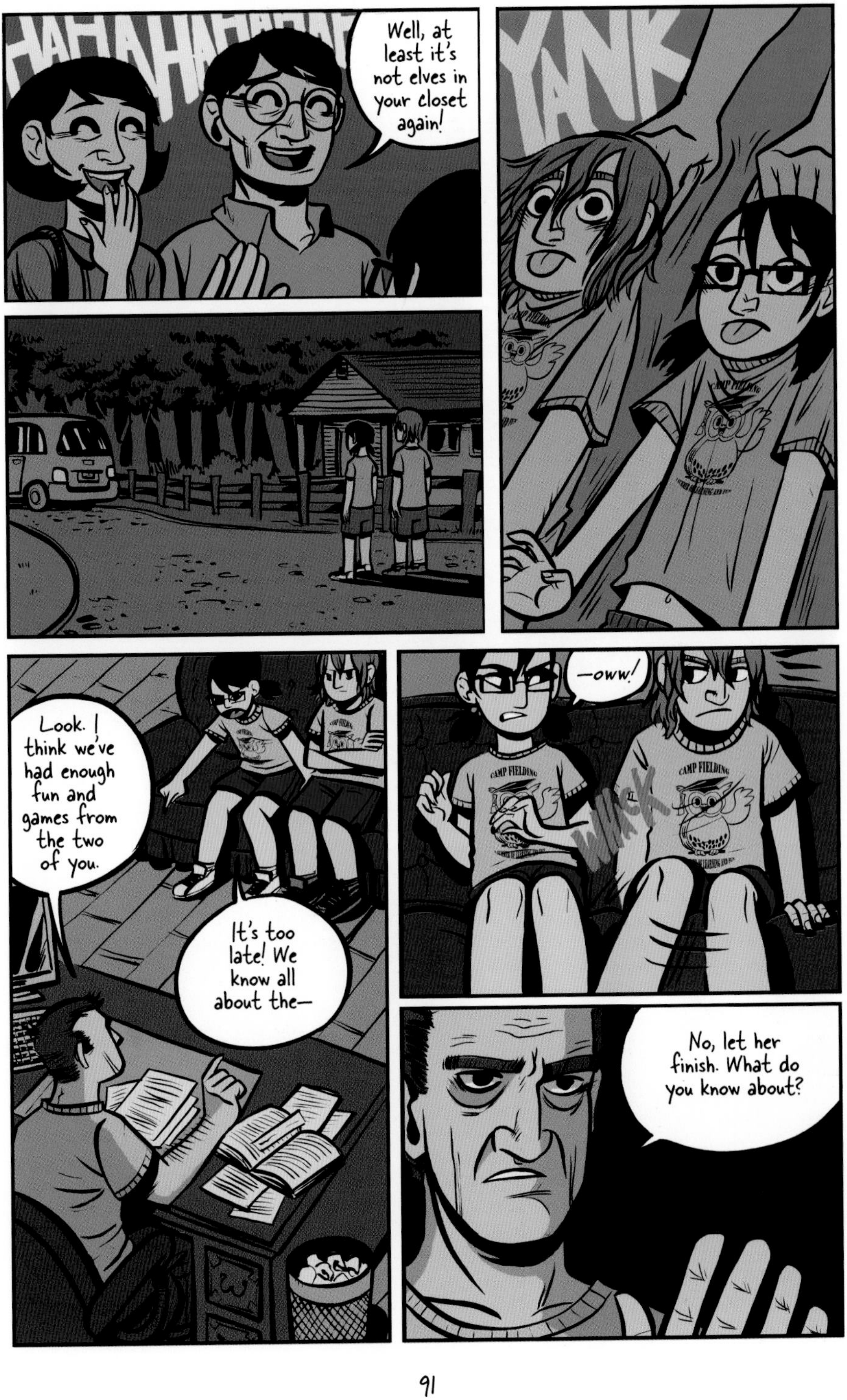
HAHAHAHAHAHA
Well, at least it's not elves in your closet again!
YANK
Look. I think we've had enough fun and games from the two of you.
It's too late! We know all about the—
—oww!
WHACK
No, let her finish. What do you know about?

—that everybody here has some kinda disease! And we're the only ones who don't have it... yet!

... What if I told you you were right?

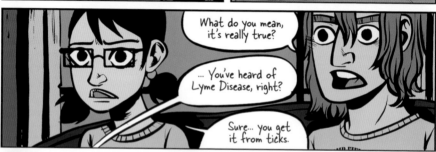

What do you mean, it's really true?

... You've heard of Lyme Disease, right?

Sure... you get it from ticks.

There's a similar disease here... a very rare disease that, if not treated, is fatal.

Come on... I want to show you two something.

92

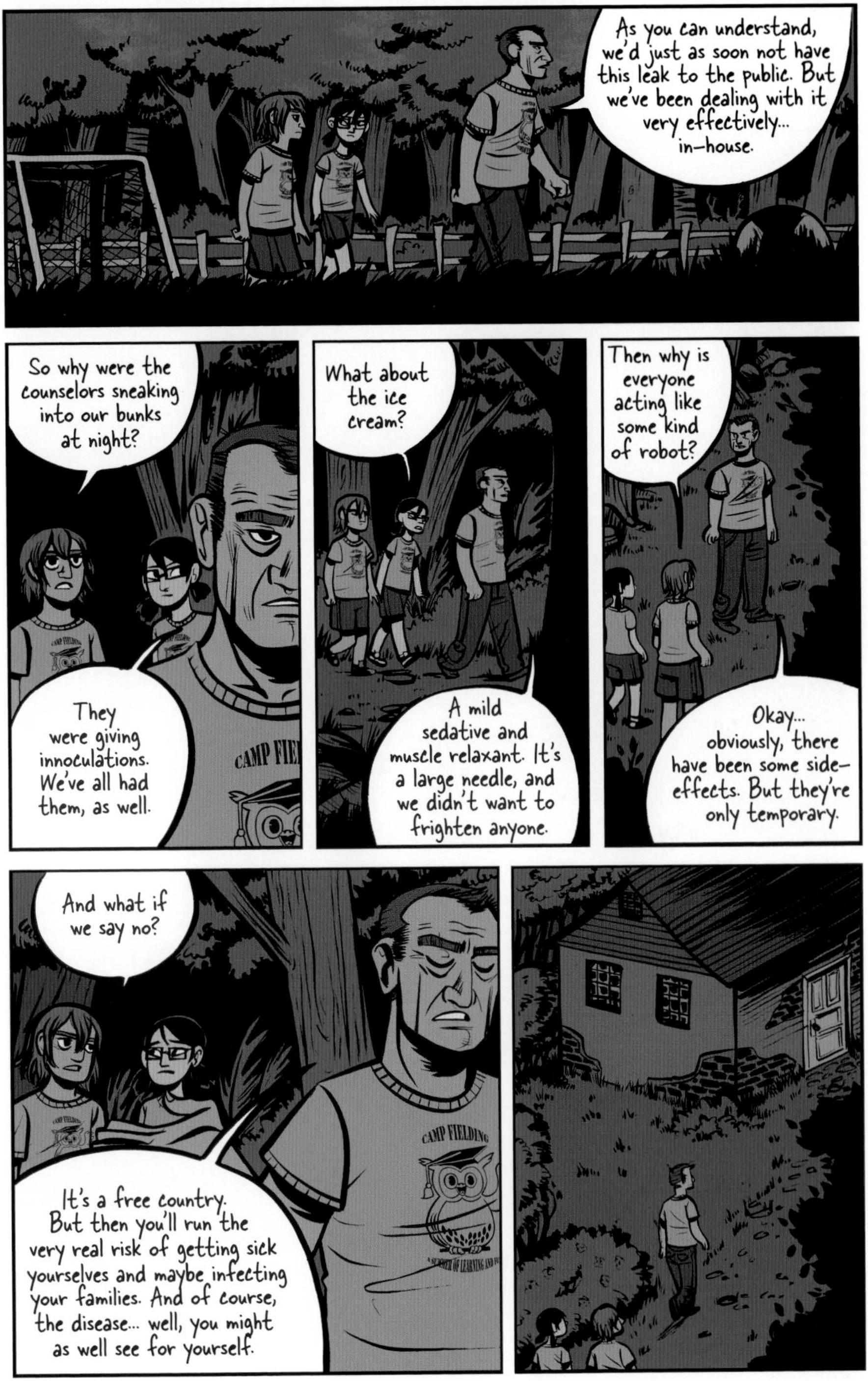
As you can understand, we'd just as soon not have this leak to the public. But we've been dealing with it very effectively... in-house.
So why were the counselors sneaking into our bunks at night?
They were giving innoculations. We've all had them, as well.
What about the ice cream?
A mild sedative and muscle relaxant. It's a large needle, and we didn't want to frighten anyone.
Then why is everyone acting like some kind of robot?
Okay... obviously, there have been some side-effects. But they're only temporary.
And what if we say no?
It's a free country. But then you'll run the very real risk of getting sick yourselves and maybe infecting your families. And of course, the disease... well, you might as well see for yourself.

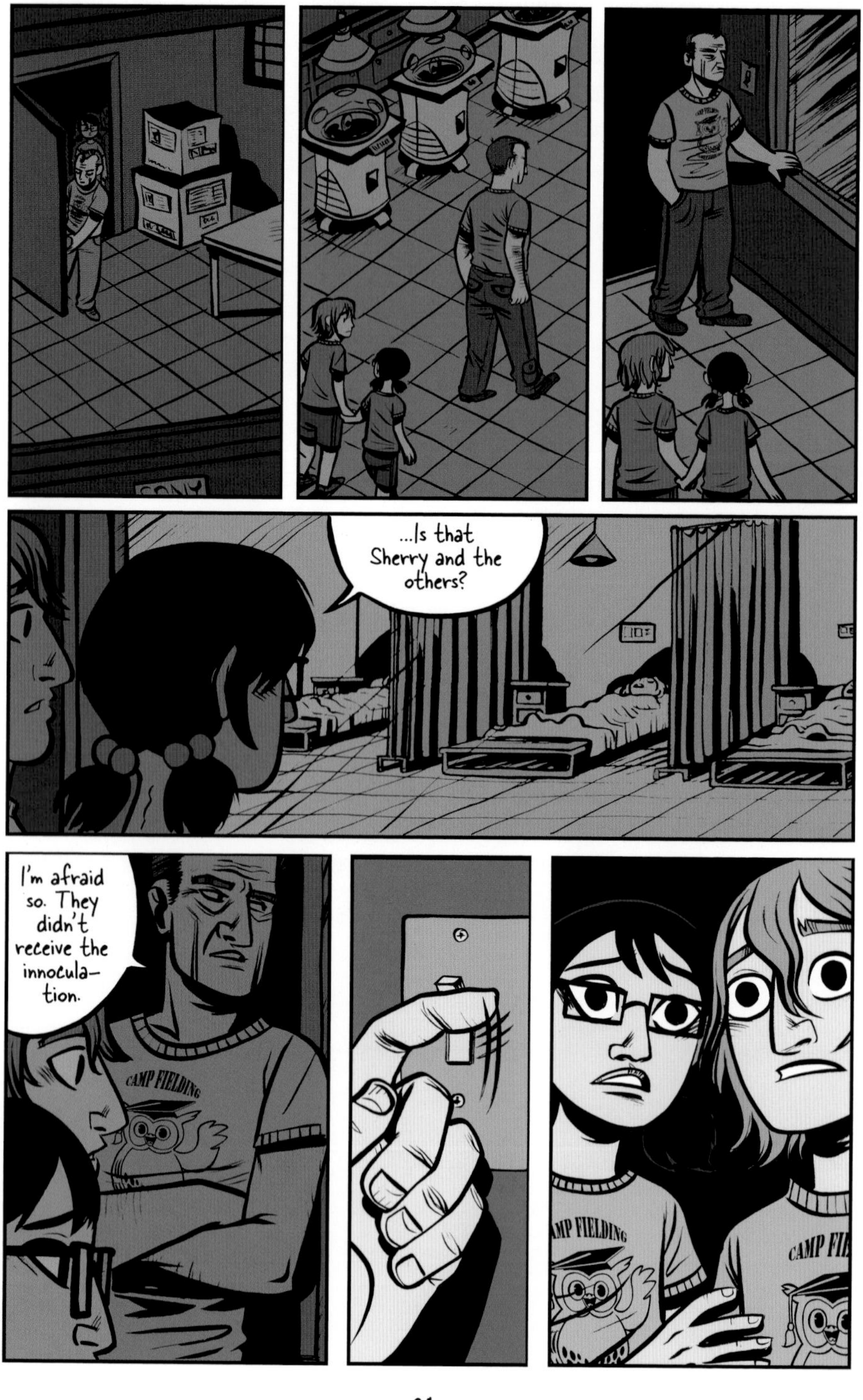
...Is that Sherry and the others?
I'm afraid so. They didn't receive the innocula-tion.
CAMP FIELDING
CAMP FIELDING

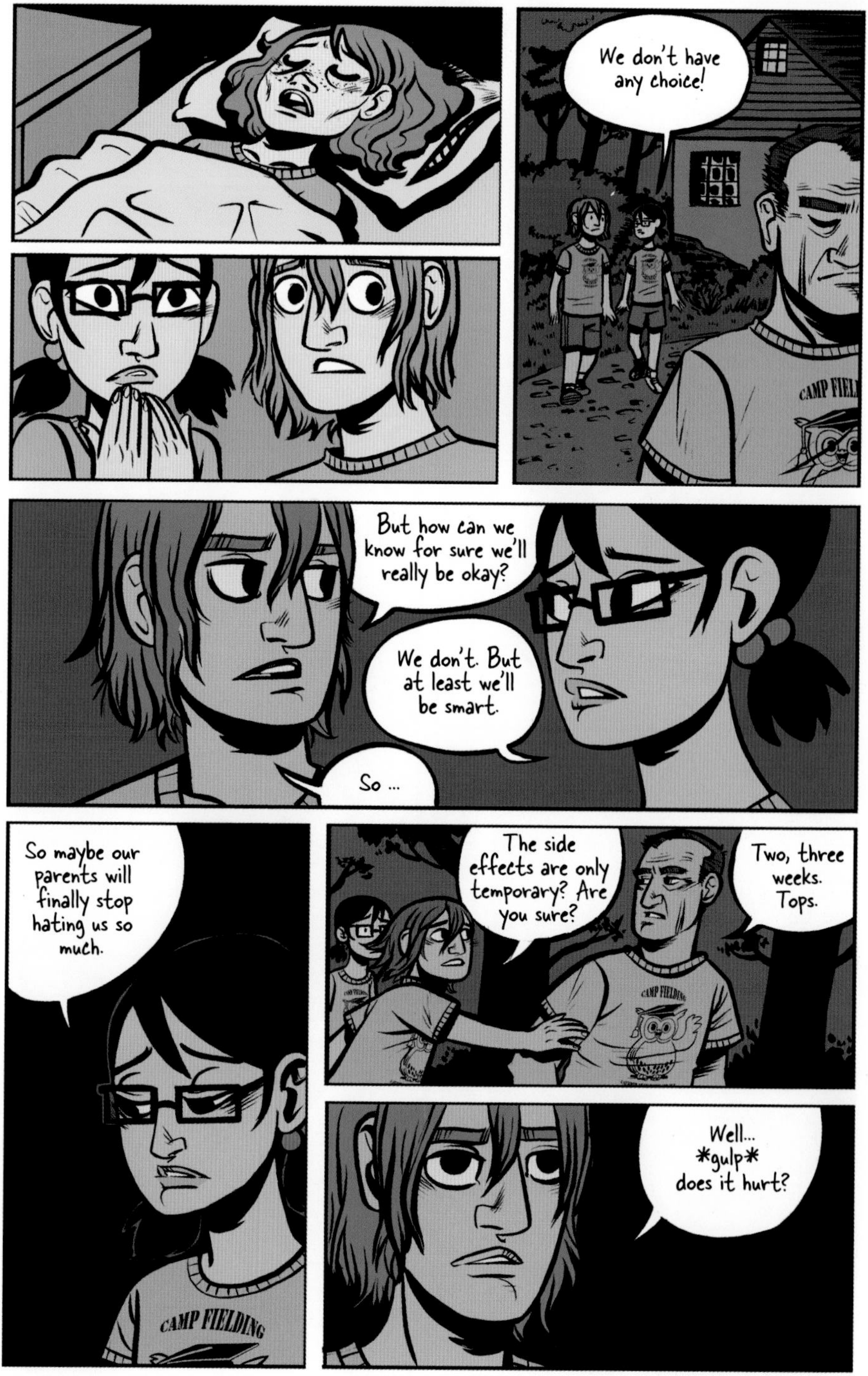
We don't have any choice!
But how can we know for sure we'll really be okay?
We don't. But at least we'll be smart.
So ...
So maybe our parents will finally stop hating us so much.
The side effects are only temporary? Are you sure?
Two, three weeks. Tops.
Well... *gulp* does it hurt?
CAMP FIELDING

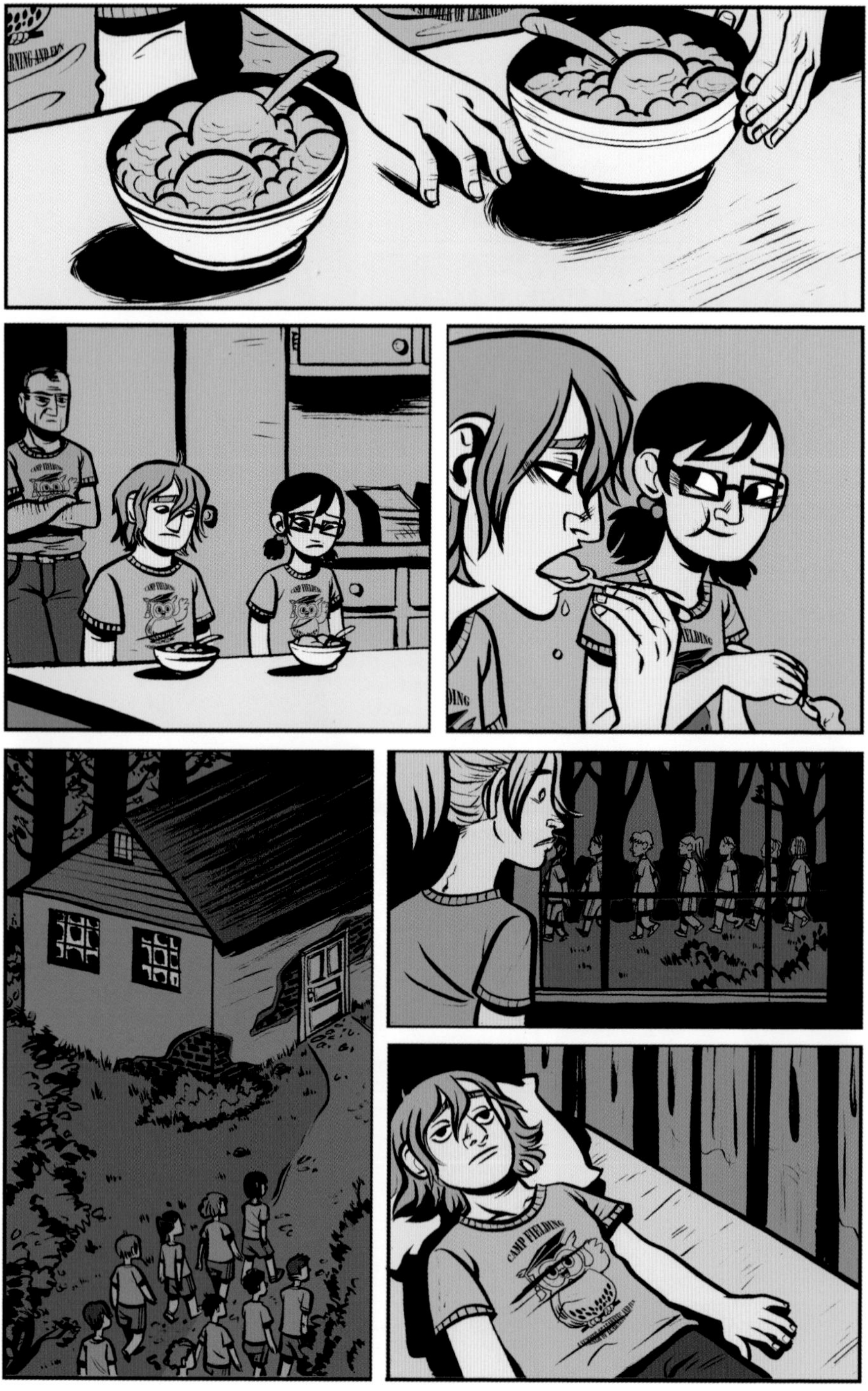
CAMP FIELDING

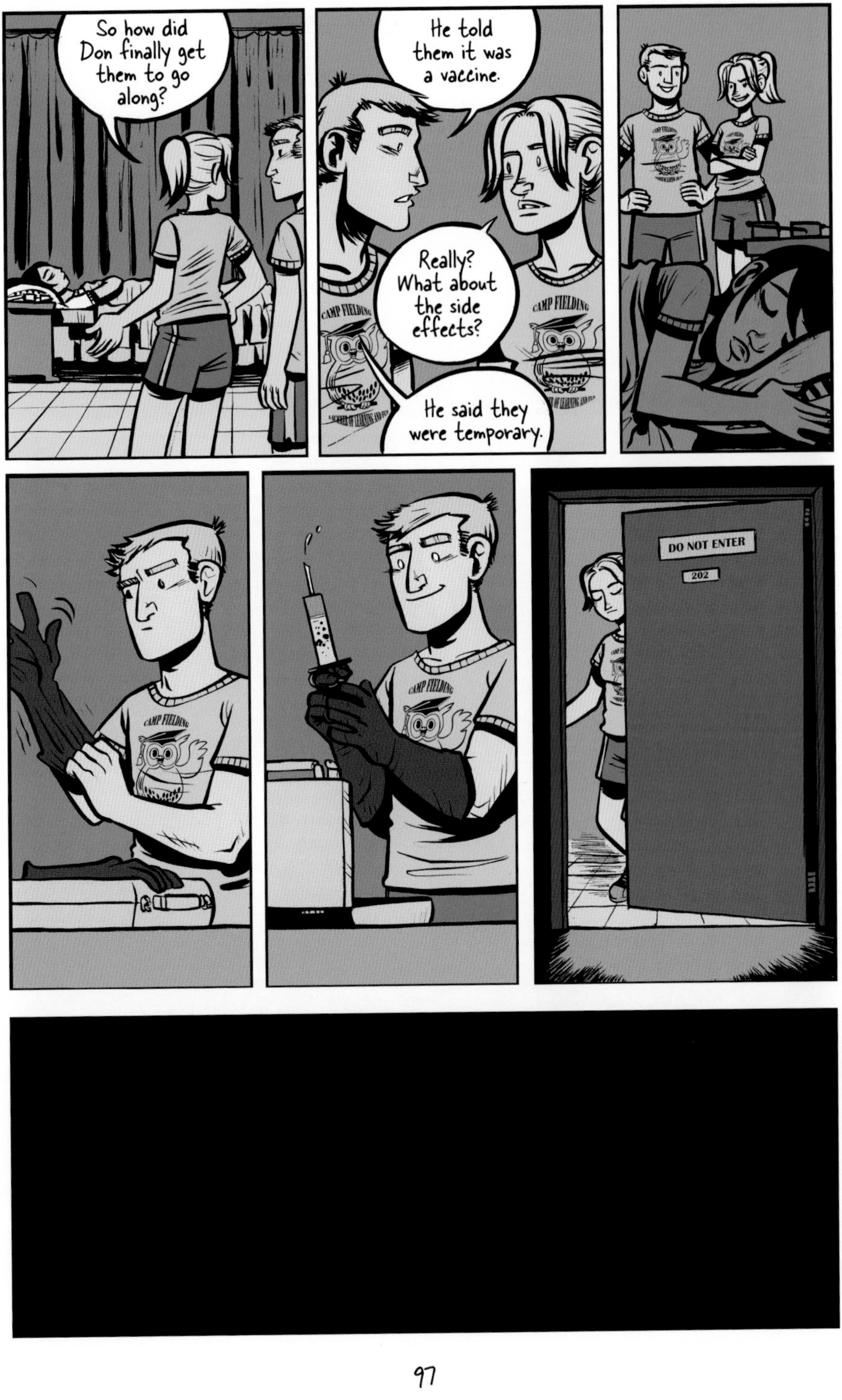
So how did Don finally get them to go along?
He told them it was a vaccine.
Really? What about the side effects?
He said they were temporary.
CAMP FIELDING
DO NOT ENTER
202

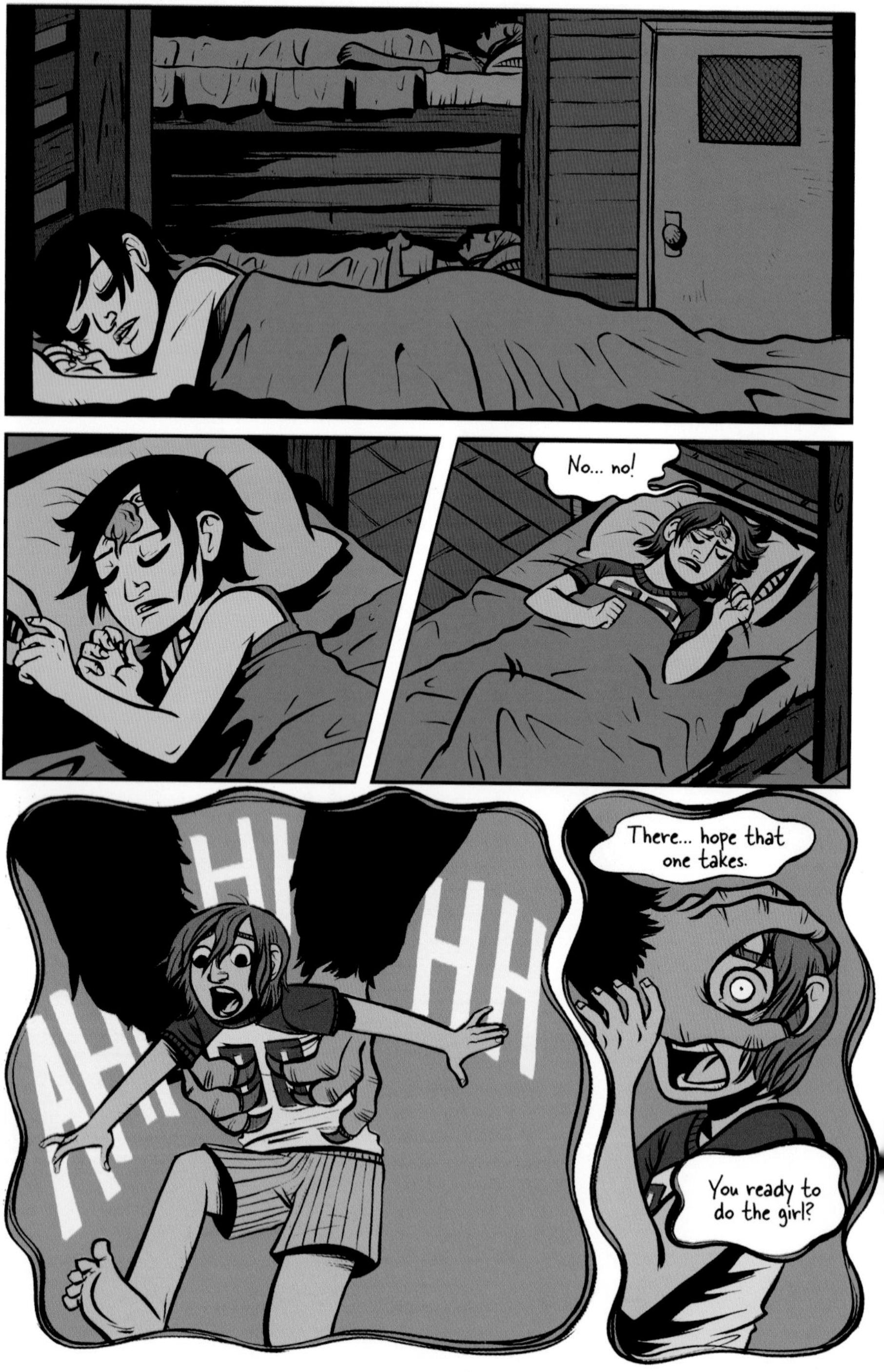
No... no!
AHHHHH
There... hope that one takes.
You ready to do the girl?

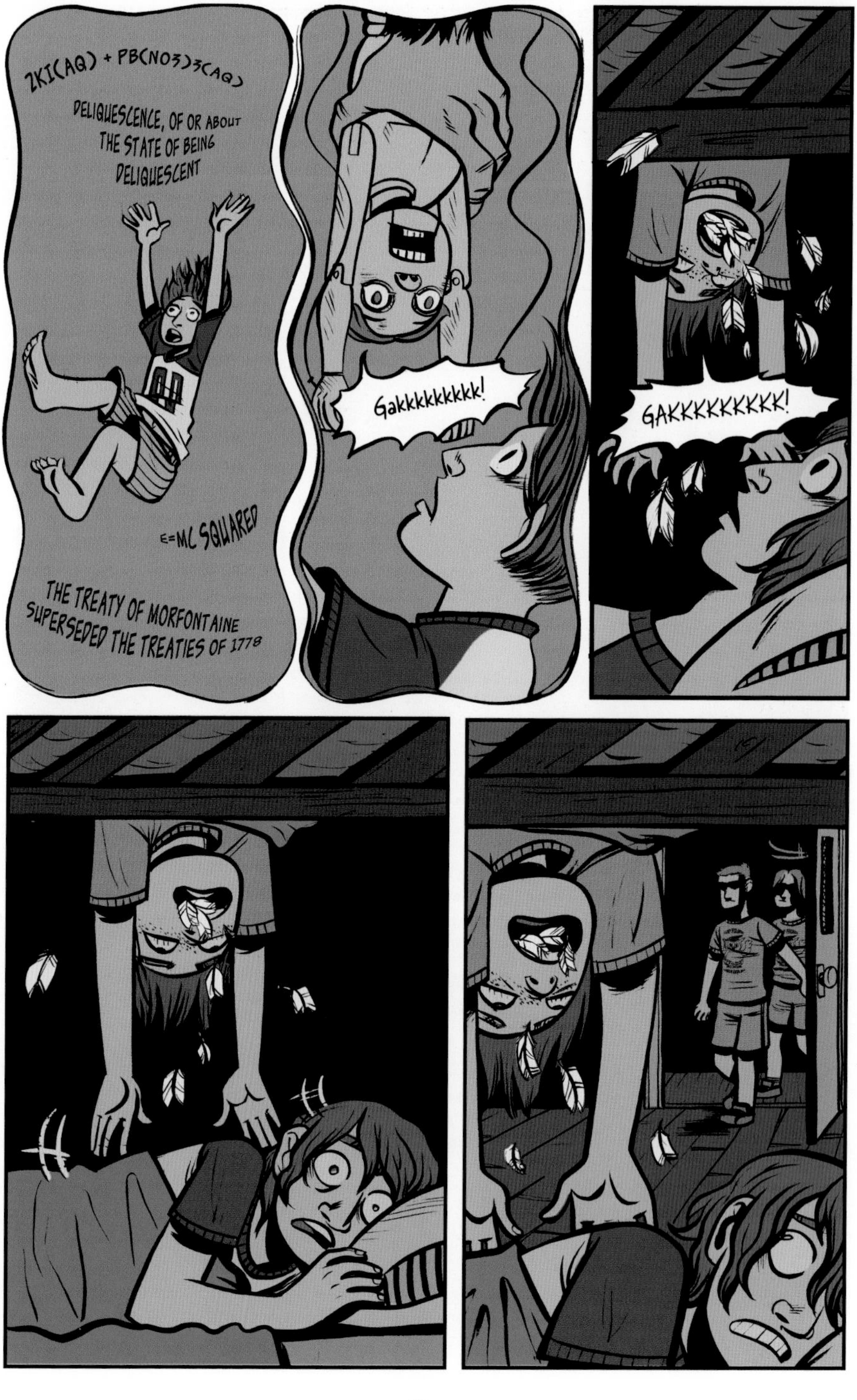
2KI(AQ) + PB(NO3)3(AQ)
DELIQUESCENCE, OF OR ABOUT THE STATE OF BEING DELIQUESCENT
E=MC SQUARED
THE TREATY OF MORFONTAINE SUPERSEDED THE TREATIES OF 1778
Gakkkkkkkk!
GAKKKKKKKK!

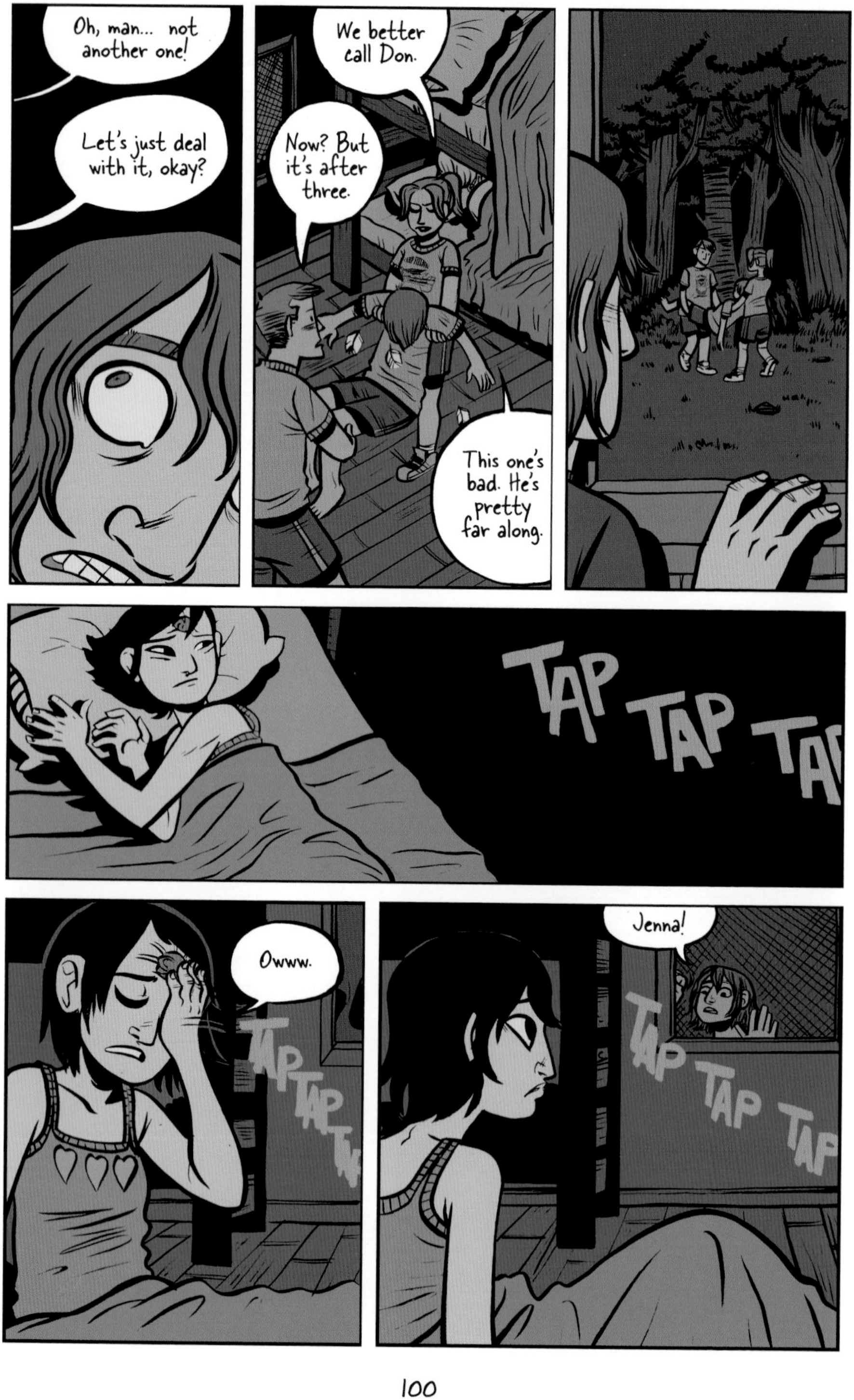
Oh, man... not another one!
Let's just deal with it, okay?
We better call Don.
Now? But it's after three.
This one's bad. He's pretty far along.
TAP TAP TAP
Owww.
TAP TAP TAP
Jenna!
TAP TAP TAP

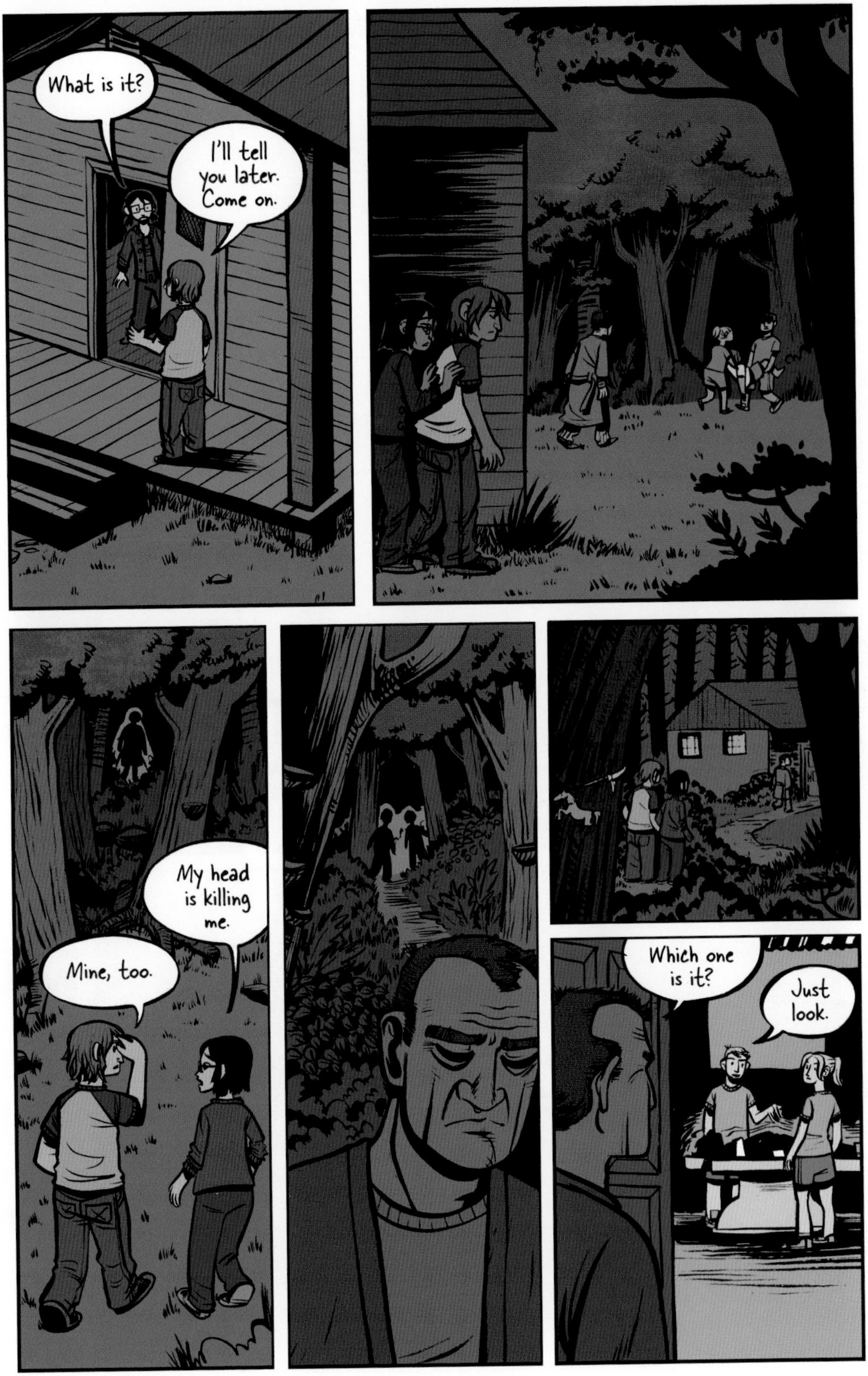
What is it?
I'll tell you later. Come on.
My head is killing me.
Mine, too.
Which one is it?
Just look.

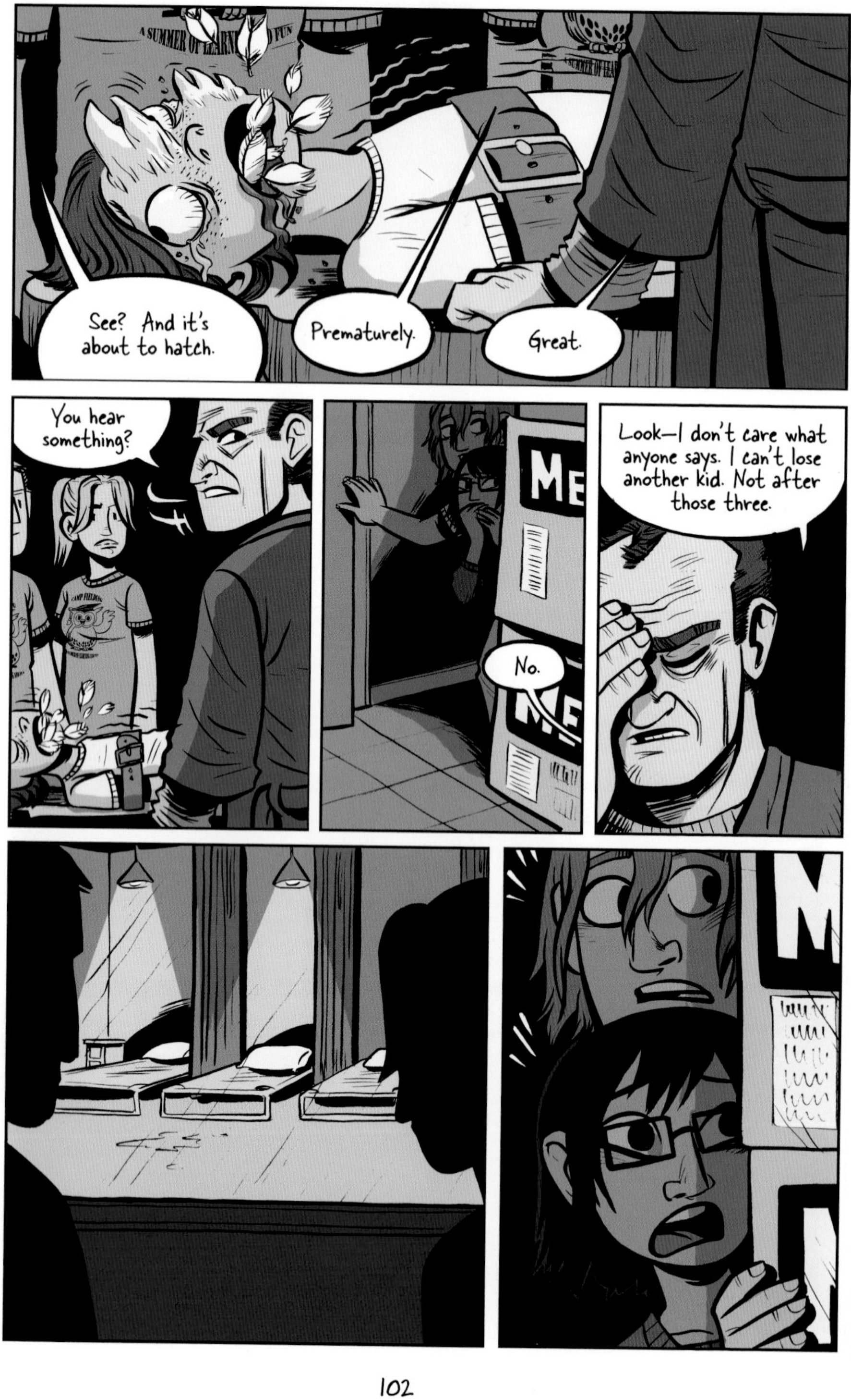
A SUMMER OF LEARN... FUN
See? And it's about to hatch.
Prematurely.
Great.
You hear something?
No.
Look—I don't care what anyone says. I can't lose another kid. Not after those three.

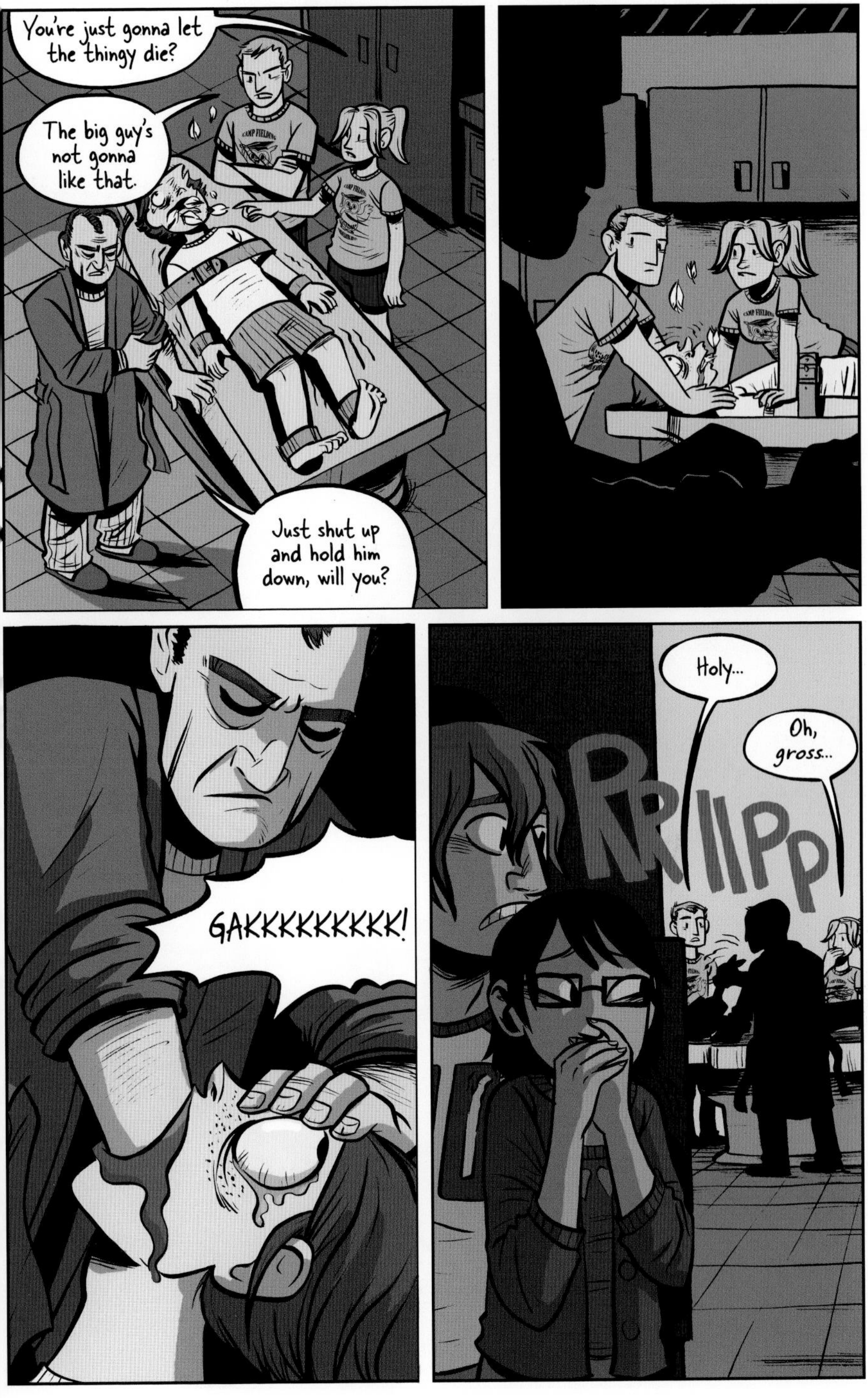
You're just gonna let the thingy die?
The big guy's not gonna like that.
Just shut up and hold him down, will you?
CAMP FIELDING
GAKKKKKKKKK!
Holy...
Oh, gross...
RRIIPP

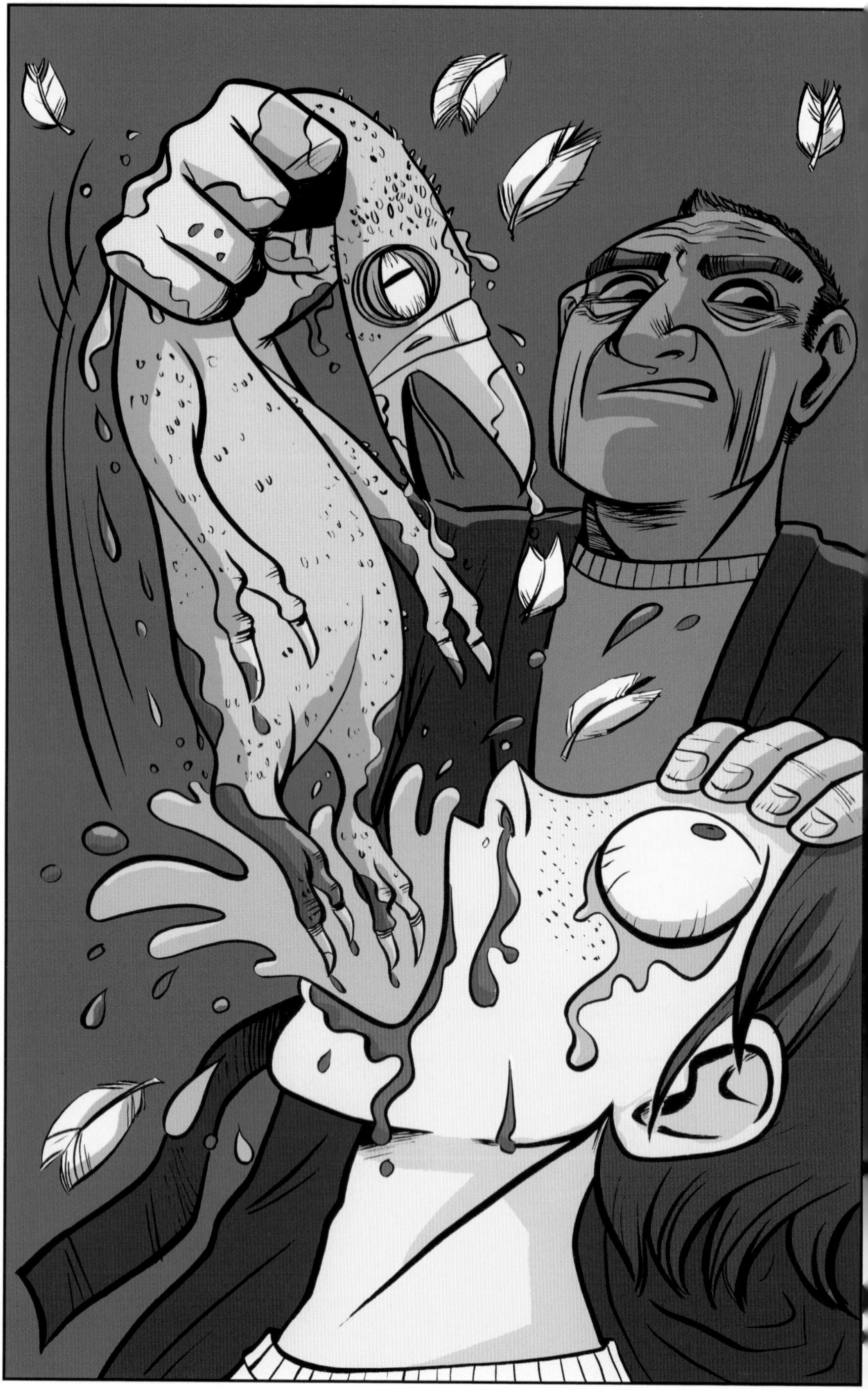

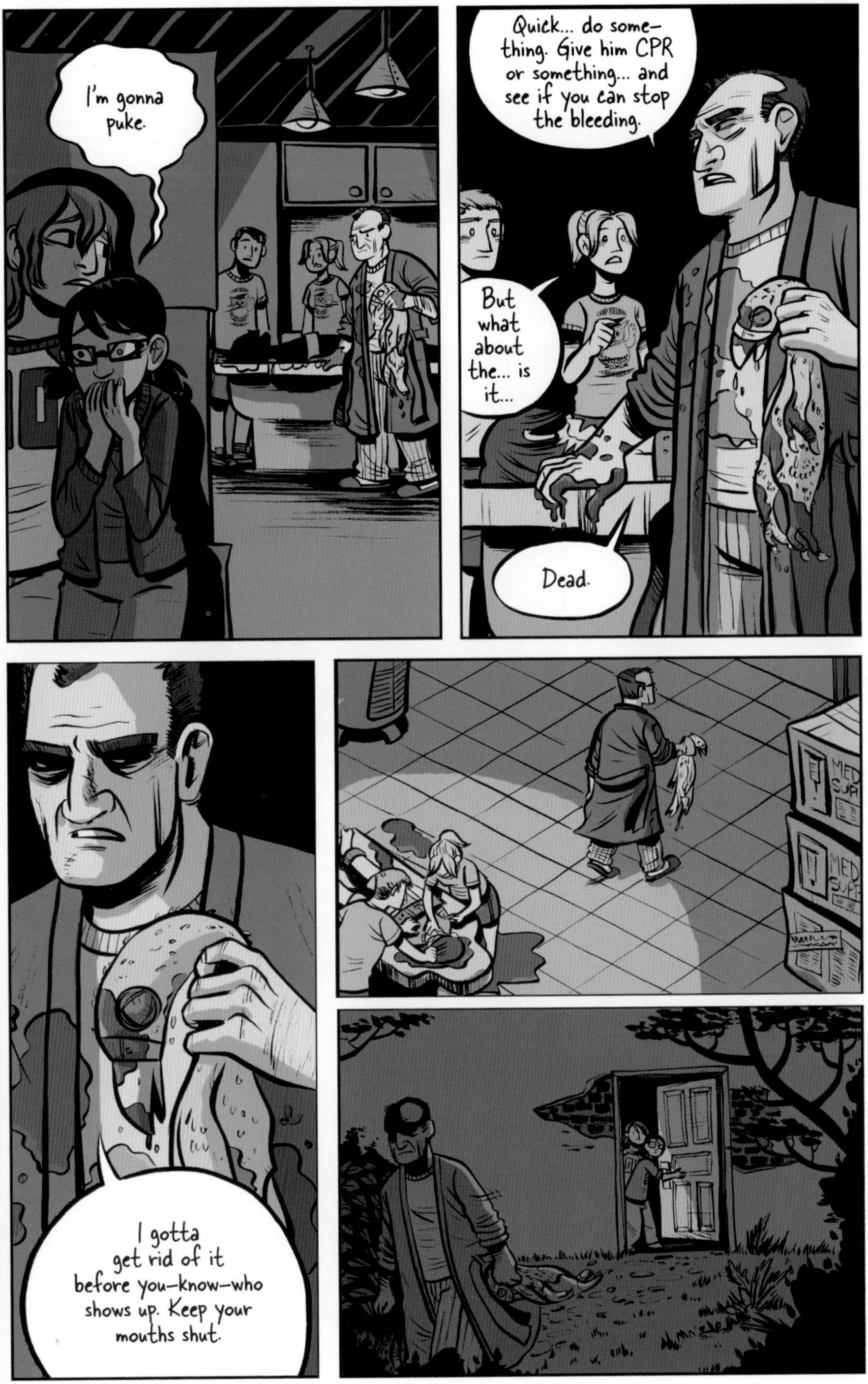
I'm gonna puke.
Quick... do something. Give him CPR or something... and see if you can stop the bleeding.
But what about the... is it...
Dead.
I gotta get rid of it before you-know-who shows up. Keep your mouths shut.

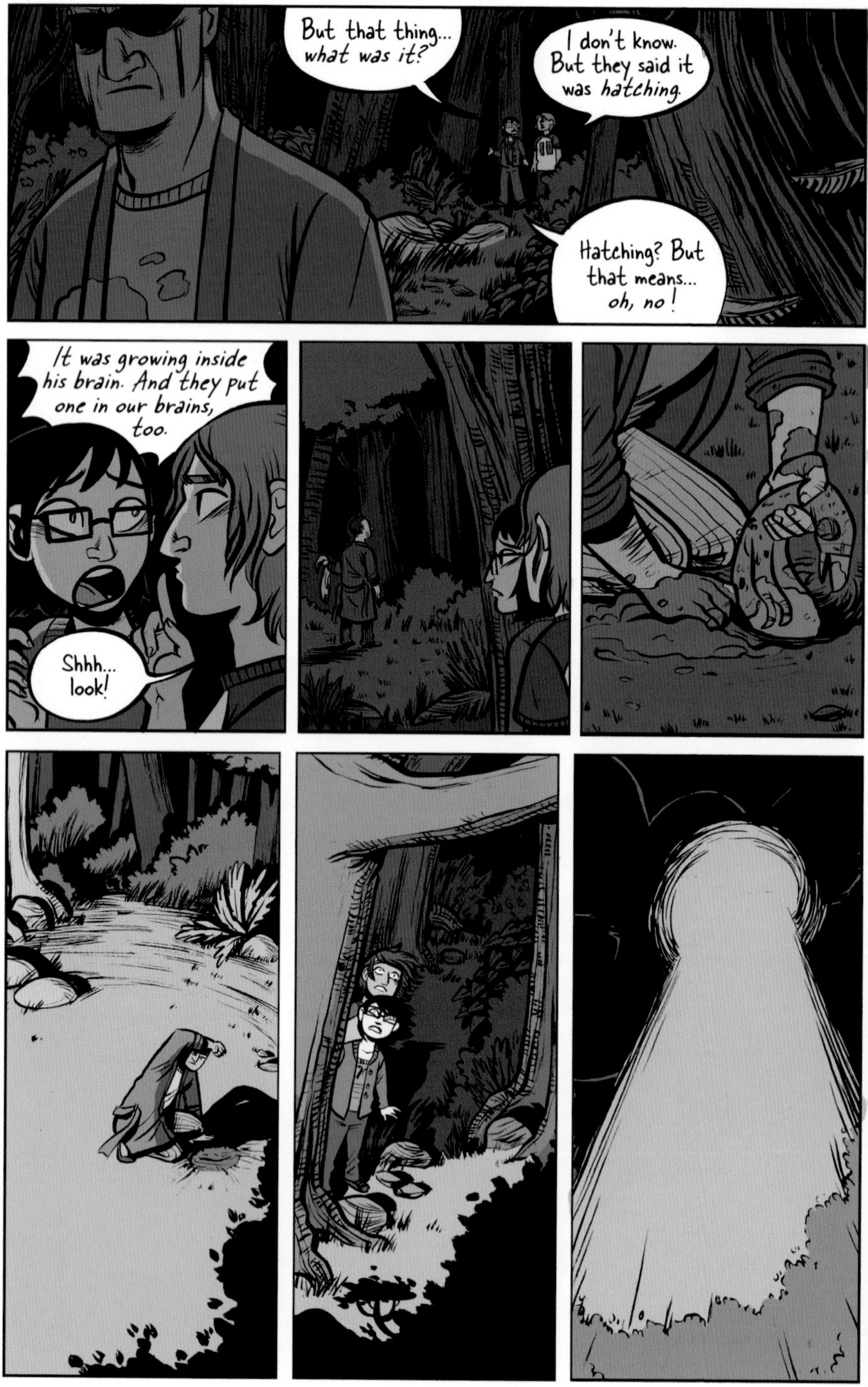
But that thing... what was it?
I don't know. But they said it was hatching.
Hatching? But that means... oh, no!
It was growing inside his brain. And they put one in our brains, too.
Shhh... look!

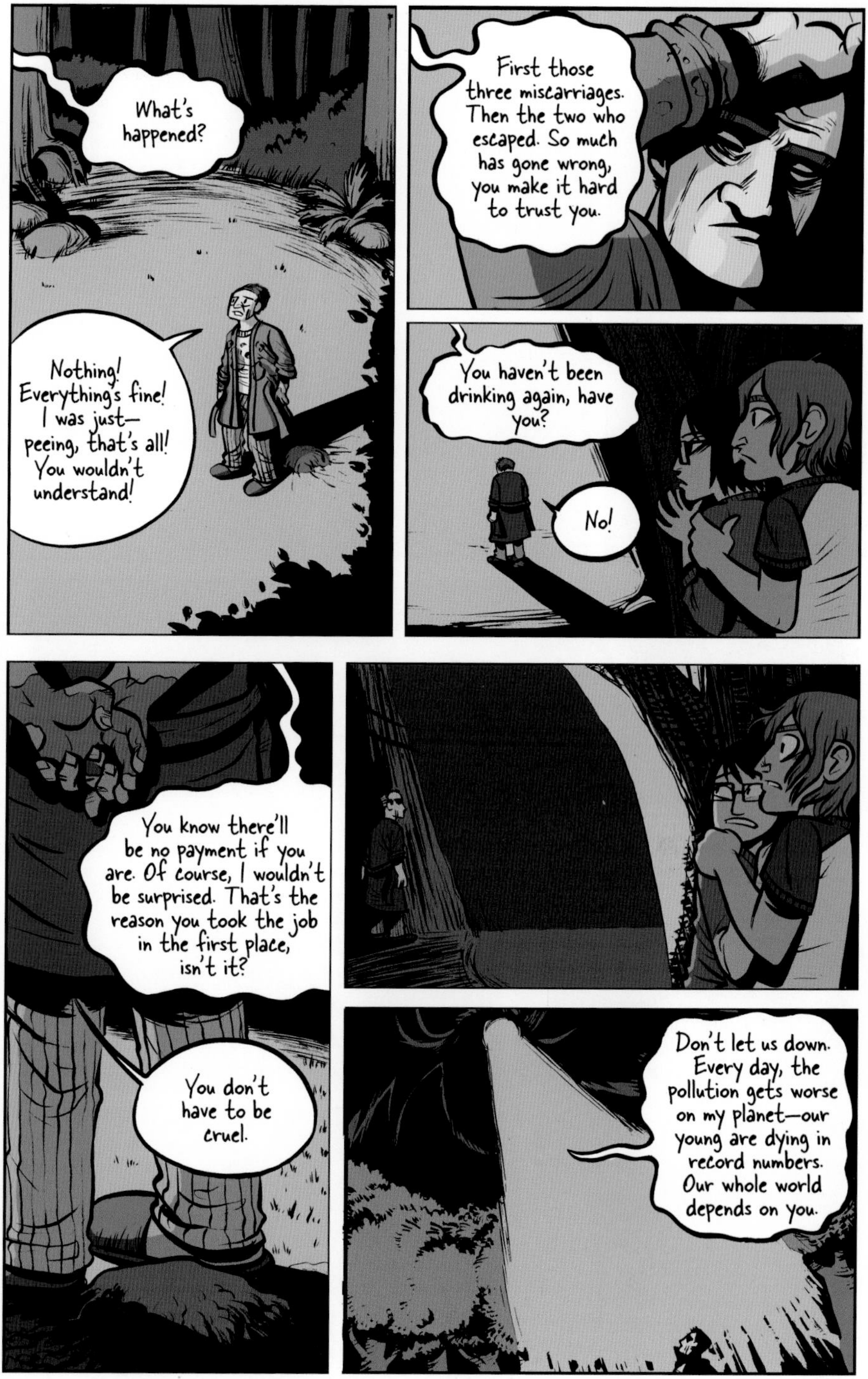
What's happened?
First those three miscarriages. Then the two who escaped. So much has gone wrong, you make it hard to trust you.
Nothing! Everything's fine! I was just— peeing, that's all! You wouldn't understand!
You haven't been drinking again, have you?
No!
You know there'll be no payment if you are. Of course, I wouldn't be surprised. That's the reason you took the job in the first place, isn't it?
You don't have to be cruel.
Don't let us down. Every day, the pollution gets worse on my planet—our young are dying in record numbers. Our whole world depends on you.

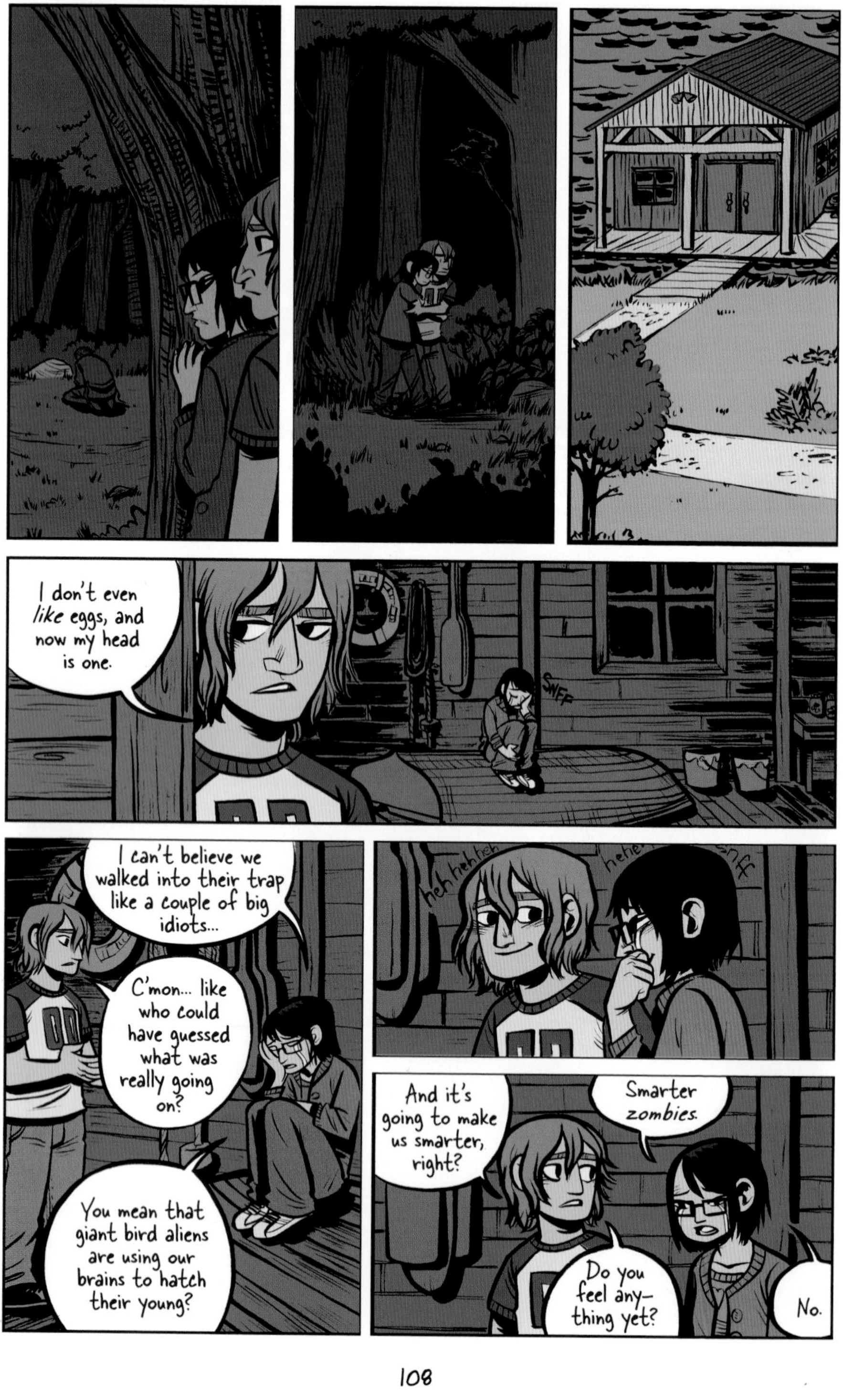
I don't even like eggs, and now my head is one.
SNFF
I can't believe we walked into their trap like a couple of big idiots...
C'mon... like who could have guessed what was really going on?
You mean that giant bird aliens are using our brains to hatch their young?
heh heh heh
And it's going to make us smarter, right?
Smarter zombies.
Do you feel any-thing yet?
No.

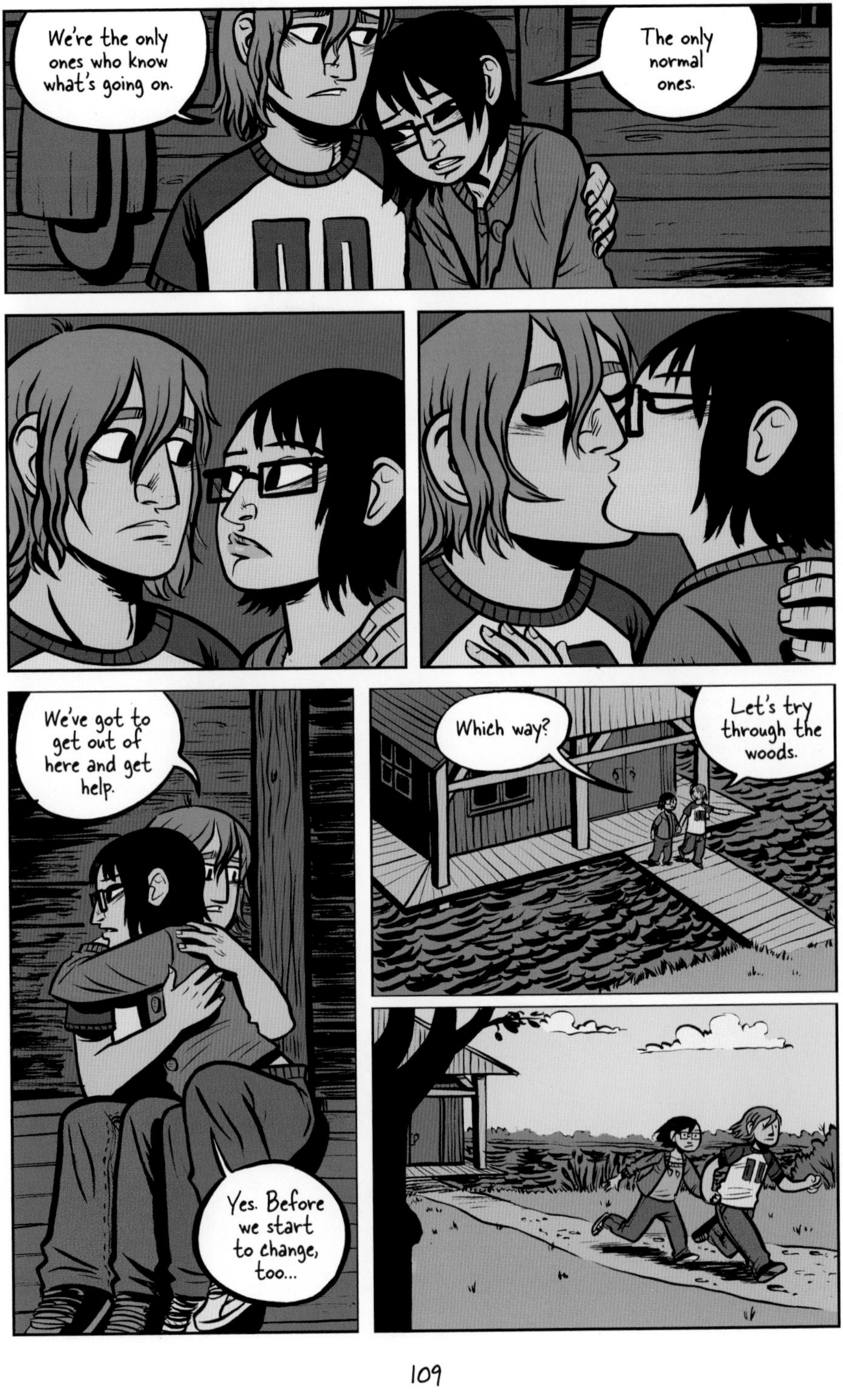

We're the only ones who know what's going on.
The only normal ones.
We've got to get out of here and get help.
Yes. Before we start to change, too...
Which way?
Let's try through the woods.

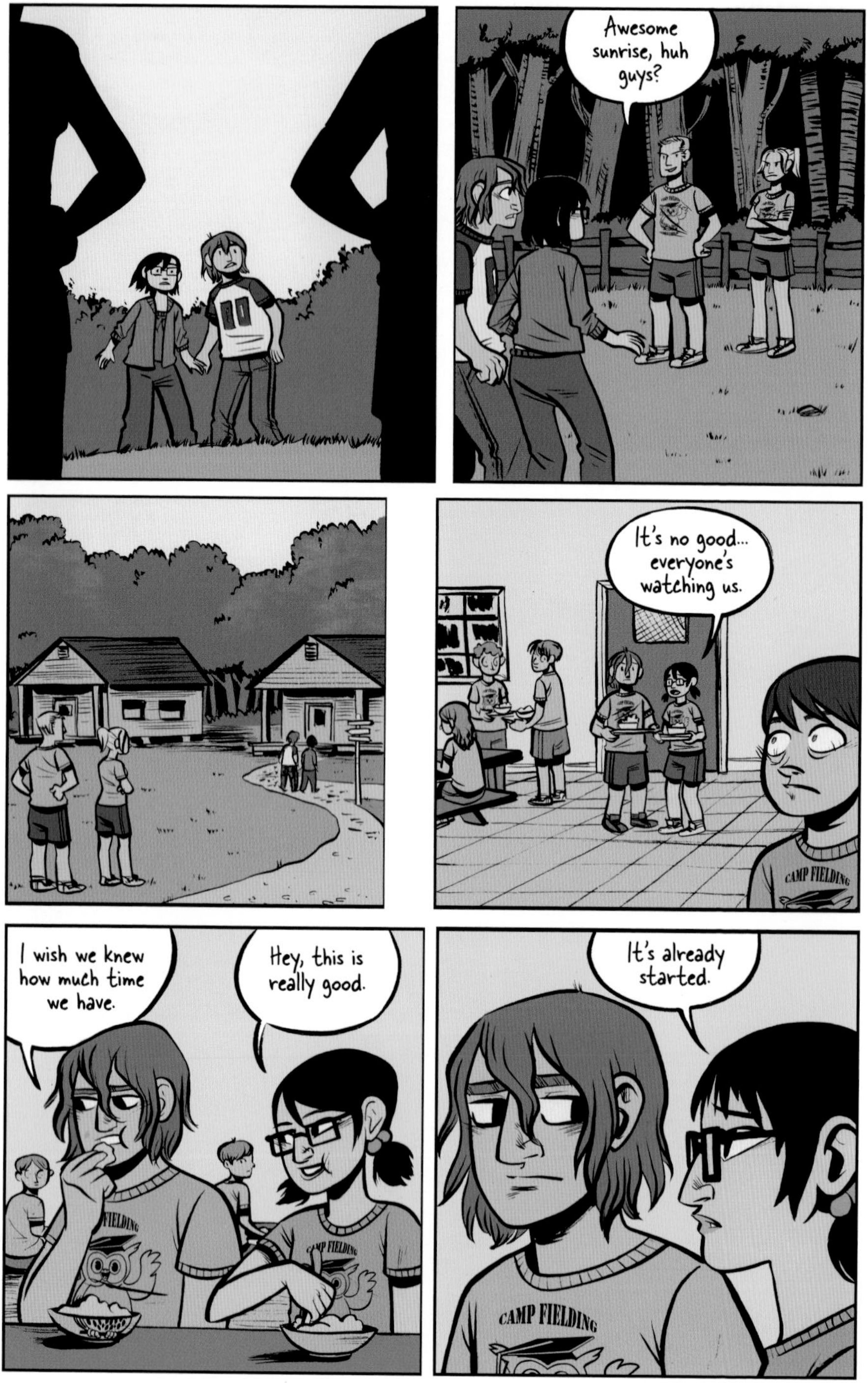
Awesome sunrise, huh guys?
It's no good... everyone's watching us.
CAMP FIELDING
I wish we knew how much time we have.
Hey, this is really good.
CAMP FIELDING
It's already started.
CAMP FIELDING

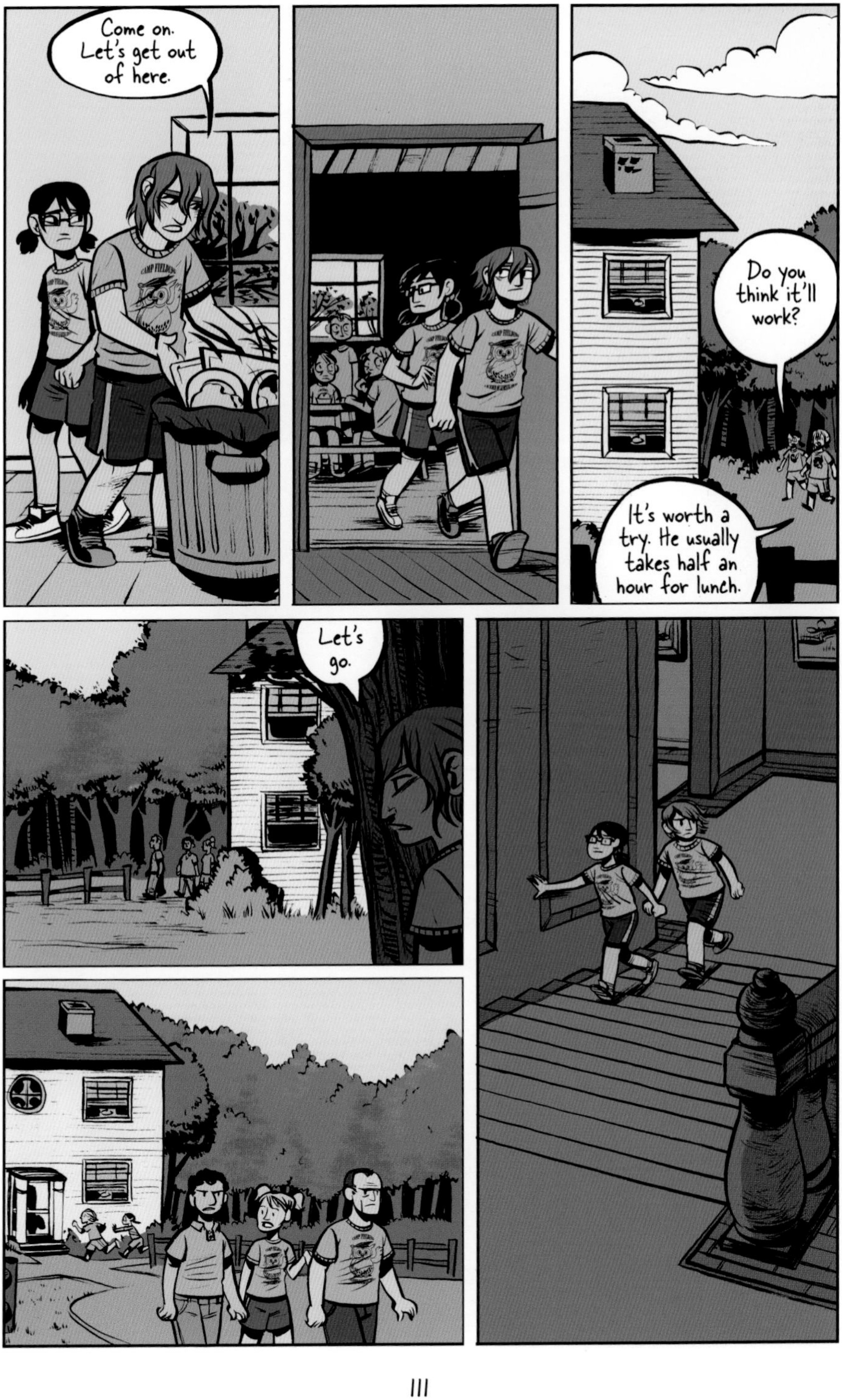
Come on. Let's get out of here.
Do you think it'll work?
It's worth a try. He usually takes half an hour for lunch.
Let's go.

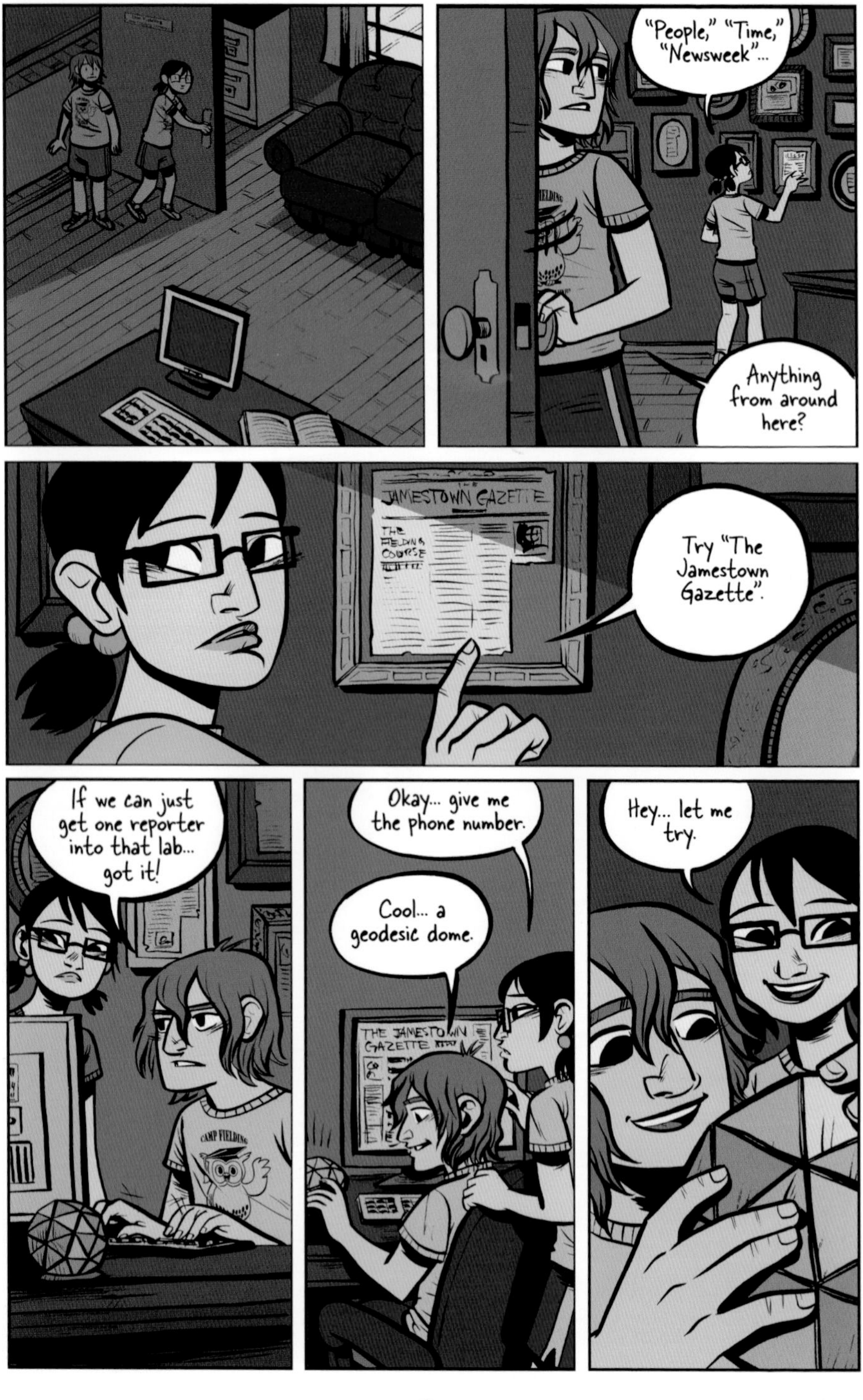
"People," "Time," "Newsweek"...
Anything from around here?
JAMESTOWN GAZETTE
Try "The Jamestown Gazette".
If we can just get one reporter into that lab... got it!
Okay... give me the phone number.
Cool... a geodesic dome.
THE JAMESTOWN GAZETTE
Hey... let me try.

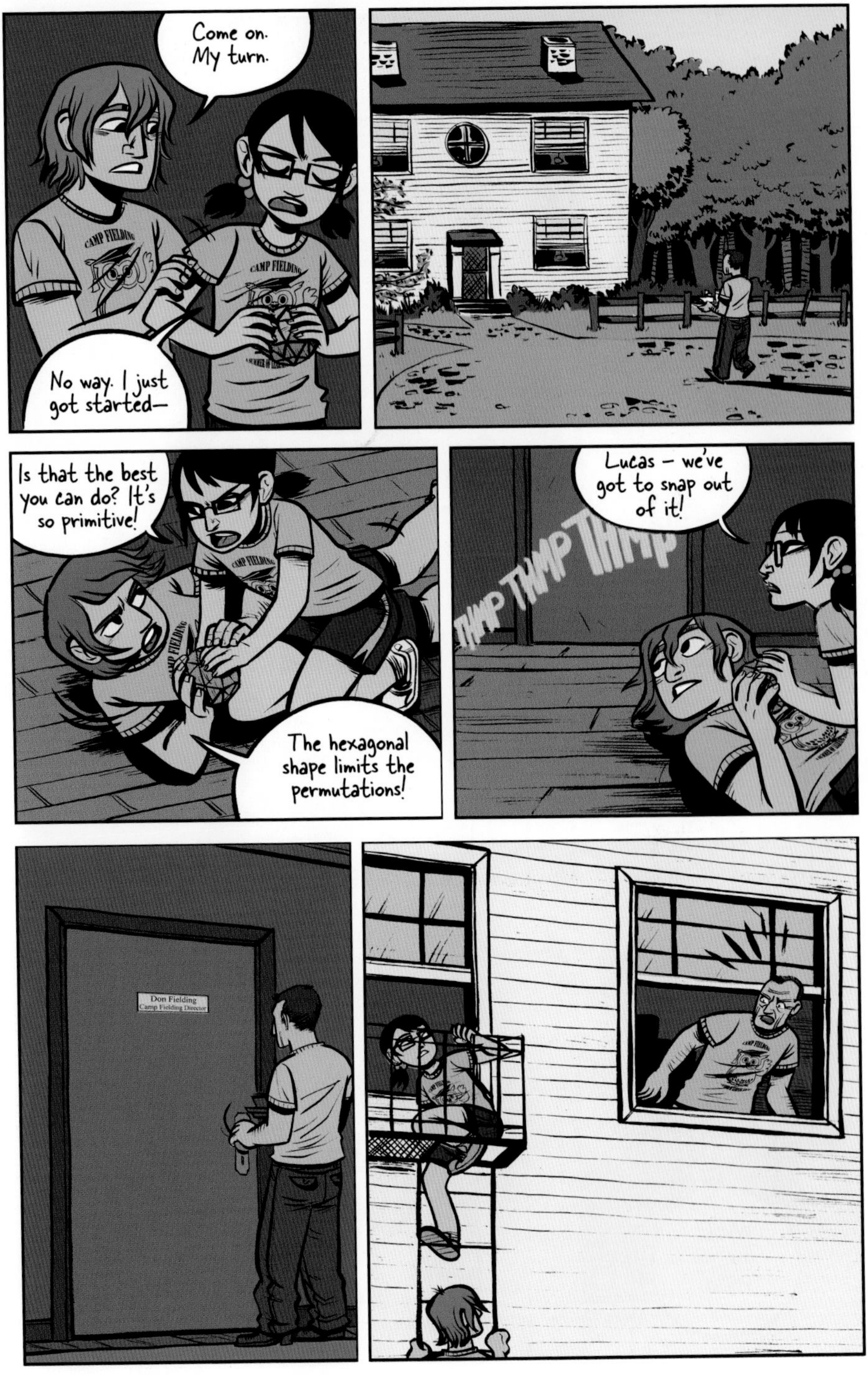
Come on. My turn.
No way. I just got started—
Is that the best you can do? It's so primitive!
The hexagonal shape limits the permutations!
THMP THMP THMP
Lucas – we've got to snap out of it!
Don Fielding
Camp Fielding Director

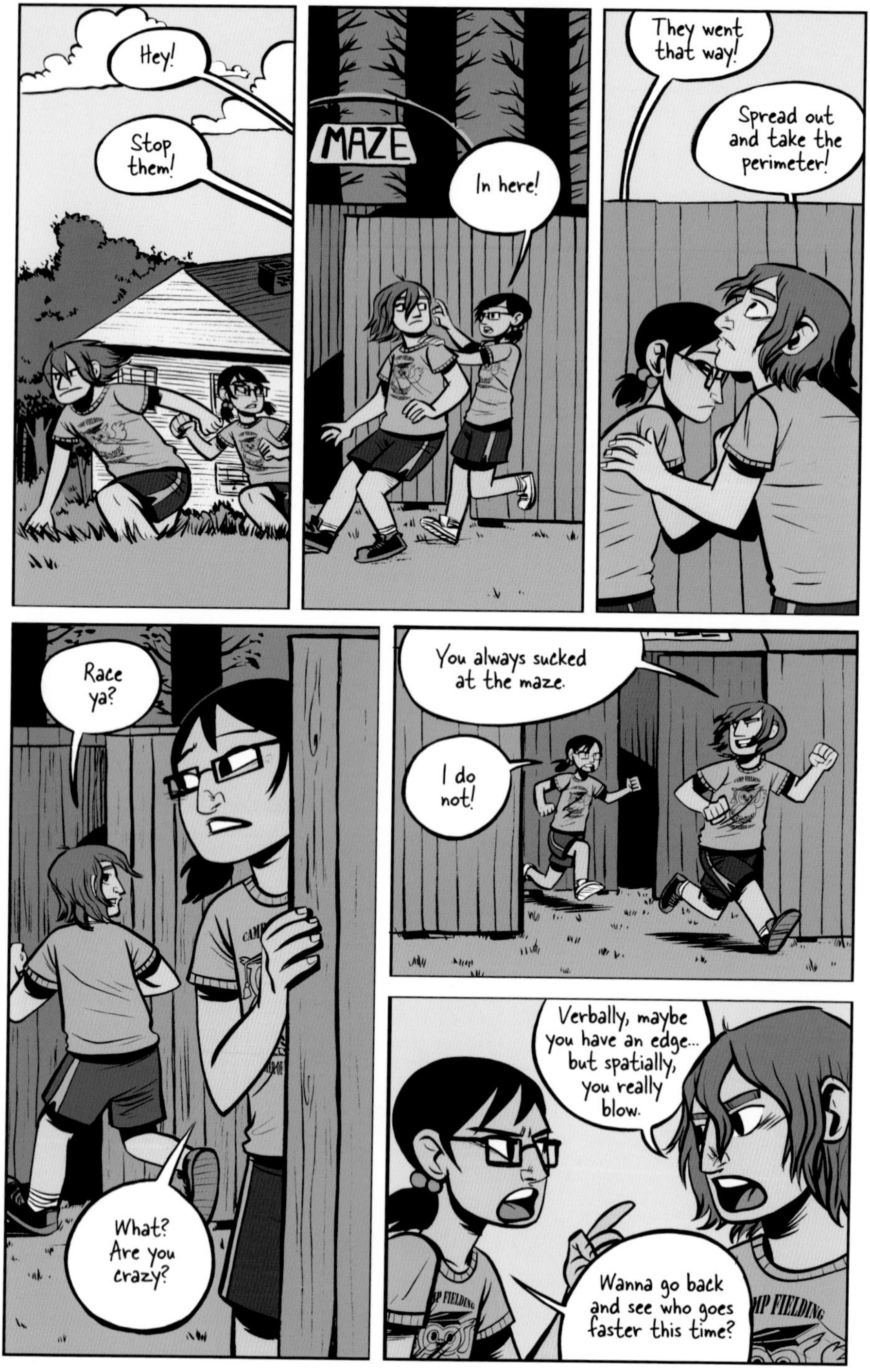
Hey!
Stop them!
MAZE
In here!
They went that way!
Spread out and take the perimeter!
Race ya?
What? Are you crazy?
You always sucked at the maze.
I do not!
Verbally, maybe you have an edge... but spatially, you really blow.
Wanna go back and see who goes faster this time?

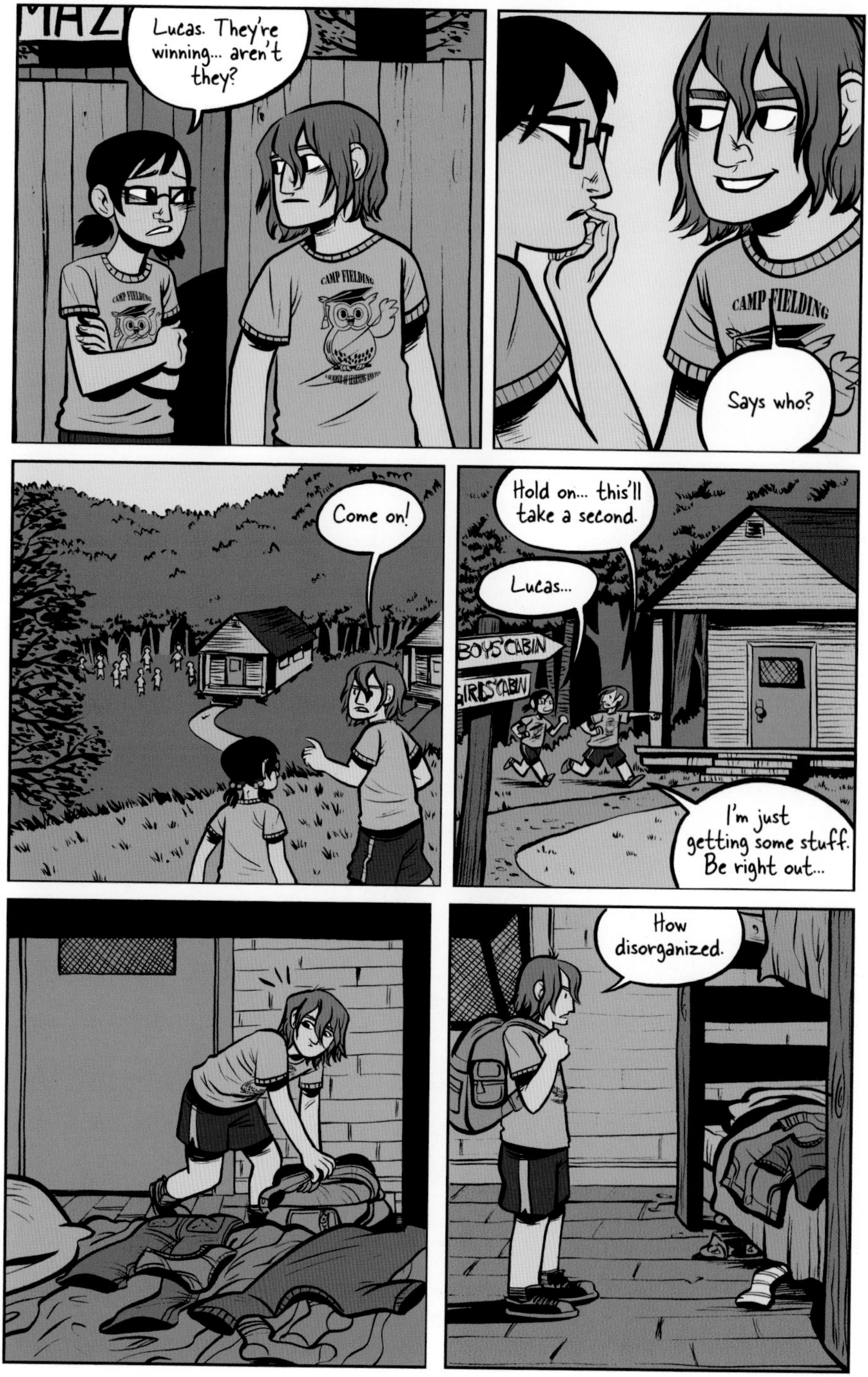
MAZ
Lucas. They're winning... aren't they?
CAMP FIELDING
CAMP FIELDING
CAMP FIELDING
Says who?
Come on!
Hold on... this'll take a second.
Lucas...
BOYS' CABIN
GIRLS' CABIN
I'm just getting some stuff. Be right out...
How disorganized.

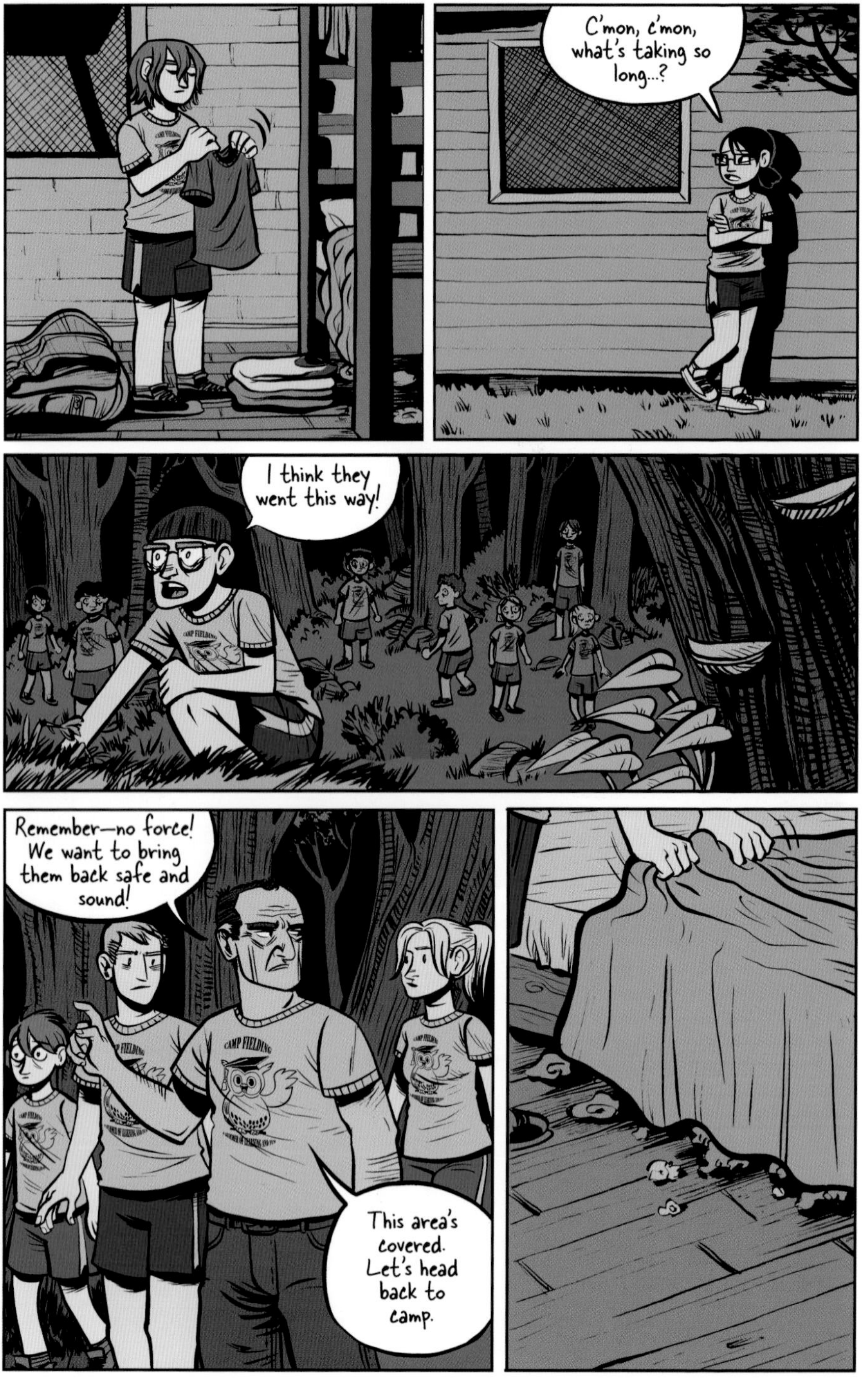
C'mon, c'mon, what's taking so long...?
I think they went this way!
Remember—no force! We want to bring them back safe and sound!
This area's covered. Let's head back to camp.
CAMP FIELDING

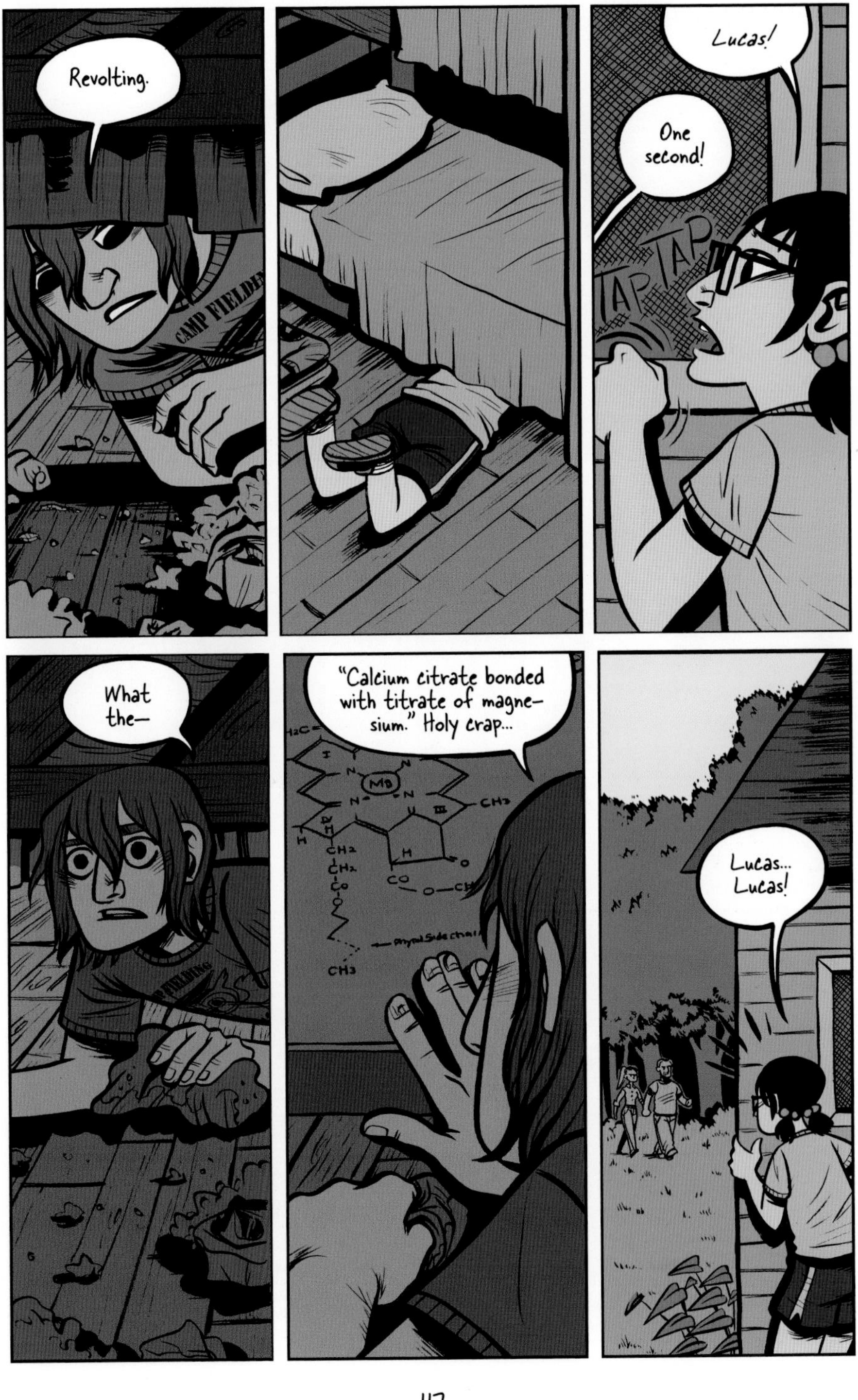
Revolting.
Lucas!
One second!
TAP TAP
What the—
"Calcium citrate bonded with titrate of magnesium." Holy crap...
Lucas... Lucas!

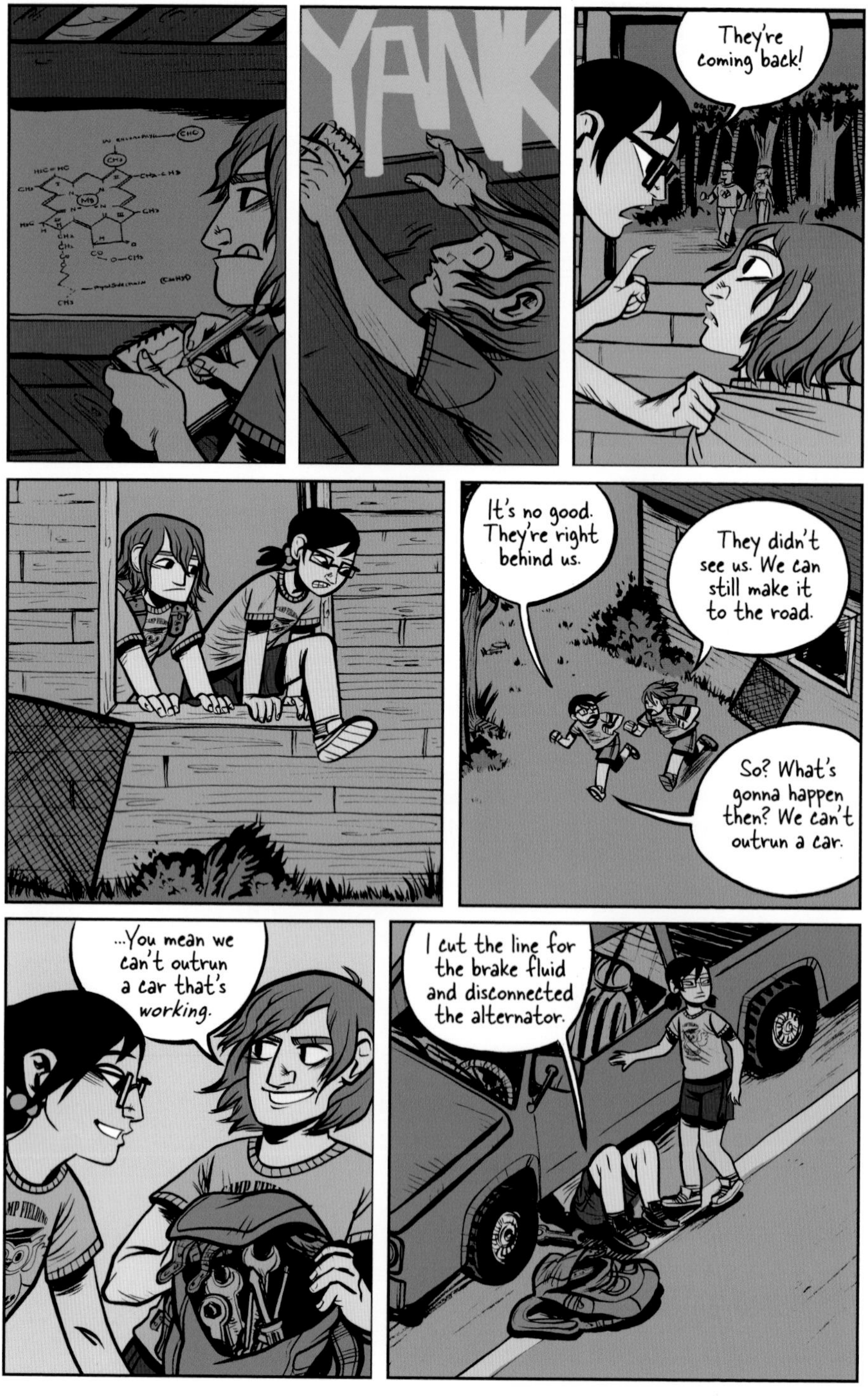
YANK
They're coming back!
It's no good. They're right behind us.
They didn't see us. We can still make it to the road.
So? What's gonna happen then? We can't outrun a car.
...You mean we can't outrun a car that's *working*.
I cut the line for the brake fluid and disconnected the alternator.

Now there's one thing you've gotta help me with...

Help me get this down.

It's going to be crude... but I think we can rig up a working model...

A working model of what?

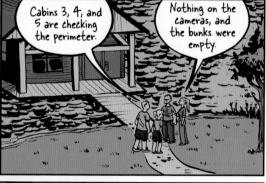

Cabins 3, 4, and 5 are checking the perimeter.

Nothing on the cameras, and the bunks were empty.

Maybe it's better if they make it off campus, out in the open.

How do you figure?

They may be smart, but they're still kids. How far can they get on foot?

CAMP FIELDING

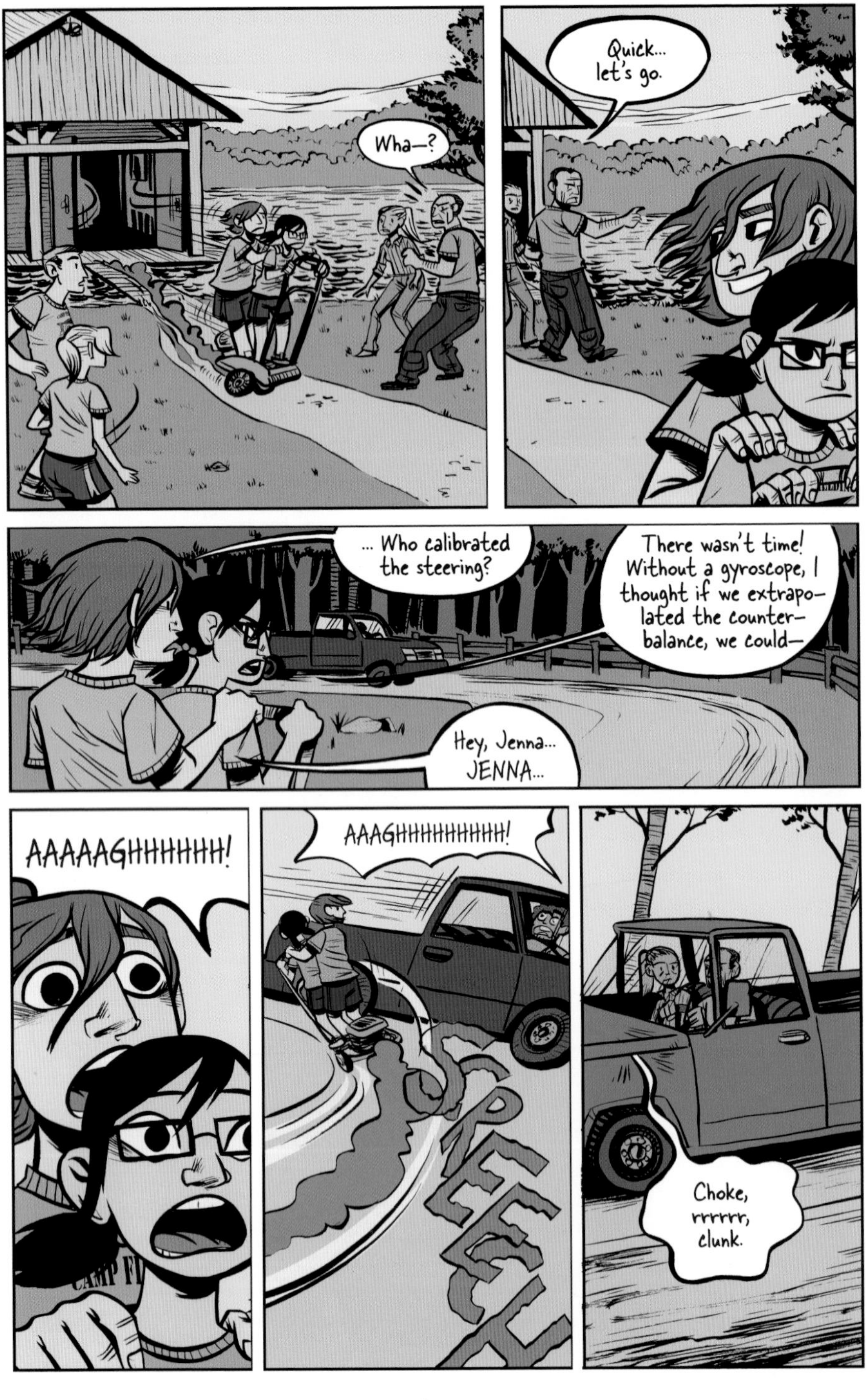
Wha—?
Quick... let's go.
... Who calibrated the steering?
There wasn't time! Without a gyroscope, I thought if we extrapolated the counterbalance, we could—
Hey, Jenna... JENNA...
AAAAAGHHHHHH!
AAAGHHHHHHHHH!
Choke, rrrrrr, clunk.

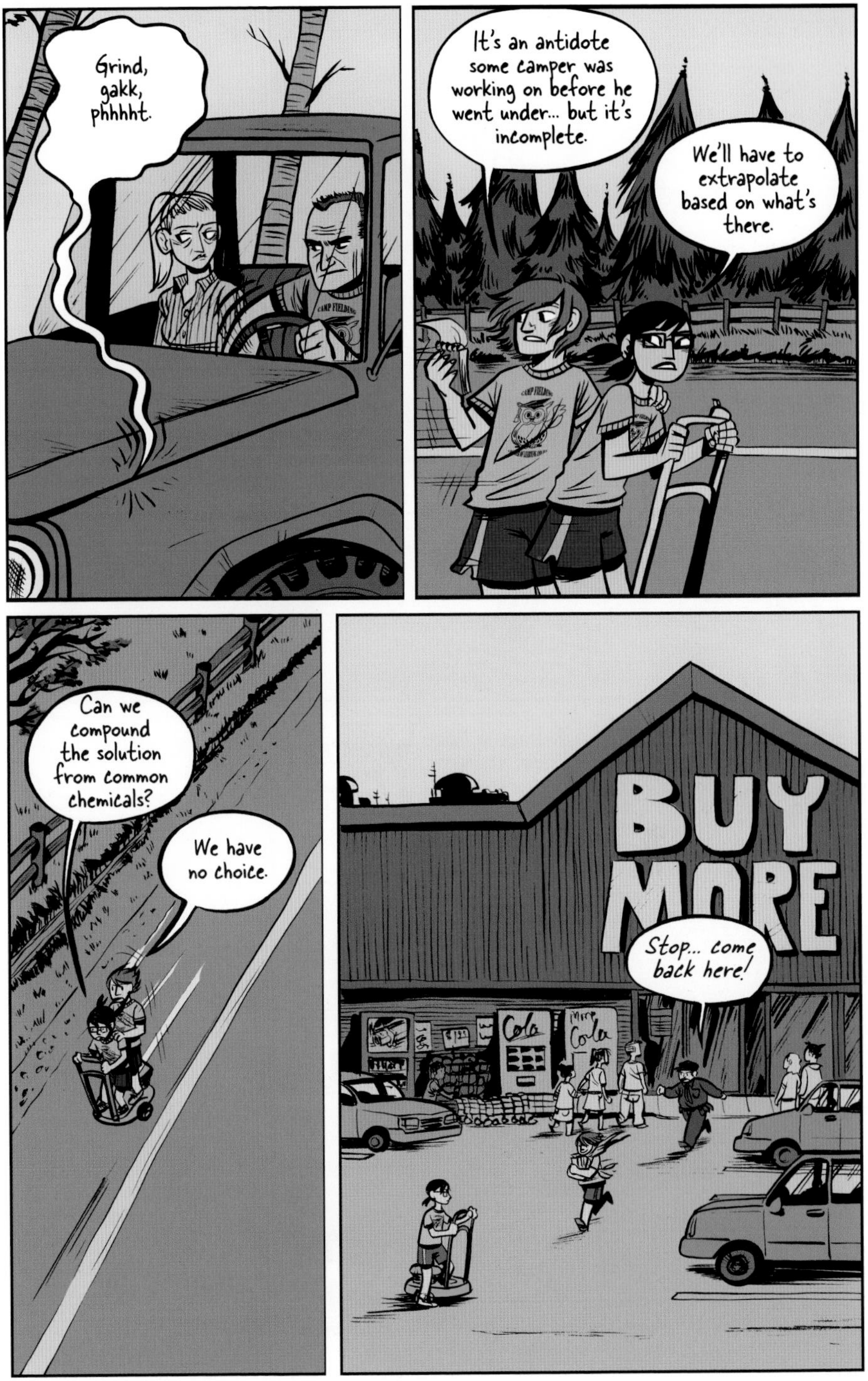
Grind, gakk, phhhht.
It's an antidote some camper was working on before he went under... but it's incomplete.
We'll have to extrapolate based on what's there.
Can we compound the solution from common chemicals?
We have no choice.
BUY MORE
Cola
Stop... come back here!

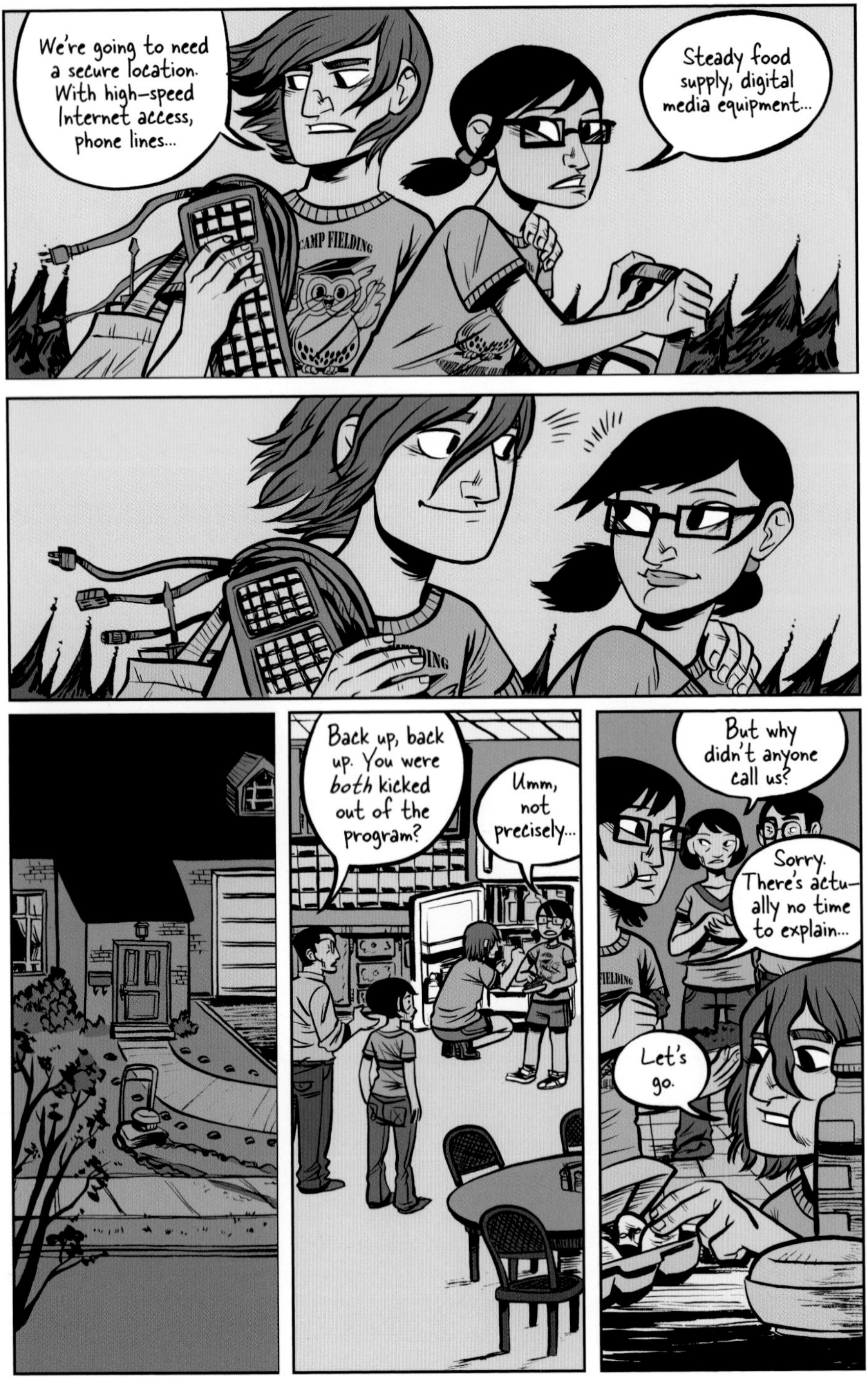
We're going to need a secure location. With high-speed Internet access, phone lines...
Steady food supply, digital media equipment...
CAMP FIELDING
Back up, back up. You were *both* kicked out of the program?
Umm, not precisely...
But why didn't anyone call us?
Sorry. There's actually no time to explain...
Let's go.

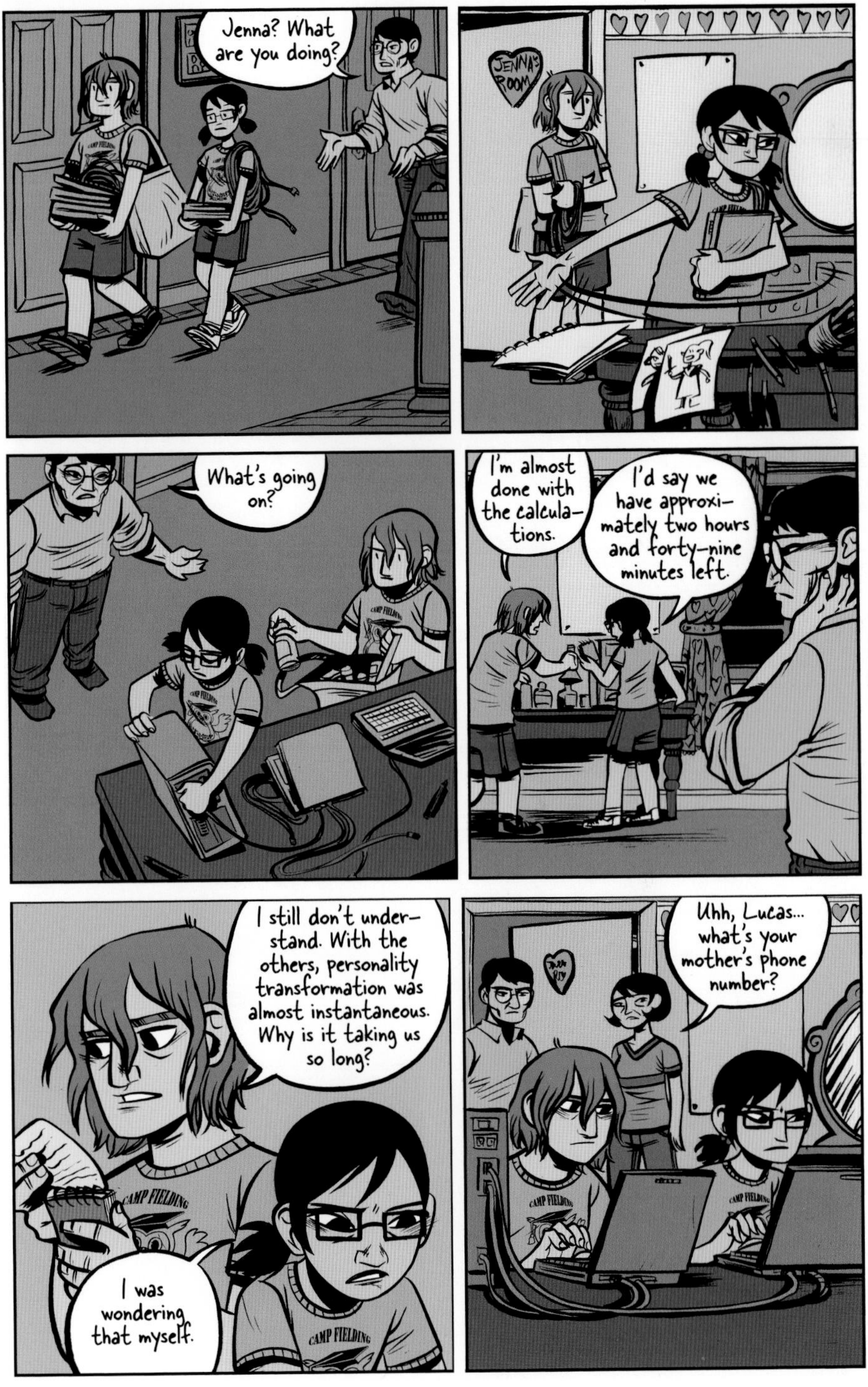
Jenna? What are you doing?
JENNA'S ROOM
What's going on?
I'm almost done with the calculations.
I'd say we have approximately two hours and forty-nine minutes left.
I still don't understand. With the others, personality transformation was almost instantaneous. Why is it taking us so long?
I was wondering that myself.
Uhh, Lucas... what's your mother's phone number?

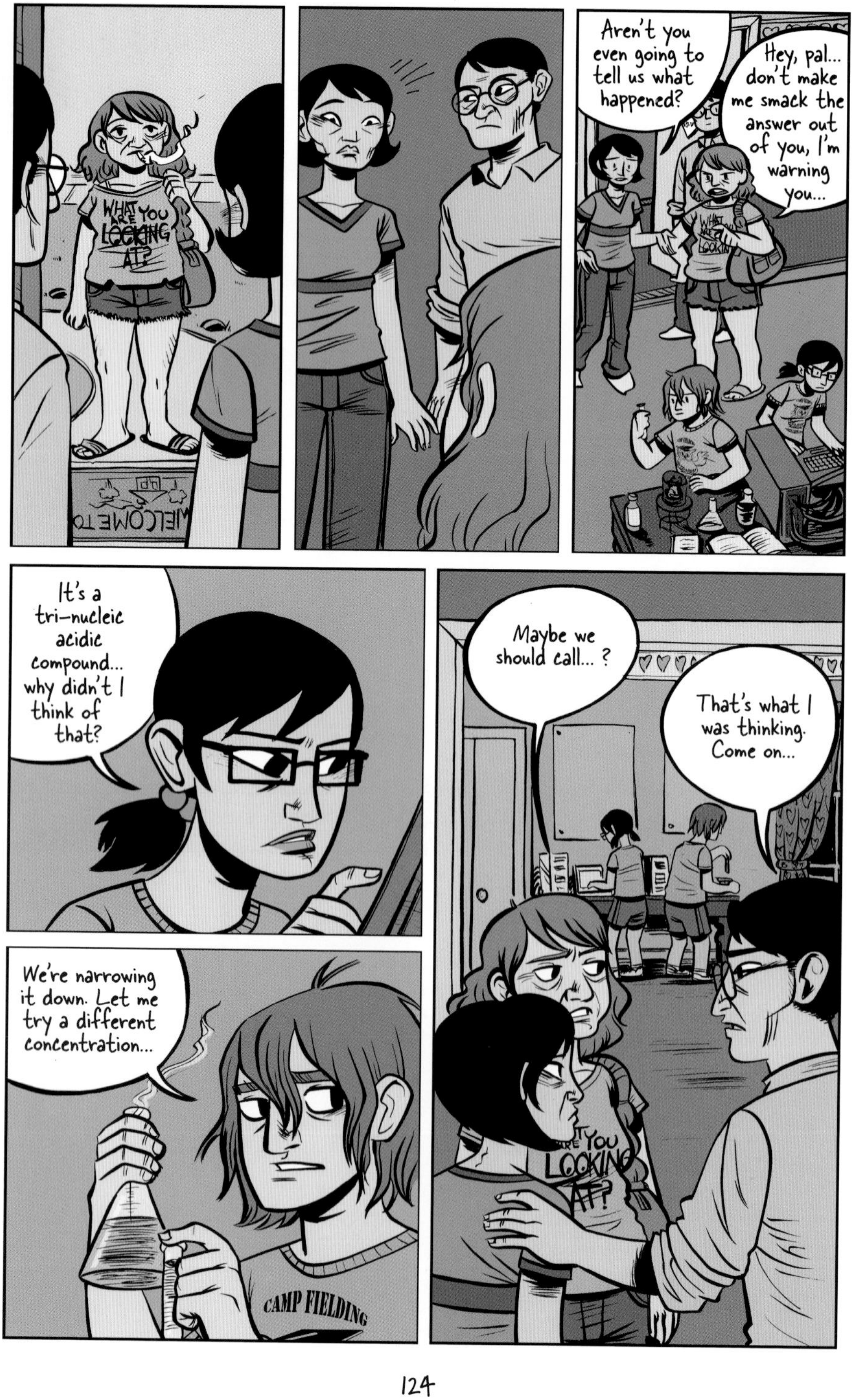
WHAT ARE YOU LOOKING AT?
WELCOME TO
Aren't you even going to tell us what happened?
Hey, pal... don't make me smack the answer out of you, I'm warning you...
It's a tri-nucleic acidic compound... why didn't I think of that?
We're narrowing it down. Let me try a different concentration...
CAMP FIELDING
Maybe we should call... ?
That's what I was thinking. Come on...
YOU LOOKING AT?

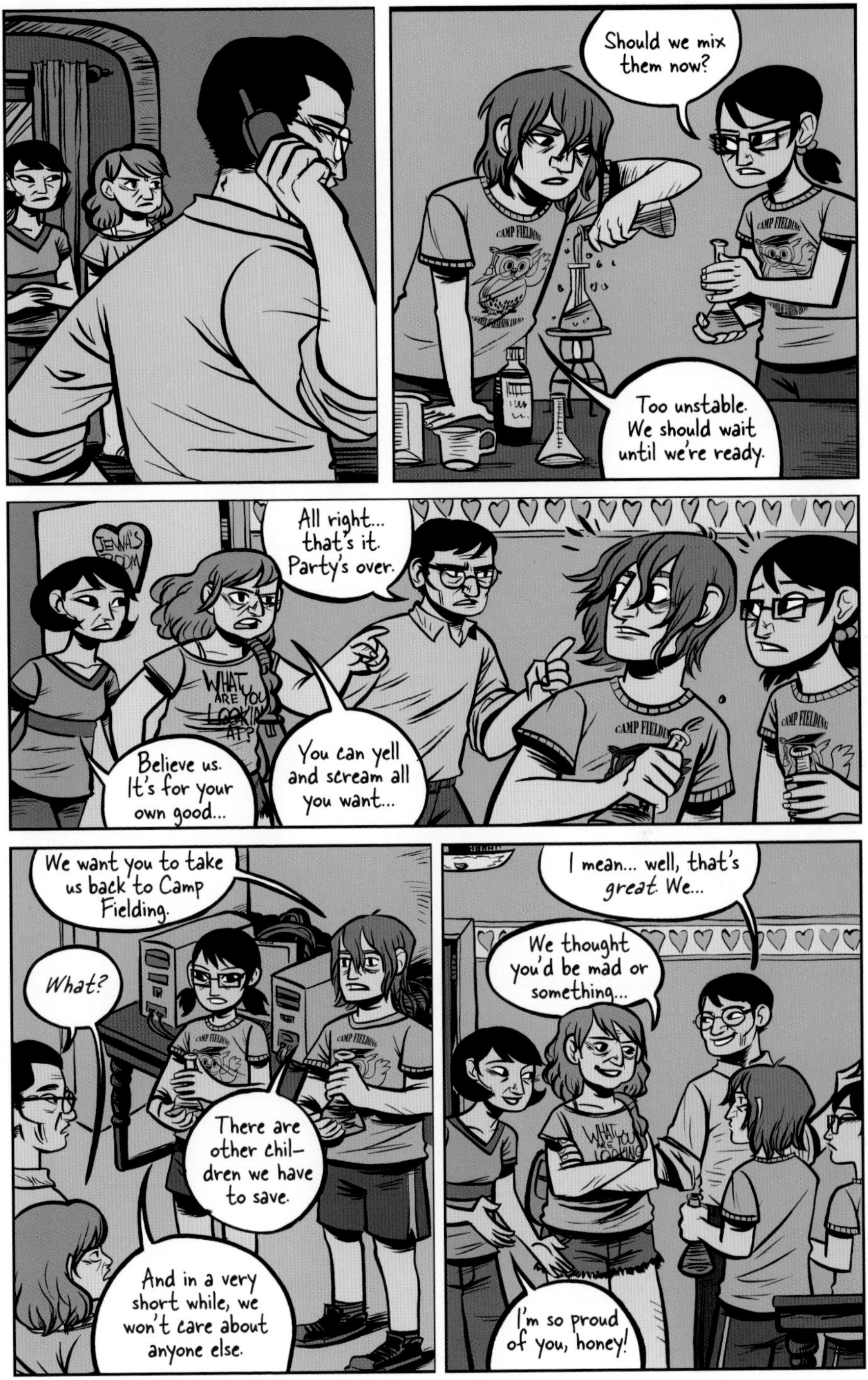
Should we mix them now?
Too unstable. We should wait until we're ready.
All right... that's it. Party's over.
Believe us. It's for your own good...
You can yell and scream all you want...
WHAT ARE YOU LOOKIN' AT?
CAMP FIELDING
We want you to take us back to Camp Fielding.
What?
There are other chil- dren we have to save.
And in a very short while, we won't care about anyone else.
I mean... well, that's *great*. We...
We thought you'd be mad or something...
I'm so proud of you, honey!

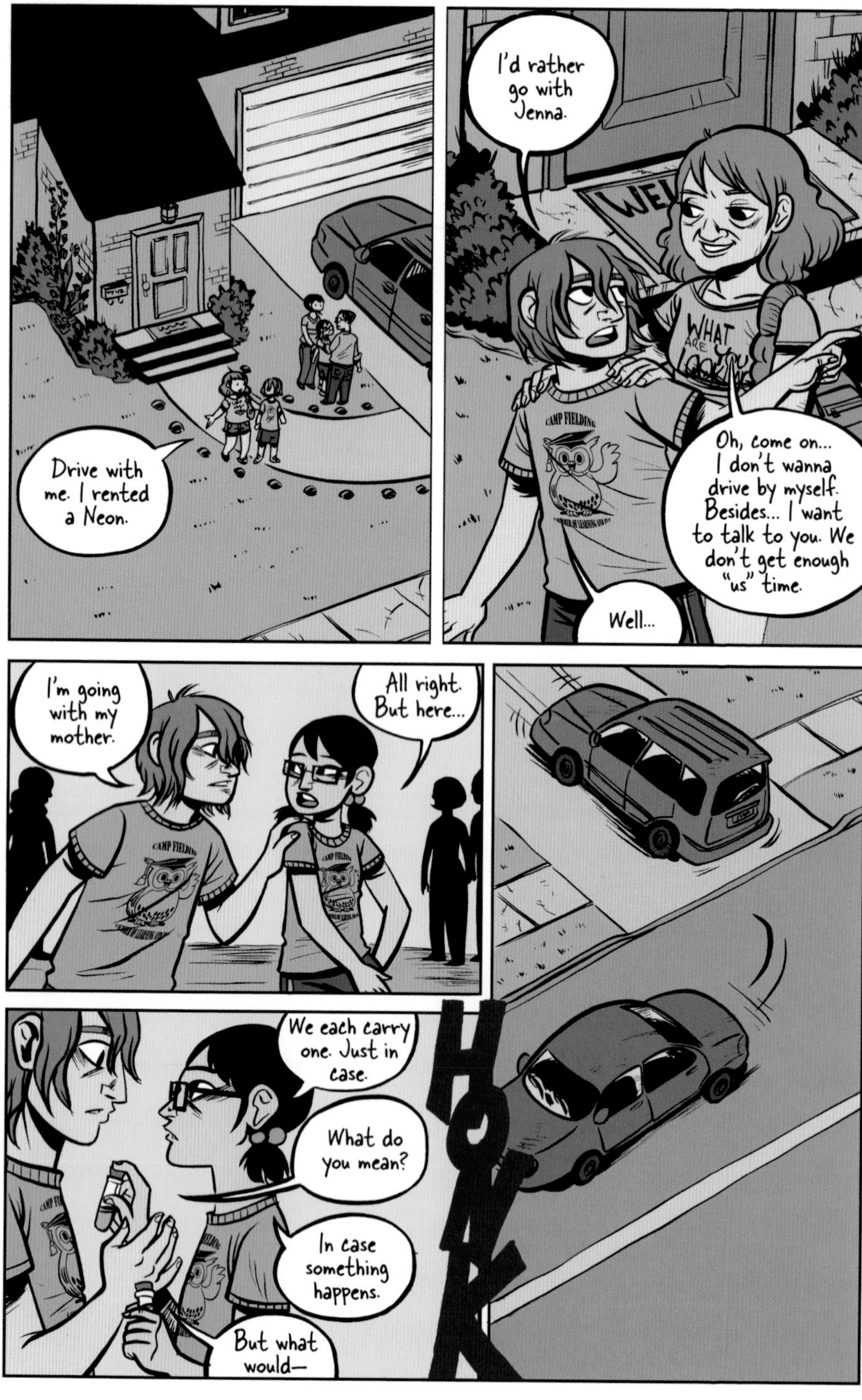

Drive with me. I rented a Neon.
I'd rather go with Jenna.
Oh, come on... I don't wanna drive by myself. Besides... I want to talk to you. We don't get enough "us" time.
Well...
I'm going with my mother.
All right. But here...
We each carry one. Just in case.
What do you mean?
In case something happens.
But what would—
HONK

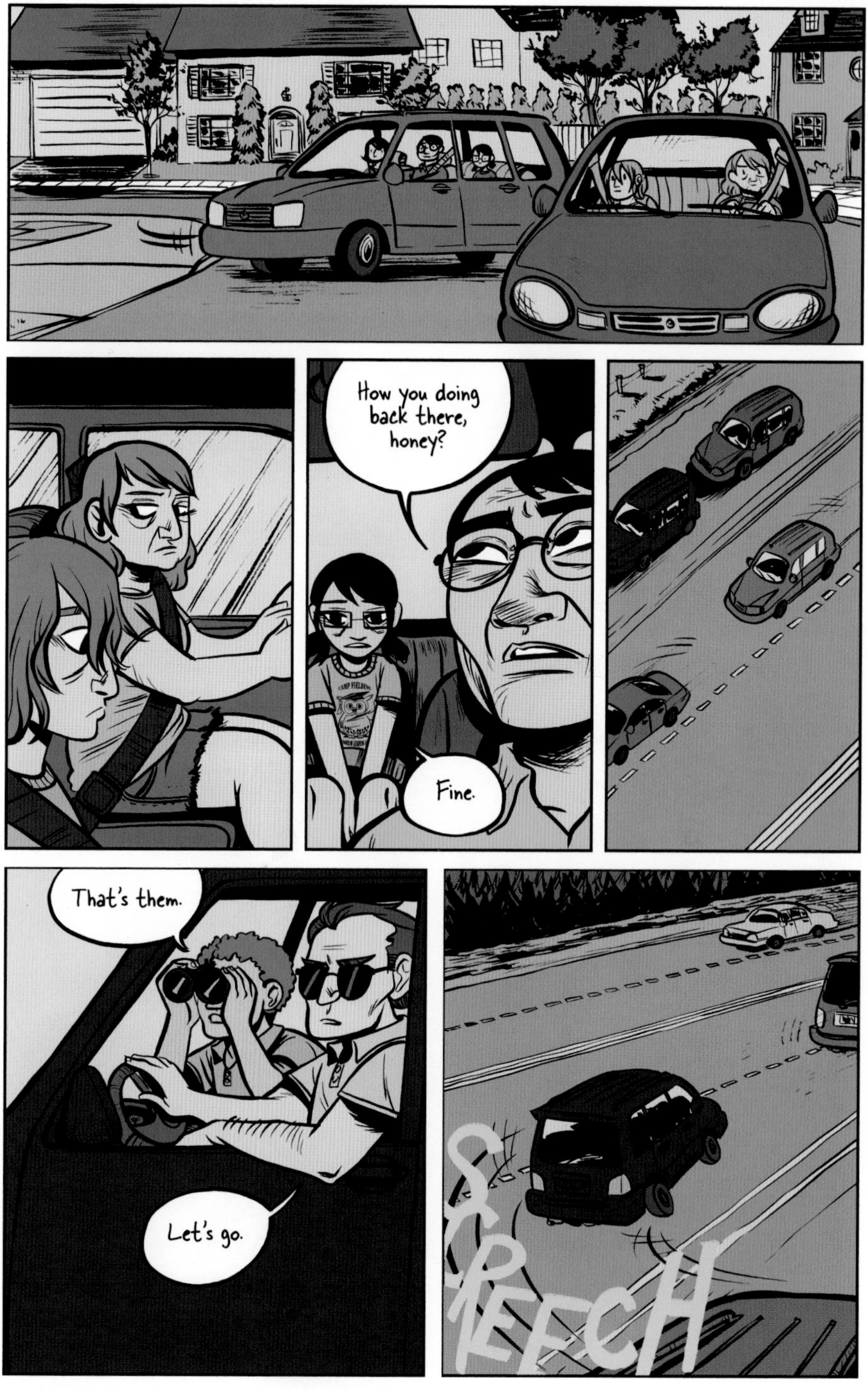

How you doing back there, honey?
Fine.
That's them.
Let's go.
SCREECH

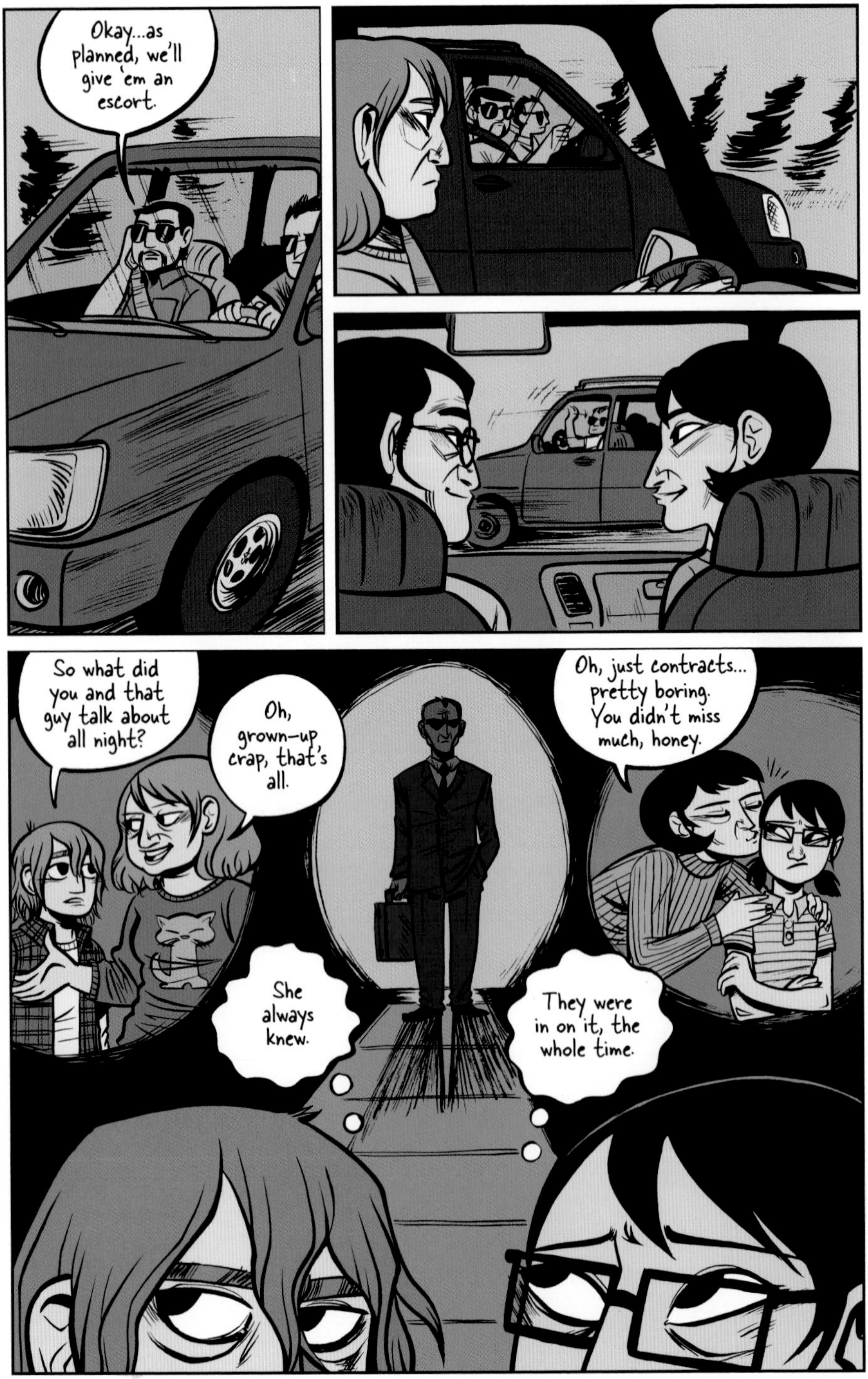
Okay...as planned, we'll give 'em an escort.
So what did you and that guy talk about all night?
Oh, grown-up crap, that's all.
Oh, just contracts... pretty boring. You didn't miss much, honey.
She always knew.
They were in on it, the whole time.

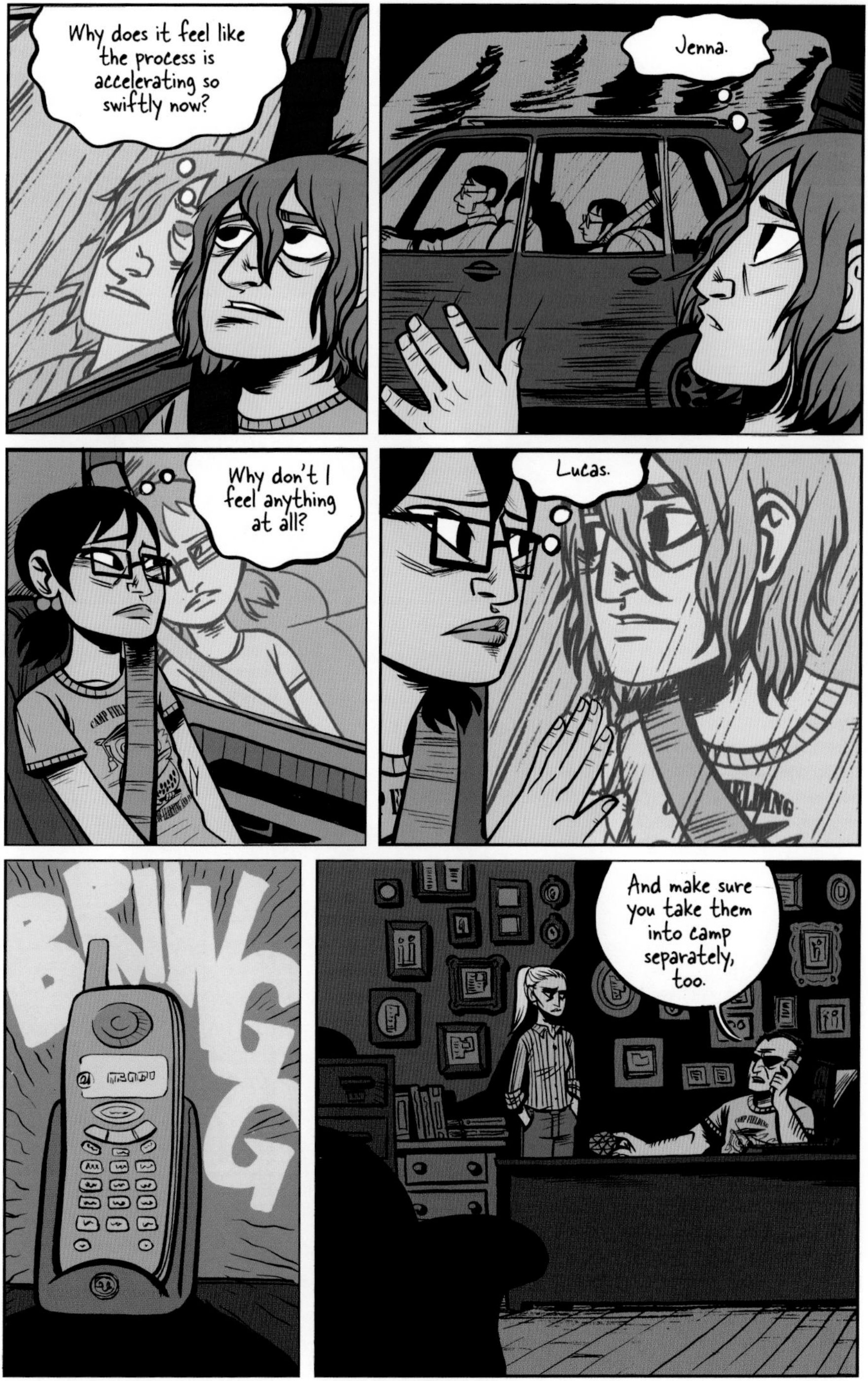

Why does it feel like the process is accelerating so swiftly now?
Jenna.
Why don't I feel anything at all?
Lucas.
BRING
And make sure you take them into camp separately, too.

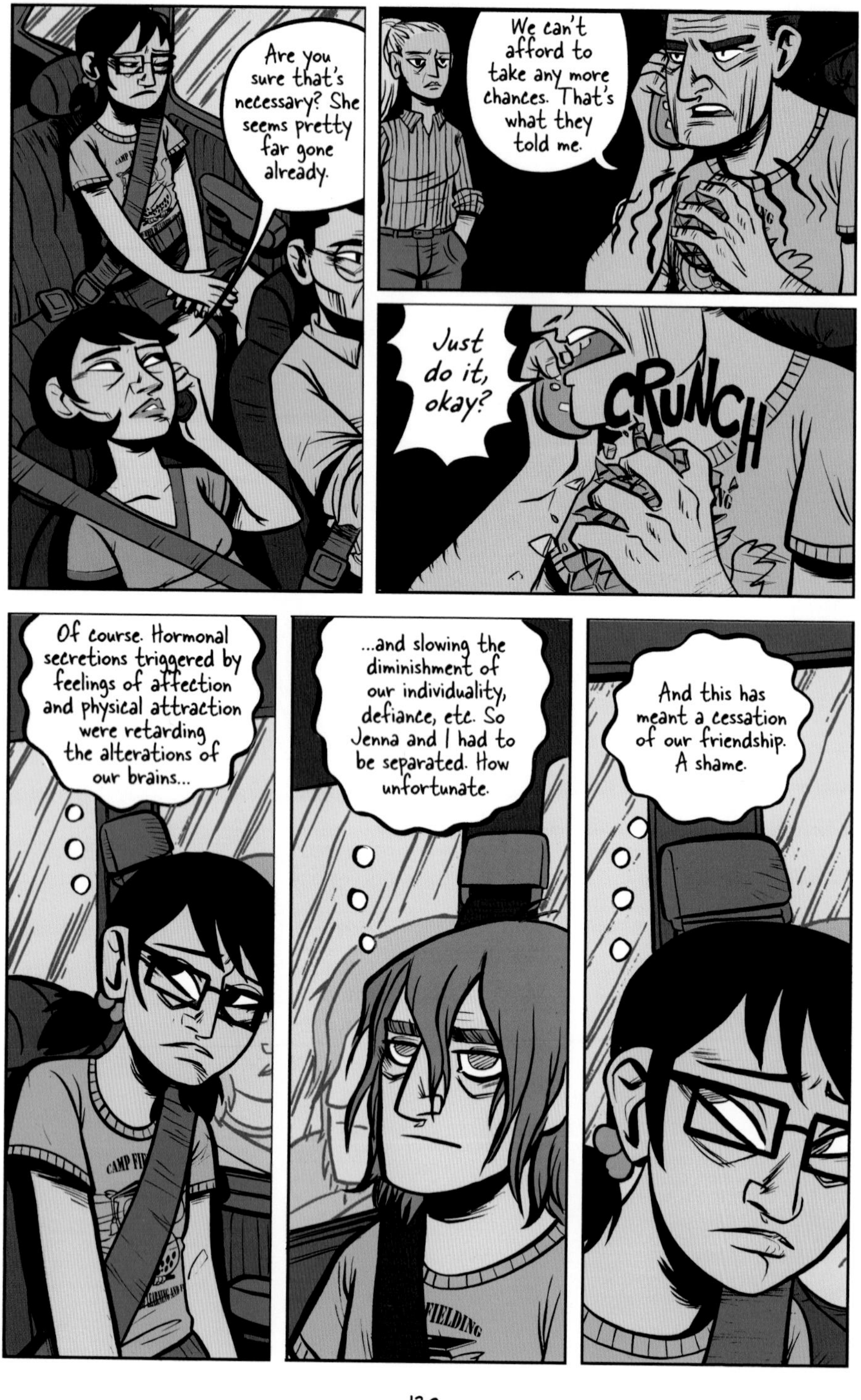
Are you sure that's necessary? She seems pretty far gone already.
We can't afford to take any more chances. That's what they told me.
Just do it, okay?
CRUNCH
Of course. Hormonal secretions triggered by feelings of affection and physical attraction were retarding the alterations of our brains...
...and slowing the diminishment of our individuality, defiance, etc. So Jenna and I had to be separated. How unfortunate.
And this has meant a cessation of our friendship. A shame.

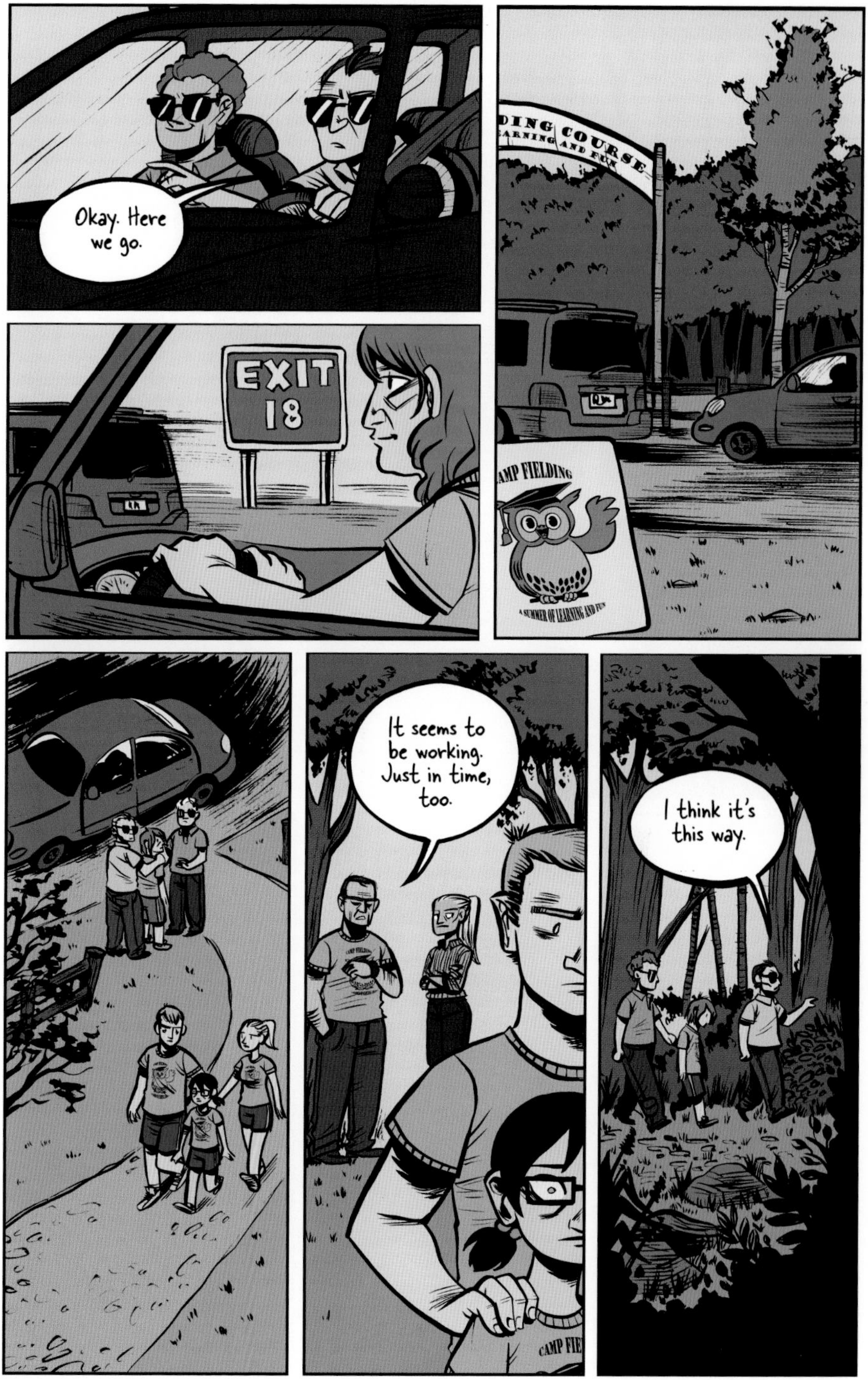

Okay. Here we go.
EXIT 18
CAMP FIELDING
A SUMMER OF LEARNING AND FUN
It seems to be working. Just in time, too.
I think it's this way.

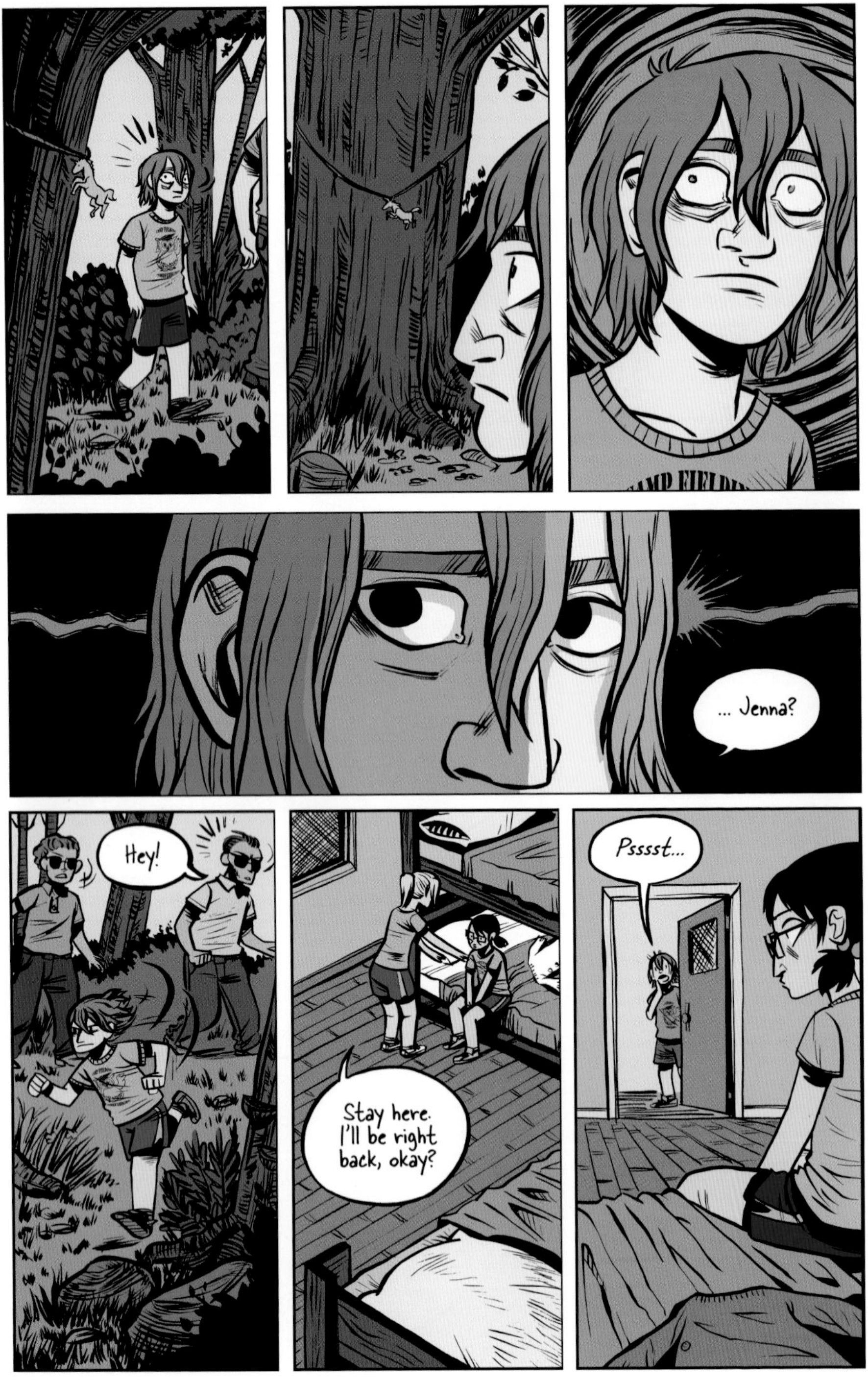
... Jenna?
Hey!
Stay here. I'll be right back, okay?
Psssst...

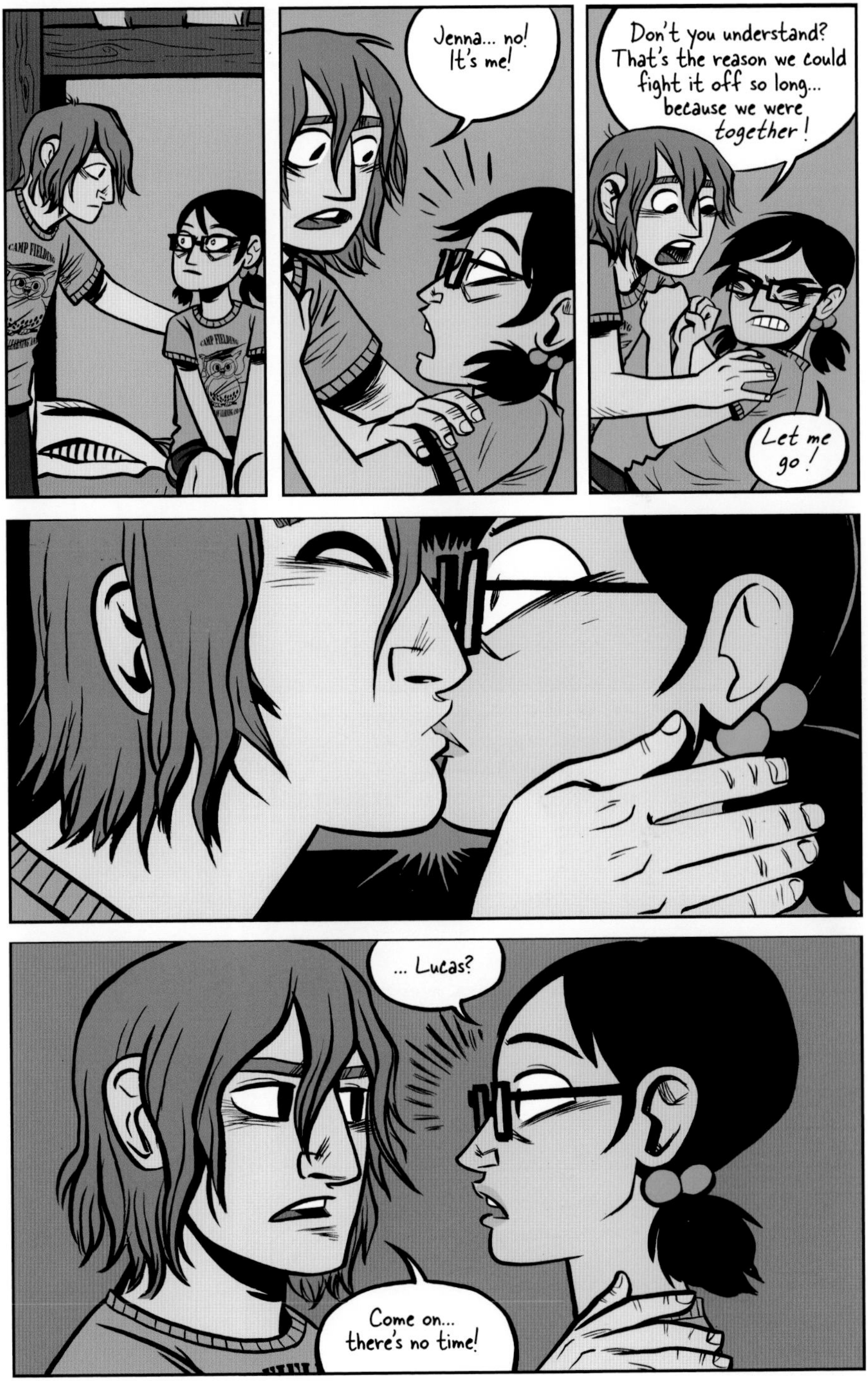
CAMP FIELDING
CAMP FIELDING
Jenna... no! It's me!
Don't you understand? That's the reason we could fight it off so long... because we were *together*!
Let me go!
... Lucas?
Come on... there's no time!

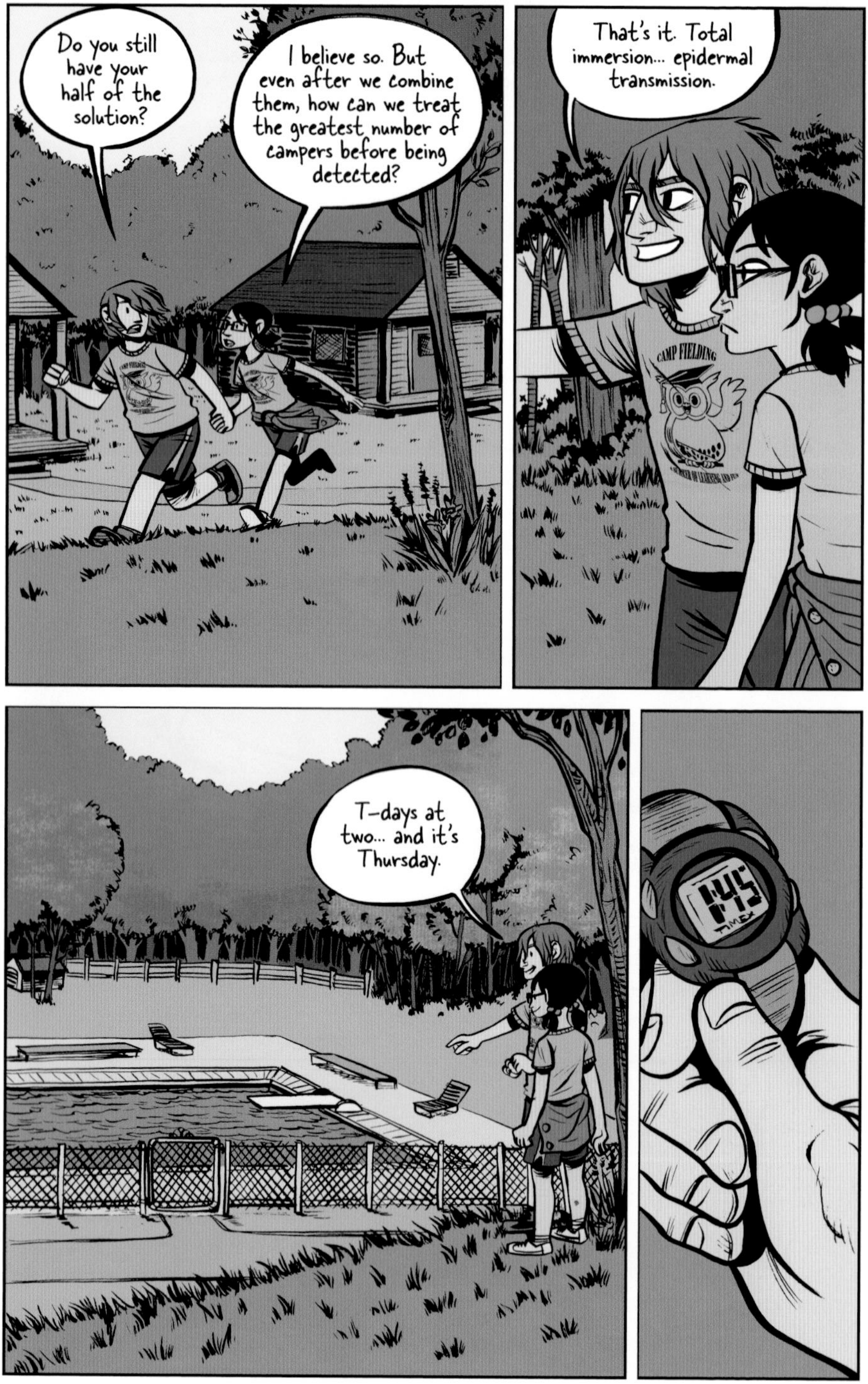
Do you still have your half of the solution?
I believe so. But even after we combine them, how can we treat the greatest number of campers before being detected?
That's it. Total immersion... epidermal transmission.
CAMP FIELDING
T-days at two... and it's Thursday.

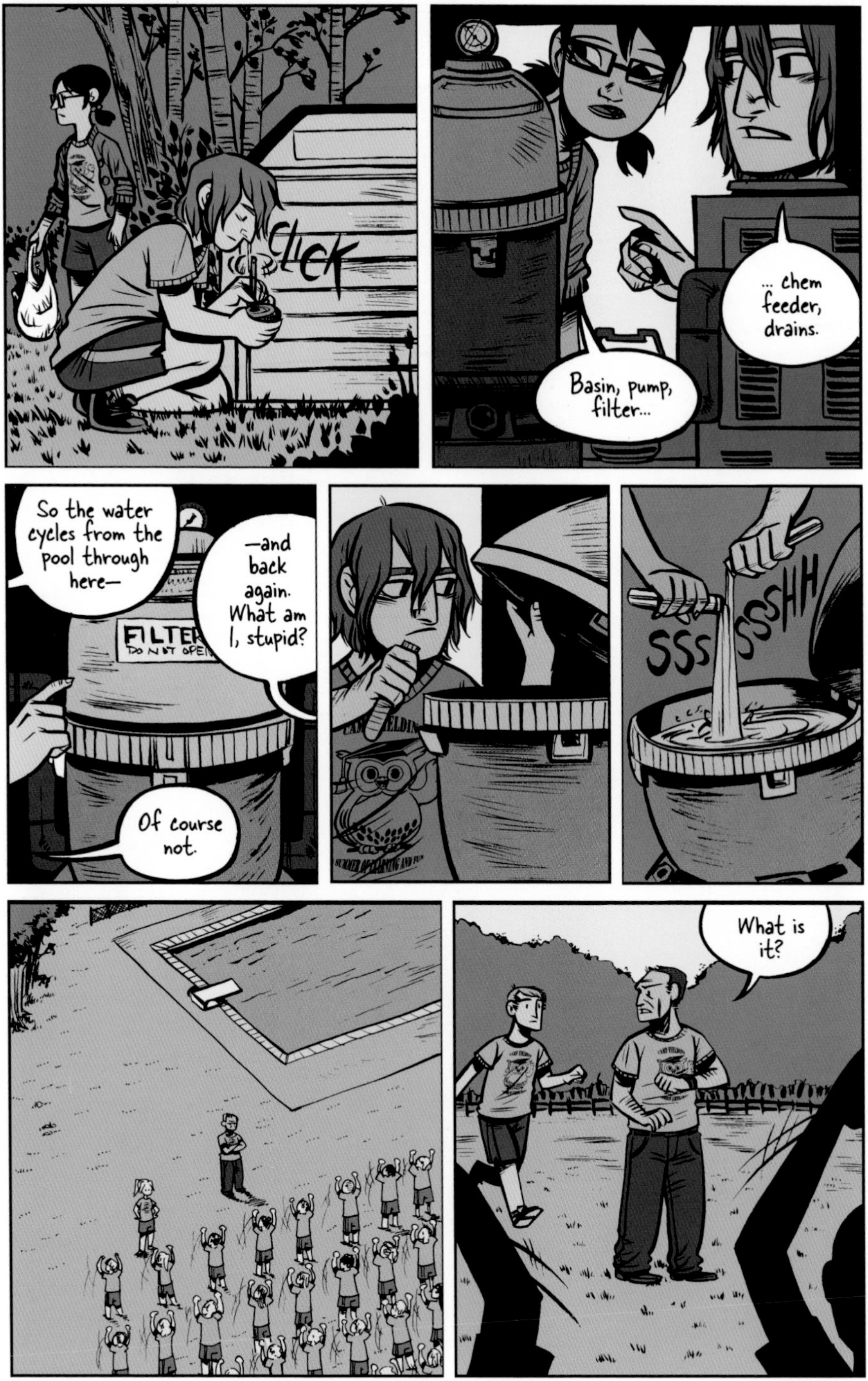
CLICK
Basin, pump, filter...
... chem feeder, drains.
So the water cycles from the pool through here—
FILTER DO NOT OPEN
—and back again. What am I, stupid?
Of course not.
SUMMER OF LEARNING AND FUN
SSS SSSHH
What is it?

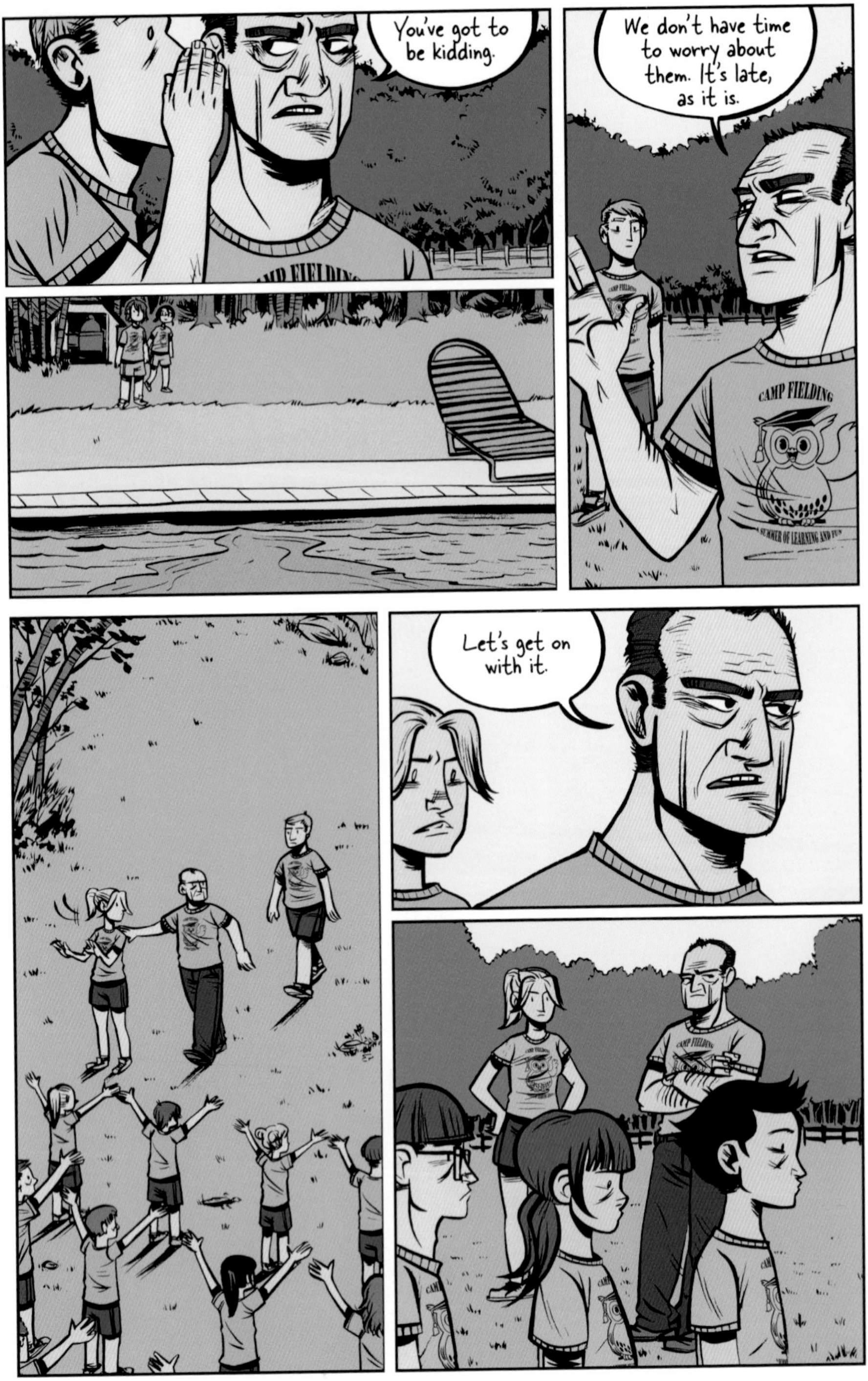
You've got to be kidding.
CAMP FIELDING
We don't have time to worry about them. It's late, as it is.
CAMP FIELDING
SUMMER OF LEARNING AND FUN
Let's get on with it.
CAMP FIELDING

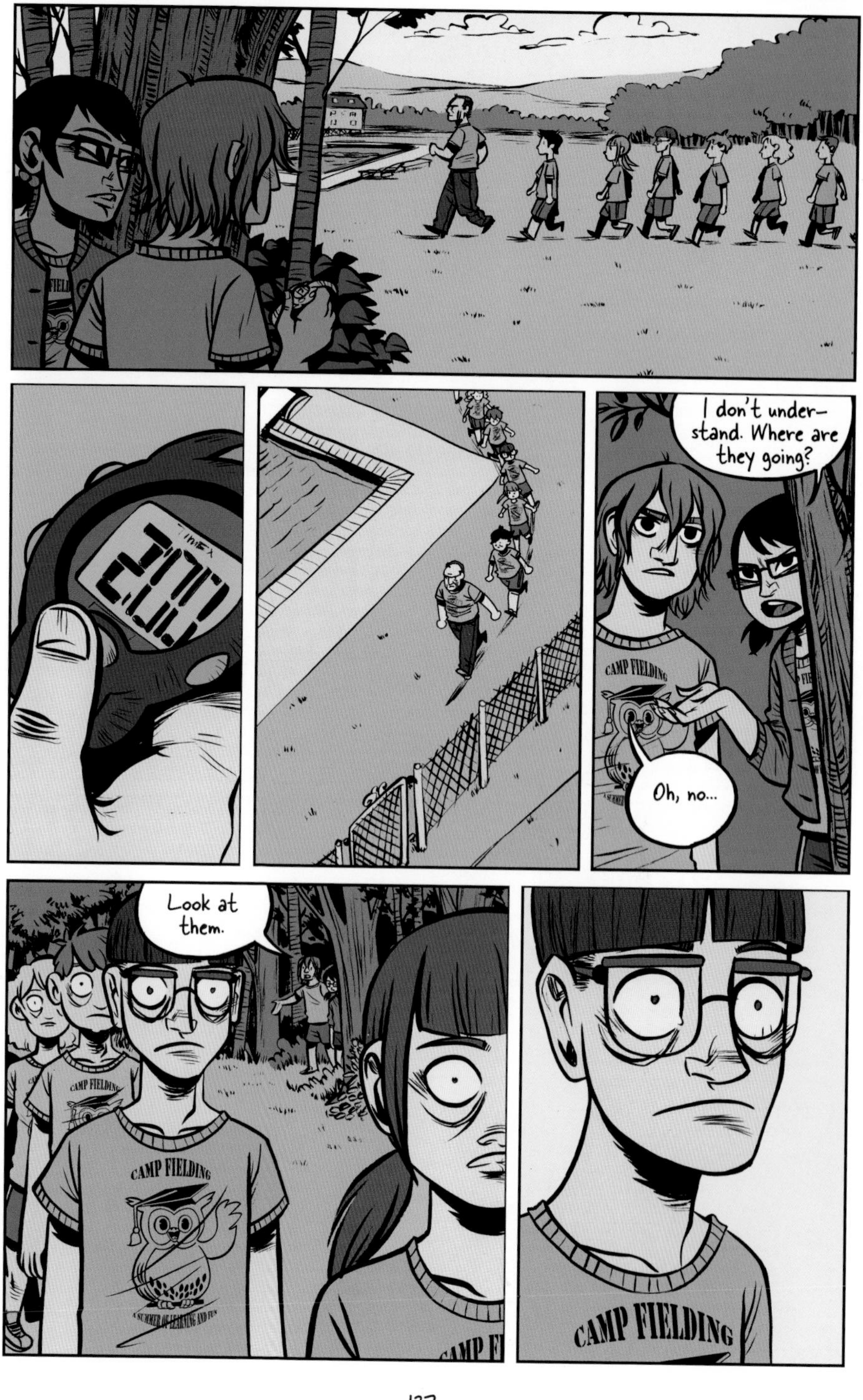

I don't under-stand. Where are they going?
Oh, no...
Look at them.
CAMP FIELDING
A SUMMER OF LEARNING AND FUN
CAMP FIELDING

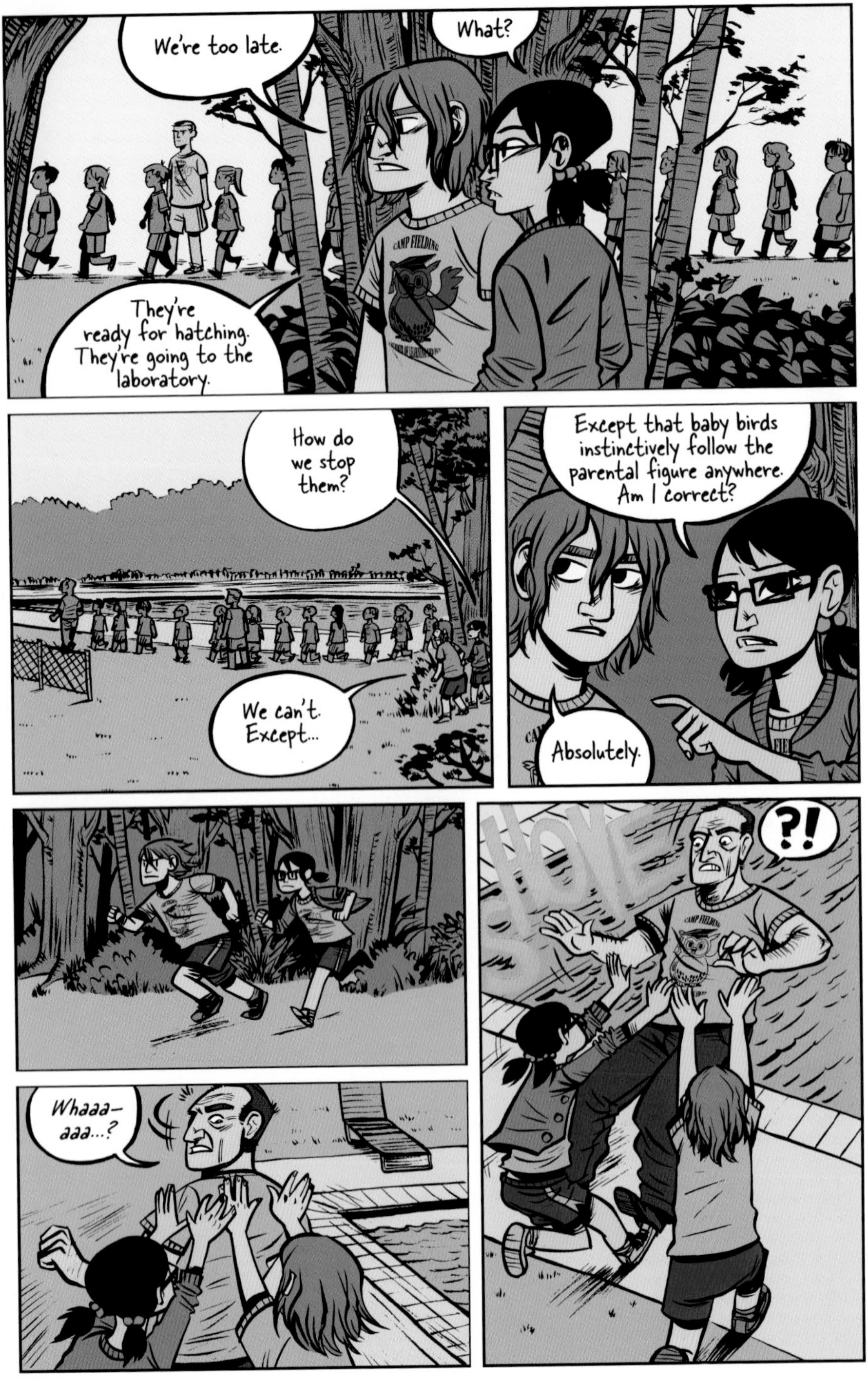
We're too late.
What?
They're ready for hatching. They're going to the laboratory.
How do we stop them?
We can't. Except...
Except that baby birds instinctively follow the parental figure anywhere. Am I correct?
Absolutely.
Whaaa-aaa...?
SHOVE
?!

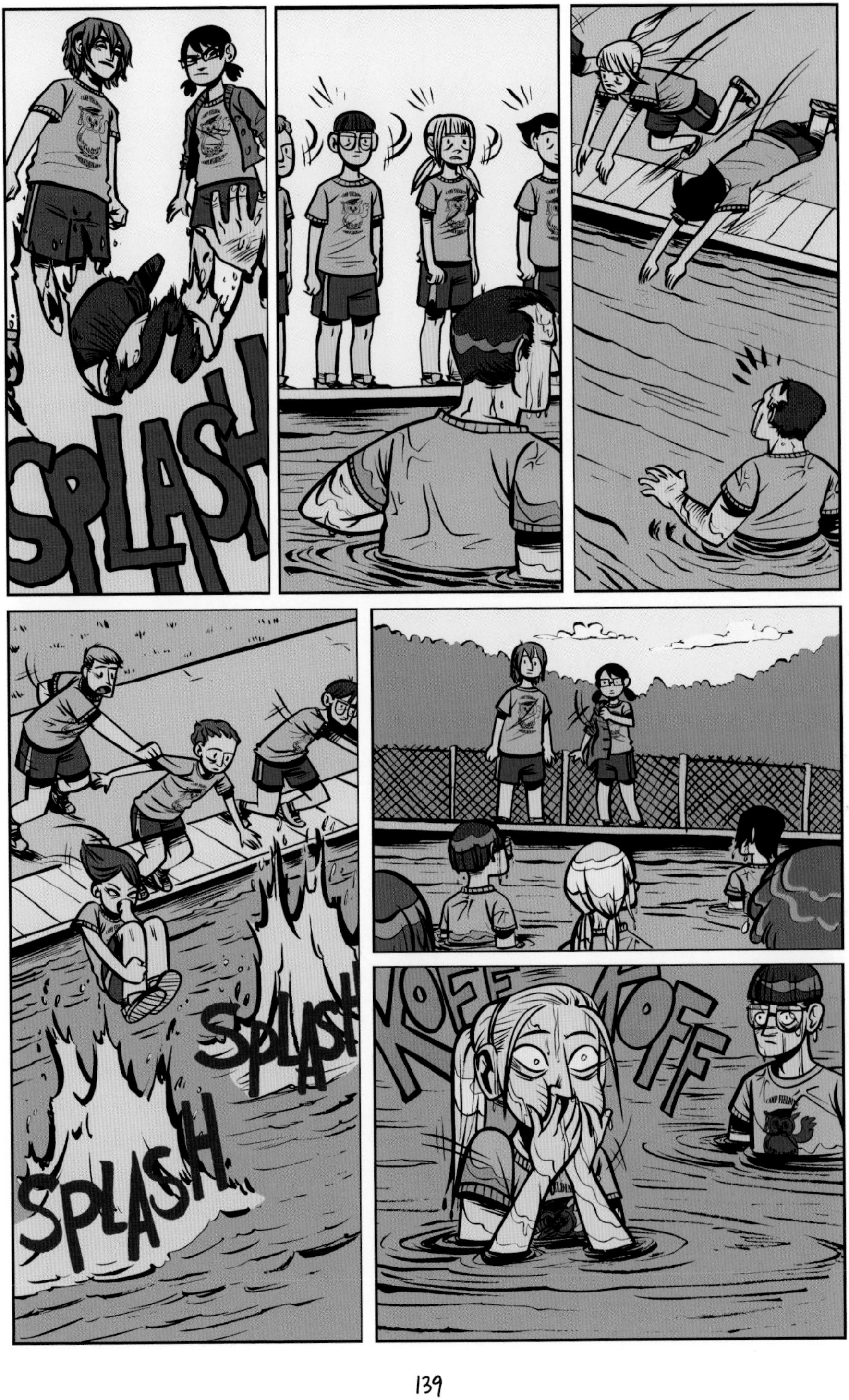
SPLASH
SPLASH
SPLASH
KOFF
KOFF

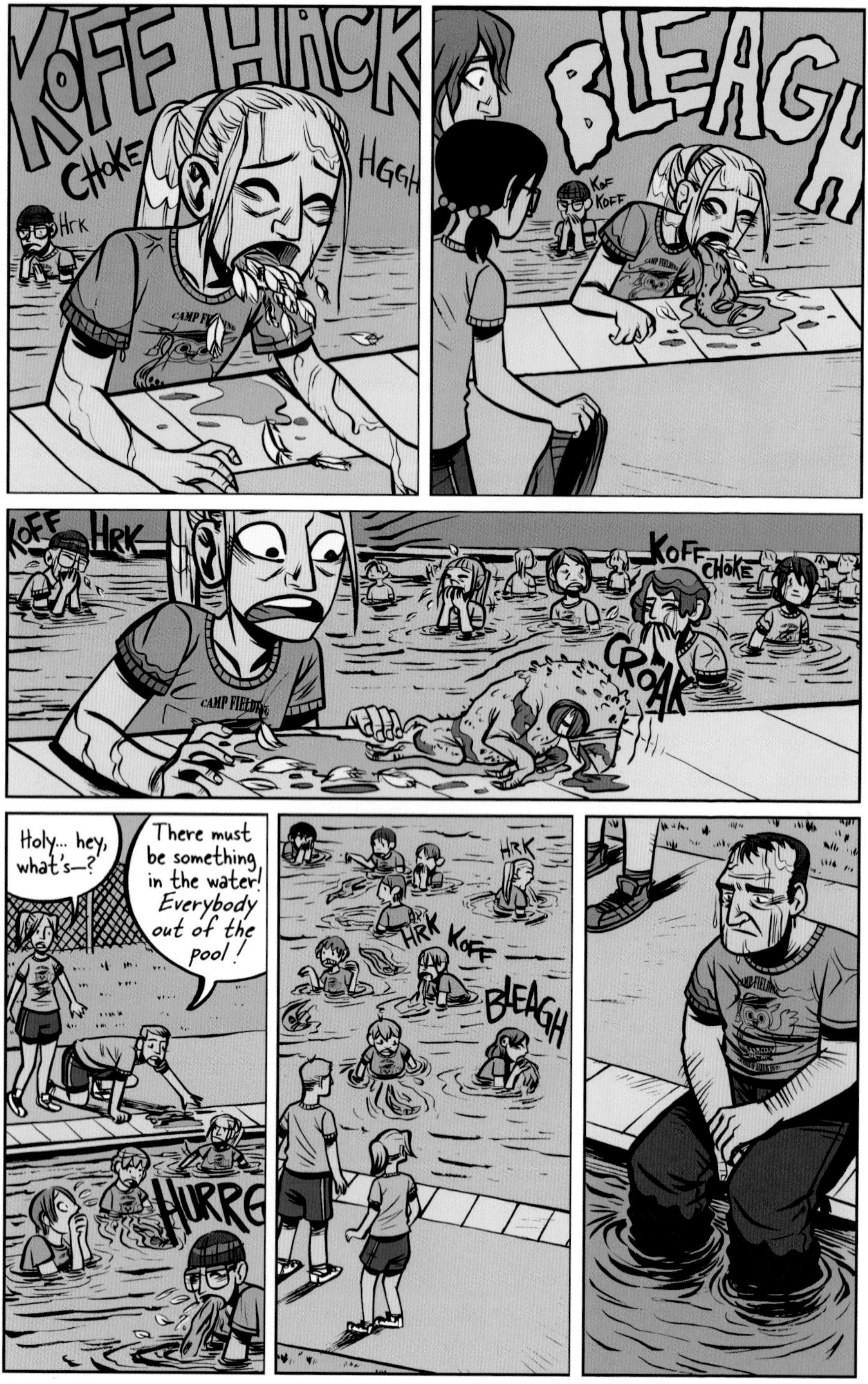
KOFF HACK
CHOKE
HGGH
Hrk
BLEAGH
KOF KOFF
KOFF
HRK
KOFF CHOKE
CROAK
Holy... hey, what's—?
There must be something in the water! Everybody out of the pool!
HURRG
HRK
HRK KOFF
BLEAGH

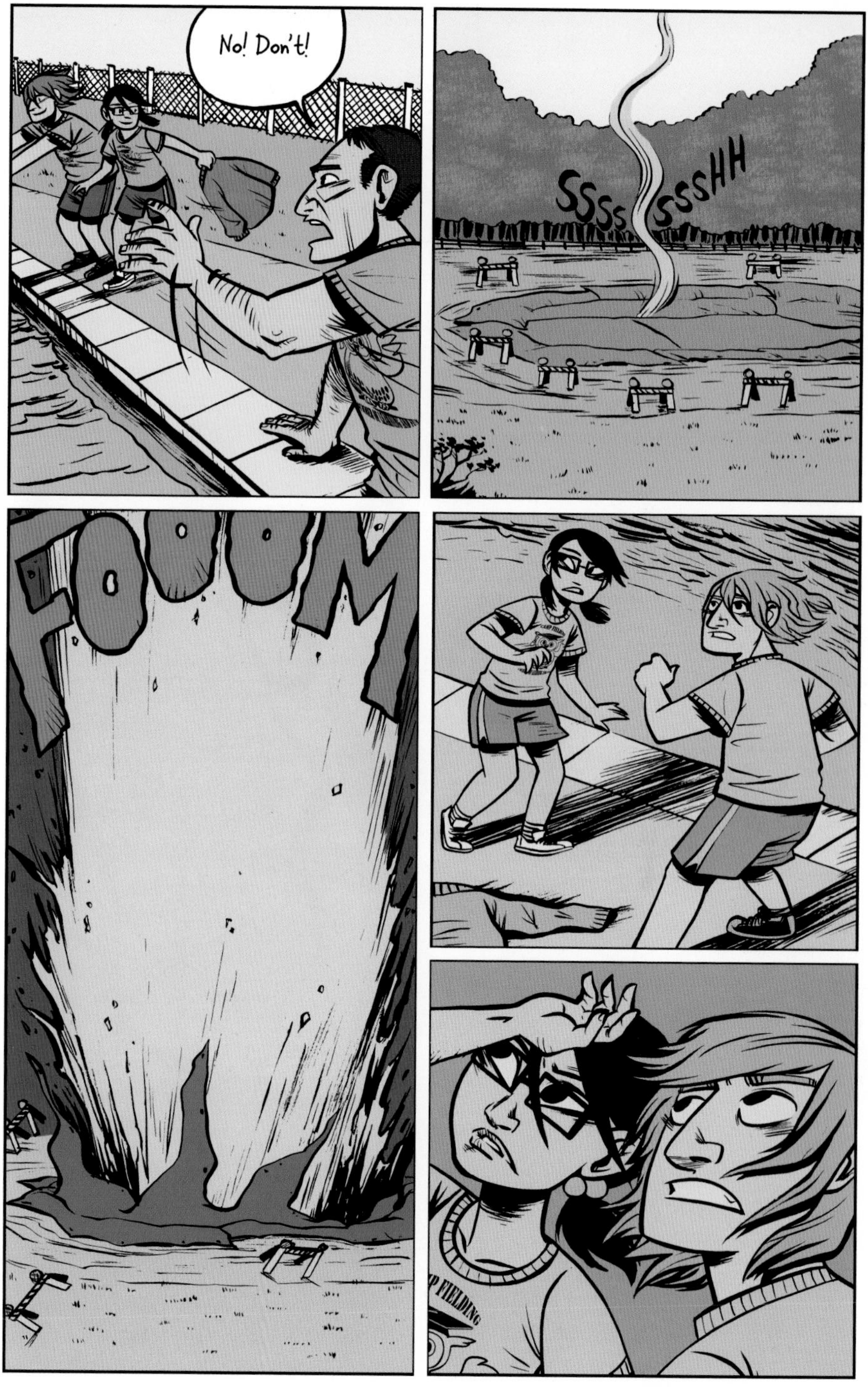
No! Don't!
SSSSSSSSHH
FOOOM
CAMP FIELDING
P FIELDING

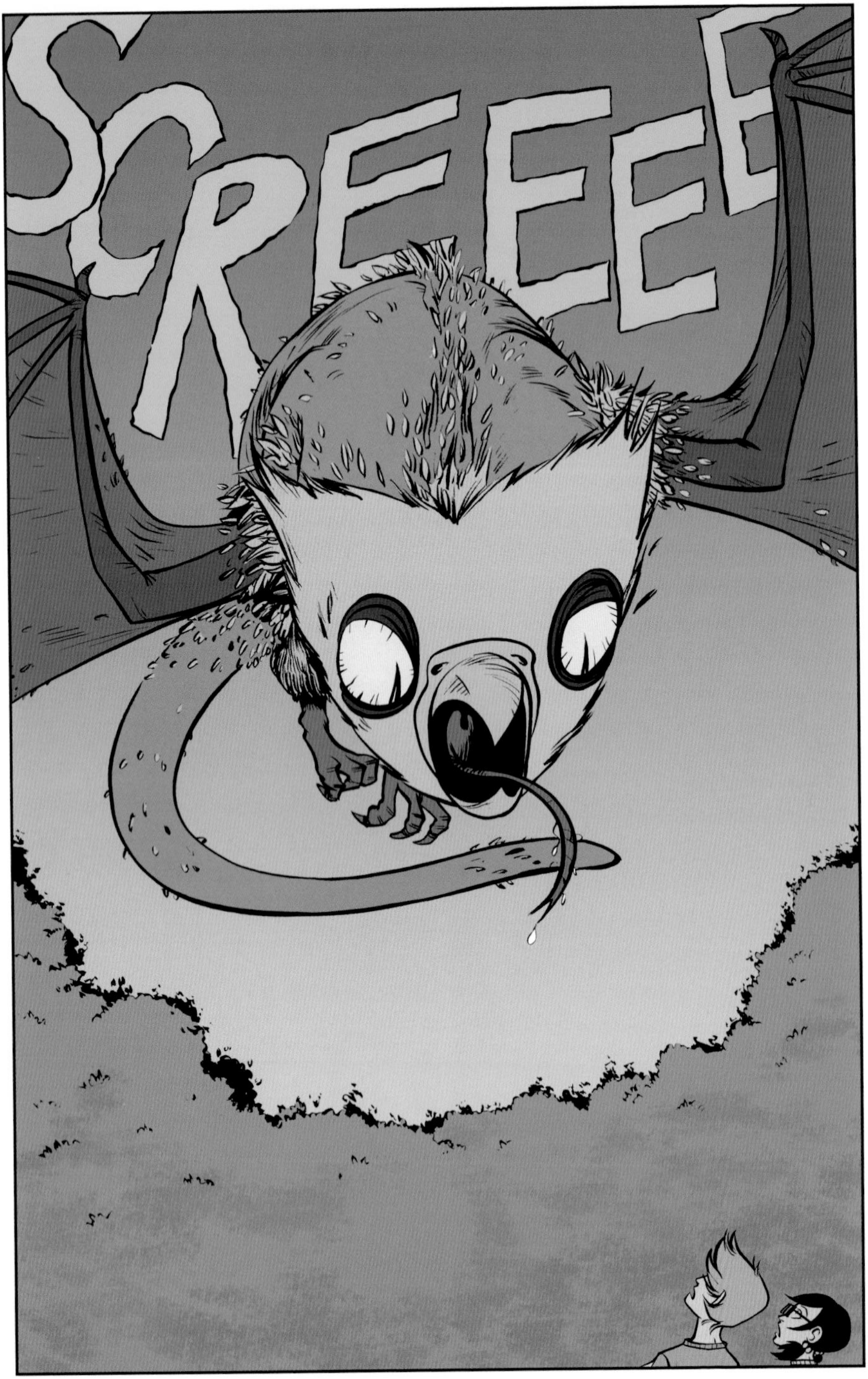
SCREEEE

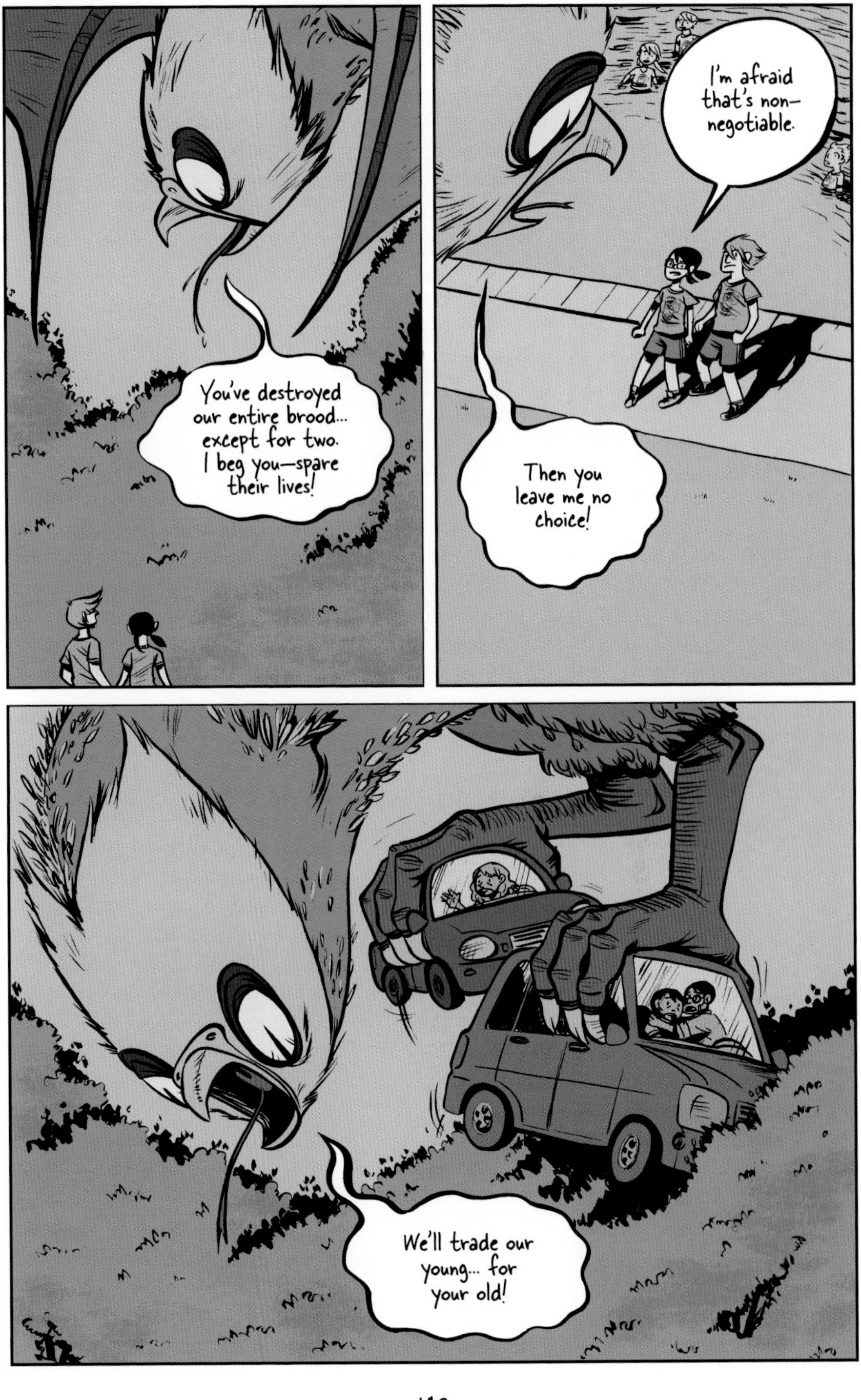
You've destroyed our entire brood... except for two. I beg you—spare their lives!
I'm afraid that's non-negotiable.
Then you leave me no choice!
We'll trade our young... for your old!

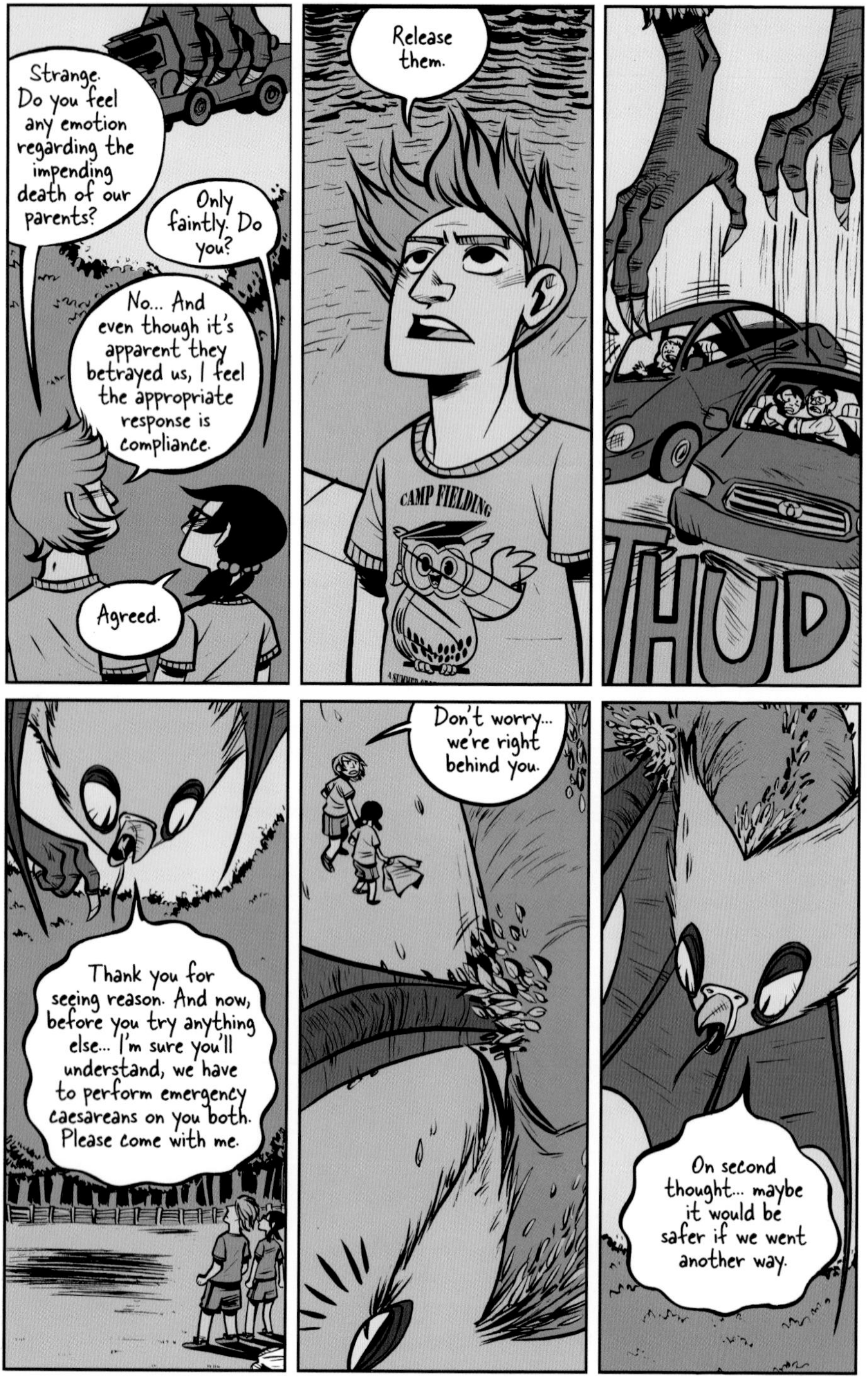
Strange. Do you feel any emotion regarding the impending death of our parents?
Only faintly. Do you?
No... And even though it's apparent they betrayed us, I feel the appropriate response is compliance.
Agreed.
Release them.
CAMP FIELDING
THUD
Thank you for seeing reason. And now, before you try anything else... I'm sure you'll understand, we have to perform emergency caesareans on you both. Please come with me.
Don't worry... we're right behind you.
On second thought... maybe it would be safer if we went another way.

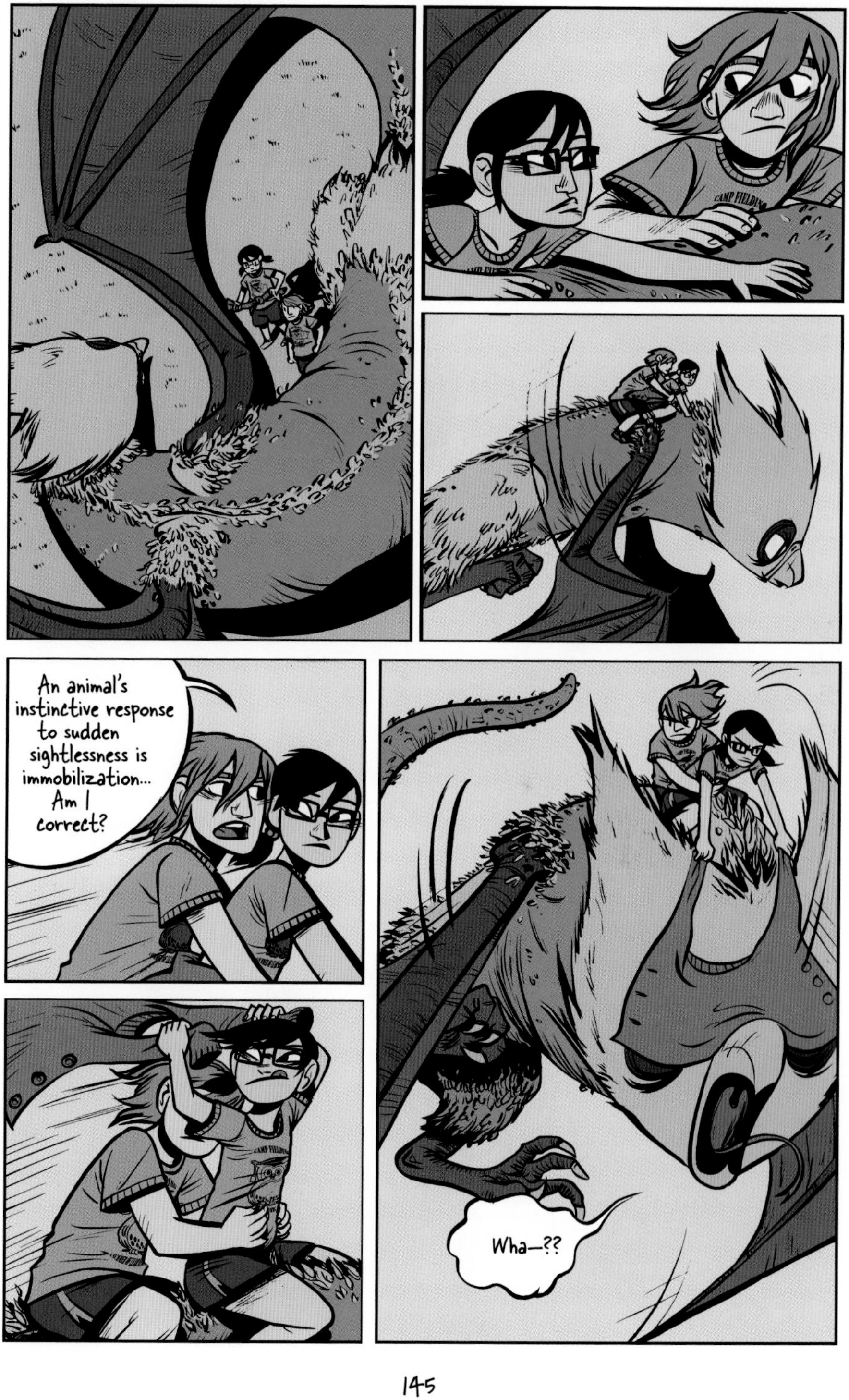
CAMP FIELDING
An animal's instinctive response to sudden sightlessness is immobilization... Am I correct?
CAMP FIELDING
Wha—??

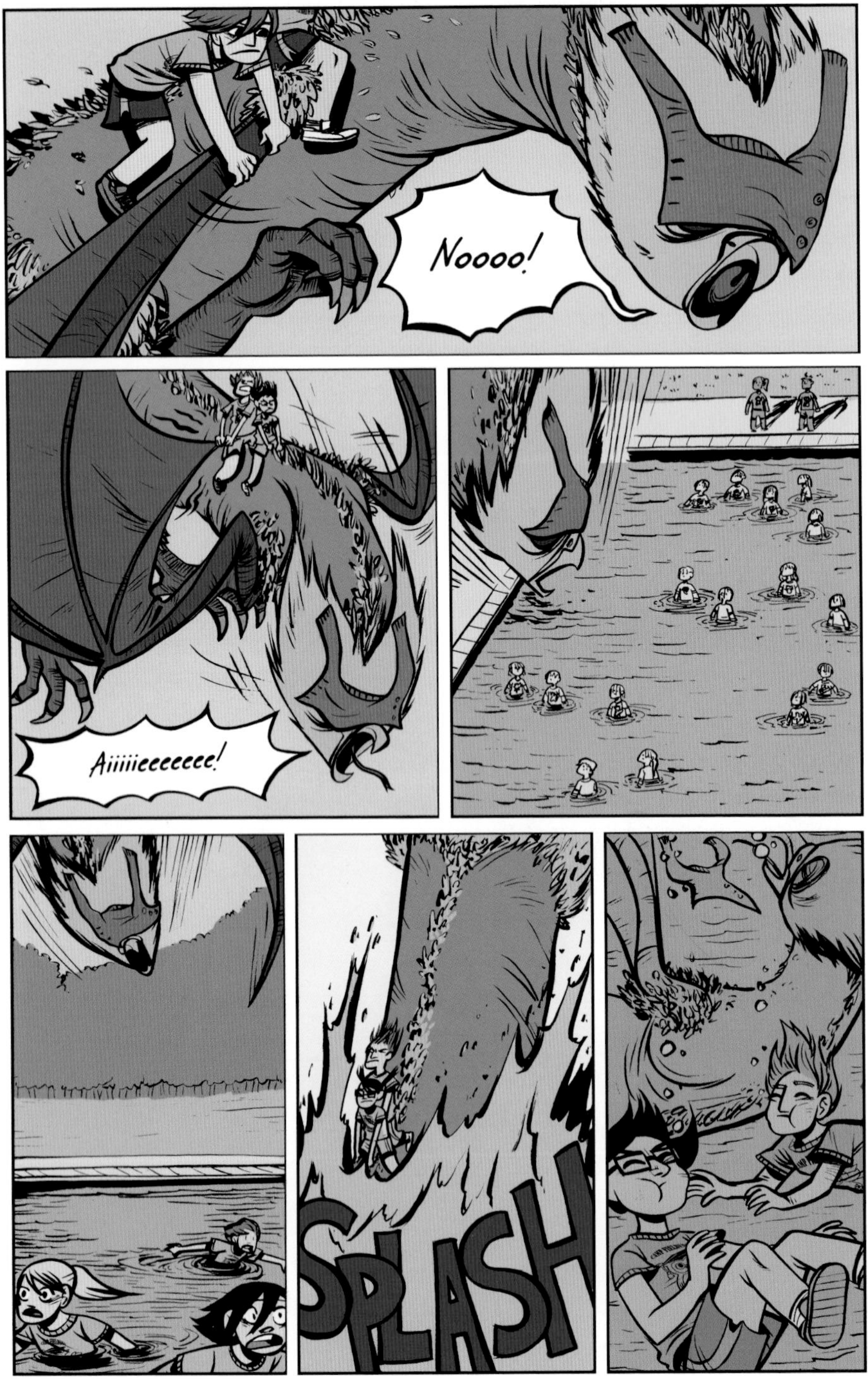
Noooo!
Aiiiiieeeeeee!
SPLASH

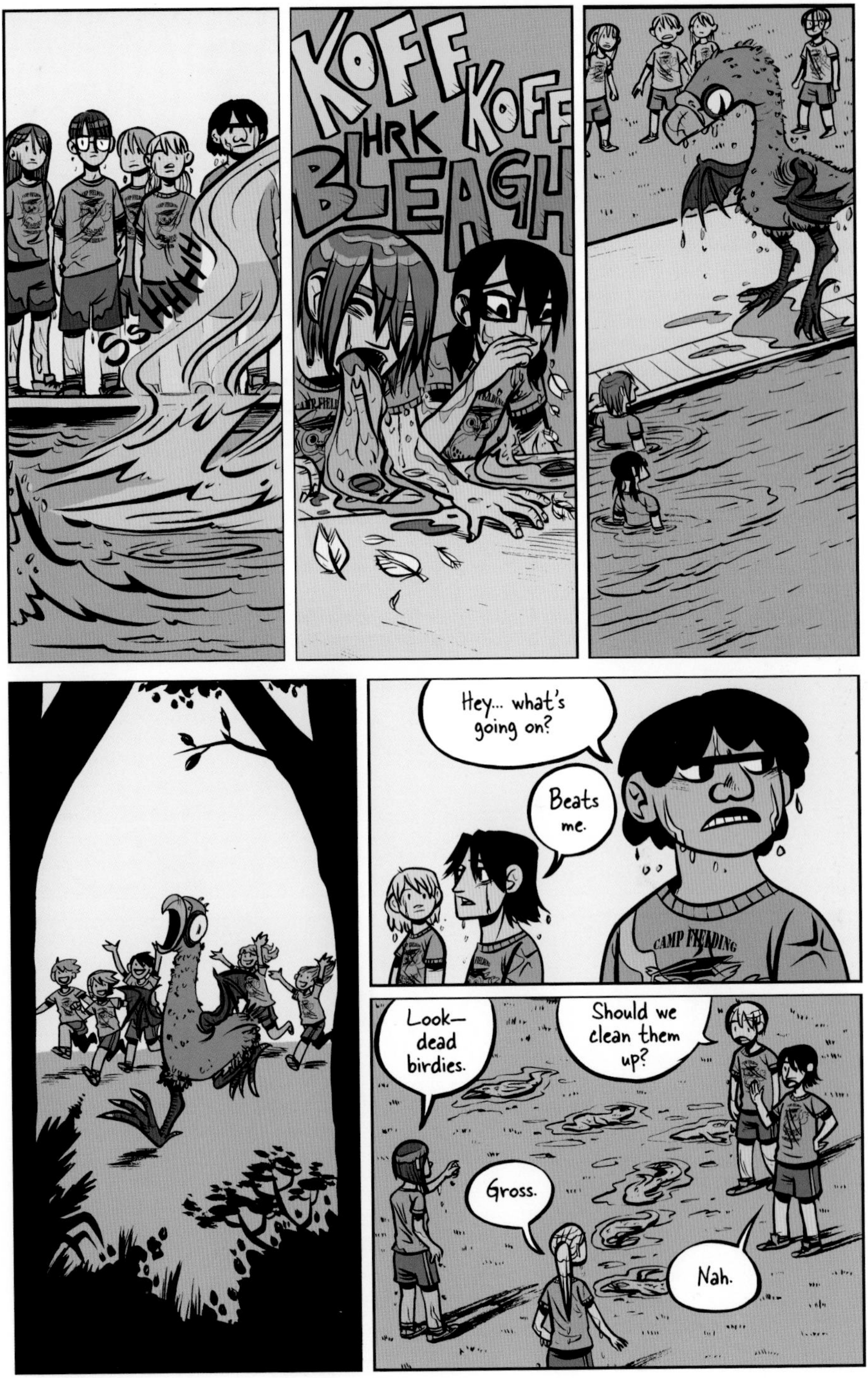

SSHHHHH
KOFF KOFF
HRK
BLEAGH
Hey... what's going on?
Beats me.
Look— dead birdies.
Should we clean them up?
Gross.
Nah.

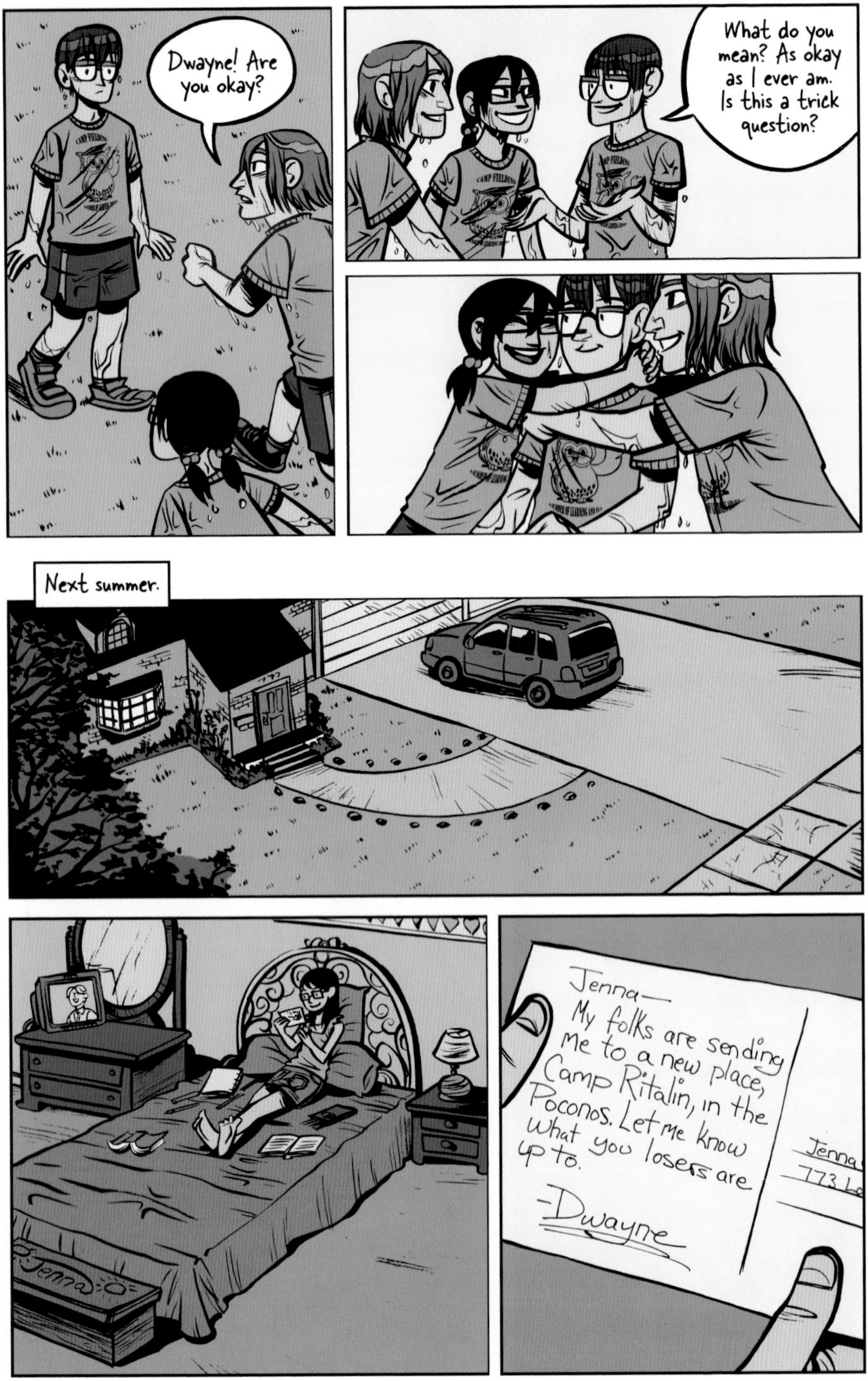
Dwayne! Are you okay?
What do you mean? As okay as I ever am. Is this a trick question?
Next summer.
Jenna
Jenna—
My folks are sending me to a new place, Camp Ritalin, in the Poconos. Let me know what you losers are up to.
-Dwayne

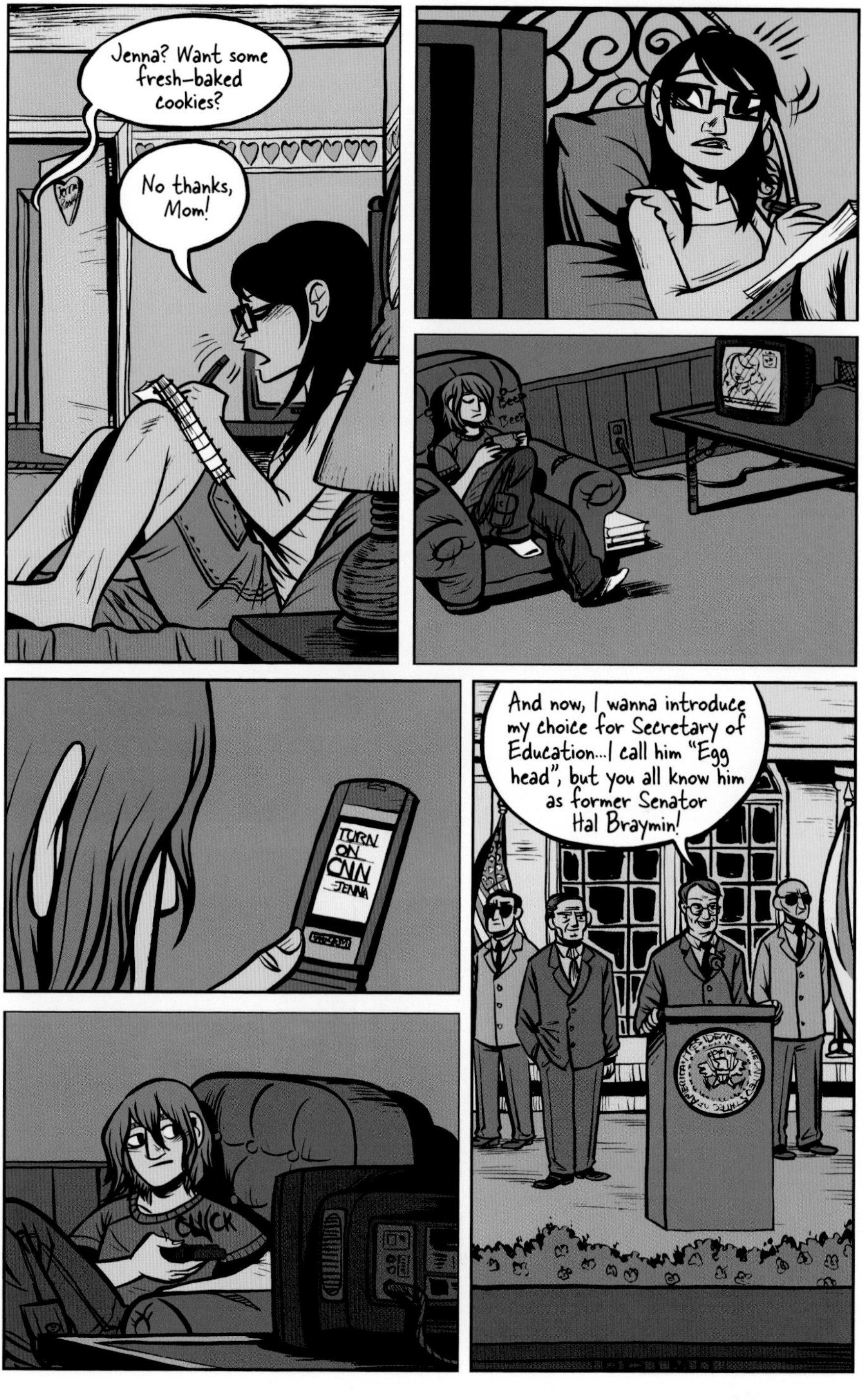
Jenna? Want some fresh-baked cookies?
No thanks, Mom!
BEEP BEEP
TURN ON CNN -JENNA
CLICK
And now, I wanna introduce my choice for Secretary of Education...I call him "Egg head", but you all know him as former Senator Hal Braymin!

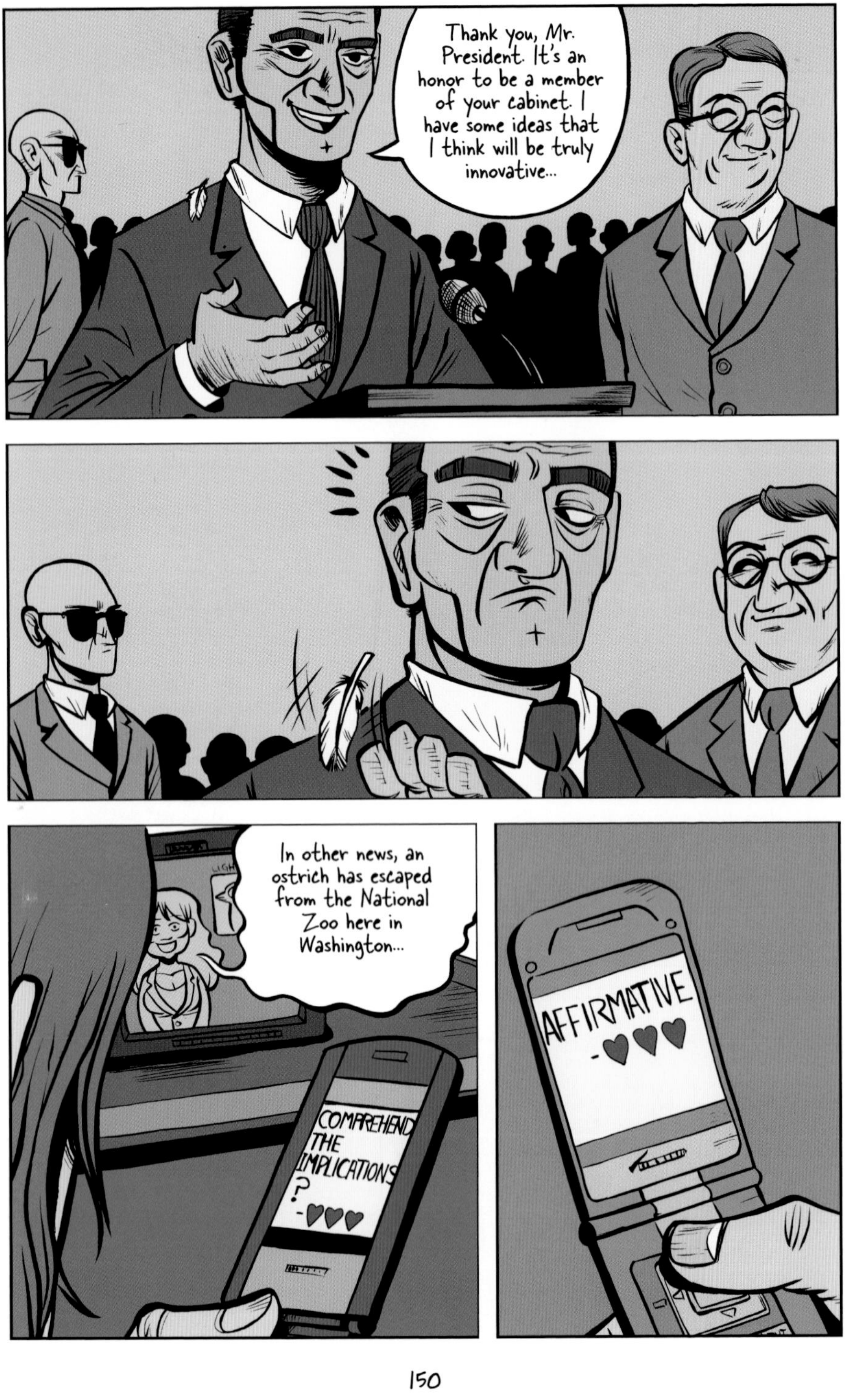
Thank you, Mr. President. It's an honor to be a member of your cabinet. I have some ideas that I think will be truly innovative...
In other news, an ostrich has escaped from the National Zoo here in Washington...
COMPREHEND THE IMPLICATIONS? -♥♥♥
AFFIRMATIVE -♥♥♥

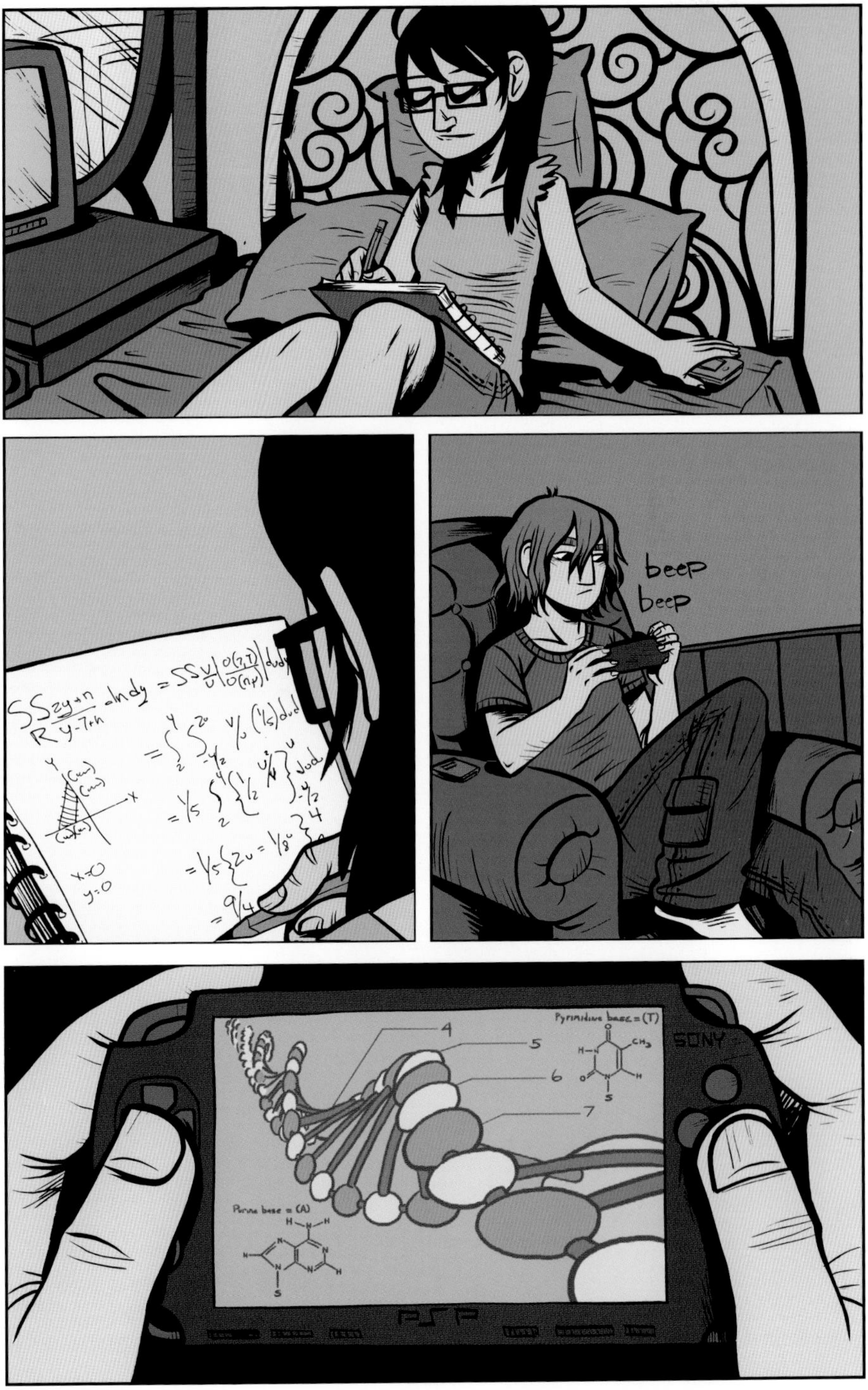
beep
beep
Pyrimidine base = (T)
4
5
6
7
Purine base = (A)
SONY
PSP

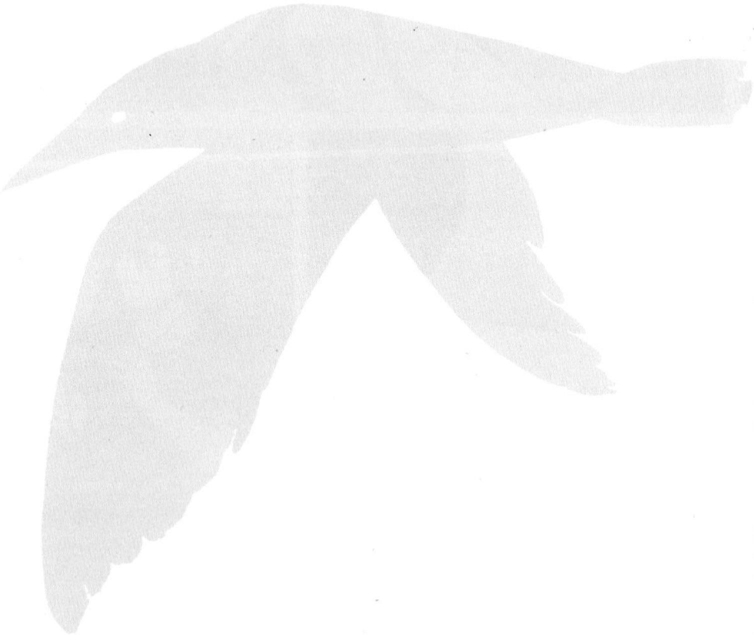